Mike Leonard was born in SE London and studied Medicine at Bristol University, working as a junior hospital doctor in a variety of specialties in that fair city.

Before settling into a long career in general practice in Weston-super-Mare, Somerset, he worked in Australia, Canada, and, for two years, as the sole Ship's Surgeon on a cruise ship sailing principally in the Caribbean and Mediterranean.

The first draft of **A Certain Persuasion** was completed in 1996, with revisions up to 1998, when it was placed in cryogenic suspension for the next 23 years while he got on with serious NHS work.

It was finally successfully resuscitated and revived in early 2022.

A Certain Persuasion

Mike Leonard

First paperback edition 2022
Cover design by Publishing Push
Itinerary maps by Denise Coreas

ISBN
978-1-80227-495-0 (paperback)
978-1-80227-497-4 (hardback)
978-1-80227-496-7(ebook)

Published by Mike Leonard

Website: http://mikeleonard-author.com/
Email: mike@mikeleonard-author.com

To my wife, Phyl (my one-time ship's nurse) and my amazing daughters, Kim and Tamara, for their ongoing love and support – and for bringing young George and the irrepressible Freya into our lives.

A Certain Persuasion

Prologue

Maryland, USA: October 1996.

At what precise moment they finally succeeded in breaking her, it would always be difficult to say. At what point too, in those past painful weeks, the sheer futility of her hopes of a military career hit home, likewise. If they wanted her out, they had succeeded. Though no one ever promised it would be easy – that much went without saying – physically, at least, she'd been prepared for it. It was just all the other unholy crap they'd thrown at her from the very first moment she'd started, she could contend with not a single day more.

A chill wind whipped up from the south that night as she stood there – icy blasts from the dark October reaches of the Chesapeake Bay, swirling mercilessly over the low marshes and gentle hills of Harford County round about her; taunting her, testing her still. Few others were in evidence out on the base just then, she noticed: guards over at the check point way in the distance, dutifully rigged and efficient; anonymous audible voices, now and again, from points closer by when the wind dropped; the stark hollow cough in the night.

She could feel their eyes upon her now though, from every watchful window nearby. And there was stifled laughter too (or was that simply her imagination?); an understandable paranoia, perhaps, in the circumstances.

There'd be laughter aplenty, no doubt, when word got round that she had gone. Amusement, as ever, for the Boys. Affirmation, in a way, of all those bastards had levelled at her from the start. Too soft, they'd said; too pretty – drummed into her at every available chance. Drummed like a military tattoo – though no tattoo, she was sure, could ever have been so painfully acquired. (She had the marks on her arms still to prove it). Drilled by the Drill Sergeant with orthodontic precision, chipping away relentlessly at her innate feminine weaknesses; the perceived rot in their system. And all those others too, tuned in uncannily to her personal cyclical issues, then goading her. Red rag, one might say, to their menstrual bull. The bastards, every one. Too soft; too pretty – though she hardly looked too pretty now, they might have to agree, with her jaw set firm and her hair so deliberately hacked. Yet another ploy that had signally failed to appease them.

How the other female trainees coped, she could not begin to imagine. Their commitment more extreme, perhaps? Their tolerance greater? Welcome to the Boys' Club, they had told her right at the outset. Wrong – you're goddamn welcome to it, her ultimate reply.

She found herself thinking of Marianne just then – her only real friend since she'd been there – and how badly affected she'd seemed by her news.

"You're leaving here? You quit? Now, you sure you thought this thing through?"

"Uhuh."

"So where will you go?"

"Far away from here, for a start. Away from here, from Baltimore, from NYC."

"And what'll you do?"

"Who knows?"

She went back in to find Marianne now that the car was loaded, and hugged her awkwardly goodbye. It felt strange – such a large woman compared to her.

"Sure gonna miss you, Honey."

"You just hang on in there, Marianne. You've been here a long time now – far, far longer than me – and only a few short months to go."

"Don't you worry, I will."

As she drove past the checkpoint for what she hoped was the very last time, the large illuminated sign caught her eye.

U.S ARMY ABERDEEN TEST CENTER
DEPT OF DEFENSE (DOD)

It was also known as the Proving Ground. The irony of the term did not escape her. So, what, in her case at least, had it really managed to prove?

She drove on to Baltimore and the small apartment she still kept there, thinking all the while of what they'd intimated when she earlier announced her decision. An official complaint hadn't really been uppermost in her mind, not that she'd bothered to tell them. All she wanted to do was get away – not bogged down in endless bureaucracy. Besides, her case was pretty trivial, particularly if you believed some of the allegations flying around the base just then. But they were defensive alright, there at the meeting. And something more when she thought back to the actual phrases they had used. An element of threat, perhaps?

Could she possibly be imagining it – or had the Boys' Club really been warning her off?

PART 1

VENUS — THE GOOD SHIP REVISITED

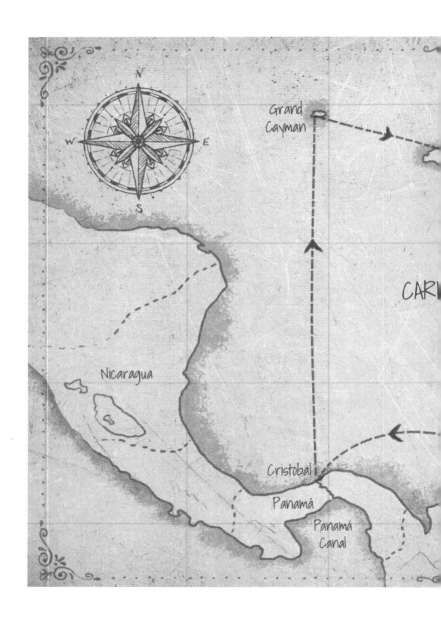

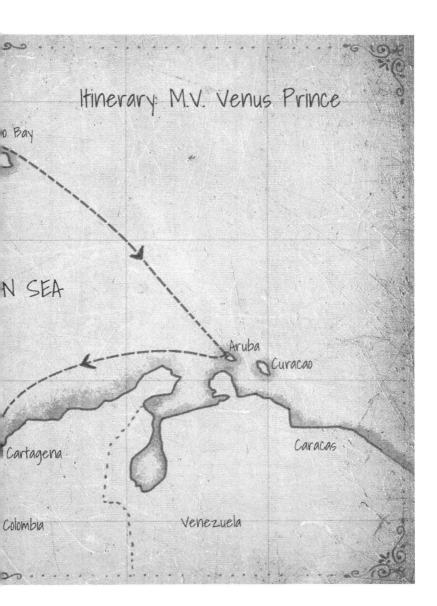

Itinerary: M.V. Venus Prince

o Bay

N SEA

Aruba

Curacao

Cartagena

Caracas

Colombia

Venezuela

Chapter 1

Caribbean: Sunday, December 8th 1996.

I

There was little ceremony that night as the body was moved.

With the lifeless, glazed-eyed fish shoved cold and unblinking to one side, the black bag containing the dead Colombian sailor slid noiselessly into the ship's refrigerated hold.

Stavros Crystakis, Staff Captain of the 21,000-ton M.V. Venus Prince – the ship at that time nine hours from Aruba in a calm southern Caribbean – looked on impassively. Short, staccato orders issued at measured intervals from somewhere behind the blackness of his moustache – a large and triumphant moustache, still visible and even more threatening there in the half-light. The two young Honduran crewmen, selected solely on the basis that fifty dollars was most likely to guarantee their silence, acted unquestioningly. Their only concession to the grim reality of the situation had been to cross themselves quickly and mutter a quiet benediction in their native Spanish, before moving the crumpled body from the engine room floor twenty minutes earlier.

There had been a definite agitation in the Captain's voice when he gave Stavros the order earlier that day – the sort of agitation only another Greek could be sure of. To an outsider, much of what Captain Ioannis Symiakos said seemed to have an agitated air about it – but perhaps, to some degree, that was merely a cultural thing. This time, though, there had been no raised voice, no gesticulation.

"The fools that did this have left us in a very awkward position, Stavros," he said quietly. "It's fine, of course, for our little 'arrangement' having Delgardo put his own men aboard as crew, but for one of them to be so obviously taken out like this is just not acceptable. Not on my ship, anyway. If he needed to deal with wayward employees, surely he could have taken care of them on shore, not while we're at sea."

"Or at least have the decency to get his men to dispose of the body overboard. Has he no idea of the paperwork, the formalities we'll have to deal with when we reach port with this damn corpse on board?" replied the Staff Captain vehemently. "It's bad enough when passengers, or crew, for that matter, die from natural causes on ship. That might take two, maybe three hours to clear. But a murder... or accident... whatever the hell you'd like to call it? – God knows how long this will hold us up for."

"Well, I've spoken to Delgardo himself by Sat-com already and discussed the situation. We won't be reporting the death when we arrive in Aruba tomorrow – just keep the body in the cold store. The port officials won't think to look there. The mortuary itself will be empty, of course – thankfully, no deaths to report among the passengers this week. In fact, Stavros, we must let as few people know about it as possible just yet. That Hotel Manager, for instance. If he gets wind of it, we will have the Company on to us before we know it. Delgardo says to wait till Cartagena to formally report the death, in three days' time. He'll fix it so there'll be no questions asked by the Colombian authorities when we arrive."

"What about the medical certification, Ioannis?" asked the Staff Captain.

"I've spoken to Dr Rodriguez already. He'll do the necessary. As you know, his time with us is nearly up – only another couple of weeks to go. Funny how even the strict ethical code of our old and respected ship's doctor can so easily be broken by the simple offer of a fat terminal bonus."

"What of his replacement? Have we heard yet?"

"The Company's arranging short-term cover initially. Flying in from Cayman, I believe, to meet us in Montego Bay on the twenty-first. Bringing his wife and kids, apparently – must think it's some kind of vacation. Shouldn't think he'll last long."

"At least that old drunken fool, Rodriguez, had the good sense to not ask too many questions," said Stavros. "Personally, I'll miss him for that. Just filled up the syringe with Penicillin – not too many questions... hey, Ioannis?"

They laughed together as they had laughed together many times before.

"But this business with Delgardo, it's very serious, Stavros. I've told him that he must arrange his business with us with more care if we are to work together."

"What did he say to that?"

"He apologizes well enough, that Delgardo. As you know, he's charm itself to your face. But," said the Captain, his small troubled eyes narrowing in on the man in front of him across the desk, "I'm afraid, Stavros, he is far too powerful a man for us to ever hope to threaten in any way."

Friday, December 13 1996.

II

An hour or so before daybreak – the northwest coast of Jamaica just now in view up ahead – a shore light flashed surreptitiously across the water. To the casual observer at least, had one for any reason been present at such a time, it might well have gone unnoticed. The cruise ship's smooth onward passage gave little immediate clue to its significance. The order from the Bridge held the key, but few on board were privy to it. Only then did the Venus Prince begin to slow – gradually and almost imperceptibly – in the darkness.

There existed now a sense of calm about the ship, the sort achieved only reluctantly on the last night of a cruise: typically, about three hours after the last of the bars had finally closed, or an hour or so after even the most ardent or erotic of farewells had given way to practical repose.

The Caribbean waters had once again been kind. With few exceptions, that week's 428 passengers rested peacefully in their cabins – bags packed, heaped high in designated mounds around the ship, ready for disembarkation later that morning. Bus boys in cramped quarters turned in their bunks and peered at forty-dollar fake Rolexes in the dark. Time only to doze before duty beckoned once more; wondering whether the tips that cruise would sufficiently repay the calculated servility of yet another week – at least compared to the one before, which was a bitch in anyone's language.

Not long after – to experienced ears at least – the dull chug of a tender was just discernible drawing up alongside, and a small shipside door on the starboard side towards the stern clunked slowly open. Low voices in heavily accented English – from elsewhere further south in the Caribbean – mingled with others, more immediately local.

Minutes later, the tender pulled away, disappearing quickly landward with an urgency that seemed to grow with the fast fading of the night.

Others on shore, primed for its arrival, waited. The next phase of the operation – smoother and even more complacent with every simple repetition – would soon be underway once again.

The truck, laden high with island produce – plantain, mangoes and bananas – was there at the ready on the narrow track by the secluded cove. The transfer of the small wooden case from the tender would take ten minutes, no more. Time then to disperse: the rickety truck, its illicit cargo well-hidden on board, off across the island, attracting little or no attention along the way. The tender also – its job now complete – back to its moorings to the west. The sea yielding bountifully once more. "Dear Lord," that Jamaican prayer would go, "we give you thanks for another fine day's catch – if you know what we mean, Lord."

The Venus Prince sailed on with a sedateness of motion well befitting its name. It would be an hour or so before its early morning risers, keen not to miss out on the last island encounter, would emerge slowly on deck.

The dawn about to greet them that day would reveal, rewardingly, the north coast of Jamaica lying there lush and still against the skyline.

An image in perfect monochrome.

Chapter 2

USA: January 1997.

I

Almost precisely sixteen hundred miles to the north, and three weeks later, New York city awoke to yet another steely January dawn.

Ed Jamieson, owner of Venus Cruise Lines – in what amounted to one single convulsive movement – found himself propelled curtly from a half-sleep that had pursued him relentlessly throughout the night. Sweat soaked and palpitating, as he had been on an ever-increasing number of very similar occasions of late, he quickly gained orientation and flopped back heavily onto the bed. Lying there in the grey stillness, he began to analyse what he could of that last contorted dream sequence. Something told him that from somewhere deep within its turmoil, an answer had somehow surfaced. But what exactly?

Ed looked over at the sleeping form of Ellen, his wife; a handsome woman – once beautiful even – though Ed hadn't really known her then. He'd seen photos, of course – she in her air-hostess uniform, short skirt and flouncy scarf, from the early seventies. He'd even entertained the idle fantasy of getting her to put it on once again, just for him this time. It wasn't often an out-of-shape sixty-year-old got to seduce an air hostess – even a sixty-year-old as rich as he.

That she loved him, he had little doubt. And he loved her too, he guessed – especially for taking the chance she had with him at this time in her life. Yet, no matter how he tried, he just couldn't get this thing with Sophia out of his mind. It had been seven years since she'd left him, but the hurt was still there, cutting deeper and deeper into the very substance of his soul. Not a single week went by when he wasn't somehow reminded. Okay, so it was now an obsession. Then there were those nightmares...

Over recent months, and with a scathing disregard for any more formal psychological analysis on the subject, Ed Jamieson had come to identify a total of three, very distinct, recurring dream types, all involving the same person. Not only that, each revolved around much the same theme, and all, too, shared the same overall end-point; the slow, humiliating torture of George Mitchell. Progressive constriction featured most popularly, he'd found; in dream type one, for example, of his fat ugly neck, and two – with no small measure of angular torque thrown in – his bastard dangling ballsack.

Satisfying enough as far as these dreams went, (and type three certainly went pretty far), they were not without their own ultimate frustration. The realisation when he awoke, perspiring and agitated like he was now, that in the final analysis – at the precise point of retribution, the very coup de gras – the consequences had hit home and, racked by fear, he had bottled out. Not only that, but, as he did so – finally relinquishing his grip on Mitchell's progressively cyanosing and distorted body part – there would be Mitchell's unabashed face in front of him, smiling, gloating over his cowardice. Still, and as always, the winner.

And now, just the thought of that coming week was almost more than he could bear. Not only had he to face what would have been yet another anniversary – this his and Sophia's twentieth – but the Annual Cruise Convention there in NYC, too. It wasn't that she'd actually be there with Mitchell, though – she rarely showed her face in New York these days. Not since that asshole had taken her off to live in Florida, after so flagrantly stealing her from him.

Sure, he had been putting in a lot of hours in those days, often out of the country – but hell, that's what the travel industry was all about. However, no matter how he looked at it, he couldn't help wishing that he hadn't been out of the country for that particular Convention – the one Sophia had attended on his behalf. The one where she'd met that dumbfuck George.

A lot, of course, had happened since then – much, it would seem, as a direct consequence. If he hadn't at that time had his mind firmly focused on Mitchell, owner of Palm Cruises, Florida, he probably wouldn't have given the cruise business a second thought. All his years in the travel industry had been devoted to virtually all other areas of the trade. It wasn't until his chance meeting with Dan Forsbrook, however, that he fully realised the attraction it might hold.

That Dan Forsbrook just happened to be George Mitchell's right-hand man and that he, Ed Jamieson had found him ripe for headhunting, had naturally played their part. And in many ways, it was only this that had kept him going. As he looked back at events, even now he tried desperately to imagine, in all possible satisfying permutations, the full extent of Mitchell's chagrin.

Not that he'd had any further direct contact with him – not even after he'd acquired his small fleet of cruise ships and set up Venus Cruise Lines six years before, with Dan Forsbrook as Head of Operations. Their paths, neither business nor personal, ever seemed to cross.

But such retaliation had never been nearly enough. He knew this for certain now – reminded of it almost nightly by those dreams. But their way was wrong – certainly for him. He knew himself well enough to realise this. Another way was needed. A real-life way, without the ultimate constraints of the justice system. A here-and-now way – less dramatic, perhaps, but practical and, above all, achievable. A subtle way, no less.

Ed rose from his reverie and went through to the bathroom to shave. His face in the mirror looked back ponderously, tired and less handsome than he liked to remember it. He recalled the meeting he'd arranged for that day, and then – quite suddenly, in one startling flash of enlightenment, it hit him.

The very answer that had eluded him since he first awoke that morning.

And as he thought it through, Ed began to realize just how good it really was.

II

Dan Forsbrook was late. As his cab turned into Palisade Avenue, Jersey City, he looked at his watch once again. Only ten minutes so far, and most likely no more than fifteen by the time he'd made it to the sixteenth floor of the Fairfax Building – but Ed Jamieson wouldn't like it. He could imagine his boss at that very moment, pacing the boardroom floor up there in Head Office, itching to get the meeting underway. How little it would matter to him that he had barely gotten over the flight back from Hong Kong, touching down as he had late the previous night.

Still, he reflected – as the car drew up outside the undoubtedly once impressive art-deco building – it was all part of the job; a job that, all told, suited him extremely well. Particularly with such a degree of freedom. Freedom of movement, for one. For the most part, he was on his own – in far-flung places, working at more or less his own pace, coping with the multitude of potential problems of the four Venus cruise ships. Wheeling and dealing in the way he knew best, with all manner of persons: from local suppliers to beleaguered shore-side agents; from distant airlines to obscure and often dubious coach tour operators. All with the power to snag the delicate wheels of motion of the operation – wheels that could be oiled so smoothly and surprisingly into life only by the liberal application of the mighty dollar. Deals he reported and those he didn't. Favours he gave and those he owed. And, more importantly still, time for his other diversions.

"Good morning, Mr Forsbrook, and how are you today, sir?" asked the doorman as he entered the large foyer.

Dan muttered a suitably polite but not quite so cheerful reply and made his way directly over to the elevators. Alone inside, he pressed the button, and – once underway – quickly drew back his jacket, checking his shirt once more for signs of blood. The makeshift dressing, he was pleased to note, seemed to be holding out just fine. It wouldn't do, he knew, to openly broadcast either the existence or severity of the stab wound – let alone its cause.

"Ah, there you are. Good morning, Dan," said Rachel, Jamieson's secretary, from the midst of a mid-morning, big city, office hum. "How was your trip?"

"Fine," said Dan, "if you exclude the ten-hour airport delay and complementary jetlag. I take it all the others are here?"

"Yeah, in the boardroom. The coffee's in there, too. Mr J, incidentally, you might be pleased to know, seems in a strangely buoyant mood today for some reason."

"Odd indeed," said Dan, "– still, there's got to be a first time for everything."

He headed across for the meeting, practicing, as he went, a face he hoped might appear somehow sufficiently apologetic.

Chapter 3

Somerset, England

I

As he watched, the clouds moved perceptibly faster to the east, onward towards the Mendip Hills nearby, and a frail sun shone through over the centre of the English Victorian seaside town.

From the upstairs window of the first-floor consulting room, Dr Luke Darius, as on a number of similar occasions that morning, found himself restlessly gazing out over the dull brown roof tops to the grey corrugated sea and beyond.

The phone rang irritably, somehow louder than usual.

"Oh, Dr Darius, I know you've finished your morning appointments, but a patient has just turned up here at reception – name of Christine West – asking to speak with you urgently. Her computer number is 3742 – she wouldn't give any details."

"Okay, I've got that," said Luke, jotting the number down.

"And also, Dr Darius, I've been asked to remind you tactfully of your meeting with the other partners at 1.00 pm."

"Right; thanks, Lizzie. You've reminded me extremely tactfully. Now send her up, if you would, please."

Luke looked up from the computer screen as the knock came at the door, a little sooner than he'd expected. He rose to open it.

A woman's face, strangely familiar he thought, smiled nervously at him. It was fine-featured and pleasantly framed by straggly blonde tendrils, which flowed down over the collar of her long, unbuttoned coat.

"Oh, hello, it's you..." he said uncertainly. "What a pleasant surprise. Listen, would you mind just waiting out there for a minute? You see, I'm expecting one of our patients any moment now. Shouldn't take me long."

"Christine West?"

"Yes, that's her name. How did you know?"

"I'm Christine West."

"You mean you're a patient in this practice?"

"Yes, we have been since we moved here three years ago."

"We?" said Luke, suddenly aware how embarrassingly little he had bothered to learn about this woman.

"Me and my husband."

"Your husband? You mean..."

"Listen, Dr Darius," she said, perching herself rather tentatively on the edge of the chair Luke had offered her, "I thought I ought to come and clear the air. What happened that night was, I'm sure you might have already guessed, very much on an impulse. I hadn't planned that it should happen that way – with you or anybody else, for that matter.

"To say I wasn't flattered by your attention would be a lie. It's not every day that a forty-two-year-old not-so-happily married woman gets the attentions of a good-looking younger man – and a doctor, at that. I was flattered. It made me feel somehow significant again. I certainly don't regret it – and I hope you won't, either."

Luke looked into her eyes as she spoke; a watery blue with make-up applied rather unevenly – in an attempt, he supposed, to hide the obvious swelling beneath. She stared straight ahead for the most part, at the shelf over to his left – empty, he noticed, except for a small plastic model knee joint, donated recently by a drug company. He chanced a glance at her legs, peeping out enticingly from behind her open black coat.

Now those he certainly did remember. The last time he encountered them they were draped almost halfway round his neck. And very definitely the fun way.

"Of course I won't regret it," he heard himself saying, remembering to look away again, in that nonchalant way he'd learnt to develop for situations like this. Well, not unless the Ethics Committee of the General Medical Council or the gutter press get to hear of it, he thought to himself. Then I'd absolutely, unmistakably, bloody well regret it.

He looked straight ahead into her eyes, hoping he'd hit just the right level of sincerity with these words. She smiled weakly back at him and then ahead again silently at the shelf.

Luke found his eyes straying over to the blank computer screen on the desk in front of him. How he wished he'd taken the time to tap in her computer number before she'd arrived. There was still the chance that she'd never actually consulted him personally in the past – even though she was on the practice list. Still a chance, in fact, he was in the clear. Well, comparatively in the clear. If she had consulted him, he certainly held no recollection of it. He could at least hope.

"I'm sorry, Dr Darius..."

"Luke," he interjected. "I think, if you recall, we were very much on first name terms that night. In fact, I don't remember you calling me 'Dr Darius' once." If only you damn well had, he thought to himself, it would have been pretty bloody obvious you were a patient, and we wouldn't be sitting here like this, now would we?

"Well, Luke, as I was saying – I'm sorry if my coming here today in this way has caused you any embarrassment. I really didn't know how else to warn you. The thing is, a friend of my husband has told him that he saw me with someone at the nightclub that night – obviously enjoying myself, and leaving with the same man at about ten past one. Gerry, my husband, knows I didn't get home until after 3.30. I told him at the time I'd been back for coffee with the girlfriends I'd gone out with earlier."

"I see," said Luke, fearing the worst.

"He obviously suspects there's much more to it, and I'm pretty sure he's put the feelers out to find out just who exactly the man was."

"So, at the moment, you're saying he really has no idea it was me?" asked Luke, trying to extort whatever comfort he could from this observation.

"Well," she said slowly, looking directly at him now, "although we weren't actually followed back to your flat, I understand the registration number of your car was taken – the one out there in the car park."

"Matter of fact, that's not mine," Luke countered quickly, clearly a little more shaken by this latest twist. "It's a courtesy car lent to me by the garage. Managed to smash mine up pretty badly a few weeks back. They tell me it should be ready any time now."

"Anyway, I thought I'd best warn you he may be trying to track it down. I'd hate for you to be involved in anything unpleasant. As you may recall, he can be an extremely jealous and violent man."

"No, I don't," said Luke. "How would I?"

"Perhaps, then, you've forgotten. It was the only time I've ever been to see you here before. I came about two years ago – after he'd begun getting a bit violent during some of our arguments."

Luke suddenly understood the significance of those swollen eyes. If he wasn't mistaken, there was also some well-camouflaged bruising below the right one.

"Our marriage had started going wrong soon after he came back from the Gulf. That war, you know, changed him completely. That and the eighteen months he recently spent in prison for criminal assault. You were very kind and supportive at the time, by the way. Extremely understanding."

II

Luke went to the common room just after 1 o'clock. The three other partners were all there, and Luke noticed how their rather hushed conversation quickly tailed off as he entered. Dr Mark Hammond, only a year or so older than Luke, stood up quickly, gesturing to him the vacant chair near the window.

"Well, we may as well get started, now that we're all here," said Clive Walsh, assuming his role of Senior Partner. "I've called this partnership meeting, as you all know, because of my concerns over patient complaints in the light of our recently increased workload. The Government, in its wisdom, has pushed on to us poor GPs the responsibility of making some of its more recent and controversial health reforms work. The more cynical amongst us..." Luke knew precisely to whom he was referring, "would no doubt say these reforms are misguided in terms of true patient benefit, and the onerous task of auditing that we have been obliged to undertake will produce a meaningless set of statistics which the Government will then be able to use out-of-context in their usual way to show how well the National Health Service is performing in the run-up to the next election. I think that's about it isn't it, Luke?"

"Couldn't have put it better myself," Luke agreed, smiling.

"The problem, of course, is that we're all finding it pretty tough going. What with our ongoing on-call commitments, etc., and what has been shown to be an ever more demanding public. However, no matter what the demands are of the job, our patients have the right to expect courtesy at all times from their doctor."

Luke sat a little uneasily. He had a fair idea what was coming.

"Well, anyway, the point is, Luke, we've had an increasing number of complaints about your manner. You are an intelligent man and your abilities as a doctor unquestioned. But tolerance is a virtue and success in general practice, as you know, requires being able to suffer fools gladly, which we've noticed you seem somehow less able to manage nowadays.

"We know what you've been through this last year with your divorce, and that can't have been easy for you. Perhaps it's time for you to take a break – arrange a sabbatical or something and get away for a while."

Luke found himself only half-listening. The truth was he was still feeling more than a little shaken over his earlier encounter with Christine West. He wondered what tone their practice meeting might take in the future should his partners ever get wind of that little faux pas. Despite her assurances that she was as keen as he to keep things quiet, it alarmed him greatly that her potentially violent husband might be on his track.

The idea about the sabbatical suddenly seemed very attractive. And the sooner he could get away the better.

Back in his consulting room, the phone rang. It was Louise, the receptionist, with more less-than-welcome news.

"Dr Darius, I have your brother Martin on hold. Shall I put him through?"

"Luke, how are you?" he began. It constantly surprised Luke just how unfamiliar his younger brother's voice seemed to have become these days. He wondered when he'd gravitated towards this particular highly polished version.

"I won't keep you long – I know how busy you medical types like us to think you are," he went on, in an amused, self-satisfied sort of way. Luke said nothing.

"Just to remind you it's Father's birthday celebration this coming Saturday. You didn't reply to the invitation, by the way. You'll be expected at Wetherfield by seven, so you'll have time to get ready before the other guests arrive. It's nothing too formal, but I'm sure you'll be keen not to let the side down. As you may know, there'll be quite a number of extremely important and, dare I say, influential people coming – not just from the Party, you'll doubtless be relieved to hear. By the way, will you be bringing a partner?"

Neatly slipped in, thought Luke. This was one of Martin's typically loaded questions, and somehow he resented it. He couldn't be bothered puzzling over possible implications but decided to hold back nonetheless.

"Shouldn't think so," he said vaguely; "I haven't really given it much thought."

"Right." Martin seemed reasonably satisfied with this. He went on: "Mother is so looking forward to seeing you and having the family all together at home once more. She's been preparing for this gathering for months. The old house hardly knows what's hit it recently – what with the decorators, and now the caterers..."

Luke let him continue, only half-listening by now. The large fern in the corner, he noticed, badly needed watering.

Not long after, he finally managed to put the phone down. Pompous asshole, he thought to himself. Strange how so short a conversation could reaffirm all those previous feelings he'd built up towards his brother over the years.

Two years younger than himself, Martin was a highly ambitious and, at times, Luke suspected, a pretty ruthless schemer. His seemingly endless circle of contacts never ceased to amaze Luke, who generally preferred to keep his distance. The truth was they seemed to have virtually nothing at all in common – except, of course, their parents. And it galled Luke to think of Martin content to ride on the back of their father, Sir Roger Darius' good name, in this, his latest venture.

For whatever reason, Martin had now decided to turn his attentions to politics – in his usual, almost obsessional way. Sadly, he shared few of his father's true virtues, apparent during the many years of his political career as a Conservative MP. Whatever dictionary Martin Darius kept in his study, old-fashioned words like 'integrity' and 'honesty' were apparently missing from it.

As far as Luke had become aware, he was now preparing to contest a marginal seat in the upcoming General Election with, he had little doubt, his own highly organised and equally underhand campaign.

Luke found himself contemplating the coming weekend with surprisingly little relish.

III

In London, the following day, Health Minister Harriet Fursdon gazed out fleetingly over the grey Thames from her

Westminster office, then resumed her dictation. The last letter complete, she turned to her secretary seated in one corner:

"That'll be all for now, Naomi. Send in Mr Darius on your way out, would you please?"

Almost before she knew it, Martin Darius had not only entered and shaken hands but sat himself down. He was now, as she watched, leaning back expansively in his chair admiring the decor. It appeared to meet with his approval.

The Health Minister had had, as far as she could recollect, no dealings at all so far with this young man – yet there was already something about his manner she disliked. There was a kind of smugness about him for a start. But, then again, some quite high-ranking ministers she knew spoke highly of him. Other colleagues in the House of Lords had apparently known his father, Sir Roger Darius, before he retired from politics some years before.

"Thank you for coming, Mr Darius. I'll be brief as I am sure, like me, you are extremely busy. I have here an article in one of our leading medical journals – one of a number recently, I may add – that has been particularly outspoken in its criticism of our recent health reforms. It was written, you might be interested to learn by a Dr Luke Darius. Some relation of yours, perhaps?"

"Yes, he's my brother. A family doctor in the West Country."

"Well, I need hardly point out to you the potential embarrassment to a Conservative Government caused by such articles in the run-up to an Election – especially if taken up by those, shall I say, 'politically unsympathetic' areas of the media over which we have absolutely no influence. The

Opposition would have a field day – particularly if it became clear they were written by the brother of a prospective Tory MP."

"I couldn't agree more. But regrettably, that's my brother for you. All I can say, knowing him as I do, is that the criticism is almost certainly not particularly politically motivated; he's far from being a political animal. More simply, a sort of harbinger of injustice as he sees it. Pretty harmless, really. Still, it certainly puts us in an awkward spot."

"Could you talk to him?"

"I could try, though I doubt it would get me anywhere. Luke and I have never really seen eye-to-eye – even from our earliest days. My simply appealing to him would, I'm afraid, almost certainly have just the opposite effect. Nevertheless, I agree: this problem must be curbed, and as soon as possible before it's too late. Leave it with me, Harriet – you don't mind me calling you Harriet, by the way? – I'm certain there must be some way of dealing with this."

IV

Having successfully got through what remained of that unusually eventful week, Luke Darius set off for Wetherfield House – his family home in Surrey – and his father's party. Although he'd finally managed to persuade the garage to part with his own car, Luke was still feeling a touch paranoid. He found himself checking out each vehicle following him in his rear-view mirror until he'd safely left the coastal town well behind him.

As he picked up speed heading east on the M4 motorway, Luke felt his gloom slowly begin to lift; a gloom which, when he thought about it, had been with him for several days now – following him around like his own pet cumulonimbus.

It was, therefore, pretty lucky for the hitchhiker, standing there in the drizzle at the exit of the Membury Service Station, that Luke's desire for company on the trip at that moment coincided so well with his overriding need for fuel.

She couldn't have been more than thirty, Luke guessed, hair drooping limply over her face, showering him with cold droplets as he grabbed her bag and threw it into the back seat. Her coat sagged despondently in a heap around her as she finally struggled free, shivering and damp on that darkening winter's afternoon.

Yet somehow, from amidst such apparent adversity, Luke had glimpsed something else, fresh and vital – an unfettered smile of gratitude; a willingness to talk, to share; an open warmth that radiated from her; a playfulness in her speech that drew him to her. Not physically – not in the usual way, at any rate.

Her name was Sarah; Sarah Wright. She was, Luke discovered, a junior reporter with the Herald, and had only recently returned to work after a pretty long layoff to have her son, who was now three. Things were fairly tough for her at the moment, she had confided – what with being a single parent and having a boss who insisted she should stick with pretty vacuous articles of 'female interest' only. A chauvinist of the old school.

But, despite it all, she was out to prove him wrong. The piece to finally change his mind was out there, she told Luke, just waiting to be written. And such was her conviction, and the earnestness of her face as she said it, that Luke couldn't help but believe her.

They talked easily and freely – she about her aspirations as a journalist and he about himself, his divorce and his own recent lack of conviction in what he was currently doing with his life. He told her about his own dabblings in medical journalism, and she seemed keen to hear more. Time passed quickly on the journey, the countryside flashing by virtually unobserved in that growing dusk.

It was then, as they approached London and the place he was due to turn off, that he got the idea. It was pretty devilish he had to admit – guaranteed to irritate the hell out of Martin, his brother. It was, therefore, definitely worth a try.

"Say, Sarah," he said turning to the rather bedraggled form in the passenger seat beside him, "how would you fancy coming with me to a party tonight?"

Chapter 4

Fairfax Building, New York

I

Back in the boardroom earlier that week, Ed Jamieson was just getting into his stride.

"Now, I think you'll agree, folks, from the data discussed at our last meeting, most of our problems seem to focus on one ship, and one ship alone – the Venus Prince. To recap briefly..."

Ed Jamieson looked up from the notes in front of him on the large shiny boardroom table and took in, in one brief sweep, the faces of the three other men seated around him. All but Dan Forsbrook – who, at that moment, seemed more interested in the contents of his coffee cup – looked attentively back.

"The first and main concern, of course, is the poor level of bookings since we started on the southern Caribbean itinerary three years ago. After the initial surge of interest came a fairly stable but unspectacular period. This, as you know, was followed over the past eighteen months by a definite and painfully slow decline.

"The second point is the vast number of complaints reaching us here at Head Office, from passengers of the Venus Prince. This level of complaint is strangely at odds with the findings from the passenger satisfaction questionnaires filled out at the end of each cruise and sent on to us from the ship every month. It almost suggests doctoring of the forms before they reach us."

Ed became aware of a slight murmuring amongst those present. Looking up from his notes, he couldn't quite ignore the suggestion on one or two faces of smiles strenuously suppressed for his benefit. If there was a joke, once again he'd missed it.

"Point three," he said quickly pushing on, "relates to some serious discrepancies noted in the last auditor's report. That, you will recall, was carried out on the ship last month, and raises many questions. Point four relates to the higher-than-expected turnover of staff compared to our other ships. We have no precise indication as to why this should be."

Ed looked around the desk to try to gauge the impact these facts had made on those present. Precious little or so it would appear, he concluded.

"Just what is it about this goddam ship that has caused it to become such a problem for us? I haven't even mentioned the increasing number of accident claims from passengers onboard having to be settled out of court. We aren't even able to contest them in most cases due to inadequate or missing reports, and poor documentation of events by key personnel on board. Not least of all, I might add, by our Mexican ship's doctor. Thank Christ he's just retired. Our legal boys don't stand a chance unless our Company protocol is strictly adhered to. I needn't remind you that the indemnity premiums have become a huge expense to us, and seem to be rising out of all control.

"As you guys well know, in the face of the current world recession and its effects on the cruise industry, there is stiff competition for a limited cruise clientele. Venus Cruise Lines just can't afford to have one of its four ships not pulling its weight. It's clearly time for some action."

Ed Jamieson paused – but long enough only for the keenest of interruptions. There were none; the facts without dispute. Chad Tomlinson, Dan noticed, was nodding slowly, as was his custom in these meetings, and John Warringer leaned back on his chair and gazed ceiling-wards in a reflective kind of way – as if at least attempting to unearth some kind of solution.

Dan had a few things of his own on his mind that morning – not least of all Hong Kong and how he'd better remember not to turn up there next time without a substantial amount of money. Not if he wanted to leave in one piece, that is. His time awaiting the rescheduled flight had been enjoyable, but not altogether profitable, at that back street gambling joint. At the time the fight broke out, he owed several people money – all of them, if his memory proved correct, named Wong.

Even now, he was sure the incident in that dark Kowloon alley a half-hour later was unrelated. He'd slipped clean away when the chips started to fly – something he'd become increasingly adept at over the years. But these were crazy times alright in Hong Kong – less than six months now till the handover – and tension in all quarters running high. The kind of place you couldn't guarantee not getting brutally attacked for the worthless contents of your attaché case; particularly if, like him, you were so transparently from out of town and alone.

32

He'd heard the muted footsteps behind him – a gentle padding sound, increasing in both frequency and intensity as they approached – and had timed his turn to perfection. The glint of the knife blade was the first thing to catch his eye. What happened next owed more to instinct than cold appraisal. An instinct, he was relieved to note, that had endured well since those long-ago days back in 'Nam.

He'd offered the case with the deceptive terminal thrust of a Kenny Rogers' fastball, and – in the vital second that followed – jumped his assailant, homing in very much on the knife arm. Forced hyperextension of the elbow swiftly loosened the blade, and three seconds later it was holstered neatly once more – only this time, fully up to its hilt in a surprisingly compliant rib cage.

It was only then, looking into the shadowy face before him – its features a frieze of utter disbelief – that it finally dawned on him. His assailant was little more than a child; a girl, he guessed, barely fourteen years old.

Only later still did Dan come to realise that he, himself, had not survived the encounter totally unscathed.

II

"The first thing, which I think is pretty obvious, is that we need to somehow keep a real close eye on just how the Venus Prince is operating, and insist on a much higher level of accountability by all those in charge. We must also take this opportunity of getting a far more efficient ship's doctor who can be briefed as to precisely what is required concerning accident reports and possible litigation."

"Would you suggest an American doctor, Mr Jamieson?" asked John Warringer, glad for the opportunity of at least contributing something to the meeting, in the face of what he feared was fast becoming another Jamieson monologue.

"No, they're far too expensive, John. We'd have to pay a US physician probably double what we're paying the Captain – not only is that an unnecessary expense, but it wouldn't go down too well with all the other Greek officers on board if they ever got to hear about it."

"Yeah, God help the poor Doc in that situation. They'd make his life hell," quipped Dan.

"No", continued Ed, "I've already given the matter some thought. The obvious answer is to recruit a British doctor – as we have on two of our other ships. They're well-trained, don't expect an outrageous salary, and can be taught to speak very acceptable American."

Chad Tomlinson took his cue and laughed appreciatively.

"By the way, Dan, I haven't had the chance to mention it to you before, but my niece, Tara, has been on to me about giving her a job in one of our overseas offices. She's keen on spending a little time abroad – now she's dropped out of military training down in Maryland – so I sent her over last week to London, and she's helping out there. I'll call her later today to get some ads out for the post of ship's doctor – ready for you to interview when you're over there soon. Okay?"

"No problem," said Dan.

"Now, gentlemen, my main proposal for the Venus Prince is bold, I'll admit, but the time has come for significant change. From the start of next season, the Venus Prince will abandon its present Southern Caribbean itinerary and sail instead out of Miami on shorter, more profitable, three or four-day fun cruises."

Holy shit, thought Dan Forsbrook, almost choking on the dregs of his coffee, the guy must surely be kidding! Had he really thought this thing through? And why the hell had he not consulted him first: his so-called 'Head of Operations' – the title Jamieson so fondly and repeatedly reminded him of? Hadn't he, after all, had years of experience running cruises out of Miami before he joined Venus Cruise Lines? Didn't he know all there was to know of the possible pitfalls? Just what on earth was Jamieson thinking of here? Such colossal overreaction! Had he no concept at all of the work that would be involved to bring this about? – work that Dan knew would undoubtedly fall squarely on his shoulders. And besides, wasn't it obvious to Jamieson that, by taking a ship out of Miami, he would be stepping directly on his old boss, George Mitchell's toes?

And Dan had no particular wish to run into George Mitchell again. Should the itinerary change happen, there was good reason to think that their meeting up would be somehow inevitable.

Dan tried to compose himself, curbing his urge for immediate combat on this one, knowing Jamieson would be waiting for his response. If there was one thing he had learned about Ed Jamieson over the past six years, it was that the best direction of approach for attack was never head-on. Rather than lock horns with the guy who paid the cheques, it always proved best to come in obliquely from the side, run with him a while, then try to veer him off his chosen course. Rather than come right out and tell the old asshole his idea was crazy, allow him to gradually see it for himself.

"Well, yes, that surely would be one way of dealing with the problem," said Dan slowly, "and in my experience, the shorter cruises – once properly set up with all the extra demands for more frequent baggage handling on embarkation and disembarkation etc. – can be made to run quite smoothly. It would, however, take a great deal of work to prepare for a new itinerary, and – in the case of the Venus Prince – considerable financial investment to get it up to standard for the strict US Public Health and Coastguard checks that would be needed. These, as you know, can be a real pain in the ass to achieve.

"Presumably sir, what you're intending then is to have the full galley refit and upgrade of the water system carried out at sea in the next couple of months, say, prior to perhaps a preliminary 'test cruise' up to Florida for the necessary certification checks – which, if successful, would give us the all-clear for booking next season?"

"Er, yes, Dan. I think that's more or less the scenario I had in mind," said Ed Jamieson uncertainly, trying to hide the fact he hadn't really thought it through quite that far.

"By the way, John," said Dan turning to the man on his left, "have you managed to get hold of that latest analysis looking specifically at recent changes in booking levels on the Venus Prince on its present itinerary since the Panama Canal stop was included six months ago? I understand they're quite encouraging."

It soon became clear to Dan though, looking back from this aside, that Ed Jamieson was no longer listening. He had already tuned in elsewhere to some inner voice. No matter what else was said that morning, Dan knew from experience that the meeting was now effectively over.

This latest development had been one hell of a surprise, to say the least. It was obviously some kind of knee-jerk reaction, but Dan had no real idea what could have prompted it. The galley refit and water system work for a start, would, he guessed, almost certainly cost in the region of three to four million dollars. The Venus Prince had been running for more than twenty years with the current galley set up – out of sight of passengers and barely reaching even minimum standards of hygiene. How a serious outbreak of gastroenteritis had been avoided since Venus Cruise Lines bought the vessel, he wasn't sure. In all other respects, though, the ship was four-star luxury, with countless millions spent on the initial major refit. But all its deficiencies would be woefully exposed if it applied to include a US port in its itinerary.

Dan had a feeling Ed Jamieson was in for a shock when the full estimate for works was prepared. In fact, he was pretty sure it would really only be a matter of time before this whole damn-fool proposal was completely retracted.

If not, he'd surely have to find a more certain way of persuading him.

Chapter 5

I

Wetherfield House, unruffled by time and serene in its quiet North Surrey setting, had played willing host to many a party of this magnitude over the years; three hundred and seventy-two years to be precise. Various historical documents attested to this, filed neatly away in the old library next to the billiard room.

Two Royal personages, apparently, had visited Wetherfield in the past – briefly, it was recorded, and on separate occasions – occasions, it turned out, separated by well over a century and so directly Royal, that Luke at that moment could no longer remember precisely who they were. More recently, though, Churchill had stayed overnight at some pre-war house party. Luke remembered wandering into the vast drawing-room on a number of occasions after discovering this, imagining that whiff of cigar smoke which, were it still present, would have been stale to the tune of some forty years.

The closest Luke could remember the family coming to actually raising the metaphorical rafters in his lifetime, had been the joint graduation party held for himself and Martin thirteen years before, on leaving their respective universities.

Although there were two years between them age-wise, Luke's basic degree in Medicine had taken two years longer than Martin's Economics course. A joint graduation party, therefore, seemed the obvious answer to their parents at the time. God, that seemed like a lifetime ago. Especially with all he'd been through since then. Probably the last time, in fact, that he and Martin had displayed any semblance of closeness.

Even then, though, Martin had pretty soon pissed him off, trooping his effete Oxford cronies around the place like he damn well owned it – like the rest of the family didn't exist and never had. Like he knew and really felt something special for the place.

But how could he? Unlike himself, he'd never really spent time there. Or precious little, at any rate, over the years. What with boarding at Eton, then going up to Oxford – sure, he'd fulfilled the family tradition right enough, and Father was pleased with that, he knew. But Martin had come away with, among other things, a sharpened sense of his own destiny. That very soon became clear – and God help all who dared get in his way. And the house always seemed to be there for him too, somewhere in the background – vast, impressive, yet curiously devoid of his own feelings and memories. A clear sign, though, to those he met of where he had come from and *ergo* where he was headed.

Luke, on the other hand, had resisted boarding school and somehow got away with it. He couldn't remember exact details, but somehow it just didn't appeal. Thankfully, his parents had relented, his mother, he seemed to recall, quite distressed by it all at the time. He had been moved to a day school nearby.

Academically he'd excelled – fairly effortlessly really – but it came as no surprise to his father that this son, at least, wouldn't be taking the traditional route to Oxford. In fact, neither Oxford nor Cambridge – unrivalled in the university prestige stakes – held much interest at all for Luke. Instead, in collusion with a group of like-minded school friends, he had soon devised 'the system'. This, like all serious statistical approaches, employed both intense mathematical analysis and, in this case at least, the reference publication 'Which University?' pilfered earlier from the school library.

Hidden there amongst the wealth of detailed information on each institution were some highly crucial sets of percentages – for each course offered, and for the university in question as a whole. And it were these sets of percentages, along with figures for total student numbers, that enabled Luke to make a vastly more informed choice.

For Luke Darius had been going through what his Biology 'A' level studies firmly reassured him was a thoroughly normal adolescence. And no way, he quickly realised, would university prestige alone be a worthy substitute for the opposite sex. With only 1 in 10 students at Oxford at the time reportedly female, its C.C.I (Critical Chick Index) – as it soon came to be known – drooped way down at 'totally flaccid' on the scale.

Luke's first choice, though, offered the rare combination of a healthily turgid score, strikingly beautiful city surroundings, and – by way of a bonus – considerable prestige in the subject he'd chosen: Medicine. And Bristol University had well lived up to his expectations. He could remember it all now as if it were yesterday: Clifton Village, the Downs, Gorge and Suspension Bridge; doing the rounds of Saturday night parties – a flagon of cider in tow to show willing and get you across the threshold; bright young women who'd take your drunken bullshit with the giant pinch of salt it deserved – good-humouredly, giving back as good as they got and more besides.

And it was mainly because of it all that, so many years later, Luke still found himself working in the West Country. The coastal town of Weston-super-Mare lay no more than twenty miles to the south – a resort of surprising beauty when the tide was in and the sun shining. But Luke had also come to know it on those many days when the sun didn't shine and the tide seemed to be out forever – and somehow he'd remained.

It was also the town he'd now just fled so ignominiously; the town he now knew he would have to leave behind him, at least for a while. Just as soon as the opportunity for that sabbatical presented itself.

"You don't mean to tell me that's it," said Sarah as the car turned in through the tall wrought-iron gates. The long winding drive lay ahead, the house itself clearly visible now about a mile away, high on the downland ridge.

"That's it alright," said Luke, "though I must admit I hardly recognise the old place with so much illumination. The floodlights around the house, by the way, are new. I rather fear that – like so much tonight – my brother will have had a fairly major hand in organising those. In fact, I doubt Father would really have had much of a say in it once Martin decided that was how he wanted to show the place off."

"They're certainly effective alright – particularly if, say, you wanted to come by helicopter," quipped Sarah.

"Don't joke. Nothing at all would surprise me as far as Martin's concerned. The guest list, too, I would guess. With the exception of a well-chosen dozen or so old friends of Father, I bet it reflects more on Martin's latest ambitions than on Dad's lifetime achievement. Either way, you might well be forgiven for thinking you'd just stepped slap into the middle of a Conservative Party Conference."

"Why so?" said Sarah with sudden interest, the journalist in her aroused. "And who on earth is likely to be there anyway?"

Luke kept her guessing, smiling to himself as he drove slowly on along the meandering driveway, darker now under a canopy of trees. A fox darted away to one side, out of the glare of his headlights and into a nearby hedge.

"And you're sure this dress will be okay – even though it's so spectacularly creased?"

It was the only one Sarah had with her – only slightly damp, she'd found, once it had been finally fished out from the bottom of her bag. She'd slipped it on in the back seat of the car in the darkness not long before, while Luke had taken a judicious roadside leak.

The road had been pretty much deserted, Sarah noticed at the time. She also noticed a sudden curious thrill of vulnerability she hadn't remembered feeling before – maximal at the very point her jeans had become momentarily stuck fast round her ankles. But he had waited, smiling and fooling about in the moonlight for her benefit. Running exaggeratedly on the spot to keep warm. Doing some kind of ridiculous dance moves. Safe and non-threatening, though she barely knew him. And somehow she appreciated that.

"Ready? Let's go."

Sarah glanced over at the house. All the ground floor rooms seemed a-buzz with activity. Luke watched as she shivered a little in the dark beside him, nervously in anticipation.

"Lead on," she said after a pause, her old confidence returning. "And don't stop till we hit the drinks table. I think somehow I'm in need."

"Relax, enjoy it. I'm sure, at the very least, you'll meet some incredibly 'interesting' characters here tonight – old farts, young farts.... oh, and not forgetting some incredibly boring middle-aged farts, too. You might even get material for that elusive story you've been after. You just never know."

II

Luke was pleased to see that his father seemed to be enjoying himself. At least enough of the old buffers – presumably from the House of Lords – had turned up to see him. Luke knew Sir Roger's recent bout of poor health had meant he hadn't been able to get up to London quite as often as he'd have liked. Members of his Club had also missed him – or so a jovial military-looking type with a drooping white soup-strainer moustache seemed to be telling him at that precise moment. A small trickle of red wine leaked gently from the left corner of his mouth as he spoke, Luke noticed, then on down his chin. The old man remained oblivious to it.

There had been a definite hush in the immediate crowd as they'd entered. The large entrance hallway looked somehow different – probably because Luke had never before seen it and the elegantly sweeping staircase adorned with quite so many people. People, he couldn't help but notice, so exquisitely dressed. The whole event so obviously without compromise. What else had he seriously expected when Martin was running the show?

Sarah stood there beside him, smiling yet again – her hair uneven, slightly clumped at the back where it hadn't quite dried. Her dress – already the subject of hot debate amongst women and men alike – hung limply and slinkily, right down to where it stopped abruptly mid-thigh. He noticed his mother rushing over through the crowd. A woman in her early sixties, she possessed a natural elegance; plainly dressed but tasteful. Understated as always.

"Ah, there you are, Luke, darling. How are you, and how was your journey down?"

"Fine, Mother, on both counts. By the way, I'd like you to meet Sarah... Sarah Wright – a very recent acquaintance, but already a good friend. She was at a bit of a loose end this evening, so I thought I'd invite her along."

"Pleased to meet you, Sarah. You're very welcome, of course."

Helen Darius had never let her two sons forget her comparatively humble origins. Born in Streatham, South-east London, of solid British lower-middle-class stock, she had trained as a nurse at King's College Hospital, no great distance away. A bright and attractive girl with an easy and reassuring bedside manner, she had secretly won the heart of Roger Darius all those years ago. Employed at the time in a private capacity at Wetherfield, she had been nursing his infirm father.

Captivated by her charms – so Luke's father had often admitted – the young and idealistic politician had worshipped her from afar. Although pursued by a number of fresh-faced debutantes, he showed little enthusiasm for their company. Eventually – taking the plunge – he proposed to Helen and shortly after, it seems, they were married. An ending, Luke had often joked on hearing the story yet again, of the truly fairy-tale variety.

Luke supposed she had been part of his reason for wanting to study Medicine in the first place. As barely an adolescent, he'd been intrigued by her stories of hospital life, questioning her about it repeatedly. And there could be no disputing in his mind the influence of her obvious respect for the medical profession. And somehow, deep down, he'd always so much wanted to please her.

"It's quite a bash," he said, now that Sarah had left them to get some drinks. "I hadn't realised there'd be quite so many people here."

"Neither had I until about a week ago," his mother said drily. "It was so kind of Martin to let me in on his plans. Still, at least Daddy seems happy that a few of his oldest chums made it along."

"How is he? Still on the treatment for his chest infection? This one certainly seems to have knocked the stuffing out of him; still looks pretty pale to me."

"He's definitely not his old self yet – physically or mentally. I'm afraid he had a bit of a further setback last week when he heard George Hobbs had died quite suddenly.

You remember George – MP for Oxford South? Collapsed in his bathroom. Two years younger than your father as well. It's quite shaken him up. The first thing he did was to call over his solicitor, John McPherson, to update his Will. Keeps saying how he's now really feeling his age. Have a chat with him, Luke, later on, if you get a chance – I'm sure he'd appreciate it. By the way, are you staying over tonight or have you got to get back?"

"Got to get back, I'm afraid. I'm on duty tomorrow."

"That's a shame. Incidentally, Sarah seems very nice. Known her long?" Luke smiled and looked at his watch.

"Not long," he replied mischievously.

Luke caught up with Sarah some ten minutes later. He saw her first in the distance at the far end of the drawing room – the bright yellow of her dress, for one thing, standing out loudly in the crowd.

"You know, it's amazing how different these Conservative politicians look in real life; and much more willing than I'd imagined to open up in this sort of party setting. Incidentally, I've been laying some pretty fine ground bait, in various directions. Hopefully, it'll pay off later with material for that story. Can't wait to see Sam Reynolds' face when I present it to him. He's my editor, by the way – the guy I mentioned earlier. I hope to open his myopic orbs once and for all to my immense potential."

They laughed together, enjoying, for what it was, their little conspiracy. Luke felt relaxed – more so than he had since they'd arrived.

"Do you know, these damn politicians are as randy as hell?" said Sarah quietly in his ear. "Especially the older ones. You wouldn't believe some of the propositions I've had – sometimes just a few feet away from their wives, too."

"There's Martin, by the way – my brother. Over by the grand piano," interrupted Luke, careful not to make his guiding nod too obvious.

"We've met already, actually. He stopped me not long back and wanted to know who I was and who I was with. Gave me the impression he thought I might be a gate-crasher or something. I told him I came with you."

"Good; that'll keep him guessing. By the way, do you want any food? It's through in the dining hall. I must admit I'm feeling a wee bit peckish."

"No, you go," said Sarah, a wicked gleam in her eye. "I'm off to stir up the suited gentry – just to see what happens."

III

Martin Darius was reasonably satisfied with the way things were going so far that night. The house had been presented just right, his father catered for well enough to feel the party might well be his, and nearly all of the right people had turned up. All the people, in other words, who really mattered at that moment in time, in the real scheme of things; those, that is, who could help him reach his political objectives.

For Martin Darius was not only a man of great ambition but also one who had long ago become acutely aware he was destined for bigger things. A man, too, who believed quite fervently in the advantage of the short-cut. Better to arrive than travel hopefully.

Sure, most of the really important guests – the elder statesmen of the Conservative Party – had come to honour his father. It was obvious too, though, that seeing Sir Roger in such a comparatively frail state of health, they would immediately make the subconscious mental leap of viewing his young, vigorous and politically ambitious son as his natural successor.

If he played the game right with his father over the coming months, there would be little cause for such an assumption to be refuted. A cleverly calculated ploy, he felt, which would give him excellent advantage at minimal cost. All he had to do after that was to con the electors. Not such a big deal, surely, to a man of his talents.

There had now, however, surfaced one particularly annoying fly in the proverbial ointment. The one made so clear to him by the Health Minister, Harriet Fursdon just recently – *the* Dr Darius, who had become more and more outspoken at such a critical time about the Government's failures in running the National Health Service. His very own brother, Luke, who, by association, could ultimately wreck his political aspirations.

He had to find a way to deal with him.

And the sooner the better.

Although Harriet Fursdon, the Secretary of State for Health, had been among those on the guest list, she had been included late – hastily following on from their recent meeting. So far, she had not turned up. Martin was not unaware of the opportunity to get a Senior Government Minister on his side, should he accomplish a solution to the problem before any real damage was done. Like stored Grace in Heaven – you just never knew when it might come in handy. When he might decide to call in the favour – as he most assuredly would at some point, however subtly, and for whatever purpose in the future.

And if what he'd recently overheard his mother telling his father was in fact only part way true, there was more than just a glimmer of hope for a solution. Sooner than he'd ever dared imagine. He'd better not miss the chance...

"Luke, there you are. Good to see you. Glad you made it down." Martin's voice boomed out loudly, easily filling the dining hall and reverberating effortlessly off the beamed and vaulted ceiling. A slightly delayed cringe of embarrassment at the sheer extravagance of the greeting interrupted Luke's half-eaten sausage roll on its way to his mouth. Faces turned towards him with sudden interest. He proffered a hand, a touch greasy he knew, there in the semi-darkness. Not such a good move, he thought, as it was suddenly clamped tight by Martin in a frenzy of joyous bonhomie. Just who the fuck does he think he's kidding? Luke asked himself, teeth gritting more and more tightly under his smile, and wondering just when the charade would end. And for who's benefit exactly?

"Hello, Martin," he said at last, quietly with finely-gauged reticence.

"You decided to bring someone after all. Met her earlier – very attractive girl," said Martin drily – quieter now, no longer playing to the audience. Definite sarcasm, though.

Luke relaxed a little. This was more how he remembered it. He took that bite of sausage roll; a measured pause while he ate it.

"And yourself, Martin – who are you going out with these days?" he asked, a touch tauntingly. Thinking about it, he couldn't remember being introduced to too many of Martin's lady friends over the years.

"No time, old son. Too much on for that sort of thing just at the moment. A politician's work, you know, is never done – particularly with an Election to fight. Quite a turnout here tonight, eh? How's the practice, by the way?"

"Fine."

"I hear you're considering a sabbatical?"

"Could be. Who told you that?"

"Oh, it was just something I overheard Mother mentioning to Father, that's all."

"Well, it's true that I'm considering taking a spell away from the practice. Let's face it, Martin, general practice under this Government isn't quite what it used to be," said Luke smiling, overtly tongue-in-cheek. "Nothing's arranged yet, though. Still examining the options."

Martin smiled back – a slow smile that said he was not prepared to be baited so simply. Certainly not there. Certainly not in those circumstances. Besides, he'd heard first-hand all he needed to know – and by sheer luck, he found himself in a position to act on it immediately. His American guest had made it along – fortunate indeed as he'd only just flown in from New York – and was here, he noticed earlier, with a smart young female colleague.

And now was the time to call in the outstanding favour he was owed.

"I haven't noticed, by the way, any of the top brass from the Department of Health here," said Luke "- or have I missed them, perhaps? One or two things I wouldn't mind discussing. It's possible they might even value my input – you know, as one of the grassroots GPs so regularly shat upon by successive governments over the years."

"No, I'm afraid there doesn't seem to be anyone here I can put you on to."

They were now walking through together into the drawing room – cigar smoke hanging in the air, but certainly no Churchillian overtones that night. At the far end of the crowded adjoining room, through the open double doors, Sarah could be seen, clearly deep in conversation with three men: one older – tall, thin and slightly aloof-looking; two middle-aged – grey lounge suits and fairly loud ties. One of them, Luke soon came to discover, with a laugh to match.

A woman whispered something to Martin in passing and he immediately broke away, following her over to the drinks table in the corner. The conversation at the far end of the adjoining room was becoming more animated. Sarah seemed to be holding her own – at least Luke could see her still smiling – sipping from her champagne glass at intervals, obviously making the most of the occasion; her mental notebook now clearly at the ready, open for business. Luke looked on, secretly amused. He was pretty sure not one of the assembled crowd that evening was quite prepared for Sarah Wright in her present mood.

Martin returned looking, if anything, a little flustered.

"By the way, Luke, your partner…?"

"Sarah?"

"Yes, Sarah. Where is she from?"

"Lives somewhere in Chiswick, I believe – I'm not entirely sure."

"You're not sure? How long have you two been together, if you don't mind me asking?" There was definite agitation in Martin's voice as he said it. He was trying, however, to sound casual.

This was it, thought Luke. Certainly a moment he was about to enjoy.

"We met this afternoon, as a matter of fact, on my way here."

"This afternoon?" blurted Martin in astonishment.

"She was hitchhiking and it was pissing down, so I took pity on her."

"And you thought it appropriate to bring her here?"

"Why not? She seemed genuinely interested when I asked her – keen to meet you all, in fact."

Martin digested this for barely two seconds.

"Oh, and why was that, do you think?" His look betrayed a sudden suspicion.

"Well, of course, besides being transfixed by my stimulating company, I believe she thought the experience might be useful to her in her line of work."

"Which is?"

"She's a reporter, as a matter of fact; a junior reporter with the Herald..."

Silence accompanied this remark as the blow struck home. Luke knew just what pains Martin would have taken to exclude the Press from a function of this sort.

"Oh really," was all he managed to say at last, before retreating once again behind his wine glass into a silence even stonier than the one before.

Luke left Sir Roger to his cronies, swapping stories about the Commonwealth. As far as he could be at that time, he was satisfied his father's countenance reflected more the slow recuperation phase of his recent illness than any fresh exacerbation of his chronic chest condition.

He had no wish to alarm him by probing too deeply. Besides, there had been a tacit agreement between them from his earliest days of qualifying, that he wouldn't blur the boundaries of their relationship by brandishing the tools of his trade. Father-son, not doctor-patient. His stethoscope, therefore, stayed firmly put in his doctor's bag back in Weston. In any event, Luke trusted his father's own specialists implicitly. He also knew that his father appreciated his gentle questioning, and took comfort from the love and concern it obviously represented.

A jazz band had started playing in the ballroom – New Orleans style – reminding Luke of his early days in Bristol, down at the Old Duke on King Street. Heading through to watch, he suddenly caught the glance of a young and strangely beautiful face, which – even now as he looked again just to be sure – still appeared to be aimed in his direction. A smile and a set of perfectly white teeth accompanied it. Luke's first thought was that the girl mistakenly thought she knew him. He smiled back automatically, forcing himself not to stare too long – not to be too greedy in attempting to take her in, all in one go.

His second thought, however, was that perhaps he'd inadvertently done something amusing or clumsy along the way – tripped someone up, maybe. Or that someone behind him that she knew was gesturing to her; and that instead, she was really looking straight through him as if he wasn't there. Just to be sure, Luke turned quickly on the spot and looked behind him. Then, a split-second to take stock, readjust, turn back, and look cool again. Or at least as cool as anyone could, having just gone through so complicated a procedure. Before he knew it, she had spoken. Definitely to him – and definitely in an American accent.

"Pardon me?" said Luke softly – so softly, in fact, he wondered whether this woman could hear him at all with the band just starting up another number. "I didn't quite catch what you said."

"I said, would you care to dance?"

"Sure. Thanks for asking. I'd be delighted."

And so it had happened. Her body was lithe but soft in the two slow dances that followed. Then they moved apart as the tempo picked up – Luke secretly glad as, besides the warmth of her body, he wanted to look at her face once more. Directly, there in front of him as they danced; their body movements, as time went on, less stilted, more carefree. The silent language of smile as the music engulfed them.

They had to go next door to talk – far enough from the band, but not too far, Luke decided a little guiltily, in case they should run into Sarah just at that moment. He felt he needed a little time to talk to this girl, alone and uninterrupted.

"What's your name?" he asked when eventually they'd found a quiet corner.

"Tara," she replied. "Tara Scott. And yours?"

IV

Tara Scott's trip to England had so far, by and large, lived up to all expectations. She had needed to get away from the US – that was for sure – after all that had happened to her in the past few months, and Uncle Ed's offer of work at the London office of his cruise company had come at just the right time.

Her mother, Kathleen, was shocked at first that she was going, but had finally come to accept her reasons. She hoped and prayed, though, that it would be only for a short time and that, Please God, Tara would work this travel bug out of her system once and for all, and come back to settle down with Hugh Gotley, there in Sheepshead Bay.

Hugh, a steady hardworking man, three years older than Tara, had been equally shocked but ultimately philosophical in the face of such adversity. Despite the age difference, they had nevertheless been childhood sweethearts. He, High School football hero; she, aspiring young cheerleader. Hugh always kept in his mind the times, after he'd left school to start work, that she'd been so obviously proud in front of her friends when he'd arrived to pick her up in his old Ford. He'd drop her off home, then return to the hardware store he'd inherited from his ailing father. Then, at the weekends, he'd take her to dances, and afterwards, they'd sit outside her mother's small clapboard house near the waterside, and talk in the darkness about their futures and how they might one day entwine.

Tara's mother liked him too: reliable and always charming – bringing her flowers when he came to lunch after late Mass on Sunday mornings.

But that was all before she'd gone to university – New York's own Columbia – staying weeknights in a tiny run-down apartment shared with two student friends who lived over in the centre of Queens. She had returned at weekends to see her mother but found all too soon that she'd changed – her horizons, her aspirations. And there, cloyingly in the background, was Hugh; and he'd never changed.

Hugh, she knew, had taken it badly when she first moved down to Baltimore on a short-term contract selling life assurance. And worse still when she announced one day, out of the blue, that she was planning to join the army.

Kathleen's only serious concern – and the subject of many of her prayers – was that Tara wouldn't have to go through the problems in life that she had. Her own grandparents, she was told, had come over to America from Ireland in 1911, settling in Brooklyn and working hard to survive during the many lean years ahead. Later, sometime after the Depression, the family had moved out to Sheepshead Bay into a house far grander than the one Kathleen and Tara later occupied there. Kathleen had married Johnny Scott, an attractive rogue it turned out, who drifted away out of their lives when Tara was barely seven.

Only by hard work and the generosity of the close Catholic community at St. Theresa's church did Kathleen ever manage, taking on whatever jobs she could to get by. Tara had been brought up strictly, but wanting for little that really mattered – with the exception, that is, of a father's love.

Kathleen Scott would accept no hand-outs – not even when her brother, Edward, seemed to be making it big with his travel business and offered to help. Only when it became all too clear that they lacked the resources for Tara's college education did Kathleen finally relent – nervous in asking him when it came to it, as by then they had grown considerably further apart.

Now, with Columbia long behind her, and with this latest work abroad he'd offered her in his cruise company, Tara was still the only real link between them.

Arriving in England, it had naturally taken a few days to adjust.

The office staff at all levels appeared friendly enough. This Tara found particularly comforting as only one or two knew she was related to the boss of the company. A surprisingly cosmopolitan crowd, too, she discovered. A couple of girls of roughly her age sported loud Australian accents – crude and confident together in this distant land. Another, notably meeker, sounded Italian. Her name was Loretta. The Australians, Keri and Gail, were staying in Earl's Court, she learned, and almost immediately invited her over for drinks one night, arranged now for that coming week.

The fax from her uncle in New York arrived only a week or so after she had, infinitely quicker, she quipped to the other girls at her desk as she read it, and considerably less jet-lagged. Under its directions, Tara had spent a pleasant few hours preparing, then distributing, the advertisement. It had gone first to the British Medical Journal (GP issue), then to 'Pulse', followed by 'GP' magazine, and then 'Doctor'.

The response had been tremendous. Almost immediately, resumés had poured in from all quarters; doctors of all ages and of all shapes and sizes. Accompanying photos, submitted as requested – reluctantly it would seem in many cases – bore silent witness to this. With the carefully ambiguous wording of the ad, as her uncle had instructed, and no doubt much as anticipated, few female doctors applied.

Then Dan Forsbrook had turned up. Tara knew from the fax that he'd be coming, and in a sense, she'd been looking forward to it. An impressive enough looking guy she'd found him – greying hair, six feet tall and slim, and probably, she guessed, in his early fifties. He dealt quickly and efficiently with a whole host of queries that had built up pending his arrival. Tara had shown him the bundle of applications for the Venus Prince position, and he'd squinted through them – mainly at the photos – intermittently chuckling to himself.

"Don't seem too many here that fit the image," he'd said at last, turning to her.

"How do you mean?"

"Too many of these tweed jackets. Your uncle's given me some pretty clear ideas of what he thinks this new ship's doctor should look like – you know, youngish and reasonably suave – for our new itinerary. Between you and me, I think he's been watching too many movies."

It was then Dan invited her to accompany him to the party there at Wetherfield House. It belonged, Dan told her, to an old business colleague he'd not seen for a while; someone who'd heard he was over in London and had contacted him. She hadn't recalled Dan mentioning at the time, though, that the man in question was, in fact, a politician.

One of the first things to strike Tara Scott had been the deportment of the other guests present that night. Though clearly not a black-tie event, it was certainly everything but. Some unwritten dress code was evidently in force that unfortunately she had no access to. It left her a little apprehensive about what she, herself, was wearing. Was it too brash, she wondered? A tad too unsophisticated for the company?

There were surprisingly few guests of her own age there, she noticed, for any helpful comparison to be made. She had stayed with Dan for the most part, straying off only once or twice as curiosity for what might lie in the next room on finally got the better of her. There was certainly more than a hint of mystery about the place, she thought. And so essentially English – at least as she imagined England ought to be.

Out of the corner of her eye just then, Tara noticed Dan talking quietly with his friend, the host of the party, behind strategically cupped hands. She had been introduced briefly earlier, not long after their arrival. A girl, perhaps the closest so far age-wise to herself – and wearing an outfit so outrageous that Tara immediately felt better about her own – was causing something of a stir among the small group at the far end of the room.

It was then Dan returned, smiled at her, and proceeded to outline precisely what it was he'd like her to do.

"A doctor? Get outta here. You're kidding me, right? Now, there is a coincidence."

"Why's that?"

"You're not going believe this."

"I'm not?"

"Well, you see, just so happens this company I'm working for in London, they're looking for a doctor right now. Getting pretty desperate about it, too, by all accounts."

"To do what, exactly? What sort of company?"

"A cruise company. One of the smaller ones – Venus Cruise Lines. You may possibly have heard of it. They need a doctor to work on one of their ships in the Caribbean. Great job for the right person, I understand. But obviously, they need somebody free at the moment – you know, to drop everything and get out there right away."

"To start when?"

"In the next week or so. As I understand it, they really want someone not too old, and single ideally. You wouldn't happen to know of anyone who might be interested, by any chance? One of your colleagues, perhaps – or yourself, even?" She threw this last part in seemingly as an afterthought; half jokingly almost.

"Wow. Sounds exciting. Could be interested myself, as a matter of fact. I'd need more details, though."

"Well, why not contact the London Office first thing Monday morning? Ask for a Mr Dan Forsbrook – he's the guy dealing with it while he's over from the USA. Tell him Tara Scott sent you. I'm working with him at the moment, by the way. Here; take my card."

"Thanks a lot," said Luke looking down at it briefly, knowing full well he hadn't one to offer in return. It told him some of the things, at least, that he needed to know about this rather fascinating creature.

V

A little later, with Tara now gone, Luke went off in search of Sarah. He was aware, particularly after this latest unexpected diversion, that he'd left her very much to her own devices over the past hour or so. Having seen her at work earlier on, though – clearly well in control of the situation – he had little doubt as to the potential of those devices.

He wandered from room to room looking out, initially at least, for her rather distinctive dress. The place had thinned out significantly. Older guests, on the whole, seemed to have already left. The main core of serious revellers had by now found their way through to the band, still playing in jaunty fashion in the ballroom. Sarah was not amongst them.

Luke made his way through to the drawing room which was fairly empty, and then the room adjoining where he'd last seen her. Two of the group she'd been with earlier were still there talking. Luke approached one of them to ask. Sarah, it seemed, had left the group roughly forty minutes before, and gone for a stroll with Martin on the terrace.

Luke went out through the French window nearby into the cold night air. The floodlights that had so powerfully illuminated the terrace were no longer on, he noticed, a little to his surprise. The clouds of earlier were thinning now, and at that moment an almost full moon appeared on high, bathing that side of the house in a subdued silvery glow. From where he stood, it was obvious: the terrace was empty.

He glanced at his watch, then turned quickly to resume his search indoors.

Ten minutes later, it finally sank in.

Sarah was absolutely nowhere to be found.

Chapter 6

I

Luke watched in silence as his brother patiently ushered out the last of the Old Guard into a waiting Daimler. Patient, however, was not something Luke himself felt just then.

"Say, Martin," he said at last when he found he could hold back no longer, "any idea where Sarah might have got to?"

Martin looked up briefly, letting slip for a second a facade of nauseating smugness. He flashed a cool glance over at Luke, then reverted fawningly once more to his guests.

"Sarah?" he asked vaguely, as the large car, at last, pulled sharply away.

"Yes, you know, the girl I brought with me tonight. I heard you took her for a stroll on the terrace earlier on; I don't seem to be able to find her now."

"You mean she didn't catch up with you before she left?" There was surprise in Martin's voice as he said this. "She intended to, as far as I know. Began feeling unwell and said she needed to leave. I managed to get a lift for her with friends heading back early to town. It's possible, of course, she might have noticed you otherwise engaged at the time and decided against interrupting."

"What sort of time was that?" Luke glanced at his watch, pointedly ignoring the inference. It was now 11.32 pm.

"About a quarter to eleven, I should think."

"What were you two talking about, anyway?"

"Oh, nothing specific; this and that, you know."

Luke bade his parents farewell, embracing his mother affectionately. He shook his father's hand – firmly but not aggressively so – their eyes locking briefly for a second, conveying more than simple words could ever hope to. His father's grip felt noticeably weaker, his hand somehow bonier than he remembered it.

"Let us know when you get something definite arranged for your sabbatical," his mother called as the old Citroen pulled throatily away.

At the end of the driveway, Luke stopped abruptly. Something on the floor of the passenger's side had caught his attention. The small leather purse was Sarah's, obviously left by mistake earlier. He looked at it triumphantly, pleased that he now had both reason and, hopefully, the means to see her again. Surely there would be something with her address on inside? If so, he could return it in person – then remembered with some embarrassment what Martin had intimated about her finding him with Tara and not wanting to interrupt.

Would she really have been offended, he wondered? He barely knew her, after all. There was little doubt in his mind, nevertheless, that he needed to see her again. For the first time in ages, he felt he had found a true ally; a kindred spirit. Besides, he wanted to know how she was feeling; whether or not she had recovered from her sickness.

The Chiswick address was there on the front of her driver's licence.

As Luke's car disappeared out of sight down the drive, Martin Darius reached into his inside pocket and took out a slim mobile phone. The person awaiting his call answered promptly. It was local traffic cop, Dave Watson; yet another person who owed him a favour.

Martin returned the phone to his pocket moments later, more than ever pleased with the way things were looking. It was completely fortuitous that his old acquaintance, Dan Forsbrook, had been there at all that evening at the party, and even more incredible that he'd been in any position to help him out. No doubt the promise of that ten grand had helped. If initial feedback was anything to go by, there was more than an outside chance his brother had been lured by the bait. He'd know for certain within a few days.

If doubts remained in Luke's mind as to which job to go for, the sudden loss of his driver's licence for a spell should make him realise the difficulties he'd now face working in the UK. And he had every faith in Dave Watson; he'd seen the way Dave worked in the past.

II

"Dr Darius? Come in and take a seat, won't you? Give me half a minute." The tone of his voice was deep, warm, American. He indicated the empty chair across the desk from him and returned to what he was writing.

Luke sat down and began looking around him as best he could, trying not to turn his head too far, or too obviously, in the process.

On the wall behind Mr Forsbrook hung a huge map of the world. It was peppered, Luke noticed, with an array of pins with large brightly coloured tops. These were clearly arranged in four discrete clusters – each cluster made up exclusively of pins of the same colour. Luke became suddenly aware of a strange surge of excitement somewhere deep inside him, seeing the whole world laid out so simply before him in this way. England was little more than a speck from where he sat, having finally located it just below the 'E' of Europe.

Just then, the American jumped up from his chair and, much in the manner of a quick-draw cowboy, thrust a sudden hand out towards him.

"Luke – very pleased you could come. I'm not sure just how much you know about the company."

"Only what I managed to read in one of your glossy brochures outside."

"Okay. Well, we're a US company with our Head Office in New York, and have four ships sailing in different locations around the world – one in the Far East, one in South America, one in the Med, and one in the Caribbean." He turned indicating the map on the wall. Four clusters of pins; four different itineraries.

"This one here in the Caribbean is called the Venus Prince," he added more specifically, pointing to the yellow group and pronouncing 'Caribbean' the American way, as if it had lost its first letter 'a'. "It's the one that currently has the vacancy for a ship's surgeon. Nearly all of our officers are Greek, by the way – a great seafaring nation if you're wondering why. On each of the ships, there are twenty or more nationalities among the crew alone. In the case of the Venus Prince, a 21,000-

ton vessel, there are about 340 crew serving the needs of a maximum 750 passengers."

Luke listened keenly, attempting to digest at least some of these facts – particularly about the number of nationalities on board. He was starting to wonder how well the French 'O' level pass he'd achieved at school, years before, and a rudimentary grasp of Latin – updated only by uneasy learning of anatomical landmarks at Med School – might see him through in the language department.

"Don't worry," said Dan sensing some apprehension. "There might be twenty-some nationalities onboard ship, but thankfully, only a few key languages – English, of course, being the main one. Besides, you can always find someone or other to act as interpreter. As far as the crew is concerned, though, from a Company viewpoint, the doctor's job is simple; you look after them and you keep them working, or, sign them off and send them home – particularly if they're likely to be out of action for more than just a few days. We can get a replacement in quick then, and keep the show on the road. After that, of course, there are the passengers."

"Where do they mainly tend to hail from?" asked Luke.

"Ninety-five per cent, I'd say, from the USA. No language problem there, on the whole – though I've got to admit, as a nation, we're a pretty mixed bunch. The main point is, though, that being American, they're going to expect a high level of service all round."

"What sort of medical facilities are there onboard?"

"There's a small hospital – only one or two beds; though, of course, more can be made available in an emergency by vacating some of the crew cabins nearby. Also, there's a small operating area, X-Ray cubicle, doctor's office and dispensary, as well as an adjacent waiting room – such a compact set-up, in fact, you'd hardly believe your eyes."

"Just the one doctor?"

"Yeah, and a nurse."

"On duty continuously?"

"Effectively, yes. The doctor has office hours for passengers and crew separately, morning and evening, but he must, of course, be on call for emergencies outside those times. The itinerary is arranged on a weekly cycle, as you can see," he said, pointing to the map once more. "Most days, you'll be pleased to know, the Venus Prince spends a fair deal of time in port. The passengers leave the ship on shore excursions and there's a good chance then for the crew to spend some time themselves away from the ship. During these periods though, either the doctor or nurse must remain in attendance onboard, just in case."

"How much actual surgery gets done on board ship these days? Surely the facilities are a little limited for anything too major?"

Luke wondered if Dan Forsbrook had sensed the level of anxiety he felt over this issue – either in the tone of his voice, or the rather oblique way he'd phrased the two questions. It had been years since he'd removed an appendix – back in his hospital days. Then, he recalled, he had had a highly organised theatre – the operating trays neatly set up in preparation, with all their instruments in the right places, and a skilled and attentive theatre nurse on hand. Not to mention the anaesthetist, often as junior as he, quipping away encouragingly at the top-end, or calling out instructions from some manual of surgical practice – more often than not in the wee small hours when the hospital was at its quietest, and the junior staff took on the bulk of incoming emergencies.

"The idea," said Dan, "is to operate only when there's effectively no other alternative. As I mentioned earlier, itineraries are arranged so that there are only fairly short hops between ports, in most cases. Our policy tends to be to get emergencies off ship whenever we can, to appropriate shore-side facilities. Both the Company and our insurers recognise the limitations of the onboard medical set-up. The insurers are particularly keen that, with passengers especially, we act as defensively as possible and take the utmost care not to leave the Company at risk of litigation. So, no cavalier attitude to surgery – or other aspects of treatment, for that matter. If there's any doubt at all that the medical approach in any serious situation could be questioned later, we encourage getting a second opinion from a local specialist as soon as reasonably possible. The doctor, of course, needs to know the quality and range of medical facilities available locally – many of which, by the way, in the Caribbean are pretty limited. He also needs to judge when to refer for treatment, or when indeed it might be better to keep the passenger onboard ship.

"Okay, Dr Darius, let me take you through a little scenario – just to give some idea of the other practical decisions to be made whilst at sea. Let's say you've got a frail eighty-year-old passenger who's fallen and broken her hip on board. You've X-Rayed and made the diagnosis. Due to her general condition, you want her to go to hospital ashore as soon as possible. The ship is 500 miles from your next port of call. What kind of options can you envisage here?"

"How d'you get on?" asked Tara Scott when he emerged ten minutes later from Dan Forsbrook's office.

"Fine. He offered me the post."

"Way to go, Luke. Say, when do you fly out?"

"Three days' time – Friday morning, actually. Mr Forsbrook's given me copies of inventories of medical equipment and supplies currently on board to look through in the meantime. Apparently, if there's anything I feel is particularly required, the Company will simply order it and fly it out as soon as possible to meet the ship."

"Yeah, the Company's good like that," said Tara. "Uncle's never been one for skimping on necessities."

"Your uncle?"

"He owns the Company."

"Mr Jamieson? Is that him? Dan Forsbrook mentioned his name earlier."

"Yeah, that's right.

"Oh," said Luke, barely able to disguise his amazement. He reflected silently for a moment; something had just occurred to him. "You didn't go pulling any strings to get me the job, by any chance?" he asked quietly, looking her full in the eyes.

"No way. I'm just a lowly office hand here, after all. My uncle took pity on me and gave me a job for a while so I could spend some time abroad. Other than mentioning the post to you at the party the other night, I've had absolutely nothing else to do with it."

What Tara had actually said was true enough in itself. The only bit she held from Luke was the strange way Dan Forsbrook had asked her to approach him, get talking, then let it slip about the job. Okay, so the guy was being headhunted – nothing so terrible in that these days, surely?

"Right," said Luke, evidently satisfied with this, "well, I for one am in the mood for celebrating. Care to join me for dinner this evening?"

"Not possible, I'm afraid. You see, I have this prior engagement."

"I understand," said Luke, clearly a little deflated. "Perhaps just a quick drink, then, when you finish up here. What time would that be – about six?"

"Okay," she replied at last, "but it'll have to be quick. I've got to get home and get ready; I'm being picked up at eight."

"Great," said Luke, not wanting to enquire too closely who exactly was doing the picking up. Though just a hint might help.

Chapter 7

I

As he sat there on the westbound tube from Hyde Park Corner later that evening, it occurred to Luke he'd so far given little thought to his impending travels. The drink he'd had with Tara had gone fairly well – she'd at least laughed at his jokes, and talked once or twice as though there might just be some level of interest. But, conversely, she had insisted on repeatedly looking at her watch – three times, he recalled – eventually prevailing on him to wind things up after about forty minutes so she could get back to her Chelsea flat and prepare for her evening out.

What it was about her that attracted him so, he couldn't, even at that time, really begin to say. She was beautiful, yes – undeniably – though not in any overt, up-front sense. She wore little in the way of makeup, for a start – her hair, he'd noticed, strangely unflattering in both length and general style. No, it was her eyes, quite definitely, that had it. Playful yet unsettling eyes he found them, welcoming your gaze then drawing you effortlessly in. Troubled eyes, now and then when you studied them, which seemed to hold secret a story from some other time.

What was that story, Luke wondered? She had hardly proved forthcoming so far. He'd given her space to tell him without too obviously being seen to pry, but she'd remained strangely evasive. Two possibly quite unrelated facts, though, had emerged at different times that evening. One was that she was working here in England not simply for the experience, but as an antidote to some more restrictive alternative back home. The other – more surprisingly, perhaps – was that she had apparently undergone the beginnings of some form of military training.

The other very important thing he knew little of even then, was, quite simply, her plan for that night. He sensed a certain reticence (or had he imagined it?) when he'd tried to enquire earlier, as discreetly and obliquely as possible. If there was a rival for her affections – which Luke somehow felt certain was the case – either she'd known him from before, or he'd got in pretty smartish since her arrival in England only two weeks back. And what possible chance would he have now that he was to fly out in the next few days? Sure, he'd be back – but when? And would she still be around when he arrived?

II

"I must say it was extremely good of you to come all this way just for a purse."

It was thirty-five minutes later when Luke had finally made it along to Sarah Wright's Chiswick address.

"No trouble, really. Besides, I wanted to see how you were."

"Just fine, thanks. Can't remember when I've had such an enchanting few days." The sarcasm in her voice was almost palpable. Luke was puzzled but persevered. Her eyelids were red and heavy, he noticed, and she seemed to be avoiding looking directly at him where he sat.

"I meant about the party. You got home okay?"

"Not exactly," she said at last. "I had a bloody awful time, in fact."

"Why, what happened? The last time I saw you, you seemed to be enjoying yourself – right in the thick of things with some pretty hardened politicos."

"Yes... yes, I was," she said reflectively, "and at that point, I really felt I was getting somewhere."

"Well, what happened then? I heard you went for a stroll with my dear brother."

"That's right. Your brother came over, told me he'd like a word in private and took me off somewhere quieter where we could talk. As we walked through one of the rooms, there you were with some very attractive woman you seemed to be pretty friendly with. I happened to mention 'Oh, there's Luke', and your brother replied 'Exactly, and that's what I wanted to talk to you about.' We then went out onto the terrace."

"And what did he have to say to you out there?"

"He told me he'd invited an old flame of yours to the party without you knowing, thinking you would be coming alone. Said your family was keen for you two to get together, following on from what he termed your 'rather messy divorce.' Apparently, there'd been family concerns over your mental state since your marriage break up, and relief that you and this woman seemed to be hitting it off once again. Your brother said you had decided to take up your parents' offer to stay overnight – as this friend of yours was also staying, by prior arrangement."

"You're kidding. He said that?" said Luke, hardly able to believe what he was hearing.

"Yes. He then told me, as party host, how embarrassed he felt – as it was quite clear you'd forgotten all about me, and how would I now get home?"

"The scheming bastard! What then?"

"Well, hearing that I had to get back here to Chiswick, he told me he'd try to organise something. He left me waiting for a few minutes, then came back with this chap Alex, just leaving and heading back this way, who would be able to drop me off. They had with them my hold-all from your car – but, of course, I'd forgotten about the purse. Apparently, this Alex was in some kind of hurry, so I had no chance – nor was I encouraged, by the way – to seek you out to say goodbye. Your brother gave me the impression it wouldn't exactly be a good idea. So off I went, there and then."

"I see," said Luke gravely. "The plot thickens. I should have guessed something like that might have happened. Martin or one of his cronies must have broken into my car to get your bag out without making it too obvious. Anyway, how did it all turn out?"

"Fine until we arrived in the outskirts of London. Then he got a call on his mobile and, after that, his whole attitude suddenly changed. Said he had to get somewhere urgently as a result of the call and had to drop me off, therefore, virtually right where we were.

"I managed to get a taxi eventually," Sarah went on, "though it took bloody ages. The streets, of course, were pretty much deserted at that time of night. When I finally arrived back in Chiswick and discovered I was without my purse, I had to go call on my mother; I had no money at all to pay the cabbie and no keys to my flat. It was pretty late and naturally, she got herself into a bit of a state. Not something I'd care to repeat, thank you."

"Christ, what can I say?" said Luke. "Really, I had no idea. I'm afraid you've experienced first-hand precisely how my brother works. It's pretty clear he wanted you out of the way. Probably felt you were stirring up trouble. He told me, by the way, you'd had to leave because you'd suddenly felt unwell. Also – according to him – so desperately offended were you by my attention to some other girl, you really didn't feel like saying goodbye. A girl, incidentally, I hadn't met before in my life – nor someone known to my family in any way, as far as I'm aware. Fresh over from the States – in the past couple of weeks, as a matter of fact. Interestingly enough, when she heard I was a doctor, she told me of a position going in her company, on a cruise ship out in the Caribbean. I applied to her boss, who interviewed me today, and I got the job. I'm flying out on Friday."

"Lucky for some – having the chance of that sort of work. Work, by the way, is a bit of a sore subject for me at the moment."

"Why's that? What about the party – didn't you manage to get any material at all for a story?"

"Oh, I got material of sorts, alright. Even, in my excitement, started turning some of it into an article the very next day. Oddly enough, the article in question – the first of two or even maybe three, I was hoping – wasn't even too provocative: 'How the Tory Ministers let their hair down in the evenings', that sort of thing. A fat lot of good it did me."

"How do you mean?" asked Luke.

"Well, I approached Sam Reynolds, my editor, with my first draft today. He took me into his office and listened closely – or so it seemed – to what I was saying. Even asked some questions and I thought I'd finally cracked it – that, at last, I'd produced something that really impressed him; something that had made him finally take me seriously as a journalist. Instead, his tone suddenly changed and he became extremely serious. I remember the look in his eyes – I'd never seen it before. He told me that he'd had longstanding concerns over my attitude and that this piece merely highlighted how my views were so clearly out of line with the political viewpoint of the paper. He incensed me so much – especially being so totally dismissive of all my work to date, and ticking me off so insultingly in that chauvinistic way of his. Then promising to keep 'a really close eye on me in future'. I knew exactly what it meant – effective demotion, that's what it meant. As if that were in any way possible. I'm already only one step off tea-lady since coming back after my time off having young Toby here. The sod put it in such a heartless way too, it became clear my position was totally untenable. I told him as much, but he didn't seem in the least put out. So, I handed in my resignation. It gave me a little satisfaction, at least, at the time – but I rather fear, by the look in his eye, that it gave him a hell of a lot more."

"My God," said Luke. "What will you do now?" His eyes swept around the apartment as he said it. Not luxurious by a long chalk, but no doubt costing enough rent-wise each month – particularly there in the London area.

"My only option, I suppose, until something else more permanent comes along, is to go freelance. No guarantees, of course, that anything of mine will ever be taken up. No real security at all, in fact. I'll just have to sit down and prepare a whole batch of articles as a stock, ready to send out to all and sundry. Only trouble is, I'm feeling so totally fed up with it all. Can't imagine how I'm going to be able to concentrate enough to produce anything even remotely worthwhile."

"You'd be more than welcome to any of my unpublished articles – there are a few I haven't quite got round to submitting yet. One or two even have a little research work attached which you could easily rehash for more general consumption under your own name. Wouldn't worry me in the slightest. Besides, I'll be out of the country for several months at the very least, I should think. I could send them on to you before I leave."

"Thanks, Luke – I might well find them useful. Got to admit I'm definitely feeling a little desperate now, thinking about it all." She paused for a while, her face set, her chin somehow more accentuated in its profile as he looked at her. "Do you know what's just occurred to me – bearing in mind all that happened the other night, and everything, of course, that's transpired since?"

"No, what?" said Luke, intrigued.

"Your brother might well have had something to do with this latest incident at work today. You know, with Sam Reynolds and the way he acted towards me. I can't be sure, of course, but the more I think about it, the better it fits. What a complete and utter bastard, if it's true. Think it's possible your brother could have been in touch with him?"

"I'm afraid nothing would surprise me about Martin. He has a huge network of contacts and, knowing him, a fair amount of influence where he needs it most."

"Well, I promise you one thing, Luke: I'm going to find out for certain, one way or another, whether or not it's true. If it is, I vow to you now, I'll do everything in my power to expose him for what he really is." The bitterness of her words gave way abruptly to steely silence.

"Do you think it might serve any useful purpose if I had a word with him?" asked Luke. "Let him know we know all about his filthy scheming?"

"No, I don't. It would only put him on his guard. For the moment, at least, it's clearly more to my advantage that he remains unaware of the precise motivation behind any vendetta he may come to suspect against him." Luke could appreciate the logic.

They were both standing now, Sarah holding her son.

"Well, good luck," said Luke, kissing her gently on the cheek. "I'll write to you, if that's okay. I can't help but feel somehow responsible – having taken you to the party in the first place. You will let me know if there's anything at all I can do to help?"

As he waited for her reply, the three-year-old suddenly relaxed his grip around her neck and let out a long, soft snore.

It was only then Luke realised that he and Toby hadn't even been properly introduced.

Chapter 8

I

What struck him most forcibly there on the Sea Grape Terrace of the Half Moon Club early that evening, was just how submissive the fleeting Caribbean dusk had been in giving way to night.

Standing there right from the very time that day-worn sun had first bowed out over the horizon – somewhere in the direction of Negril to the west – Luke Darius had hardly a chance to finish his first Daiquiri. Admittedly, he'd taken it slowly; slow sips interspersed with long pauses as he tried, amongst other things, to analyse the precise derivation of the music drifting over to him from somewhere down by the beach. Calypso? – well, one or two of the numbers he'd heard might fit. Then there were the steel drums, ringing out in truly characteristic tone. And there, steadfastly behind it all, the purest reggae pulse he'd ever heard. Ever felt, even. Produced there for him so effortlessly, so teasingly, by mere kids – some, he would wager, barely twelve years old. Then, and then again, the sort of tantalising rim-shot punctuation and drum fill that had provided for him such percussive delight over the years. There in Jamaica. There in the land it first began. He could hardly take it all in.

Night was different here. Even darkness itself was somehow different. It descended and engulfed, joining almost seamlessly with the tall, lushly-silhouetted vegetation. There all around him – warm, humid and thrilling, trapping within its midst all manner of nameless scents.

Luke looked out over the lively crowd assembled round about in the hotel grounds. Behind them an occasional glint of light over the calm waters of Montego Bay. Before that day, the place had been little more to him than a song title. A memorable enough song though, admittedly.

Luke's introduction to Jamaica had begun several hours before, as the BA flight direct from London Gatwick touched down in the small airport of Montego Bay itself. It had proved a tiring enough ten-hour trip which had begun early that same morning in a not untypical English drizzle. Luke found himself pleased to leave it behind him as the plane swept up through the thick cloud cover, into the bright and altogether more cheerful world above.

He was resigned now, in his mind, about Tara and the only possible option open to him as far as pursuing her. Things had happened rather quickly since they first met, barely six days before. Although his feelings for her were clear, he was old and experienced enough to understand there was slim chance of anything more ever coming of it. He was also sufficiently realistic to know that the reference point she stood for in terms of desirability would undergo, with time, a natural recalibration, along with the inevitable broadening of his horizons. In fact, from where he sat at that moment looking out into endless sky, he was aware the broadening process was already underway. Not a hint of any horizon was visible.

A limbo contest was getting underway not far off. Luke sat on his barstool under the circular straw canopy of the beach bar, and craned his neck a little to watch. A crowd had gathered already. A round-faced man with glasses that Luke recognised from his flight earlier, had just bowed out early – principally, it seemed, because he'd forgotten to bow at all, either forwards or backwards. A sizeable paunch hadn't exactly helped. His effort though, such as it was, was greeted with equal applause. The man smiled proudly by way of response and wiggled his portly torso beneath his first, carefully selected Hawaiian shirt as if to show he, too, was into the swing of things. No party-pooper he. Then, without stopping, in one enviably flowing movement – danced no doubt to some secret calypso of his own – he continued up the beach to his waiting barstool. Luke moved slightly to accommodate him.

"Thanks," he said a little breathlessly, though clearly trying not to show it. "You need another drink?" His voice was soft and slightly nasal – from somewhere in the north of England.

"Cheers, same again, thanks." Luke pushed his empty beer glass towards him along the bar. "I'm Luke Darius, by the way."

"Duane Dalton," said the man, amidst the noisy chatter round about them. Luke thought he must have misheard. The name had a slightly unlikely ring about it, particularly for a northerner.

"How long's your vacation?" asked Luke, taking a mouthful of pale beer through an inch and a half of froth.

"I'm not over here on holiday," said the man. "I've come to work. I'm joining a cruise ship tomorrow."

"Really?" said Luke. "Me too – the Venus Prince."

"That's the one," he said. "What's your line of work then?"

"I'm taking over as ship's doctor. And you?"

"Oh, something far more important, I'm afraid. In fact, I often wonder how any ship could ever dare leave port without someone of my expertise on board. I'm a stage-hypnotist – one of the entertainment and cruise staff. Last week, a flatulent working men's club in the north of England; tomorrow, the world. Duane Dalton, by the way, is my stage name. Real name's Harry Egglestone."

Luke looked at him slightly in awe for a moment or two. He'd heard of the kind of things these guys could get up to. His time on ship was promising to be even more interesting than he'd first imagined.

"Well, here's to a great time on board," said Luke raising his glass.

"Hear, hear," said Duane Dalton, once more putting his alter ego firmly behind him.

They drank a few more beers together – in honour of Venus Cruise Lines and its touching faith in their respective abilities – then turned in for the night.

II

Tassos Demetriou, First Engineer, climbed the steps from the engine room deep inside the Venus Prince at 11.30 that following morning. His standard-issue V.C.L overalls clung sweatily to his ample body, such had been the temperature down there that past hour. His forehead was oil-stained, wiped carelessly by the back of an occupationally greasy hand when he wasn't thinking. Or, more precisely, when he was thinking – but concertedly so about something else entirely.

The temperature in the engine room seemed to have altered little since the Venus Prince had first docked there in Montego Bay, some three and a half hours before. The necessary maintenance that morning had kept him a little longer than he'd anticipated. All he wanted at that moment was a quick mug of coffee in the mess – thick and black as he liked it – and a slow cigarette or two. Trouble was he'd smoked his last, and most of his compatriots had by now all gone ashore. He sat for a while alone in the deserted mess-room wondering idly about lunch, or what passed for lunch in those glorious hours between cruises when all the passengers had disembarked and the new ones were yet to arrive.

The menu posted on the mess door by the hapless Italian waiter – relegated out of disfavour to the task of serving only crew – promised much as ever. Tassos, though, found he was getting increasingly tired of the fancy Italian names used, week after week, to describe just one type of meal. It amazed him that there were so many variations in that noble language for the simple word 'leftovers'. Trust the Italians to do it so stylishly tongue-in-cheek.

Tassos Demetriou – as all who knew him would tell you – was a big friendly Greek man with a hearty laugh, a ready smile and two prominent gold teeth. There were others of other colours too, as it happened – ranging from off-white to black – but not many. Though his gait was slightly lumbering and ungainly, he possessed a charm and generosity of spirit few could ignore for long.

He had been at sea now almost half his life, and away from his wife and family for a spell of seven months so far, this time around. Tassos thought of them often, at night alone in his bed, and what they might be doing back home. He could readily picture in his mind their little house on the hillside outside Salonika, and how it would be looking at different times with the changing seasons.

Only four months more, his contract complete, he could return to his beloved country once again. Perhaps, after that, he'd find a ship that plied its trade closer to home. Or maybe even try something completely different – as he'd promised himself on an ever-increasing number of occasions as time had gone on. Sure, he'd get lucky in the disco on some of the cruises after the Captain and other senior officers had had their pick. And yes, some of those American girls could be really hot stuff – back there in his practical cabin with the token double bed; the only size of bed, he'd come to discover from bitter experience over the years, that could seriously hope to rest all of his massive frame at the same sitting.

But he was getting to an age now, he was aware, when the odd fling provided scant recompense. He'd hardly seen his kids grow up, and he wanted to be closer to his parents – now both old and feeble. He knew above all that he'd never forgive himself if either of them died while he was so far from home.

Tassos finished his coffee – now even thicker as it had cooled and settled in the bottom of his mug. He needed those cigarettes with a vengeance he suddenly realised. It wouldn't take a minute to pop ashore to get some from the nearest bar. Few people were about just then, so it mattered little that he was still in his overalls. He'd clean up later and relax a little before the new passengers arrived for boarding.

As he walked down the gangway, Tassos was struck once again by the rare beauty of the island. Palm trees edged their laden canopies close to where he stood, shadowy and welcoming in the midday sun. He'd seen many beautiful islands on his travels, but few really to compare with this.

He strolled through the open gates of the port enclosure – a token wire-mesh fence – and spotted the bar, a low flat building, barely three hundred yards ahead. A tune from the ship's disco came to mind, and he immediately attempted to whistle it. Barely ten bars through, he ground to a halt. Music had never been his strong point and besides, it had just come to his attention that he was not entirely alone; something of a shock to a person whose whistling was as tuneful as his.

A young local girl appeared before him. There, suddenly, from out of nowhere, just as he had rounded the first bend in the path. Small and slight-of-build, she was strikingly pretty; her hair a cascade of fine plaits each terminated by a small pink ribbon. Tassos stood like a giant above her looking benevolently down. Despite her size, she spoke up directly and confidently:

"Hey, Mister. You want fucki fucki?"

"No, thank you," he said, shaking his head concertedly and walking on.

"Only fifty dollars US," she said, managing somehow to keep up with him along the path.

"No, thank you, really."

"Forty dollars then?"

"No, really, thanks – I'm only just going to the bar for some cigarettes. Then I've got to get straight back to ship to work."

"You want sucki sucki, then? It's a bit quicker if you're in a hurry."

"No, thanks."

"Only thirty dollars."

"No, really..."

"Twenty dollars then, Mister, and I give you real nice sucki sucki."

"No, I'm sorry. I've only just got enough with me for my cigarettes."

"You're not telling me the truth, Mister. Show me then."

"Look," said Tassos, fully confident on this point. He dug into his overall pocket and pulled out the few creased notes from within.

"Only twelve dollars with me, and as I said I need that for... "

"That'll do fine," she said, deftly snatching the money from his open palm. Before he could ever hope to react, she had lifted her short white skirt right up to her navel and tucked the notes quickly, if not a little provocatively, down the front of some alarmingly skimpy knickers.

"Come," she said triumphantly, ignoring all protestations and leading him determinedly by his large oil-stained hand towards the dense undergrowth nearby.

III

It was 3.30 that afternoon when Luke Darius arrived at the quayside to board the Venus Prince. Although the ship wasn't due to sail till nine that night, passengers, he knew, would begin boarding at 5.15. It struck him, therefore, that he couldn't seriously leave it much later. Besides, his desire to see as much as he could of the island – or at least that part in the immediate environs of Montego Bay – was countered by an ever-increasing curiosity about the ship he was about to join. The ship that would be his home for several months at the very least, if all went well. And who knew what, after that?

He recognised it at once in the distance as he approached, from the photos in one of the brochures he'd seen. Its outline was quite distinctive, managing – despite its size – to look somehow sleek and streamlined. The large funnel, projecting high from the rear aspect of the vessel was itself swept-back looking; a little like the dorsal fin of some huge amiable shark. A logo of sorts was inscribed on it; the Company's no doubt, Luke surmised. Towards the front – he'd have to start learning the technical terms for these things soon – there was an even taller projection skywards, somewhere above the Bridge. The radio mast surely, with – if he was not too much mistaken – a satellite receiver halfway up. Two rows of streamers came from the pinnacle of the mast back towards the base of the funnel, flapping jauntily in the gentle sea breeze.

As his taxi got closer still, Luke found his eyes focusing on a series of lifeboats forming a neat row along the side of the vessel, taking up a good chunk of the mid-section. Above that deck, he counted three others. Below it, he couldn't really be sure.

A sailor stood at the foot of the gangway setting up some bunting, and Luke nodded to him as he made his way, fully-laden, up the gangway. The foyer he found himself in was large and circular, with various kiosks around its periphery. One bore the sign **PURSER**, and another **CRUISE OFFICE**, with a sub-heading below it, which somehow made more sense to Luke just at that time: **RECEPTION**

"Ah, hello Doctor, we've been expecting you. How was your trip?"

"Fine," said Luke.

"I'm Martina, by the way, one of the cruise staff. I'll just call the nurse, who'll hopefully be able to show you around – your cabin, the hospital, etc. You have office hours this evening from seven to nine, so you'll have plenty of time before then to sort yourself out. I'll let the Captain know you've arrived; he'll no doubt want to see you at some point. Incidentally, you should find that some temporary uniforms have been delivered to your cabin already. They should do until your own arrive – next week I should think."

The nurse, when she arrived, was of medium height, slim and tanned, a point emphasized by the cool whiteness of her uniform dress. Her hair was dark and shoulder-length, tied back neatly.

"Welcome to the Venus Prince," she said amiably, shaking his hand. "I'm sure you'll find it an interesting experience at the very least. I'm Kate McColl, by the way."

"Luke Darius."

They walked off out of the foyer, down a wide, illuminated corridor towards the rear of the ship. Luke carried his bulging suitcase as elegantly as he could; Kate, obligingly, a smaller item of luggage. They soon entered a smaller corridor off the main one, set at right angles to the first.

"This is the hospital area, and our cabins are both further down there," said Kate pointing ahead. "Yours is number ten – one of the biggest, by the way, with a double bed. Apparently, they're only given to the top knobs on board. I'm a junior officer, so-called, but I had to fight like hell even for a single cabin. They gave me one eventually, when it became obvious I needed a phone. You see, the old Mexican doctor who was here until a few weeks back just wouldn't – or should I perhaps say, couldn't – respond to night calls. Before that, I'd had to spend the first three months here three in a cabin, sleeping on a top bunk. But believe me, even that's luxury compared to how some of the other crew live. You'll see for yourself when you get to know the place. Up to twelve in a cabin some of them, with only a tiny curtain across their bunks for privacy."

"Sounds horrendous – especially for months on end. Who, by the way, occupy the other cabins along here?"

"Mainly entertainers and cruise staff. Some of them, at least. The band members do. And the magician, and a few dancers and cabaret singers. A lot of the entertainers, you'll find, double as cruise staff during the day."

They entered the hospital through the main door, bypassing the small waiting room. Kate pointed it out to the right, through an interconnecting door. It had eight seats grouped fairly tightly around a low coffee table. A few magazines were scattered on top in customary fashion.

The doctor's office area housed a desk and a few shelves with reference books. The ones Luke had specially ordered – included in the list he'd phoned to the London Office before departure – would soon add to those. He wouldn't feel half as confident till they arrived – especially the book of surgical techniques. Behind the desk, one of the hospital's two portholes poured natural light in across the clean linoleum tiles of the floor.

An adjacent small room, stacked high with lockable cupboards and glass-encased narrow shelves, lay in virtual darkness until the light was switched on. Bottles and boxes of all shapes and sizes lined the remaining shelves of what was clearly the dispensary. A stainless-steel sink and worktop took up most of one wall, with further storage units below. In one corner stood a tall refrigerator that housed, among other things, certain injectables requiring cold storage.

Kate led the way back into the main part of the hospital. A second desk was positioned in a partly partitioned-off nurse's station, close to a small passageway with two separate cubicles housing beds. Another area boasted an old operating table bolted to the floor. Some of the handles and knobs for adjustment to its many potential positions were missing, Luke noticed on a cursory glance. Looking at it, he wondered above all when it might have been last used for treating anything approaching major.

Nearby, a large glass cabinet proudly displayed an array of surgical instruments. These included, among other things, a couple of bone saws and some barbaric-looking obstetric forceps. There were other instruments too, that Luke had never encountered before. A large shiny metal construction stood oddly nearby, in one corner of the room. An assortment of pipes entered and left at various positions – almost symmetrically, but not quite. Two gauges were visible near the top. Luke fancied it looked a little like some kind of old-fashioned discarded robot, trapped in an unnatural pose and desperate to escape.

"That's the autoclave," said Kate pointing to where it stood. "Don't worry, it seems to work okay once it's been cranked up. Over there," she said indicating a slightly narrow doorway, "in that tiny room is the X-Ray machine. We've rarely used it since I've been here. More usually, we'll get x-rays done in port – and reported on too."

"Hmm, good idea," said Luke eyeing it dubiously. A lot of equipment had clearly been on this ship for considerably longer than the six to seven years Venus Cruise Lines had owned it. He wondered how safe this machine might be – and if, or when, it had ever been serviced.

They were now walking towards the door. "You probably want to check out your cabin and unpack a little," said Kate. "You might even have time for a quick look around the ship before we open up this evening. Though you'd better hurry; the passengers will be joining us soon. Then we'll have the usual chaos for a few hours or so, till they get settled in."

IV

Luke found cabin number ten and went in. The bit about the double bed was true enough. The only thing – and he couldn't help being struck by it immediately – was that it took up virtually fifty per cent of all available floor space. Much of the rest was encompassed in an extremely small en-suite shower and toilet. When he dropped his bags on the floor around him, he found himself pretty much marooned and had to quickly pick them up again and transfer them to the bed. There was a shelf under the porthole by the side of the bed that looked to Luke as though it might prove useful. Just in from the door, a built-in wardrobe of reasonable size promised to take all he'd brought along, five times over. A compartment at the top housed a life jacket. A few items of uniform hung separately on hangers. Luke removed them for inspection. They were obviously clean enough – the laundry tags were still affixed with pins and bore some squiggles in what looked like Chinese lettering. Clean enough – but would they fit? And even if they did, which bits should he wear for what? The smarter of the two types would presumably be for wear in the evenings.

Luke stood in front of the full-length mirror on the outside of the wardrobe door five minutes later, smiling absurdly at his reflection. They fitted after a fashion, yes – but what sort of fashion were we talking about here, he wanted to know?

The shirt, white and short-sleeved, billowed out uncontrollably – even after tucking it into his over-tight white trousers – paying little heed at all, he was aggrieved to note, to his fairly trim figure beneath. Having dutifully put the shirt on, the only things he realised he'd forgotten were the epaulettes – three-striped and no doubt highly significant in seafaring terms because of it.

Luke found he felt like a bit of a fraud as he struggled to fix them on, after all, proper seamen, he was reminded, spent half their lives earning their stripes. Here was he, barely half an hour aboard only the second ship he'd ever set foot on in his life, and he was handed three of the things on a plate. Only one less than the Captain. In fact, from the display of photos of the senior officers in the foyer he'd noticed in passing earlier on, only three or so officers had more. Honorary stripes only, he told himself as he ventured, a little self-consciously, out of the cabin soon after.

Luke looked at his watch as he walked down the corridor back towards the foyer. It was 4.55. There were signs of a lot more general activity as he approached. A deck plan was displayed on one wall, and Luke studied it keenly. He was currently on, he discovered, the Riviera deck. One of the main staircases led off nearby, and he headed up to take a look at the deck above – the Promenade deck. This deck, while having cabins to the fore of the roughly central staircase, was taken up by what was clearly the main and rather impressive restaurant.

Looking through the large glass double doors, Luke was taken by its attractive Art-Deco style. A voluptuous buffet had been assembled at the far end. As he watched, a delicate white swan carved in lard was being set up prominently on a stand. Out through the side windows of the restaurant, Luke could see that this was, in fact, also the lifeboat deck he'd noticed earlier.

The next deck up revealed the main entertainment lounges, shops, boutiques and casino. A sign at the top of the stairs as he reached it, proclaimed this to be the Caribbean deck. Several small palms, growing in containers dotted around, were attempting to emphasise this fact. A quick look at the cost of some of the more obviously designer goods on display in the gift shops made him gasp. Then, remembering the brochure prices of the cruises, it occurred to him that – to many of the passengers at least – these prices would probably not seem so very outlandish.

More cabins were to be found to the fore of the next deck, the Panama deck. To the aft were various other public rooms, including a games room, reading room, piano bar and – furthest to the stern – the nightclub.

Climbing the stairs once more, Luke finally reached the top. He found himself in an empty café on the Lido deck, looking out through its windows and open doorway to a poolside bar where a number of early arrivals were refreshing themselves in the growing dusk. He walked through, ever conscious of his uniform, smiling by way of greeting to the café and bar staff as he went, and emerged onto the reassuring hardwood of the deck. Hardly had he a chance to orientate himself when someone close by spoke:

"Say, Officer, could you tell me what speed the ship will be making between here and Aruba – and what kind of stabilisers have we got?"

"I'm afraid I'm only the doctor – and I've only just joined the ship at that. I'm sorry, you'll have to ask a proper seaman."

Luke moved on swiftly, feeling more than slightly embarrassed, and even slightly more useless. Two minutes later, he was stopped again.

"Say, you wouldn't be the Captain, by any chance, would you?" said a kindly, well-preserved, but clearly ancient face.

"No, I'm sorry – I'm just the ship's doctor," replied Luke almost meekly now.

"Don't worry, sonny. You're far more important on this ship to someone of my age, and don't you forget it."

His morale visibly lifted by the worldly wisdom of an eighty-seven-year-old from North Carolina, Luke chatted for a while then headed back to his cabin. A quick rest, a coffee and a shower, and he'd be ready to face evening office hours.

By the time the hospital had been open an hour, Luke and Kate had seen six passengers and two crew members, and then sat talking, waiting for further business.

The passengers they had seen so far, Kate told him, had been pretty typical for the onset of a cruise. Three had come merely to 'register' with the doctor, bringing notes from their own physicians back home 'just in case'. One fellow in his seventies arrived breathlessly brandishing a diagram of his recently bypassed coronary arteries – only three weeks before, it turned out. Luke cringed inwardly at such blind faith in the medical set-up on the ship but said nothing. He quickly resolved, however, to check out their resuscitation equipment directly this guy had gone, and promptly did, much to Kate's amusement.

Word came through before they closed up that the Captain wished to see him in his cabin at noon the following day. Luke was left wondering what precisely in the wording of so simple a message had successfully managed to convey such an aura of foreboding.

Chapter 9

I

When Luke went to seek out the Captain's cabin at 11.50 the following morning, he had already become well acquainted with his voice.

He had been reminded by Kate about lifeboat drill that first morning at sea as he sat with her through a fairly quiet morning surgery. Sure enough, at nine o'clock precisely, a very foreign-sounding voice rang out over the ship's tannoy. Luke found it quite a strain trying to take in exactly what was being said. Eventually, having become, to some degree, accustomed to the style of enunciation during an interrupted and somewhat puzzling preamble, he could distinctly make out the phrase "go to your lifeboat stations." Kate had instructed him the previous evening in what it was he was expected to do. She'd even taken time out to show him exactly where he needed to go when the final order came.

Wearing the lifejacket he'd earlier taken from his cabin, and a very unfamiliar-feeling officer's hat, he set off carrying the orange resuscitation case he'd checked out the night before. A nearby flight of stairs took him towards the stern of the vessel on the starboard side. There, already assembled at his lifeboat station, an assortment of crew-members waited, chatting amongst themselves. Luke joined them and soon found his feelings of uncertainty quashed by their ready acceptance of him.

"Hey, Doctor," said one holding up a pale-brown palm. "You are welcome, indeed, amigo." Luke slapped it playfully in a high-five, a trigger for others to greet him likewise.

"You – Americano?" said another.

"No, English."

"Ah, English – very good. Very nice English gentleman," he said in a mock BBC World Service accent.

Just then, a particularly stern-looking, thickset figure in uniform came into view. Instantly, the disorderly crowd around him transformed themselves into a fairly close impression of an orderly line. Luke's efforts to follow suit sadly failed. Almost before he knew it, he found himself face-to-face with undoubtedly the thickest, and most evil-looking moustache he'd ever encountered in his life.

The man attached to it stopped dead and peered down silently to where Luke had left the bulky orange case neatly blocking his way. Spotting this, Luke obligingly dragged it into line beside him with his foot.

"You are the new doctor?"

"Yes," said Luke.

"Well, please, Doctor, adjust your hat. Officers, you must understand, need to set an example to all these others working on board." He gave a slow, disdainful look along the line, then turned away and began muttering into his walkie-talkie in voluptuous Greek.

"Who was that?" Luke asked of the man nearest him as the line visibly relaxed.

"That's the Staff Captain."

"Looks a pretty tough cookie."

"You're not wrong there, Doctor. Sure don't do to get on the wrong side of that man."

II

"Wait there," said Demitri the steward, rather officiously, as Luke arrived outside the Captain's quarters later that morning. "I'll tell him you're here."

Luke looked around him while he waited, attempting vainly to catch a glimpse of his reflection in a window nearby. He still didn't feel any more comfortable in uniform – particularly one that, in part at least, resembled a fully blown sail. Would the Captain pass comment, he wondered?

The room Luke entered was spacious and tastefully appointed in a more traditional nautical fashion. Various charts and ornaments adorned the walls, along with one or two framed photographs. Luke had little chance to study them. The focus of the room was a large teak desk. The Captain, sitting behind it, looked up as he approached.

"Sit down, Dr Darius. Tell me, have you worked on a ship before?"

"No, Captain."

"Well, don't worry. My Staff Captain and I will instruct you in all you need you know. Where have you come from, by the way?"

"London – I flew out from London yesterday morning."

"And you were recruited by the London Office?"

"Yes, Captain – by Dan Forsbrook, while he was over from the US recently."

"Mr Forsbrook himself interviewed you for this post?"

"That's right. As I understand it, they wanted a British doctor. The London Office advertised and by some luck, Mr Forsbrook offered me the job." Luke, noticing the Captain's deferential use of the title 'Mr', decided against a repeat of his earlier over-familiar use of Dan's Christian name.

"You are clearly too modest, Dr Darius. But you strike me – if you don't mind me saying – as a little young for this type of posting. I must admit, I am more used to a doctor on ship being of... more mature years. Won't your career suffer at this stage, coming away to sea like this?"

"Hopefully not in the long term. The truth is, I'm taking a bit of time out to review just where I'm going with my career. And my life in general, for that matter."

"I see," said the Captain viewing him quietly.

Luke guessed he was in his fifties, observing the facial wrinkles and brownish areas of pigmentation from sun damage to his exposed scalp. The crown of his head was almost totally bald, save for a cluster of longish strands crossing over optimistically from one side. When he spoke, the Captain's thin lips parted into a half-smile; pleasant enough in itself, if one ignored the heavily tobacco stained teeth revealing themselves uninhibitedly at intervals behind.

The Captain's shirt too – like his own – spilled out unceremoniously over the band of his trousers as he sat there. Luke was aware, though, that this was due mainly to material far less easy than mere cotton to tuck in.

"There is a list of rules you will be issued with, Doctor, and expected – like all others working on ship – to adhere to."

"I guessed as much, Captain," said Luke, looking him squarely in the eyes once more and putting all thoughts of liposuction as a possible solution to the other man's shirt problem firmly out of his mind.

For a moment, Captain Symiakos said nothing.

"You will be expected at the Cocktail Party this afternoon, to be introduced to the passengers. Wear your other uniform – the non-formal evening uniform – for the time being. In future, providing it turns up, you will have the formal one to wear – short white jacket, black bow-tie, cummerbund and black trousers. Now, Doctor, there is just one thing I think I ought to mention to you."

"Yes, Captain?"

"I feel I run what some might describe as a 'tight ship' – at least, I believe that's your English expression. Everyone working on board has his own job to do. In my experience, it is vital that everyone sticks firmly to his own area of business and expertise and avoids interfering in other people's. Do you understand me, Doctor?"

"Yes, I think so," said Luke. As he thought about it sitting there, he managed to convince himself it did seem to make some sort of sense.

"Just concentrate on making sure your own department is running efficiently. That's all that is required."

III

The senior officers formed themselves into a line behind the Captain in some clearly pre-determined order of importance, and Luke found himself about halfway along.

Most of the others round about him seemed either very burly or very surly – with the exception of the Staff Captain who managed successfully to combine both. Any worries Luke might have had regarding his appearance in this, his other type of uniform – the white, high-necked evening one with matching white trousers – were instantly dispelled as he studied the others and their obvious sartorial disregard. He was by far the youngest of those present, though he had seen other younger junior officers as he wandered around the ship earlier.

Few present there appeared to Luke to have any real heart for the proceedings – that is, with the obvious exception of the Captain, Cruise Director and Hotel Manager, involved just then in formally welcoming the passengers. A few of the officers, notably the Chief Engineer and Chief Radio Officer, bore a distinctly tortured look. Others, he noticed, merely looked vague and resigned. The resident band, a clearly accomplished seven-piece, played quietly in the background on the stage nearby. Over by the bar, a cluster of wine waiters prepared to distribute hundreds of glasses of fizzy wine, lined up on trays and masquerading quietly as champagne.

Soon after, the Captain was introduced. He stepped forward to the microphone, speaking clearly and confidently, though in the same voice of occasional mispronunciation that Luke had heard earlier that day over the tannoy. After a short while, the audience began to become a little restless. It revived slightly, Luke noticed, when the Captain turned to introduce the senior officers.

One by one, the senior officers trotted out as their rank and name were announced, forming a new line directly across the floor. Each was greeted with a short, polite burst of applause. The officers ahead of Luke all seemed, at most, faintly embarrassed by it all. Next would be his turn...

"As usual, Captain, the ladies on the list I've marked would seem to be available. Three of them will be on your table at dinner tonight. You can take your pick. The rest I've sent flowers from you, and an invitation for other nights. I trust that is okay?"

"Indeed, it is, Demitri. Good work, my friend. That will be all for now."

"You have an excellent system, Ioannis," said the Staff Captain, as the Captain's steward left. "I must congratulate you – although I'm afraid you may now find you have competition judging by the applause that young doctor got at the Cocktail Party earlier."

"Don't worry, Stavros. I can deal with that side of things, no problem. I'm afraid, though, my concerns about this man are far more serious than that. Have you seen this telex?" The Captain held it out for the other to read.

"I see," said the Staff Captain after a pause.

"First of all, this guy is handpicked by Forsbrook himself in London, and now – as you've read – Forsbrook is on his way right now to join us in Aruba tomorrow. Just for a day, mind you – and specifically, as he's mentioned, to spend time instructing this new doctor. And in what exactly?" The Captain paused here, looking closely at the other man, and began slowly shaking his head. "No, Stavros, my concerns are far, far greater. There seems something very odd about the way this man has been recruited by Venus Cruise Lines. I hope I'm wrong, but I rather fear this doctor has to be some sort of spy for the Company."

PART 2

A CERTAIN PERSUASION

Chapter 10

I

At about the same time Luke Darius had first boarded the Venus Prince the day before, Ed Jamieson, at his weekend cottage in the Catskills, had just begun the second detailed reappraisal of the precise wisdom of his idea.

The estimate for the galley refit, and other works to the Venus Prince, had finally come through. John Warringer had knocked on his door at Head Office just after 2.30 the previous afternoon and brought it in for his immediate attention. Keen to avoid the worst of the Friday afternoon build-up on the Turnpike, and get a good early start for their weekend away upstate, Ed shoved the document into his attaché case and set off home.

It had remained unopened long after he and Ellen had left their house near Lincoln Park. Halfway to Mount Trumper, where they were headed, it was well forgotten.

Ed was reminded of it first as he unpacked the car sometime later. He promptly forgot it again as Ellen called for his help in getting the fire going, claiming, as usual, that the woodpile was somehow damp. Ed laughed and told her she'd never make a boy scout. He then allowed himself a brief fantasy of how she might look filling out one of those uniforms. Why was it always Ellen and uniforms, he'd often wondered? The kindling finally caught as the old flame flickered briefly within him once again.

It was only after they'd eaten and Ellen had handed him his brandy – which he took over to the fireside chair – that he eventually remembered it. When at last he did open the large Manila envelope and read it through, he knew he'd mistimed it all completely.

He should have known better. It was bound to have played on his mind. Should have left it for the office on Monday. Too late now though. The bottom line – and Ed Jamieson's trained eye always steered itself straight for the bottom line – was a figure considerably higher than he'd ever seriously considered. Holy Christ, he thought to himself. Not a lot short of four million dollars. Outrageous, alright – and was it really going to be worth it?

Ed gulped his brandy almost reflexively, hardly tasting it, and composed himself to tackle the actual detail of the text of the accompanying report. Perhaps within it lay the answer to at least some of his questions. Then, maybe, he'd sleep on it, and after that – if the knot in his belly still hadn't sufficiently unravelled – he could always try catching a word with Dan in London. Why was Dan always somewhere else when you needed him? Perhaps he should have listened more to Dan to begin with. Damn the man – why was he always so goddam right?

II

Dan Forsbrook stood half-naked in front of the mirror in his London hotel room that following day and viewed with a certain satisfaction the fully healed scar of his chest wound. It had taken time, admittedly, and still hurt like hell when he coughed, but he was walking straighter now – and, more importantly, no one had really noticed all along. It had been a close-run thing early on, though – particularly on that occasion he'd twisted awkwardly, bending over in the office in front of his colleagues, and almost blown his cover. Visibly wincing and staggering slightly with the pain, he'd attracted much concern from those all around him. Quick-wittedly, he'd clutched his back, not the wound site; an upper lumbar sprain rather than the deep intercostal haematoma diagnosed by the physician outside DC with such a reputation for discretion in these matters.

It was just then that the hotel switchboard announced the incoming call from Thailand. There was really only one person it could be.

"That you, Bill? What's happening, buddy?"

"We've gotten ourselves a bit of a problem out here right now, Dan. Getting some hassle from the father of a young boy from one of the outlying villages. Traced him right here to the Thai Orchid. Of course, we ain't admitting nothing. Persistent kinda guy, though; could be trouble. How d'you think we should handle it?"

"Same as last time, Bill – though you'd better be careful. Things are one hell of a lot more high-profile now than ever before. If the guy's on his own, it's simple; you deal with him discreetly one night. If, on the other hand, there are others with him and they start causing a stir, just move the kid somewhere else for the time being then clear the decks for a while. Last thing we want are the authorities poking around."

"Got you, Dan – no worries. Hey, how was Amsterdam, by the way?"

"Haven't made it over there yet. Though if all goes well, I should be leaving tomorrow."

III

Back in the Catskills that same day, Ed Jamieson and Ellen strolled through the woods and skied a little where the meagre snow allowed, but Ed had no real heart for it. He tried not to show it, but Ellen had guessed long ago something was up.

"You seem awfully tense, Honey. Problems at the office?"

"No, nothing too serious. Nothing I can't handle easy enough, anyway. C'mon, let's get some coffee. I'm chilled through."

Ellen noticed he was still a touch preoccupied when they called in on their old friends the McFaddens, also up for the weekend, in the neighbouring property. Only later, when they'd left and returned once again to their impressive six-bedroomed 'cottage' did Ed acknowledge the need for a more rational approach. Ellen left him alone in the study, doodling away on a large blank sheet of paper while she went to cook supper and watch TV.

Now, what would the real cost of this proposed itinerary change be? Ed asked himself as he sat there. He looked at the various ball-park figures he'd scribbled down on the paper in front of him. And how much of a gamble, going for it in so short a time?

Dan was right – major work would be needed to get the ship up to the required standard. But not just structurally. The running of the ship itself had been lax – he mustn't forget that. And there had been all manner of other concerns he'd brought up at their meeting only two or three weeks back. An awful lot of systems needed to be in place and functioning smoothly before the ship would be deemed fit for what was under consideration for that coming season. Could it seriously be achieved in the next three months? At what point, for instance, should they print new brochures and start booking – and cancel those they'd already got for the present itinerary? Wouldn't it be better, after all, to delay the start date to later in the year, just to be sure? Was this really the answer to the Venus Prince and Venus Cruise Lines' problems? And, if not, what was the point of it all, anyway?

"Honey, there's something on TV you might be interested in," said Ellen popping her head round the study door. "Some cruise company or other – one of the bigger ones, I think – getting some kind of industry award. It'll be back on in a second after the commercials. C'mon through – supper's almost ready now, anyway."

"Okay, dear. I'll be right there."

"I've missed the exact name of the award, Hon," said Ellen as Ed walked in and sat silently at the table. The commercials were still running. "Some Gold Standard Award for excellence in travel. They're apparently just about to interview the winner."

Ed wasn't fully concentrating. He found he couldn't help his mind wandering back to his own dilemma. He was just recalling precisely where he'd got to in the debate when the programme flashed back on the screen.

Instantly his body tensed. The face of the interviewee was certainly one known to him.

"You know, that guy looks somehow familiar – though I can't for the life of me place him," said Ellen, her eyes fixed intently on the screen. "Who is he, Ed? Any ideas?"

"Yeah, that's George Mitchell – owns Palm Cruises down in Florida. An old acquaintance of mine." Ed spoke slowly, trying hard to make his voice sound relaxed. It came out, though, a little woodenly.

"Well, Palm Cruises are obviously doing well for themselves."

"Evidently so," replied Ed simply.

"And if that place they're interviewing him from is his home," said Ellen, indicating the almost palatial residence in the background, "then he's got to be absolutely raking it in."

"Guess you're right." Ed spoke morosely now as he watched his old rival George Mitchell playing up to the camera in an appalling riot of modesty, tempered with a kind of calculated sincerity. Sure – George was saying just then – this really was a great honour, and one that he, himself, was not entirely sure they fully deserved. But yes, of course, they were a company that took customer relations very seriously indeed and hoped to improve their operation still further, if they possibly could. And no, certainly none of this success would have been possible without the right people behind him.

Then, to Ed's horror – and as an example, no doubt, of one such wonderfully supportive person – out trotted Sophia, his ex-wife. She walked over to where George Mitchell was sitting poolside – obviously picked up by another camera – then kissed him fondly for all the viewing public to see.

Ed found that long after this piece of gloriously choreographed 'real-life' was over, it was somehow impossible to take in anything further that was being said. He remained in a state of semi-shock until his wife broke the silence moments later.

"Why, that's your ex-wife, isn't it, Ed?" said Ellen turning to him when at last she'd recognised the woman's face on the screen.

"Oh, yeah – you know, I do believe you're right: it is Sophia. Sorry, Ellie, I was miles away just then. Had my mind on something completely different. My, she's changed, hasn't she? I'd hardly have recognised her. Must be the way she's done her hair. It's shorter, and a touch darker, I think."

For some time now, Ellen Jamieson had known something, at least, of Sophia's existence. Ed had given her basic details of their marriage, soon after they'd first met. He hadn't dwelt on the manner of their break up though. This was partly – he'd very soon had to admit – because of the strength of the feelings he still had for Sophia. But it was also because he felt he'd been shown up; usurped, for perhaps the first time in his life by another man. And how it galled him still; more so now than ever before, in fact, as he sat there watching in silence, powerless to respond in the way he would have liked, there in Ellen's presence.

In the end, he simply stood up and, feigning disinterest, went back to the study and closed the door. Ellen heard him mumbling something about needing to tidy away one or two things before supper. The reality of the situation, though, could not have been more different. His brain had now finally reached saturation point – completely overwhelmed by the bombardment of so many disturbing visual images. Ed knew immediately that they would remain with him for a long, long time to come; perhaps, at his age, till the very day he died. A strange panic rose within him.

Ed sat in the study for a minute or two more, trying to compose himself – trying desperately to get some handle on his emotions. Memories of seven years ago flooded back, and he was powerless to ward them off. Suddenly, all became very clear to him. He had loved Sophia and now he found he hated her; he had never loved George Mitchell and now he found he hated him even more, if that was in any way possible. Hated the man with a vengeance. Headhunting Dan Forsbrook had really never been enough. The son-of-a-bitch was happy and prospering – that much was clear. Something else had to be done. Something to put an end to that sickening complacency. Something to let him know that he, Ed Jamieson, still existed. Something to keep that bastard on his toes. Damn him to Hell!

Ed wasn't sure how much Ellen was able to guess about his inner conflict or the reason for it. He continued, therefore, in his attempt to hide it from her. Supper, despite this, was a pretty subdued affair. Soon after, Ellen kissed him on the forehead and took herself off early to bed. Under her arm was a book she'd already started; another of those mystery stories she so readily immersed herself in. Ed was not surprised by her retiring in this way – she often did about this time when they were up at the cottage.

Ed stayed on, telling her he had one or two business calls to make. What he didn't tell her was that he needed to contact Dan Forsbrook urgently. Nor did he mention the reason why.

IV

"That you, Dan? How's it all going?" There was stunned silence for a moment at the other end, then an audible recovery.

"Mr Jamieson? You got any idea what time it is here in London? Almost three in the morning. I take it you're not ringing to enquire after my health. Some kind of emergency, right?"

"Not exactly. Sorry about waking you, Dan. Just wanted to let you know it's all-systems-go for the new itinerary. The Venus Prince transfers to the Miami run from the start of next season."

"You've had the costings through, then?" asked Dan dubiously. Something wasn't right; something in his boss's voice – the timing of the call. He couldn't quite put his finger on it.

"Yeah, they came through. Sure, a bit more than I'd expected, but what the hell. It's peanuts anyway, compared to what some of these big companies pay out on an upgrade –

and it's them we're going to be competing with from now on. However, when we succeed – as I fully intend we shall – and fill up the Prince at their expense, it'll more than pay for itself before too long. One thing though, Dan – we'll have to work fast. Now listen; this is what I want you to do..."

Ten minutes later, Ed put the phone down. He went through to pour himself another brandy. The fire had died back, so he squatted down close to it and prodded the embers with a poker hanging nearby. A flame danced for a moment or two over the dull red interior. There was still some life in it yet.

As he stared into the glowing hearth, Ed could see George Mitchell's face in front of him once more. This time, though, it bore a distinct look of alarm – a look which pleased him immensely. This George Mitchell had just heard the news: Ed Jamieson wanted a piece of his action and was no longer someone who could merely be brushed to one side. Ed Jamieson was now, without question, someone to be reckoned with.

An excited thrill passed through him. He poked the fire once more and the flames obligingly reappeared. He turned to warm his back and looked out into the room.

For the first time that evening, Ed Jamieson became aware of just how fine that brandy really tasted.

Chapter 11

I

As Luke walked by on deck, he caught sight of Duane Dalton leaning out determinedly over the ship's rail, looking downwards. Such was his general degree of inclination that his compatriot's head was barely visible from where Luke stood. There was, however, little doubt who it was – his main distinguishing feature being another of those tropical shirts. It outshone even the brightest of those round about. Luke went over to join him, now that the Venus Prince had arrived in Oranjestad.

Beyond the tall palms of the busy, open roadway of the dockside area, stood the low, flat-roofed modern buildings of that part of town. Luke scanned the horizon beyond for any hint of style remotely Dutch. A row of quite distinctive gables, some distance away, finally caught his attention.

Luke's impression of Aruba, as they'd approached that Monday morning, was that of a chunk of flat, arid desert somehow transported and dumped there rather carelessly in the southern Caribbean. To disguise the mistake, a few palm trees had been planted along its powder-fine shores. Even so, it failed dismally in meeting his preconceptions of a lush Caribbean island. Judging by the town and visible road network, it was clearly extremely civilized; an air of confident, yet friendly, prosperity about the place.

"Great show last night," said Luke coming up beside him. They both stood watching as the mooring lines tensed and the ship began slowly sidling into its berth.

"Yes, it went well, thank God," said Duane after a moment or two. "Just as well it did, though. I'd had nothing but strange remarks and dubious looks since I arrived on board and the other staff discovered I was a hypnotist. Especially when it turned out I only had two shows a week – about three hours work in all, they no doubt calculated. Seemed pretty determined to let me know they expected me to make up the rest of my hours in cruise staff duties. Thankfully, after that first performance, I note a slight but welcome softening of their attitude."

"Yes, I particularly enjoyed the bit where that rather effeminate guy you had up on stage returned to his seat, then, minutes later when that carnival music played, jumped up and started trying to French kiss the Staff Captain who just happened to be sitting next to him at the time," said Luke, laughing once more at the recollection.

"Our dear Staff Captain wasn't amused though, was he?" said Duane, smiling. "A slight miscalculation on my part, I'm afraid. Trust me to pick on the very officer on the ship best able to make my life absolute hell."

"Listen, Duane, I've got to go. I've just spotted a visiting bigwig I'm due to meet up with this afternoon. Catch you later, okay? Oh, by the way..."

"Yes?" said Duane.

"When I click my fingers, you'll awaken and wonder what all the noise is about. Then you'll realise it's something only marginally louder than your shirt."

"Ha, very fucking funny. Piss off, will you? I know you're only jealous."

Captain Symiakos, too, had seen Dan Forsbrook on the quayside waiting to board the ship. He began wondering once again what it could all be about. Sure, the telex had mentioned a need to instruct the new doctor on matters of procedure, but was that really all it was?

If the truth be known, Ioannis Symiakos was still feeling considerably shaken by the death on the Venus Prince of that Colombian sailor six weeks before. And to be more precise, the particular circumstances surrounding that death. Not that, even now, he really knew what fully lay behind it. He hadn't dared probe too much. And neither Delgardo nor his men had been particularly forthcoming.

The cover-up under Delgardo's direction had gone smoothly enough. Surprisingly, not even one vaguely awkward question had followed his report to the officials in Cartagena. And since the sailor was not officially part of the crew, he'd felt the more left unsaid the better, where Head Office was concerned. As far as he could tell, their ignorance remained complete. In fact, with regard to all practical aspects of the incident, there had so far been an almost alarming lack of consequences. Though clearly a great relief on one hand, it left him wondering about the exact degree of Delgardo's power and influence in that part of the world, and, more than anything, the precise value he placed on human life.

Ioannis Symiakos had long since come to understand just what a grave error of judgment he had made in first allowing himself to get involved with this man Delgardo Estremosa. It had happened simply enough to start with, in the way these things so often do. Being paid a regular substantial sum merely to turn a blind eye had seemed almost too good to be true. It was certainly not the sort of offer a man of his disposition could easily pass up. More than once, he had compared his salary with that of his opposite number on other cruise ships he'd encountered along the way; men captaining ships of similar size to the Venus Prince, or even smaller. In almost every case, he had come away feeling both incensed and belittled.

And so, before long, he had begun to retaliate.

A number of small-scale schemes had presented themselves at various junctures – nothing too spectacular though. Nothing that would significantly bring forward the day he could seriously entertain comfortable retirement. Nothing until then, that was.

And so, he had consented and allowed himself the luxury of the interim contemplation of those plans – the island home and bar on Skiathos, a little sailing and fishing, and all those beautiful, unattached female tourists. His wife, if she wanted to remain his wife, would just have to learn to live with it.

The beauty of the scheme – to start with at least – was that even if the two 'passengers' working for Delgardo had been caught in possession on board, he himself as Captain could claim total ignorance of their true intent. The most he could realistically be held to account over was just how they had managed to board the ship midway through a week-long cruise and successfully occupy an empty cabin without any questions being asked. Nothing too serious, it might be agreed.

If only things could have remained that way. It hadn't taken long for Delgardo – flushed, no doubt, with initial success – to insist on expansion of the operation. Even then, it had been introduced oh so gradually, sweetened by a commensurate increase in his cut. Almost before he knew it, he found himself struggling to keep control. Two 'passengers' became four permanent crew members – then six, then eight. Now there were a dozen and they had become virtually a law unto themselves. Not only were they extremely choosy over which crew activities to participate in – and those involving serious work were rarely amongst them – they had also developed a rather worrying ability to persuade other Hispanic crew members to comply almost unquestioningly with their wishes. Stavros, his Staff Captain, had reported back his suspicions on several occasions recently. Clearly, even he was becoming alarmed at authority on board being so flagrantly undermined.

And would it stop there, he wanted to know? Somehow, he doubted it. Even on the last occasion when he'd spoken to Delgardo in Cartagena, the man had hinted at a further increase in the volume of cocaine to be transported next month. Only a small increase, and only for a short period. But that had been the story all along. Where the hell would it all end?

One thing was clear enough to Ioannis, as he stood there mulling over these points in his mind. Things had just gone way too far now. He'd saved enough of the profits in his Cayman account to make a serious and lasting impact on his personal wealth. What he needed now was some kind of way out. Not that he could ever dare suggest such a thing to Delgardo directly. He dreaded to think of the possible outcome. No, that would be foolhardy in the extreme.

What he needed was some other – admittedly, almost miraculous – turn of events. One that he, himself, could not in any way be considered responsible for.

And so far, there existed only one glimmer of hope. It had been mentioned briefly in a recent memo – though considered by whoever sent it from Head Office to be no more than something of a 'long shot'. Then, a few days later, some technicians had come aboard to measure up the main galley for a refit, and the water system too had been inspected. Little was said at the time, but surely this was an optimistic sign? Perhaps Dan Forsbrook himself might have some sort of update on these proposals when he came aboard. God, he hoped so. Or would he have some questions about that death instead? Could anybody investigating it shore-side have possibly tied up directly with the Company without him knowing it?

Ioannis forced himself to curtail this worrying line of thought. He went back in his mind to the proposals he hoped Forsbrook might have more news on and how – just to test his initial response – he had dutifully (if not a little provocatively) passed on the basic content of that Head Office memo to Delgardo. It was a little premature, he knew. Above all else, he hoped – thinking back to it – that his own voice over the satellite phone that day had betrayed none of his true feelings at the prospect.

Even now though, as he stood there on the Bridge, he was left wondering just what the Colombian might have made of it all.

II

Dan Forsbrook, by this time, was feeling pretty much resigned to the situation. His boss could hardly have made his intentions clearer in that notable early morning phone call of two days before. There seemed, therefore, little point in arguing the case further. Whatever Ed Jamieson's true reason for his decision, Dan knew he could save himself a whole lot of time and effort in the long run by applying himself wholeheartedly instead to the job in hand. He was a little annoyed he hadn't managed to get over to Amsterdam, even for a day, but there would be other times. Instead, he'd spent several, often difficult hours tying up with John Warringer in New York, getting a work schedule arranged and contractors organised. If all went to plan, both they and their equipment would soon be flying out, and the work on the Venus Prince underway.

In order to lighten his load still further, the next thing he needed was a firm commitment from those working on board. With the test cruise up to Tampa set provisionally for March 20th, less than three months ahead, there was little time to lose in getting all systems in order. The backing of the Captain, Staff Captain and medical department would be crucial in this regard. Get them fully motivated and his problems would be all but solved. Time spent addressing this issue now would, he knew from past experience, repay itself many times over.

The doctor would present no trouble, he was sure. Hand-picked and keen – and so far, untainted by sloppy practice on board – all Dr Darius would need would be a simple explanation of the vital importance of the certification checks. Would the Captain need any more convincing? Perhaps a few home truths would help. How, for example, the command of the Venus Prince – or lack of it – was currently viewed by Head Office. How an opportunity now existed for some degree of redemption. How failure would not bode well for contract renewal. The usual kind of threats. What else could one really say to the Captain of a ship?

Dan knocked on the Captain's door – more as a signal of entry than any realistic request for permission. The Captain's reply came just as the door closed behind him. He stood up quickly to greet the newcomer.

"Hello, Captain Symiakos," said Dan, extending his hand to the other man. "You got my telex from London, I take it?"

"Yes, Mr Forsbrook. We have been expecting you. But you're only staying the one night with us?"

"That's right. I leave tomorrow in Cartagena, then fly out the following day to the US. Got some business to attend to there before jetting off to Singapore to join the Princess for a few days. How's that new doctor settling in, by the way?"

Dan sat himself down on a sofa of sorts, a little like a chaise longue, at the far end of the room. He looked over at the Captain, now sitting back behind his desk.

"Just fine, so far. A pleasant enough fellow certainly," said the Captain a little warily. "Though I haven't really had a chance to see him at work so far, so to speak."

"Don't worry, he's been well-vetted. His credentials are excellent."

"I don't doubt it. I gather you're going through some procedures with him?"

"Yeah, but first I have something to discuss with you, Captain."

"Yes?" said Ioannis Symiakos a little apprehensively. The American's intonation was, he found, a little difficult to interpret.

"I gather you had a brief communication from Head Office, a couple of weeks back, about the Company's consideration of a possible change of itinerary."

"That's right, I did," said the Captain quietly, holding his breath, poised for what was to be said next. Forsbrook had brought news as he'd hoped. Would there be a let out for him from Delgardo after all?

"Well, the latest word," said Dan slowly, "is that Mr Jamieson, in his wisdom, has decided to go ahead with the changeover from the start of next season, sailing out of Miami. Four-day cruises down to the Bahamas – you know the kind of thing. We're working on the exact ports of call right now. Both Freeport and Nassau look okay so far. We'll know more soon."

"Really?" said the Captain, barely able to conceal his relief at the prospect. Dan Forsbrook need have no worries: he had good enough reasons of his own to see all went smoothly. This change of itinerary really was the only possible answer, as far as he could see, to the dilemma he found himself in. And, best of all, he himself could not be viewed as having had any part in the decision.

"We're well aware of the large amount of extra work that will be involved. A test cruise will run up to Tampa to arrive on the 20th of March, so we need the ship completely ready by then for the US Public Health and Coastguard checks. I needn't emphasize how important it is that these are passed successfully – or, indeed, how the Company would view it if, for some reason, they weren't. Do you understand my meaning, Captain?"

"I most certainly do. Don't worry, Mr Forsbrook, you have my word on it. My Staff Captain and I will do all in our power to see this thing through. The Company has been extremely fair to me over the years. I will gladly take this opportunity of showing my appreciation. And, if this doctor is half as good as you say, the ship will have no problem matching the deadline. You may rest assured, Mr Forsbrook."

III

Later that day, as the Venus Prince left the quayside at Oranjestad, Luke returned to the hospital to open for that evening. Kate was already there at her desk.

"How did you get on with the Bossman?" she asked, turning to him.

"Well enough. He was just filling me in on details of what the Company expects of the medical department. Apparently, there's a rush on to get the Venus Prince ready for some important upcoming inspections. Been a sudden change of plan as far as next season's itinerary is concerned. Forsbrook certainly seems to have put the wind up the Captain, though; not surprising really when you consider how much work there is to do. That galley for a start – and the way they store food! Stacked any old how in refrigerators of totally unpredictable temperature. I've been running some checks today. We'll have to start keeping records of all the fridges on the ship and institute regular galley inspections. Half of our problem will be to convince the Italian boys in the Catering department to take infection risk seriously – starting with the Catering Manager himself. It's all going to mean a whole lot more work for us both, I'm afraid. Do we have an up-to-date register of gastroenteritis cases, by the way?"

"Oh, the Diarrhoea Book? I found one once when I was poking through some old files in the dispensary for something or other. The last entry, if I remember correctly, was about four years ago. Certainly, there hasn't been one in use since I've been here."

"Well, we'll have to get one up and running pretty quickly. In fact, all infectious disease cases need documenting. The US Public Health will want to see a well-kept, current record when we have the inspection in Tampa, so you see, there's no time to lose. Apparently, by the way, if the number of cases reaches a certain critical percentage of the total number on board that week, the ship would be refused permission to dock."

"Well, I know for a fact we've had some cruises in the past where we've had to treat an enormous number of cases. The emphasis then, as I remember it, seemed to be more related to directing blame away from the ship – inferring that food eaten ashore, on excursions etc., was most likely to be to blame. I really can't remember much effort on the part of Dr Rodriguez spent investigating possible shipboard sources of infection."

"And the other really important thing we've got to do is get involved with the routine analysis of the water on board to ensure adequate chlorination and absence of microbes. Outlets all over the ship need checking regularly, and a record kept – potable sources and others, as well as the water in the swimming pool. There's a special kit, apparently."

"Anything else we've been omitting to do, while you're at it?"

"Yes, emergency drills involving the whole crew will have to be tightened up considerably. The US Coastguard is apparently pretty hot on procedures. I gather there'll be quite a few full-scale practices in the weeks to come, preparing us for a variety of possible scenarios. You know, fire on board, capsize, etc. And naturally, where injuries are supposedly incurred, we'll, of course, be involved. We're sure to get some practice using this," said Luke indicating the emergency stretcher over in one corner. It was like a half-cone in shape, the sort suitable for hoisting by helicopter.

"That should be fun," said Kate, taken by a particular mental image. "Especially if the stretcher team end up trying to get to someone deep in the bowels of the ship. Some of those lower stairways are quite steep, you know, with incredibly tight bends in them. As for the steps up from the engine room – they're so damn dangerous, I swear someone's going to end up getting killed down there one of these days."

Chapter 12

I

"I tell you, Dottore, these Colombian women – they are without doubt the most beautiful in the world. Of all the countries I have visited in my life, really, I have never before seen so many fana-tastic ladies in one place."

"You sound like something of an expert, Vito," said Luke with a smile, as the old Deck Steward wiped the table near where he was standing, and rearranged the white metal chairs neatly around it. This done, he paused and straightened up. A knobbly hand, the one not holding the cloth, rested on his hip in a way that almost disguised the sideways kink of his lower spine. This showed itself particularly when he walked – the resultant tilt of his pelvis giving the impression of a comparative shortening of his left leg. His limp was renowned throughout the ship and – though he was unaware of it – cruelly mimicked; particularly by his younger compatriots.

"Believe me, Doctor – I have been here many times in my life. Especially when I was a young man. These girls from Colombia – and Venezuela too – the very best. Bellissima..." He broke off suddenly, kissing fully the gnarled fingertips of one hand, throwing them skywards in a passionate Milanese gesture. Lips themselves, thought Luke, that might once have held passionate promise; now thin and shrivelled almost beyond recognition. "I would have married one too," he went on, "if only my wife had let me."

Luke laughed out loud at the remark, rendered even more amusing by the oddness of the old Deck Steward's accent.

"And you're still married to her?" he asked. "She must be an understanding woman, letting you go off for such long periods like this."

"She was a very understanding woman," said Vito quietly and with sudden seriousness, "- when she was alive, that is. You know, I miss her more now than ever before, my Margueretta. She has been dead this past fifteen years." His deep cracked voice wavered discernibly as he said this.

"Do you have children?" asked Luke.

"Three fine boys."

"At sea?"

"No, Dottore. They have more sense."

As Luke studied the Colombian coastline in the distance, a voice cut in over the tannoy. It was that of Craig Jensen, the Cruise Director, embarking on a short account of the long and colourful history of the port, spanning, in approximately twelve minutes, some four hundred and sixty years.

Luke leaned back lazily against the side rail and listened, tilting his hat a fraction to shade his eyes from the midday glare.

"Sounds quite a place, doesn't it?" The voice was Rick Tucson's, the magician on board. "Think I'll try getting a seat on one of those tour buses if there's any room. Sure as hell don't fancy wandering around any place in Colombia on my own if I can help it. Not after some of the things I've heard."

"Well, according to Craig Jensen only a minute or two back, Cartagena seems to have a reputation of relative safety amongst Colombian cities. Still, I guess the operative word there must be 'relative'."

"Yeah – these guys are really bound to say that though, aren't they? The last thing they want is a crowd of passengers too scared to get off the ship. Wouldn't do much for local trade – or, for that matter, the Cruise Director's cut from the emerald shops he makes sure are included on the tour. You know – the old back-hander. This is the first ship you've worked on, right?"

"Yes," said Luke.

"Well, you'll pretty soon discover that everyone on ship that can manage it has his fingers in one little pie or another. Mark my words – the Captain, Staff Captain, Chief Purser and some of his underlings, Hotel Manager; you name them, they're at it. You're a passenger and you want your cabin upgraded? No sweat; there's plenty spare on this ship. Couple of hundred bucks to the right person and it's yours. Some of these scams the Company knows about and almost accepts as a traditional perk of the job. Others they obviously don't and would deal with most seriously if they ever found out. These are the ones you'll find carried out here on board a little more discreetly."

"Is that so?" said Luke. "I had no idea."

"Well, if you keep your ear to the ground, you'll see what I mean. You going ashore, by the way? If so, I advise you to watch what you say to those armed military types at the dockside. No wise-cracks now."

Shortly after, the Venus Prince began drawing up to Cartagena's new Cruise Ship Dock. According to the commentary over the tannoy, this had only been completed in the past ten years or so. A covered walkway extended from the pier to the shore facilities. In the distance, Luke could just make out the San Felipe Fortress and the elaborate domes of churches in what he presumed to be the Old City.

Half an hour later, the tour group drove off en masse. Soon the convoy of buses would split; ancient sites and less ancient shops of emeralds and pre-Columbian art reproductions visited in almost equal measure. Like it or not. No debate.

As he waited for the ambulance car to arrive for his patient, Luke watched as Dan Forsbrook pulled away in a cab. Captain Symiakos, who had just seen him off, nodded to Luke as he returned to the ship. For some reason or other, he had a curiously smug look about him.

A number of young women, each of such startling dusky beauty that Luke knew immediately Vito had been so completely right, stood around at intervals chatting. Some, accompanied by certain of the ship's officers, ventured aboard. By their actions at least, it appeared they had known each other for some time. Was this then, Luke wondered, an example of the stereotypical sailor's 'woman in every port'? And if so, how did the arrangement work? Surely these ladies couldn't be – were just too breathtakingly beautiful to be – common whores?

The realisation was shocking, yet it somehow stirred him uncomfortably deep inside. A feeling – he had to admit – almost akin to jealousy overcame him, suddenly and sickeningly. An envy of these very men who, through no merit of their own, could have such women so easily. He had never been in this position before. Yet, he knew instinctively he could somehow never – no matter how much his body ached to – bring himself to knowingly partake in their game.

It disturbed him nonetheless.

Just then, as something of a welcome distraction, the ambulance car trundled into view. Luke returned to the foyer. Moments later, he emerged, wheeling his patient – Mr Arnold Christopher, retired optometrist from Wisconsin – down the gangway and over to the waiting vehicle.

II

At about the same time that Luke had left the arthritic Mr Christopher and his badly discharging right ear to the tender mercy of Dr Raoulle, ENT specialist, on the third floor of the main hospital and gone off to look around, Dan Forsbrook had not only checked in but was now enjoying a cool swim in the Hotel Caribe's Olympic-sized pool.

Dan preferred the Caribe not only for its facilities but also its soul. It was the oldest by far of the main Cartagena hotels. Colonial in style and standing in expansive gardens, he felt its position second to none. There it remained at the southern end of the Bocagrande – one eye over the Caribbean, the other, with undoubted amusement, over its more absurd-looking modern competitors along the way.

Later, as the Venus Prince sailed out from Cartagena Bay, Dan raised a glass towards Felipe, the young barman, who smiled back a little puzzled. It had all gone surprisingly well, he couldn't help thinking. His strategy had obviously proved the right one. Yet Symiakos had been even more receptive to his threats than he had first imagined he might. Why should this be?

Dan didn't ponder this for too long. Instead, he had another drink, left a large tip for Felipe on the bar and took off for a quick stroll before dinner. He liked to make the most of these enforced nights away – the ones when he wasn't actually on one ship or another. Or worse still – caught in the very act of travelling. Best of all, he liked it when he could relax – at Company expense – in some of the very finest hotels and enjoy all they had to offer. He had no family to speak of – certainly, no immediate family missing him right then. There was no one back at his bachelor apartment waiting for his call. No close neighbours, there in DC, tuned in to his irregular comings and goings. Only his special friends and contacts – widely spread around the globe. He harboured no regrets; he was well satisfied with his lot. Just as long as he could stay one step ahead of the game.

When the knock came at the door of Room 158 at 10.35 pm, Dan put his coffee cup down on the bedside table and went to answer it. He had just been debating in his mind exactly when he ought to leave for the Casino del Caribe over at the Pierino Gallo – the scene of one very notable past triumph. It stood out in his memory: there had been so few others of late. The thought of this had clearly excited him – a thought that had now been interrupted.

Who could this be, he wondered? He was not expecting anyone just then. Felipe perhaps? But surely not this early? If it was, he might have hoped for a little more discretion.

The two men standing outside the door were not known to Dan. One – the taller of the two – stood back two feet or so behind the other. His height, though, and the overall proportion of his body made his immediate appearance nonetheless remarkable. They were both wearing light-coloured suits, the closer man's considerably more casual in style. It somehow lacked the aura of true casualness though, mainly due to the sheer bulk of body within it. The taller man's face moved little as Dan looked. The other man spoke;

"Mr Forsbrook?"

"Yes," said Dan, puzzled. They didn't seem like hotel staff, though there was an air of quiet authority about them. Port officials, perhaps – or local plain-clothed police?

There were other, more unlikely – but infinitely more worrying – possibilities that occurred to Dan as he stood there. But surely to God, no way in this part of the world?

"I regret having to bother you at this time of night, but I have something of great importance to discuss with you. It is to do with the ship, Venus Prince. May we come in?"

"You are from the Port Authority?" asked Dan, standing aside to let them enter.

The first man went over towards the balcony window and sat himself down in one of the two lounge chairs located there. The other man remained impassively by the door. The briefcase he was carrying had been placed on the floor by his feet.

"Come, Mr Forsbrook, let us sit and talk," said the first man gesturing to Dan to join him in the other chair. "Excuse my friend here, Ramirez. He is a man of few words. Unfortunately, very few, even of those, can he manage in English."

The face of the man speaking, Dan noticed as he observed him close-to, was a rough-hewn, well-lived-in sort of face, sculpted and ruddied by the elements. A small, well-healed scar stood out clearly on his left cheek – largely due to its comparative pallor.

"What exactly about the Venus Prince?" asked Dan as the man made himself comfortable in the chair. This he did in a way that suggested no two-minute stay. "I guess whatever it is must be important – calling on me like this at this hour. How did you know where I was staying? The ship's agent, presumably?"

"We have our ways," said the man casually. "Mr Forsbrook, I think I must explain. I have a position of some authority in this region of Colombia. Not only do I involve myself in the wellbeing of the local community and its prosperity, but I also have my own – how shall I put it? – business interests."

"You are from EDURBE then?" asked Dan.

"Not directly – though I do, of course, have an interest in the good work of the Urban Development Corporation. The new Cruise Ship Dock, for example – which you may know was fundamentally an independent project – was, I am proud to say, something I was more than pleased to lend my support to. Now, about the Venus Prince..."

"Yes?" said Dan, still a little uncertain as to who exactly this guy was, or indeed, whom he represented.

"It has come to our attention that it is intended to change the itinerary of the Venus Prince from the beginning of May. Were this to be the case, I am afraid a lot of people in Cartagena would be extremely disappointed."

"I'm sorry, of course, to hear that. To be honest with you, though, I've had very little real say in the decision myself. The Company has greatly enjoyed its relationship with the Cartagena authorities, and, of course, very much regrets if any decision to use other ports instead will have the effect of diminishing local prosperity."

"Very nicely put, Mr Forsbrook. So diplomatic, and so very kind of you to have regard for the feelings of the Cartagenan people in this way. But, I'm afraid, there is a little more to it. The Venus Prince has, personally, always been considered a very special ship."

"How so? There are plenty of other, much larger cruise ships that include this fine city on their routes. Surely the loss of the Venus Prince would make little overall difference?"

"Admittedly, there are other ships; but actually, fewer than you might perhaps imagine. Certainly, fewer than were expected following the provision of the new dock and shore-side facilities. The Venus Prince has been one of our regulars, not just for one season, but consistently, for quite a few years now. And that we appreciate. To pull out now would, we are afraid, send bad signals to other cruise companies and the travelling public at large – especially in the USA."

"Well, I'm very sorry," said Dan, with the distinct impression that he was repeating himself, "if what you say is indeed the case. As I've said, though, the decision was taken at a higher level, and the plans for our new itinerary already underway. There's unfortunately little more I can add."

Dan looked closely at the man sitting opposite to view his reaction, hoping he might have said enough at this point to conclude their meeting. It soon became clear that this was a vain hope indeed as there was not the slightest alteration in the other's features. Dan, however, wanted to be getting on with his own plans for the evening. He felt a growing urgency within himself, now that he had mentally psyched himself up for the Casino. He glanced over at the second man who had now stooped down to pick up the briefcase. Was this the sign he was looking for?

The man opposite turned in his chair to face his companion, and the taller man leant forward and swung the case over towards him, onto a small coffee table nearby. As Dan watched him do this and straighten up again after, he was filled with sudden alarm. Something he'd glimpsed beneath the tall man's jacket left him aware that a different level of respect was now indicated. He'd only seen part of the leather strap across the left side of his chest, but he had little doubt what it was connected to. As he looked at the man now, in as expressionless a way as he could manage, he was able to just make out the bulge below his armpit beneath the loose-fitting garment.

The man seated pulled the briefcase across the table towards him and opened it. He took out a folder – a sheaf of different-sized papers sitting unevenly within – and placed it on his lap. Once there, and still unopened, he turned his attention once more to Dan.

"You disappoint me, Mr Forsbrook," he said looking directly into his eyes. "We know you to be a man of great influence in your company, Venus Cruise Lines. Little, we understand, is done without some regard for your opinion."

"How would you know that?" cut in Dan a little aggressively. "And come to think of it, how did you get to hear of the proposed itinerary change? It hasn't exactly been common knowledge. In fact, the final decision wasn't made until three days ago."

"As I believe I have said once already this evening, we have our ways. In fact, there are quite a lot of things we know about you, Mr Forsbrook. That is why we have this proposition to make you."

"Proposition?" said Dan with sudden interest. It wasn't the only question he wanted the answer to at that time. What he equally needed to know was what precisely they knew about him. Surely not...?

"It's a proposition we feel will be of particular interest to you – bearing in mind your current predicament."

"And what do you mean by that?" asked Dan, though he had a strange feeling he knew exactly to what this man was alluding. He attempted a look somewhere between disdain and indifference.

"We know, for instance, Mr Forsbrook, that a number of people in various parts of the world would very much like to speak with you at this moment on the subject of money owed to them over your gambling debts. I believe, too, that you have been seriously threatened on more than one occasion in the past two months as a consequence. Mere aliases would seem to be no longer sufficient for you, Mr Forsbrook. As you've no doubt become aware, unless you come up with a substantial sum of money soon, your life will be in serious danger. What we are about to propose could allow settlement of all outstanding claims against you twice over."

"Okay, go ahead. Let me hear," said Dan tensely. "But I think perhaps the danger you refer to is a little exaggerated."

"Not according to our sources. Anyway, as I have already said, we are aware of your level of influence in the Company. I have also stressed how important we feel it is that your ship retains its current itinerary. We propose to pay you the sum of one million US dollars on condition that you succeed in persuading your boss not to go ahead with the change of route."

"A million bucks? Mmm," said Dan, hardly believing what he was hearing. He fought to contain his initial elation. It was not a gift they were offering, after all.

"Gentlemen," he said after a pause, having attempted to digest some at least of the implications of the offer, "generous as this undoubtedly sounds, I find it difficult to believe that retaining one smallish cruise ship in this way could seriously be worth so much to you. I have a nagging feeling there's something else – some other slant on this you're just not telling me. Who exactly are you, anyway, and what are your real interests in this? What you've told me so far just doesn't seem to hold water."

"Very well, Mr Forsbrook. I will be more forthcoming with you, seeing as you insist. First of all, my name is Delgardo – Delgardo Santos Estremosa. I am known in this region more simply, I think you'll find, by the name Delgardo. It is true that I have considerable business interests. Part involves the export of certain products. Up till now, we have found good use for the Venus Prince in its potential as a type of courier transport up to business contacts in Jamaica."

"You have couriers using the ship to transport goods to Jamaica? What kind of goods, may I ask? You surely don't mean cocaine, for Chrissakes?! Does the Captain know of this?"

"No, he knows nothing at all. It is all carried out with extreme discretion, trust me."

"You're using the Venus Prince for organised drug-running and you want me to help you? I'm sorry, gentlemen. No goddam way."

Delgardo turned his head towards Ramirez, who had so far remained still. Now, however, as Dan watched, he slid his hand up slowly under his jacket until it came to rest. He looked back at Delgardo, ignoring Dan completely.

"No, relax, my friend," Delgardo said to his colleague slowly. Dan wondered later, thinking back to it, why Delgardo had said this in English. It had clearly been for his benefit. "No need to get impatient," he continued. Ramirez's hand dropped back into view. Delgardo addressed Dan once more as if nothing of any significance had occurred.

"This, if you don't mind me saying, Mr Forsbrook, would seem to be a particularly high moral stance you are adopting. Especially for someone who is not only a compulsive gambler but also someone with – how shall I put it? – dubious business interests of his own."

"What exactly do you mean by that?" asked Dan in surprise.

"Perhaps if I simply tell you we know about your special agency – what's it known as? Yes, that's it; 'Eastern Promise'. Am I right?"

"I'm afraid I have absolutely no idea at all what you are talking about here. I'm sorry."

"Come now, Mr Forsbrook. Do you really want me to spell it out? Let me remind you – the business you helped set up with your old friend Bill Newman from Vietnam days?"

Dan hesitated, then fell into a stunned silence. Delgardo continued, pressing home his advantage.

"Yes, we know all about the way the agency works. Very clever of you both to see the potential on offer. It helped, I'm sure, that your colleague has remained living out East for so many years now. He could no doubt spot the gap in the market right away – over there in Thailand. And who better to help him than his old war buddy." He said the word 'buddy' almost mockingly. "Someone who, through the nature of his legitimate employment, is in the unique position of being able to fly out and call in on the agency at fairly frequent intervals – no questions asked.

"Now, let us talk morals, Mr Forsbrook. When these – what shall we call them? – ah yes, 'gentlemen travellers'. When these gentlemen travellers make their way out to Bangkok for the vacation of their dreams, who do they call? Discretion assured – isn't that part of your boast? Yes, they call the contact agency known as Eastern Promise. And what happens then? I'll tell you, Mr Forsbrook. What happens then is that they are put onto the many child prostitutes roaming the streets of Bangkok and Pattaya. Young boys mainly, I believe – your own personal delicacy, Mr Forsbrook, if I am not very much mistaken?"

"You're quite wrong, Mr Estremosa," interrupted Dan irritably. "No way am I connected with any such organisation. The idea is preposterous. There must be some mistake."

"No mistake, Mr Forsbrook. Our information is thoroughly cross-checked, don't you worry. Oh, admittedly, we had to dig fairly deep to uncover your association with the agency. But there it was; Dan Forsbrook, one of the founder members." Dan looked shaken. "And now, where was I?" Delgardo went on. "Yes – and it doesn't end there, now does it, Mr Forsbrook? Having got these children into the hotel rooms – the hotel owned, by the way, by your company – the service you provide to your customers goes one step further. The rooms – the 'special' rooms I'm referring to now – have another facility. Am I right? Not only can your clients enjoy the very special nature of their vacation, but thanks to Eastern Promise, they are able to take away with them a detailed recording of their triumphs. Yes, Mr Forsbrook, on the specially prepared video tapes you have made for them."

"No – no, you are wrong," Dan interjected pathetically. Delgardo ignored the interruption. He went on, a wicked gleam now in his eye.

"And even then, it doesn't stop there, does it? What these poor naive fools don't realise is that the master copies of these video tapes are retained by Eastern Promise, aren't they? What do you use them for, Mr Forsbrook? Blackmail? Oh, not directly, I'm sure. That's not your style, is it? Sell them on, perhaps, for someone else to dish the dirt? That's the expression, isn't it? However, one usage we are sure of is the inclusion of certain of these 'performances' – clients faces in the main blacked out, admittedly – in the production of child video porn for potential worldwide distribution."

Delgardo paused on that note of triumph. Dan looked around sheepishly, submission now evident in his whole demeanour. Delgardo spoke again, slower and less vindictively this time.

"I am sure in the light of all this, my friend, you would no doubt like to reconsider our little offer. What we are asking is – by comparison, of course, to any imaginable alternative – very simple and well within your capabilities. In fact, so confident were we that you would ultimately agree, we have had the money paid in already to this numbered Cayman Islands account. The documentation is all here." He handed Dan some papers from the folder on his knee.

"By the way, Mr Forsbrook, it goes without saying, we will be monitoring your progress closely at all times. Be sure not to let us down."

Chapter 13

I

Out once again in the gently-tousled waters of the then dark Caribbean, the Venus Prince weaved slowly along. Its slight but regular roll paid careful disregard to the rhythm of Carnival Night on board.

Passengers adorned to varying degrees with items of fancy dress, writhed and jiggled on the dance floor of the Venturer's Lounge. Cruise staff had provided initial encouragement – a mere catalyst for those of the right personality or degree of intoxication. Or, as it turned out in many cases, both. Luke looked on in amusement.

Grant Harrison's band, it soon became clear, was more than equal to the task, performing some pretty complicated Latin pieces with both skill and gusto. Luke found himself swept in, tapping out a very passable Samba on the small circular table in front of him – barely audible though, in the general din, even to his own ears.

"Doctor, would you care to dance?" said someone from close range, bending over towards him.

He looked around. It was his old friend from North Carolina, Eunice Charlton.

"Absolutely delighted," he said, rising quickly. He slipped his arm gently through hers and led her out onto what he hoped might prove to be the least precarious part of the packed dance floor.

Dan Forsbrook had so far refrained from venturing out of his hotel room. His visitors had gone, but ever since they had – only some thirty minutes before – he had sat alone in a state of almost complete bewilderment. Only now was he able to apply some form of objective appraisal to what had just occurred.

There could be little doubt about it; he had just played host to a member – no doubt of some seniority locally – of the Colombian Cartel. Although he didn't purport to know much of their overall activities, he had heard enough rumours of some of their methods – like many others the world over – to be suitably alarmed.

It puzzled him that there should be such concern over one distribution point – if what Delgardo had said about it involving only one or two couriers was indeed true. So small an operation, he had said, that not even the Captain was aware of its existence on the ship. Really, how could this be? Certainly, if Captain Symiakos himself didn't know, then surely some of the crew – of whichever nationality – would have to be involved somehow or another?

Did these couriers board from here in Cartagena? Presumably so. Did they appear on the passenger list? He would be intrigued to know.

But surely that was all beside the point, wasn't it? That side of things he really had little control over – unless, of course, he intended to somehow have the operation busted. And who exactly would he approach to arrange that? The

Drug Enforcement Administration – the DEA, perhaps? He had heard of them, sure, but when he came to think about it, knew little of their mode of operation. Where, for example, did they hang out, anyway? They must surely have operatives working locally. But – more importantly – what would be the consequences for him, should this happen? It was almost too terrifying to contemplate. Particularly as it would be pretty obvious to the Cartel that such a move was solely down to him. Then there was the alternative – give them what they wanted. How difficult would that be? Old Jamieson seemed pretty determined about the changes when last he spoke to him. How easy would it be to convince him otherwise?

It seemed somehow ironic that he'd just spent so long over the past day or so instilling in those key personnel on the Venus Prince just how important it was that the ship be meticulously prepared for the changeover. Perhaps, though, it was just as well he had, thinking about it. Anything he might have to do to alter Jamieson's decision would have to be done surreptitiously – behind a mask of complicity. His position, as far as the Company was concerned, must not be seen to have changed even slightly while all this was going on.

Then there was the other aspect – the hold this man Delgardo now had over him. His team had certainly done their homework alright. How had they found out? How much information was really available to them? He was not unaware of the consequences should word of his involvement in Eastern Promise – and the rest – be given to the authorities back home. If that were ever the case, he wouldn't be able to show his face back in the US again, for some considerable time.

As he thought this all through, Dan Forsbrook realised it all pointed one way – and to one thing only. Time was short and he'd better get thinking. He still had five days before his next meeting with Jamieson at Head Office. It was all suddenly very clear – what he needed were ways of making certain his boss was persuaded. There was really no room for error.

Meanwhile, there was something else more immediate that he needed to attend to. Something that might offer brief but welcome respite from this latest dilemma.

He grabbed his jacket and headed off for the Casino.

II

Of all those dancing at Carnival Night the previous evening, she alone, as far as Luke was concerned, stood out. In fact, he'd found it difficult at times to take his eyes off her. The elegance of her movement, the litheness of her body, the erectness of her head; all attributes one would no doubt expect from a professional dancer – one of a mere handful on the entertainment staff.

And there she was now – purely by chance, it turned out – chatting with him. Chatting casually – disinterestedly almost, it would seem; her Texan drawl, however, allowing him all manner of mental imagery behind his shades, as he looked stoically ahead at all that was going on before them. Seductive country singer more than once came to mind.

Most of all, though, they talked about their slow but nonetheless exciting entry just before, into the first of the three Gatun Locks of the Panama Canal. Not far up ahead, as they watched, a sizeable tanker was that very minute simply rising up, albeit slowly, before their eyes. It came to an eventual stop many feet above their level.

Tall and blonde, she stood beside him, only a couple of inches in height between them. Luke pointedly held back from dwelling on other aspects of her physique; it wouldn't do his current state of ease any good at all. He knew well enough of their existence – he'd seen her on stage several times so far that week and tried to pretend he hadn't been affected. Not that she had been in any overt state of undress – shows on board were never quite of that nature.

But what bothered him most of all, if he was in any way honest about it, was something else entirely. Even now, as he thought about her standing just there – shoulder to shoulder beside him – taking in the same scene ahead, he was genuinely unable to recall any precise details of her face. For some reason or other, it remained virtually a blur. Her body – no problem – etched indelibly in his mind: a cinematic image from the dance floor of the Venturer's Lounge, in the costume of the night before. In particular, as he recalled, the high cut of her lower bodice – only a little risqué in this day and age – accentuating the length of her leg and exquisite pertness of her rear. Attractive though he remembered it to be, her face posed a different problem. What, if anything, was there of particular note about it?

But then again, what did it really matter to him, anyway? He'd lusted over anonymous, faceless bodies before – been galvanised in a paralysis of desire by a mere glimpse of the right female portion. Exquisitely presented, disconnected; the only requirement being that it had to be just right. Then, the

149

storage of the image along with the others – those countless mental snapshots, ever fading. There to be revisited when occasion allowed or needs must.

The problem in this present case, though, was that he rather feared that this particular image would not so easily go away. It would have little chance even of fading with time – constant reinforcement would see to that. And how would he handle it? Would his senses become eventually blunted to her charms as the season went on? If so, surely this could only be for the best?

Certainly, he felt no real desire for her as a person – had no wish to even try to take things further. And anyway, if he did, it would surely be a mistake – working in such close proximity, day in day out for perhaps months to come. Besides, her very presence intimidated him. Her very sexual presence. He felt somehow unequal to it. She had a power over him that thankfully she might never get to know.

And where did Tara fit into all of this? Where was the mental image of her, right now? It was there, sure enough. Always had been. But in her case, it was so completely different. Her face, for example, was with him at all times – visiting him often in the days since he'd last seen her, and with stunning clarity. Just when he least expected it.

Even though he'd only known her a short time, there had developed an odd purity about his thoughts for her. Strange for him, he couldn't help thinking. Feelings that transcended the merely sexual: part of him seemed to have somehow simply blocked these out – though he couldn't really think why.

In fact, he could recall little of the exact detail of her body – the slimness of her hips or the shapeliness of her legs. What he could clearly recollect, however, was the look she flashed at him when she smiled, and the snugness of her body against his as they'd danced; and how warm and right it had felt so close to him.

The journey, earlier that morning, in from the Cristobal breakwater and through the channel from Limon Bay, had proved one of great interest to Luke. The channel itself had only been a hundred and fifty yards or so wide, he would have guessed, and appeared to cut right through dense mangrove swamp – so close-by on one side that it seemed in places almost possible to reach out and touch the thick green vegetation.

The three Gatun Locks themselves, Luke had learned from Craig Jensen's ongoing commentary, would raise the Venus Prince fully eighty-five feet. Each of these was a twin lock, with a thick dividing wall in between, with ships on one side passing those on the other in opposite directions. All three lock chambers were of identical size – a mere one hundred and ten feet wide and a thousand feet long.

Having passed through to the south, the ship would find itself in Gatun Lake – one of the largest artificial bodies of water in the world. This had been formed by the Gatun Dam, an earthen dam across the Chagres River.

As he walked back a little later to the hospital, Luke had the chance to see, close-to, one of the famous mechanical 'mules' trundling along its track-way, one of a pair guiding the Venus Prince slowly through the narrow waterway. Luke was particularly struck by the degree of inclination it could manage, as it positioned itself ready for the next level up.

III

Next morning at eleven saw the Venus Prince anchored off Grand Cayman. Tenders from the island relayed passengers, and later crew, ashore. A handful of clearly affluent and elegantly dressed islanders came out to the ship for a look around. Luke noticed them later on deck – served at an otherwise empty deck-bar, by no less than the chief bar steward himself. Money, it seemed, in this situation at least, clearly talked.

There was, Luke found, a completely different atmosphere about this, the more northern part of their itinerary. In fact, it was only here and Jamaica, which they would be returning to tomorrow after completion of the first week-long circuit, that made Luke feel he was really in the Caribbean – as he had previously imagined the Caribbean to be. There was a welcome lushness to the vegetation on this and the other flat islands of the Cayman group; a lushness not present in their more southerly stops. The water was breathtakingly clear – almost bright turquoise in the shallows closer to shore.

As he travelled in the tender a little later on, Luke spied a wreck in the depths. Not a buccaneering wreck, but the rusting hulk of a considerably more modern vessel. He noticed the dark forms of divers investigating it as he passed, and later still, a whole host of snorkellers off to one side in the reef close to shore.

After landing, Luke took off at a leisurely pace down George Town's main street, Cardinal Avenue. He had read the Tourist Information leaflets and it was true: for such a small island group, it really was hard to believe there were so many banks and financial institutions. Several hundred in all, it proclaimed. Luke found it difficult to imagine, looking around him, where exactly they might all be housed.

The streets were clean, the buildings stylish and almost stately in a small-scale sort of way. Later, he would take a taxi to the hospital – barely a mile out of town towards the airport – to inspect its facilities. Then, if he had time, a trip down to the Plantation Village resort on Seven Mile Beach. He knew that was where some of the others had gone. An alternative – he noticed with some amusement scanning the map – would be to go to the village of Hell, to the north of the island. Something to tell the folks back home – or perhaps even send a card postmarked from there. How long would it take for the round trip, he wondered? Luke glanced at his watch. There would be no time today.

He hailed a taxi and headed off for the hospital.

What Luke Darius couldn't have known just then, however, was that his trip to Hell was already set for another place and time entirely.

PART 3

TESTING TIMES

Chapter 14

I

That night, the last of that particular cruise, the Captain's Gala Dinner was to be held.

Luke was surprised to find that he, like three or four other senior officers, was expected to preside over a table of his own. Their tables, it turned out, were far smaller than that of the Captain, there in its position of prominence at the head of the room. It was, nevertheless, a new and interesting prospect. Luke still felt slightly disadvantaged by his attire, particularly with the passengers so formally dressed. He only hoped his own uniforms would be there on arrival next day in Jamaica.

The ageing Chicago physician who sat with his wife directly across from Luke seemed particularly interested in his posting and his motives for being there.

"So why you here, Doc? They paying you much?" he asked, trampling heavily over the bush that others more tactfully might have beaten around.

Later, after the group had cordially split, Luke found himself leading two of his table up to the Venturer's Lounge. He ordered their drinks with the nonchalance of one secretly in possession of a fairly generous bar allowance, allocated mainly for the purposes of passenger entertainment. As the lights faded and they settled down to watch that night's show, Craig Jensen appeared and kicked off with his own brand of cabaret. It had a sort of washed-out, time-warped feel about it as far as Luke was concerned, but seemed to go down well nonetheless. Next came the magician, Rick Tucson, and after that the dancers. Luke tried not to make it too obvious he was secretly preoccupied with Sandy's gyrating crotch.

When the performance ended, Luke wandered through to the nightclub. The band were all there now relaxing, as were most of the other entertainers and a fair crowd of passengers; fewer, though, than he might have expected for a last night.

Not long after midnight, the place thinned out considerably so that only those passengers really determined for a final fling remained. Word went round of a crew party down in the mess. Soon after that, the disco began to waver and slowly die.

Luke joined his fellow workers; the first time he'd seen them let their collective hair down since joining ship the week before. Sandy, though, he was a little ashamed to have noticed, wasn't amongst them.

II

Mrs Charlton came by the hospital early next morning to say farewell.

"Have a safe trip home," said Luke, giving her a gentle peck on the cheek.

"Here's my address, Dr Darius. If you ever find yourself up my way, do call."

"You know, come to think of it, I've never been to North Carolina before."

Chapter 15

I

Unlike the last meeting at Head Office three weeks before, Dan Forsbrook this time ensured he was there in good time.

It was early the following Wednesday and he was in a frame of mind slightly more optimistic than it had been for days. There had been an awful lot to think about in that past week. It was only now, having set his initial scheme into motion, that his mood had finally lifted. He was not unaware though that a lot depended on his performance at the meeting that morning.

There would be no direct result today – that wasn't necessarily the intention. But he needed, he knew, to somehow plant the seeds in Ed Jamieson's mind: to get his message across without making it appear he was in any way pushing an opposing viewpoint. Bearing in mind Ed Jamieson's attention span – and general level of receptivity to any subject not on his own personal agenda at these meetings – Dan knew he stood most chance speaking first. To this end, he had managed to persuade Rachel, Ed's secretary, to oblige. Now, as he looked at the typed agenda she had produced, he was pleased to see his name there right after Jamieson's introductory preamble.

"So, there we have it, ladies and gentlemen. Admittedly, there is an element of risk, particularly with the late timing of the thing. But I feel sure, with such a talented team as those present, it should ultimately pose little real problem. The press release, by the way, is due later today..."

Well, that's answered my first question, thought Dan. He had known enough examples of Jamieson's often fickle nature in the past – decisions he'd pushed through against better advice one day, virtually fought with them over – reversed, seemingly on a whim, the next. But that clearly wasn't the case here. The old boy was being consistent for once, at least. He had to give him that.

Jamieson was still talking, though at this point, clearly winding down.

"Now, if you recall in our last meeting, a number of other concerns were raised about the Venus Prince and how it was running. Dan, I see you're first up today. I believe you've recently returned from a visit to the ship where hopefully you've been able to view the situation close to. What do you have to report?"

Dan distributed some handouts around the table then made his way over to an overhead projector at one end of the boardroom.

"First of all, folks, I'm pleased to be able to tell you that things are not all doom and gloom on the Venus Prince. Far from it, in fact. Since we last met, various issues raised have now been addressed. A new doctor – a Dr Luke Darius – has been recruited while I was over in London, and thoroughly briefed as to what is expected of him. He joined the ship the week before last and seems to be settling in pretty well.

Since arriving on board, he has undertaken a critical review of the way the medical department had been running up to that point and already instituted a number of key changes. He understands fully the importance of strict adherence to protocol regarding potential medical litigation claims against the Company. And, as well as this, he is aware of his own crucial role in helping achieve our aim of getting the ship up to standard for the new itinerary."

Dan paused briefly and glanced around at those listening. Jamieson, he noticed, looked reasonably satisfied so far. And so he should, thought Dan – he's hearing just what he wants to hear. One of the others, John Warringer – just behind Jamieson now that they'd all swivelled their chairs round towards the overhead – sat there looking slightly vacant. There were three others, two of them women, not present at their previous meeting. They had been brought in now as the itinerary changes affected the departments they themselves each headed.

"Morale is extremely good, I am pleased to report," went on Dan. "I've spoken to key personnel on board individually, and all seem to be basically happy with these latest proposals. Captain Symiakos himself, although keen to give his utmost support, has voiced certain reservations, however, about the time scale we have imposed. He feels it is totally inadequate for what needs to be achieved. He is particularly concerned about how much seems to rest on the ship getting through the checks at the first attempt and the loss of those bookings already confirmed for early next season on the present itinerary, which are now about to be cancelled.

"The Captain is also aware, as are we all, that barely scraping through will not be enough – particularly with so much information nowadays about a ship's performance openly published here in the USA, and the Company's reputation at stake. His concerns should be viewed in the light of an admission on his part that things, not only structurally but organisationally too, have been far below the exceptionally high US standard for so long."

Dan gauged the pause having said this. He carefully avoided adding any opinion of his own, as he might so easily have done on any other occasion. What he had to be seen to be doing was merely reporting the views of others – or what he chose to represent as their views, however well-fabricated and however well-slanted to suit his own requirements. He hoped Jamieson had been alert to what he'd said for there was more to come:

"Now, as far as customer satisfaction is concerned, as was pointed out at our last meeting, the official passenger satisfaction questionnaires might possibly have been a little suspect. Since I was also keen to look closer into the current state of play regarding the present itinerary – purely so that we might learn from our mistakes – I thought I'd conduct a small survey of my own while I was down there. I won't bore you all with the details of every question asked, though I do have some copies here if you'd like. The main points of interest are summarised on the handouts you have in front of you."

Dan placed a transparency on the overhead.

"It has its deficiencies, admittedly, but taken as a kind of 'spot check', you can see the results are actually fairly encouraging. Connection flights were highly rated, though airport transfers to join the ship could have been handled better. Embarkation procedures obviously went pretty smoothly..."

All very reassuring stuff, thought Dan – as long as you're still paying attention, Jamieson. That's all I ask.

Dan knew he was in danger of boring the hell out of everyone with his survey – but pure fiction always did run that risk.

"So, in summary, I was heartened by what I saw with regard to the running of the ship, and have tackled those areas where improvement will definitely be expected." Here Dan switched to the next transparency.

"Now, coming to these last few points, you can see the results of some questions I threw in regarding passenger motivation for booking that particular cruise in the first place. The main and overwhelming reason – given in some seventy-six per cent of cases you'll notice – turned out to be the inclusion of the Panama Canal. This, as you know, was brought in only seven or eight months back. It is of interest too, I think, that if we look specifically at the overall passenger uptake since that time – on the graph here, at the bottom – you'll notice a definite and highly significant upturn." Dan was speaking a little more quickly now. He was determined to slip in these final important points before Jamieson interrupted him – as he felt sure he pretty soon would.

"This other graph, incidentally – which I managed to get from the U.S.T.F Market Research Group, is of their latest survey carried out for the Panama Canal Commission in Washington. As you can see, it shows the increased numbers of tourists expected to visit the Canal in the next two years or so – leading up, of course, to when the US transfers it over completely to Panama on Dec 31st 1999."

There, he'd done it. He need make no direct reference to the figures: the graphs he'd dreamt up possessed a volubility all of their own. Jamieson hadn't spoken yet, but he could feel it coming. He purposely left the transparency on and began a quick summary of his talk. Hopefully, he had got the point he wanted across. Now a smart reversion to the party line.

"In conclusion, therefore, the Venus Prince is performing reasonably well and, following my short but productive visit last week, all key personnel will be working, like ourselves, with the clear aim of making the changeover as smooth and painless as possible. Although the Captain has reservations about the time frame we have imposed – and the risk and consequences of failure – I, for one, have no specific reason at the moment to share his view."

If Ed Jamieson had any views of his own on the more noteworthy aspects of Dan's report, he limited them to one small point of information addressed equally to all present:

"Thank you, Dan," he said with a pause, as he stood up and looked around him. "I would just like to address the point raised regarding Captain Symiakos' anxieties. To smooth the way – and generally help us prepare for these checks – I have contacted a specialist company in Galveston who deal with this kind of thing all the time. I understand they are completely tuned in to what precisely is required. Consequently, one of their top consultants will be sent down to join the ship in the next few weeks. His job will be to check how everything's

164

coming along, help deal with any specific problems we might have encountered, and basically make sure we get through when we come to be tested. I appreciate things might well be quite difficult without bringing in someone of this level of expertise – but, thankfully, they're available if you're willing to pay.

"Now, John," he said, gesturing to Warringer, "I believe you are going to give us an update on the galley refit, which, if I remember correctly, you informed me yesterday is already underway on board."

II

Two days later, that Friday morning, Ed Jamieson was sitting at his office desk in an unusually pensive mood. Rachel, his secretary, for one, had noticed clearly enough – almost immediately she went in, in fact – having been summoned in her boss's usual fashion half an hour before. What, on any other day, would probably have turned out to be a perfectly straightforward briefing – what to fix-up with whom, about what and when, with perhaps a touch of dictation thrown in – today was somehow strangely different.

There was something about the way he sat there – at times barely hearing what it was she'd said to him. That was unlike him for a start. Then there was the way he kept on about that package he'd received earlier – the one she'd signed for when the courier called. Not that she'd managed to get from her boss exactly what was in it. He hadn't said, and she didn't feel too much like pushing the point. But if he'd asked her about the guy delivering it once, he'd asked a dozen times. Well, three or four, at least. And still, all she could tell him was that he was six-one, about one hundred and eighty pounds, wearing a full-face motorcycle helmet with visor, and a black leather outfit. Perhaps, if she'd really thought it was going to be so important, she'd have leant out of the window to see what sort of motorcycle he had. She kind of imagined a Harley – but then again, she often imagined hunky, mysterious, leather-clad guys on Harleys; trouble was there were so goddam few in New York.

After Rachel had left her boss's office – with a list of things to sort out only a fraction the length of her usual at this time of day – Ed swivelled in his chair and leant across to the top drawer of his desk. Turning the key slowly, he reached inside.

It was the third time he'd examined it since it had been handed to him barely an hour earlier.

Inside the bulky outer packaging – which had reflected only poorly the shape of what lay within – had been a slim brown envelope. It was this Ed now held in his hand. There had been no markings at all on the outer package – and none either, as he inspected the envelope once again, on this.

So, who the hell had sent it – and why, for God's sake? What did it all mean? These and other questions raced through his mind as he recalled the gist of the message inside. The exact phrasing eluded him just then and he began opening the envelope to remove the note once more. As he did so, the phone rang. It was Rachel.

"Mr Jamieson, sorry to interrupt but I have Mrs Jamieson on the line for you. She says it's important."

"Okay," said Ed, "put her on." It was unusual for Ellen to call him at the office.

"Ed?" His wife's voice, he thought, sounded a little anxious.

"Ellen, hi. What's up, Honey? Anything the matter?"

"Just a letter turned up here at the house for you. Found it in the mailbox with the others. Difference with this one is there's no postal markings on it at all – just a message on the front saying 'ED JAMIESON – URGENT ', written in red. You want me to open it, Ed, or wait till you get back?"

"Open it up, Hon." Ed waited in a breathless silence till he could wait no more. "What's it say?" he said, exhaling at last and trying not to sound too eager. He listened while Ellen read it to him, struggling to remain calm, mostly for her sake.

"What does it mean, Ed?"

"Some kind of joke – that's all, Honey. Some of the guys fooling around, I'll bet. By the way, I'm planning to leave a little early today – stick around and I'll see you about 2.30, okay?"

Ed put the phone down and stared into the uncertain void before him. What on God's earth was this all about? he asked himself.

"Rachel, is Dan in this morning?"

"Yes, Mr Jamieson. He's in with Chad and Patsy, going through the new itinerary. Word's through on Nassau – dates confirmed."

"Good. Could you ask him to come to my office straightaway?"

"Yes, sir. I'll do that."

"Dan, come in. Sit yourself down. There's something I want to discuss with you – strictly between ourselves, okay?"

"Sure, Boss – fire away. What's on your mind?"

"This morning, no more than an hour and a half ago, this was delivered to me here by courier."

Dan took the sheet and read the words printed on it:

FORGET FLORIDA, RIGHT? KEEP YOUR MOTHERFUCKING SHIP WHERE IT IS IF YOU KNOW WHAT'S BEST FOR YOU. DO WE MAKE OURSELVES CLEAR?

"A threat?" said Dan incredulously. "But who...?"

"That isn't all," said Jamieson interrupting. "A further message was delivered to my home this morning – at a very similar time to the first. Ellen just rang – she read it out to me. It said simply:

DON'T MAKE US HAVE TO MENTION IT AGAIN, OKAY?

"It's kind of eerie alright," said Dan. "Whoever these screwballs are, Boss, they sure as hell know where you live. Any ideas at all who they might be?"

"None whatsoever at the moment."

"Well, they certainly wasted no time – the official press release was only two days ago. You got any enemies at all you know of? By reputation, at least – if you don't mind me saying, sir – you seem to have trodden on your fair share of toes in the past in your business life, getting to where you are today."

"Yeah, I've played hard, I'll admit that. But nothing to warrant these kinds of tactics."

"What do you propose to do, sir?"

"Well, my hunch, Dan, is that it's just some asshole – or group of assholes – trying to scare me off. Trying to test my commitment. Good chance they'll just back off when they see how serious I am to see this thing through. Besides, in terms of the works being carried out, and the cancellations on the current itinerary, we've already made a sizeable financial investment even at this early stage. And I'll be damned if I'm going to give that up so easily."

By the time Ed Jamieson got home that afternoon, he'd had time to think things through a little more clearly. He found Ellen in the lounge reading. She didn't appear too concerned by what had happened earlier, simply pleased to see him. It wasn't often he managed to get home early on a Friday – unless, that is, they were planning to go away for the weekend. He was relieved he'd obviously managed to reassure her sufficiently on the phone. The last thing he wanted was for her to be affected in any way by this incident.

With this in mind, he purposely avoided the subject of the letter for all of an hour or more. Instead, in as relaxed a way as possible, he kept her talking about everything but – about the dinner party they were due to attend the following evening; about what Eve Sanderson had said that morning at coffee round at her place and about when they'd next go up to their cottage and who they ought perhaps to invite that time round.

Then, later in the kitchen when he'd spied the envelope on the table, he said casually, laughing:

"Ah, yes – that damn fool letter that came earlier on. Don't worry, Hon, it's much as I thought. Some stupid dispute over parking spaces in our building. Young morons in one of the other companies think they can resolve things simply by making loud noises. I just told them not to be so damn childish – we'll sort it out in a civilized meeting next week. No problem. I'm afraid, though, I'll have to bring the matter of this letter up, as an example of just how puerile their behaviour has been so far."

And with that, Ed took the envelope and put it in his pocket.

III

Later that afternoon, as darkness closed in all around and the curtains of the large house were drawn, Ed went into his study; the place he always went when he wanted to be alone. Ellen understood this and rarely bothered him there, figuring that if he was in the kind of mood where he needed to be in such gloomy surroundings, he deserved to be there on his own.

Ed sat down in a red leather winged-back chair and switched on the table lamp by his elbow. He took out first the folded envelope from his pocket and then a slim diary that had, near the front, a list of phone numbers he always liked to keep close at hand.

There was someone he needed to call; someone he hadn't spoken to for some time, but who was a close friend from way back, nonetheless. He opened the envelope and looked at the wording of the message. It had the same typed lettering as the first. The other thing that hadn't escaped his attention, was the synchronicity of the two deliveries. How exactly had that been achieved?

"Jack – that you? How you doing, you old son-of-a-gun? It's Ed – Ed Jamieson."

"Ed – it's been a long time. You keeping okay?"

"Sure, Jack. Real well."

"You ain't gonna believe this but wasn't my old mother just talking about you the other day? So, tell me, Ed, what's on your mind?"

"I need your help, Jack."

"Figured that might be it. Okay, I'm listening."

Jack Buchanan, ex-NYPD, had taken to P.I. work not long after he'd left the Force, four years before, under something of a cloud. The case against him had never satisfactorily been proven, but there had been a lot of bad press at the time over the assault charge. Bearing in mind his age and ongoing suspension from duty pending the internal enquiry, retirement on health grounds, when offered, seemed the simplest solution all round.

Ed had known him for the best part of thirty-five years; first met him, in fact, down at the gym on 34th Street after his first fight. He had been an impressive figure in those days – a fast, powerful Irishman, with a crop of red hair and a left hook that seemed to come from nowhere. And somehow nearly always managed to have the desired effect.

Ed began relating the incidents of earlier on. Without really thinking, he found himself slipping back into the common dialect of their younger days. He included enough background details to allow what had occurred to be viewed in some kind of perspective. Jack listened quietly, asking every so often for certain points to be repeated as he took down notes at the other end of the line.

"Okay, Ed," he said at last. "Tell me, first of all, what's your gut feeling about all this?"

"Well, Jack, my guess is, it's a little scare tactic from someone or other – I've no idea who – just to see if I'm serious. I doubt it's been particularly well thought through, though, as the press release was only the day before yesterday."

"Who else would have known in advance of the proposals – besides, of course, those working here in your New York office?"

"No one really – except, come to think of it now, we did send a telex to the Captain of the Venus Prince warning him of the possibility. You see, we needed an estimate done for work to be carried out on board, should we be going ahead with the changeover plan. I presume also, then, the guys from the company carrying out the refit. They must've gotten some clues when they were there on board, preparing the estimate in the first place."

"And they were... the company, I mean?"

"Go under the name of OCEANWAY LTD. Their base is down in Tampa."

"Okay, Ed. Now, I want you to consider this real good. Is there anyone you can think of, who, at this moment in time, would directly benefit from your ship staying put?"

"No, not really. Not directly benefit."

"Okay, put it the other way. Is there anyone you can think of who would be seriously disadvantaged by your taking the ship out of Miami instead?"

"Not greatly disadvantaged, no. I can't see it. Not to the degree that would warrant direct threats like this. There just isn't that much at stake – in real terms, that is."

"Right, Ed. Now, listen to what I've got to say to you. We've known each other a long time; we go back a long way together, right? You're a successful guy, and over the years you've been one tough son-of-a-bitch at times too. We both know that. You had to be, to get where you are now. Goes with the territory, right? So, you've rubbed a few people up the wrong way, now and again. Who hasn't? Now, maybe, one of those guys doesn't like what happened and decides to pay you back. He may be resentful; he may be jealous. He may be a she, Ed: a broad – someone you've pissed off some way or another over the years. What I need you to do now, Ed, is think, okay? I need you to think real hard. Then, when we meet tomorrow, you give me a list you've drawn up with all the possibilities of who these people might be."

"Okay, Jack. Guess you're right. It's got to be done systematically. When do you want to meet?"

"It's the weekend now, right. How's about at your office tomorrow? Will there be anyone else around?"

"Not in the afternoon, there won't."

"Okay, say two-thirty then. And I'll need to go through all your personnel files."

"No problem. There's some on computer but they're manual mainly."

"One other thing, Ed. Whoever it is knows where you live, right? You given any thought to the security aspect of all this? It might be some crank – some unpredictable weirdo."

"Don't worry, Jack – I've got that way in hand. There's a company I've already contacted. In fact, there's a night patrol guard right outside this very minute. Besides, we're well fenced in here and alarmed to the hilt."

"That's good. Though, at this point, I feel the main target is most likely to be the ship itself. And getting at that would take someone pretty determined. Okay then, Ed, see you tomorrow."

Things seemed no clearer to Ed Jamieson late the following afternoon, there on the sixteenth floor of the Fairfax building. While Jack went through the personnel files, Ed tried adding to his own list from records he kept of past business contacts.

They reviewed their progress at five o'clock over a quick cup of coffee.

"Well, nothing's exactly jumped out at me just yet," said Jack. "But don't worry, I've taken copies of some of these records so I'll be able to go through them a lot more carefully in the next few days – with, maybe, a little cross-checking by my contacts back at the Department. Now, let's take a look at your list."

"Nothing desperately obvious here either, I'm afraid. Sure, there are one or two who might possibly have had cause for grievance – but that was years ago now. Plenty water under the bridge, as they say, since then. Not one of them, though, really seems to have any convincing motive I can see to justify going so far as to actually threaten me like this."

"Okay, Ed. Now, why don't we take a look at it from a different angle? Let me ask you for another list – but I need you to be dead straight with me, okay?"

"Whatever you say, Jack."

"Give me a list of your motives for making this changeover. You admitted earlier it was a fairly bold business move. Presumably, there were pros and cons in your mind at the time. Let me in on the kind of questions you asked yourself – or, shall I say, needed answering – in coming to the ultimate decision. What, indeed, are the true benefits as far as you're concerned?"

IV

Two evenings later, the phone went at Ed's home. Ellen answered it.

"It's for you, Honey," she said, "– a Mr Buchanan." Ellen didn't know Jack, nor of any of Ed's dealings with him in the past. This, it turned out, was probably just as well.

"Thanks, I'll take it in my study."

"Jack?" said Ed, when he was sure Ellen had put her receiver down and they were definitely speaking in private.

"Listen, I've gone through everything I have so far, and I have to agree, it don't make a whole lot of sense. I've still got a way to go, naturally, but there are two things I need to talk through with you. The first is: just because we aren't aware of a clear enough motive for such a threat doesn't mean there isn't one; the person behind the threat might be some kind of head-case – in which instance, all logic can fly out of the window. In my experience, Ed, these types of situations can potentially get way out of hand. Have you considered that? From what you say, it might not be absolutely too late to hold back on this itinerary changeover business – if not permanently, then at least 'til we get some clearer idea of what we might be up against."

"My answer is no, Jack. We've left it late enough as it is. The timing is absolutely crucial for us being ready for the start of next season. I'm still convinced it's just some crank shooting off, trying to scare me. Well, I can tell you – it just isn't going to work."

"Okay, I hear you. Had to ask, that's all. The second point is that I've gone through your lists – especially the last one where you've outlined your motives. Correlating those with all the other information, it strikes me that one possible candidate does stand out among the crowd."

"You mean George Mitchell?" said Ed.

"That's right. But only, that is, if he's as acutely aware as you of your rivalry."

"But, even so, sending threats like that's a bit extreme, isn't it? After all, all that's really happened between us so far is that he stole my wife and I headhunted his right-hand man."

"But is it? Ask yourself this: why did you headhunt Dan Forsbrook in the first place, Ed? To start up a cruise company of your own, that's why – an area you had no previous experience in at all. He steals your wife: you suddenly decide to go into the cruise business. Not content with that – a situation that brings you into his arena as a potential competitor – you go one step further and take his key operations manager in a clearly underhand way. That brings you into direct conflict once more.

"Okay, so you lie low, keeping your ships out of his way for a while. Now, though, you're planning a move that's quite obviously edging in on his territory. Only in a small way, admittedly. But, how does he know you aren't planning to eventually bring your entire fleet over to sail out of Florida and steal business away from him, right under his nose – just like he stole your wife? Nothing to stop you, presumably, if you had a mind to it. A well-planned price war, for example. I don't know exactly how these things work."

"Yeah, it's possible he's trying to warn me off. But, if it is him, I'm sure it wouldn't go much further than just the threat."

"You could be right, of course. But bear with me. Let me take you through another scenario. Just say – for the sake of argument – your ex-wife, Sophia, has suddenly realised after all this time she's still desperately in love with you and it was all a big mistake. Maybe the first flush of their romance is over right now – despite all recent appearances. I refer here to what you said about seeing them together on TV at that recent awards ceremony. Now, just supposing she starts taunting him during one of their arguments that he's only half the man you were. In the end, he's sick to death of hearing about you. Then he gets wind of this latest development."

"I see what you're getting at. In other words, it all becomes a lot more unpredictable. Well, I have to agree, Jack, he is the only person I can think of right now with any reason at all to want to dissuade me. And, believe me, if it is George Mitchell, and he wants a contest, then, by God, he's got one. See what you can find out about him, Jack. Use whatever methods you have to. I need all the dirt you can find. There's got to be something we can use if a counter-attack becomes necessary. Though, in the case of George Mitchell, I wouldn't entirely rule out some form of pre-emptive strike."

"I'll see what I can do. It'll mean a trip down to Florida."

"Whatever it takes, Jack."

"There's just one other thing."

"Yeah?"

"This man Forsbrook. You trust him?"

"Sure I do. Absolutely. Why do you ask?"

"Well, if this guy Mitchell is behind the threats, and Forsbrook used to work for him, it's not outside the bounds of possibility that Dan might still feel some allegiance to his old employer. Or that some allegiance hasn't been encouraged, one way or another – if you get my meaning. It's worth a thought, anyway, Ed. You see, we simply can't afford to leave any stone unturned."

Chapter 16

I

The next afternoon, at a calculated interval after lunch, a call went through to the Health Secretary's office in Westminster. The London weather was brighter, though considerably colder than it had been of late.

"Ah, it's you, Mr Darius. Do you happen to have anything to report on the subject we discussed last time we met?"

"Yes, indeed I do, Harriet. And the news, I am pleased to report, is excellent. At this very moment, my dear brother is some four and a half thousand miles away, working on a cruise ship in the middle of the Caribbean. And, if all goes to plan, he will be for some months to come. Well away from the NHS and British politics, and – more importantly – well out of the political limelight. My mother received a postcard just this morning, in fact."

"Excellent. I won't ask how you arranged that, but I am deeply indebted. Believe me, I have enough on my plate justifying these latest reforms, without some smartarse doctor with potentially damaging connections adding to my task. Thank you very much, Mr Darius. I won't forget your assistance in this matter."

"Very gracious of you, Harriet. I thought you might be grateful. That's why I feel so confident you might like to go a little way towards repaying the favour."

"Indeed?" said Harriet Fursdon, a little taken aback by the impudence of the remark. His tone had changed little – still softly smarmy. A harder edge, though, now suddenly seemed to have surfaced.

"My campaign team tell me we have hit a serious problem locally in the constituency with Windhope General Hospital and its proposed ward closures. Key services, as you know, are due to be switched to the main city hospitals over twenty miles away. As you'd expect, the Opposition are making as much political capital out of this as possible, and, all in all, it augurs very badly for my chances in the Election."

"You've stated the Party line about the need for increased efficiency and dedicated centres of excellence?"

"My co-workers tell me our arguments just won't wash. Local people are simply unhappy at the prospect of having to travel so far for basic treatment: paediatrics, orthopaedics, or for anything other than the most straightforward of births."

"And what, Mr Darius, do you think I can do about this?"

"A timely announcement should do the trick; in other words, get me off the hook. For a couple of months, at least."

"What exactly do you mean?"

"I want you to announce a halt to the ward closure programme at Windhope. Simply say it's being reviewed. Of course, you can revert back to doing whatsoever you like after Election success has been secured, hopefully, both for the Party and for me."

"Have you any idea at all what you're suggesting? Such a thing would be completely out of the question. Besides, I think you should remember always that the most effective electioneer knows how to express the views of the Party both clearly and firmly. Then, of course, it's simply a question of diverting attention concertedly away by first attacking, then ridiculing the Opposition's stance. In other words, one just has to learn how to turn the debate around to concentrate instead on areas of comparative strength."

"Perhaps then, I shall just have to watch your Department at work in the coming weeks. Could be interesting; particularly if we – my family, that is – are unable to put that chap from Channel 4 TV off the scent."

"I'm sorry, Mr Darius, I have absolutely no idea what you're talking about."

"I'm referring to the fellow who turned up yesterday at Wetherfield House, our family home, trying to locate a certain Dr Luke Darius. Apparently wants him for a major prime-time TV slot – 'Public Vision', I think it was. The subject, I think he said, was this Government's 'Care in the Community' programme, and how successful or otherwise it has been. Highly contentious at the best of times, I would have thought. And topical too – what with that chronic schizophrenic chappie, Denzel Brigson, stabbing the young shop assistant like that last week. Turned out into the community after how many years in institutional care? Bound to be questions asked about the wisdom of any policy that allowed someone with such a history of violence back onto the streets. People are naturally going to argue inadequacy of supervision under the new system. Especially, as I seem to recall, this is just the latest in a long line of examples over the past two years or so."

"Get to the point, Mr Darius."

"Well, it seemed this man from the TV company wanted to build an entire programme around my brother. I, for one, am not entirely sure he deserves quite such celebrity status. I mean, what has he really got going for him – other than the fact he has strong opinions and isn't afraid to voice them? Oh yes, of course, the fact he's from such a well-known political family. Anyway, Harriet, this chap seemed to think he was just the right person for the programme – due to be screened, I understand, in the next month or so."

"Did this man find out just how far away your brother has gone?"

"Thankfully, Mother was able to be nothing more than vague. She doesn't actually know which company Luke is working for, or indeed which ports he might be regularly visiting. In fact, as far as I know, she hasn't any contact address for him, for some reason. She left me to do the talking and, luckily, I was able to keep the chap at bay with one excuse or another. But you know, Harriet, how persistent these fellows can be. I really don't know how long we can seriously hope to put him off."

"Mr Darius, I hope you're not attempting to use this situation as some form of bribe to get what you want from me."

"You wrong me, Harriet." Martin Darius' voice quivered with affected indignation. "I'm merely reporting how the land lies, that's all."

"Well, as I see it," her voice was almost sneering now, "even if this person did locate your brother, surely it would take an awful lot to get him to make the trip back to the UK, virtually straight away. He doesn't sound particularly like the sort of man who would be tempted merely by an offer of money. In fact, serious as your brother appearing in such a programme at such a sensitive time would undoubtedly be, it appears to me the chance of this happening is extremely slim. As it happens, Mr Darius, I am prepared to take that chance. You, on the other hand, must be left in no doubt at all: if you think that I, a Senior Government Minister, can be manipulated in such a way, you are sadly mistaken. You have a lot to learn about politics, Mr Darius, and unfortunately, only a few short weeks left to learn it in."

Fuck it, Martin Darius thought as he put the phone down; it hadn't worked. She just wasn't buying it. And after all the help he'd given her in getting Luke out of the way in the first place. Damn the woman. And such a brilliant piece of calculated plotting – all that crap about the TV journalist. She'd believed him about that, it would seem. But still she refused to budge.

Yet it would be all so damned easy if only she'd agree; get the issue of that pain in the arse hospital out of the way – at least for the time being. For that all-so-critical time being.

Surely, it was obvious that no matter what the manifesto pledges were, a judicious temporary alignment with public opinion was mandatory at such a time as this? What were the Party chiefs up to, for Christ's sake? Did they want to win this sodding Election, or what?

In years to come, when he'd claimed his rightful position among the most senior Tory ranks, he would show them all how it was done. There was a way to play the game to win.

And perhaps he, Martin Darius, would have the job of rewriting the rulebooks.

II

A red, globular sun hung heavily over Weston Bay that evening, some one hundred and forty miles to the west. Its thin rays spread out over the water, avoiding with equal care the dark island shapes of Steepholm and Flatholm alike. To one side, the promontory of Brean Down lay wearily to rest, clad only in colours of night. Beyond, some ten miles or so on, the coast of Wales clung thinly to the horizon.

Christine West was also aware of the sunset that evening, though for no more explicable reason than it was there as she closed the lounge curtains. Behind her, slumped heavily across the sofa, lay her husband. His shirt was open to the waist; his stockinged feet dangling loafishly over one end. A television blared mindlessly in the background, a half-empty beer can poised at one elbow; his motionless body visible only partly under the untidy newspaper which had collapsed unevenly over him sometime earlier.

She finished in the lounge, tidying quietly around him, then went through to the kitchen. He would expect dinner when he awoke; he always did. Not long after, he would be off to the pub. Little changed. On the odd occasion – and only with his blessing – she would have an evening out with the girls. Though she rarely felt like it these days. And certainly not until all the marks had settled and the bruising was gone. And that wasn't so often really, when she thought about it.

Even then, she was always sure to be back by midnight. No need to tempt providence any further.

As she placed some food in the oven, the phone went. Adjusting the dials rapidly, she set off to answer it. A second later, she stopped dead: her husband had made it there first. Poised out of sight behind the half-open kitchen door, and despite the growing temperature of the smallish room, Christine West froze as she listened. The car Dr Darius had been seen driving that fateful night had, it seemed, just been identified.

She'd heard a locum doctor had taken over at the practice since she'd last spoken to him. Her sincerest hope now was that he had been sensible enough to get himself as far away from Weston as possible.

III

Back in London, Sarah Wright had just completed the first batch of articles ready for posting. She was racked, however, by momentary indecision. The three topics she had chosen to kick off with all had a medical flavour. Each leant heavily on paraphrasing articles Luke had lent her. But had she been right to quote him so directly from his work the way she had? In places, it almost came across that he was right there with her, being interviewed.

One thing, however, she did know: she had a duty by him too. Being a freelance journalist – and in her unique position – the power to direct the argument or sway it one way or the other to suit herself was hers alone. Luke's viewpoint could be represented in as biased a way as she wanted, particularly as he wasn't around to defend or clarify. The points he raised, or the statistics he offered, could be used in or out of context, however she liked; to emphasize whichever point she, alone, desired.

And what exactly did she desire just then? Articles that sold? That, of course, went without saying; she needed the money. Articles that she believed in? Yes, that had to be true as well. Her moral code would accept no less. Articles to help underline her own current anti-Government political stance? That was more difficult.

How much did this viewpoint owe to her treatment at the hands of Martin Darius, she asked herself? If she was honest – quite a lot. Even so, it would hardly be fair, she decided, to aim the weaponry of Luke's articles – aided as they were by his own original work – in such a way as to bombard his own brother and jeopardise any aspirations he might have. Clearly, this was not what Luke himself had directly intended.

No, she would have to do her own kind of research in order to even begin to get even with Martin Darius. Find out first what she could about him, and then, if possible, expose him for what he was, or for how she knew him to be. And for that, she needed to get to work. For that, she needed to dig and delve – untiringly. And there wasn't much time left to pay him the most telling blow.

How should she begin? Where ought she look first, in the hope of unearthing something that might cause him sufficient embarrassment?

Just then, something occurred to her. Not an answer in itself; just a clue as to how to proceed from here. It was obvious really. She would have to closely analyse his constituency – and, more specifically, problems he might face in ultimately winning the seat. Woking wasn't so very far away, after all. She would make immediate enquiries.

Come to think of it – hadn't there been something in the papers recently about problems at some hospital or other, down that way?

IV

Tara Scott got back from the London office of Venus Cruise Lines a little later than usual that evening. There had been a mix-up over bookings on the Mediterranean cruise, which had appeared simple at first but got more complicated the more people she spoke to in attempting to straighten it out. Her Italian was not good, and the Rome office, she felt, could have been a little more helpful. Eventually, with Loretta Pastrali's interpretational skills on her side, all was finally resolved.

It was as she began to open the large front door of her Chelsea flat that Tara became aware of its presence. The scuffing sound as the door pushed it over the rough fronds of the mat was the first indication. She continued on gingerly, and once inside, quickly retrieved the slim, padded package from behind the door. It was not large; it had obviously squeezed through the letterbox – and only half-folded to achieve this. She straightened it out and examined it.

Two things struck her at more or less the same time. The first was the small group of US Mail stamps attached to one corner. The other, as she straightened it more fully, was a penned entreaty: PLEASE DO NOT BEND.

Tara opened it eagerly. It was surely from her mother. Strange, though, she hadn't mentioned sending anything when she spoke to her last by phone only days before.

As she removed the large colour photo, backed rather optimistically by a cardboard stiffener, she realised it quite definitely wasn't. Then came the letter – fully ten sides – in a hand she recognised all too well. It was from Hugh Gotley back home. Tara perched herself on the edge of a hall chair and read.

It was with a confusion of emotions that she finally put the letter down some minutes later. As she did so, Tara noticed the photo – badly crumpled on one of its sides – lying there on the floor at her feet. She immediately bent down to retrieve it, touched by a sudden twinge of guilt as she became aware of the full extent of the damage inflicted on it in transit. A deep crease cracked the gloss surface, extending fully over Hugh's face. A face which, she noticed, was otherwise smiling – as indeed was hers alongside him.

The photograph, she remembered, had been taken a year or so before – during clearly happier times. Or so it would seem at first glance. Looking more closely at her face, though, it occurred to her how stilted the smile had really been; how uncomfortable, looking back, she had really felt posing for it. Another symbol of solidarity forced upon her by a man who surely understood, even then, that she was slipping away.

His words were more or less what she might have expected: his continued yearnings for her and, never far below the surface, intimations of undying love. All of this washed over her – largely untouched under the protective shell she had since enveloped herself in, against him.

Yet she was surprised by one thing: how unexpectedly comforting she found his homely small talk. How, for example, Sheepshead Bay was getting along without her: how the hardware store was ticking over – what new lines were selling and which weren't; what her mother had last said to him after Mass on Sunday; what their mutual friends had been up to and what they had to say for themselves; how much they were all missing her.

She skipped over the bit about Ilene and Michael who were, at last, getting married. She had never really expected any more of either of them. Besides, Tara felt their inclusion in the letter was not without reason. This irritated her a little; but then, she had never really expected any more of Hugh either. She concluded that she could read him all too well – and, on reflection, couldn't help but feel a little sorry for him too.

Tara placed the photograph on the mantlepiece, struggling a little to make it stand due to the degree of its deformity. Then, slipping off her coat, she went through to the kitchen to get some coffee. She sat at the big pine table thinking, aware that the letter had somehow affected her, but not entirely sure how.

The flat felt suddenly empty around her. Tara thought of home and her mother, and of the life in New York she had left behind. She thought, too, of Aberdeen and Marianne and the call she'd made to her two nights before. Though it was clear Marianne was missing her, there was little doubt from the assuredness of her voice that things were still going okay for her. Tara recalled her friend's pragmatism when, early on, they'd discussed attitude problems at the base. It was a pragmatism that had no doubt aided Marianne's endurance throughout her entire training so far. There were reasons behind it, too.

"Well, I just gotta accept it, right, Hon? I mean, what other choice do I have? It's expected of me, see. That's the trouble with coming from a military family like I do. My father, right, he was a Colonel in his day – only retired a coupla years back – and his two brothers, they were Army men too. He sure ain't gonna listen to any of my whining – he's made that pretty clear in the past. So, I guess I'd better just get used to it. If I flunk this, I know he won't wanna know me."

There were aspects of her school life too, which seemed to have played some part in Marianne's readiness for what was to come.

"Probably a lot different for me, Tara," she'd told her one afternoon. "You see, I've been teased and bullied pretty much all my life; mainly over my size and shape, not to mention my colour. I kinda got used to laughing it off – though, believe me, deep down it hurt. In the end, I guess I just got immune to the whole damn business. Don't worry, girl, none of that shit really bothers me now. Besides, as you know, I haven't got so very long to go."

It surprised Tara, in a way, how distanced she herself now felt from such a disastrous period in her life. She'd filed an official complaint, for what it was worth, only two days after leaving the base having coldly reflected on all that had happened – and not least of all on the callous stance of the training staff at their final meeting. She hadn't intended to stay on in Baltimore longer than she needed, but had done so long enough for that tight-lipped Government official to come and interview her over her allegations. Later, she'd made her way back to New York, determined to put the whole episode behind her.

Her plan to travel and work abroad had worked out well in this regard so far. The job itself was fine; the people she worked with second to none. But there could be no denying the very real sense of loneliness she still felt.

London itself had, by and large, lived up to her expectations. But how many museums and stately homes could one seriously visit and still hanker for more? The time of year didn't help much, either. These British winter days were damp and gloomy for the most part, even when it hadn't rained.

She had made a certain effort, though, despite this – trips to Brighton and Bath, Oxford and Cambridge, with one trip still planned. This clearly would be too much for a weekend, so she had requested a few days off. She would be leaving for Ireland the following week in search of her last remaining ancestors; not that they probably even knew of her existence. But what after that?

Her eyes drifted over to the notice board by the door. Something, in passing, caught her attention. It wasn't immediately clear why. Then it came to her. Peeping out between a Royal Ballet poster and a marginally overdue electricity bill, she spotted it – almost garish in its tropical hues. It was a postcard she'd received from Luke.

Things had been undeniably flat since he'd left, she had to admit. Not that she'd even really got to know him to any degree. After he'd gone, though, so had the only feeling of excitement she'd really experienced since she'd been over here. Brought it home to her, once more, how alone she really felt.

Was this some quality of his or a deficiency of hers, she asked herself? Was it merely his obvious decency and good manners, contrasting so greatly with all those other assholes she'd had to put up with back home on the base? And his sentiments – those expressed in the card: what did they really mean?

More than this, perhaps, how might she ever get to find out?

Chapter 17

I

Initially, disappointment was all Dan Forsbrook had felt. Then, as days had gone by, he found there was more; something else slowly creeping in, now threatening to take over. Where disappointment alone had once reigned, a growing anxiety had now come to the fore, increasing almost daily in intensity.

It was now fully two and a half weeks since his last meeting with Ed Jamieson. One thing in particular seemed to have become patently clear in that time – the asshole wasn't budging. Somehow, Dan had hoped his boss's initial response to the anonymous threat had been more a demonstration of bravado, unsustainable when the full range of possible implications hit home; heavily veiled implications, admittedly, but there nonetheless in the number, wording, and mode of delivery of the messages he'd sent on that day.

It was clear now he would have to act further; prepare himself for what had to be considered a new phase of activity. And it was pretty obvious too, what he should plan to target next.

He sealed the envelope he was holding addressed to SHIPRITE INC., GALVESTON, and put it in the office mail-tray for posting a little later that day.

II

"Captain, the Catering Manager says he needs to speak with you urgently. There are problems in the galley. The workmen have left another set of ovens disconnected – apparently more dangerous wiring discovered today during installation of some of the new equipment. There is general chaos down there, I understand. Cooks and bus boys tripping over each other's feet, and all the stuff for the refit lying around on the floor. Passengers are up in arms; the food is greatly delayed, as you can imagine, and cold when it eventually arrives on the table."

"Where is the Catering Manager now?"

"I have asked him to wait outside your cabin."

"Okay Demitri, tell him I'll be along in five minutes."

With his steward gone, Ioannis turned once more to the Staff Captain.

"It was bound to happen, of course – carrying out such a full refit mid-season at sea. No matter how well you plan these things, there are bound to be problems. But, believe me, Stavros, it is vital this work is completed, especially with Delgardo expanding his operation almost at will now, while we look on. Already we are more than a week behind schedule. Let us just pray those missing items of galley equipment turn up in Montego Bay this Saturday. And that fellow – what's his name?"

"Chuck Withers."

"Yes – the expert coming to help us get through the checks – he's due to join us there too. Let's hope he is able to guide us through this present minefield and successfully address some of the other issues we have to face. As well, of course, as checking over the new installations. God knows what kind of reaction we'll get from passengers next week when the water system is upgraded – you know, when their showers don't work and their toilets won't flush."

"The thing that surprises me, Ioannis," said the Staff Captain, "is how calmly Delgardo seems to have taken the news of the itinerary change."

"Yes, I wondered too what his reaction might be. He sounded pretty unruffled when I reported it to him. But one thing I've learnt so far in my dealings with him is that our friend Delgardo Estremosa is a very difficult man to read."

III

Late that Friday morning, Chuck Withers gazed out of the window of the DC-10 and took in the approaching coast of Jamaica. Somewhere below was situated the point on the northern edge of the island that he would be heading for later that day.

Why he hadn't managed to get a reservation for the direct flight to Montego Bay, he had no idea. Presumably, there'd been some kind of mix-up along the way. He found himself, nevertheless, rather looking forward to the journey north across the island from Kingston – provided, that was, his hire car would be there waiting, as promised by the company he was going to work for.

Making his way out of the airport terminal half an hour later, the stocky Texan was struck by it immediately. Could hardly miss it really. The sign itself was maybe two feet square, and the local man holding it was positioned prominently at the front of the waiting crowd. And there was little doubt, judging by what was scrawled across it in large black letters, precisely whom it concerned.

It read: **CHUCK WITHERS (SHIPRITE INC.)**

Chuck was not disappointed by what he saw around him – at least not once he'd mastered the clutch and got the jostling suburbs of Kingston at last behind him. As he picked up speed on the open road north, on into the foothills of the Blue Mountains, he couldn't help feeling very much at peace with the world. He drove on admiring the view, one eye always on the road ahead – though sadly none in his rear-view mirror.

Chuck didn't see the truck till it was virtually right alongside. He didn't come to understand its intent until it suddenly veered over and side-swiped him. He could see them smiling as he struggled to recover – three at least he could make out – all white teeth and dreadlocks. The mountain road was exposed there, and the drop beyond the barrier frightening. They rammed him again and he hit it, though thank God, it didn't budge; just the searing grate of metal on metal alongside him. He tried to brake and they braked. He could feel his shirt sticking to his back, the sweat running down his forehead, his heart thumping wildly in his chest. The steering wheel wrenched in his grasp once more as they charged him, and he fought desperately to regain control. He could hear the car wing buckling as the road curled away to the left – a sickening, regular jolting sound against the barrier that, as he listened, suddenly stopped.

There was no more noise.

No more sickening vibration.
No more barrier to save him.

IV

The cabaret, it turned out, was excellent. It surprised Luke a little as he sat and watched, that having seen the same line-up on several previous occasions, he still found the show even remotely interesting. His perspective, though, had clearly changed. No longer was he simply just another member of the audience. Now he had got to know these performers more as real people: their hopes and aspirations; where they'd come from to get to where they were now; what precise point in the development curve of their respective careers they were currently at – or, at least, perceived themselves to be at.

Some clearly were on their way up, potentially in a big way; Rick Tucson, the magician, for example. There was an assuredness about his stage presence, an ability to communicate with the audience at all levels, which suggested to all who saw him that no other course of events was remotely possible. Others, far less persuasive, had long since come to terms with the harsher realities of show business life. Some were arrogantly staid, defensive of the position they felt they had so far attained; others more pragmatic, content merely to continue making some sort of living at it. Then there were the relative newcomers to the profession: glistening smiles and youthful exuberance exuding through every visible pore, desperate not to put a foot wrong; egged-on by the continuing encouragement of their agents and what they could recall of that last favourable review back home.

Duane's hypnotic act had come on a long way since that memorable first – when, like Luke, he was fresh on the ship. He had learnt by degrees how to read this mainly American audience and played to them that night accordingly. Judging by his success, the formula patently worked.

Where Sandy fitted into Luke's analysis, he had no idea. Nor did he ponder the question any more fully now that she was there in front of him once again on stage. Eyes transfixed, once more in the darkness of the lounge that night, it struck him he knew all he needed to about her. And all he did know fitted neatly into the convenient fantasy world he had built up around her image. To know more could surely only threaten to shatter such a safe and comfortable illusion.

Sipping his beer in that packed auditorium, Luke began pondering, amongst other things, one of the principal reasons he was currently there on ship: why he had taken time out of his practice in England in the first place.

The incident with Christine West had been a mistake – there was no doubt about that. He had been extremely careless in his affair with her – if one short-lived incident could so poetically be described. The point was, however, that she had been one of his patients. Worse than this, it might easily be construed he had used privileged knowledge of her relationship difficulties to further his own ends, and that knowing she was emotionally vulnerable, had taken unfair advantage of her.

It was untrue, of course, but, in the context of the close local community in which he worked back home and the outcry that could so easily follow, it was the last thing he would wish on any doctor, least of all himself. Indeed, the scandal might well be going on that very moment for all he knew. There were plenty of other female acquaintances he fancied well enough to have affairs with back there – all without that taboo 'patient' label so inconveniently attached.

But the situation he found himself in now was so uniquely different. Here on ship everyone was potentially his patient. Certainly, all those working on board were; and some considerably closer now as personal friends than he would generally wish patients to be back home. There, any of the more intimate examinations of patients he knew more personally could easily be passed over to one of his colleagues. Thus, embarrassment was spared all round. Here onboard ship, there existed no such provision – not unless the closer acquaintance in question could conveniently wait for a shore-side opinion.

As things currently stood, anyone he spoke to one moment, he could – in a potential emergency – be examining rectally the next. So too, in theory, with the female crew. He could be sleeping with one, one minute for example, then taking her appendix out, or dealing with her ectopic pregnancy the next.

Just then – and with such thoughts still very much in mind – Luke found himself gazing over at some poor unsuspecting crew members on the dance floor. Thankfully, they were not privy to such contemplation. But were they really so unsuspecting? Probably not. Their relationships with him surely bore such potentialities somewhere in mind. To them, he would always be primarily the ship's doctor – trained and employed to do the best for them in any circumstance. The fact he might also be a friend, had to remain incidental.

If the thought of such enforced – though admittedly minor – alienation depressed him a little, another thought struck him at that moment. It was one which as he considered it, concerned him even more. Who the hell would treat him if he suddenly became seriously ill at sea? Kate, after all, could only do so much. Luke thought this over a little longer. He could find no satisfactory answer.

One conclusion he eventually reached was that the doctor-patient relationship in this particular type of situation had – by both circumstance and necessity – to be governed by slightly different rules. An ethical approach was naturally of paramount importance in all his actions as ship's doctor – it was just that certain other actions might be a little more difficult to justify to a third party, should one ever enquire.

But hopefully, it would never come to that. Attractive as some of the females he knew on ship undoubtedly were, he hadn't met one yet who had so far managed to dispel the feeling he still held so intently for Tara.

V

"There's no sign of him, Captain, and we're due to remove the gangway any minute now."

"No word from his company as to why he might be delayed? Damn!! Well, what of the equipment we're expecting for the galley? Surely that has arrived?"

"Not as far as I am aware, sir. The agent brought some medical supplies we requested, but that was all."

"Well, we will have to get through to Head Office as soon as possible – tell them what's happened and get them to chase it up urgently. If we don't get the help we need soon, it could be too late. We've now only three weeks or so until the checks in Florida, and there's still a way to go before we're anything like ready. I was really counting on this man Withers arriving today. From what I understood, he was due to fly in over twenty-four hours ago. I wonder where the hell he could have got to?"

Chapter 18

I

Midway through that following week, Luke was becoming more than a little alarmed. The water supply to one area of the ship or another had been shut off at various times over the past two days, as different parts of the main system had become involved in the upgrading process.

The mood amongst many of the passengers he encountered was fairly grim. Not only those attending the hospital, either. Complaints flew freely that week; complaints that – in the sharing – bred further general discontent. Complaints that, even as a fully paid-up representative of the Company, Luke found difficult to defend. Having spent so much on this luxury cruise, how could temperamental showers and obstinate toilet cisterns fail to detract?

Then something else began giving cause for concern. Having so assiduously set up the Diarrhoea Book soon after joining the ship in the hope he would have a fairly clean slate to present to the US authorities when the time came, Luke could not shy away from the trend it was now revealing. So far this week, he'd had more cases of gastroenteritis than in all previous complete weeks put together.

Was this solely due to poor hand-washing amongst the passengers, or could the water supply to the main galley be under threat too? How were food handlers coping? Then there were the problems with the refrigerators of the previous week, shut down like other appliances due to those electrical faults. Had they been satisfactorily cured, he wondered? Had alternative storage arrangements been ultimately successful? Was the food safe? If not, what potential horrors lay in store for them from now on?

It was clear to Luke – and Kate, too, when he voiced his fears to her – that a good deal of time and effort was going to be needed to avert a possible disaster. Not only would a major outbreak of food poisoning multiply their workload and strain their limited resources almost to breaking point, but it would not bode at all well for the Company either. This was a very sensitive time in the lead up to the US Public Health checks already arranged. They risked nothing short of abject failure and all its attendant consequences. But not only this; passengers seeking compensation on account of their illnesses wouldn't have far to look for evidence of a sufficiently damning nature against Venus Cruise Lines.

II

Dan Forsbrook's face registered sudden alarm as Ed Jamieson told him the news.

"And you say his company hasn't heard from him either? Christ, that is a mystery. I can only agree with you, sir; this certainly does leave us in a bit of a spot as far as the Venus Prince is concerned."

"Yeah, and they say they haven't anyone else available to take his place till at least the back end of next week. That, as you know, may well be too late."

"Damn!" said Dan convincingly. "What the hell could have happened? The flight out should have been pretty straightforward: I sent the tickets through myself. Did he get to check into his hotel, do we know?"

"Apparently not. His company, naturally, have made whatever enquiries they can, but don't seem to have gotten much further. The Captain, by the way, is extremely concerned about how things are going on the ship; seems they're having a hell of a rough time of it on board right now. And, to cap it all, one of the key electronic pump control units we supplied is apparently of the wrong spec. They can't complete the water-system upgrade until we can get another one down to them."

"Sounds like that could take a while," said Dan.

"Hopefully not. Warringer's on to it right now. If he can locate one soon, the best thing might be for you to run it straight down to the ship yourself. We can't afford any more foul-ups just now. Besides, it sounds as if they could all do with a bit of a pep-talk as well, at this rather crucial time."

"Good idea," said Dan making his tone considerably more positive now. "If they can get the unit by tomorrow night, I could meet the ship in Cayman on Friday."

III

Fresh from the island's Owen Roberts airport two days later, Dan Forsbrook arrived at the George Town jetty. The junior officer overseeing the tender operation greeted him respectfully and helped him aboard the next one bound for the ship. The leather suitcase and large package, which together made up his luggage, were carefully loaded while he watched. The main package had now all but been delivered, safely enough and very much as Jamieson expected. It was the second, however – currently secreted in his suitcase – which now occupied his thoughts.

They had dropped it off with the first; the control unit for the pump. It had been on order, apparently, for some weeks now and had somehow been overlooked. The man delivering it from the supplier the day before had told Dan it almost certainly wouldn't be overlooked for long. He had an idea that now work had finally got underway on the ship's water supply system, it would only be a matter of a day or so until this package of filters was missed. Without them, several of the new pumps were effectively incomplete, and immediately at risk of damage were they to be put into operation.

The real beauty of it – something Dan was not slow to appreciate the significance of – was that nobody else at Head Office had been aware of their delivery alongside the control unit. He had thankfully been alone at the time. Now, as he was about to board the Venus Prince, forty-eight hours on – and given his own secret perspective – it was clear the last thing on his mind would be blithely to hand over the second package right away. Further delay in the ship's preparations could only work in his favour.

The Captain's manner during the ship's inspection soon after, with its transparently superficial air of optimism regarding the works on board, served only to confirm Dan's initial impression. Despite the bravado of his words, Dan knew they concealed grave doubts over the way the preparations were going.

And it was not unreasonable that they should, he reflected with some satisfaction; the ship was in total chaos. How those working on board were managing to function even at this level, he couldn't imagine. What he could imagine though – easily enough – was the barrage of protests from irate passengers; a barrage he knew that would ultimately be directed back to Head Office.

Perhaps if he had managed to convey a little more forcefully to Jamieson at the outset the true impact this upgrade work would have, none of them would be in this mess now. But Jamieson, he seemed to recall, was far from receptive to anything he'd had to say at the time. His boss was clearly driven in his decision to change the itinerary. And having once decided, he had pushed ahead in spite of everything. Why? What lay behind it all? There had to be something.

Down in the hospital area, he met Luke. The nurse, Kate, turned up soon after, looking more than slightly harassed. It had been an unusually busy week and both of them were showing clear signs of fatigue. He was soon to understand why.

Following Luke's general report, Dan was briefed more specifically on the increase in gastroenteritis cases that week. He then viewed the other systems both Luke and he had set up together so many weeks before. Not for the first time, he was struck by Luke's efficiency. His most recent recruit was performing well. Too well perhaps, given what his own goal had now become. Though it was pretty obvious to him, even the most efficient ship's doctor would be unable to influence the course of events he had planned. Chuck Withers, perhaps the only man able to make any sort of difference, had been duly taken care of. His company, Shiprite Inc., hadn't heard from him – that much he already knew. In fact, it was just possible, knowing the kind of men he'd employed to deal with him, that very few people would ever hear from him again.

IV

Dan's alarm clock woke him at four-thirty the following morning. Something he'd learnt from his meeting with Delgardo intrigued him. He rose, dressed and quietly made his way up on deck. Positioning himself in a deckchair – comfortably out of sight towards the rear of the vessel – he waited. The coastline of Jamaica would soon be coming into view up ahead. Quite where Delgardo's illicit cargo was to be off-loaded onto the island, he had no idea. But, if it took him all of the time between now and when the ship docked, he intended to find out.

There was one other thing that interested him about this operation too. And it was possible he might get some clue while he watched. Could it really be true – as Delgardo had intimated – that Captain Symiakos genuinely knew nothing about what was going on under his very nose?

A great deal of activity began taking place onboard once the passengers had disembarked later that morning. With the ship virtually empty, and with approximately seven hours until the next group boarded, there was little reason to hold back. Installations which, mid-cruise, could only be carried out in three separate stages so as not to disrupt services on board too dramatically, were now each effectively a one-piece manoeuvre. In fact, because of this, a number of the more major jobs had been saved for just this time.

Even so, the sudden mood of optimism that accompanied this flurry of activity soon found its limits. Most of the long-awaited items of essential galley equipment had arrived – but not all. As a result, two of the main refrigerator units were still unable to function. Large areas of stainless-steel surfacing were still in need of expert fixing, and there was little prospect of this being completed that day before they set sail. By 3 pm, with still some way to go, it was clear to all that another difficult week was in prospect.

The electronic control unit that Dan had brought with him – and presented so encouragingly the day before – had finally been fitted. The lack of filters had also been noted, and their precise significance now under scrutiny. It almost seemed that with the much-anticipated resolution of one area of work came enough fresh queries to make evaluation of overall progress even more difficult.

Dan surveyed this state of affairs with quiet satisfaction. He found himself debating in his mind the merits of continuing on board for the next two days, as had been his original plan. He had already seen enough to be convinced: no way on earth would this ship pass the strict examination it was due to undergo at the hands of the US authorities in just over two weeks' time. Without the right kind of guidance, they were lost – and even by the time Chuck Withers' replacement arrived in, say, five to six days from now, it would almost certainly be too late. The whole exercise had been pure folly right from the start; a miscalculation which would ultimately work very conveniently in his favour as far as his dealings with Delgardo were concerned. He could see no reason to endure the inconvenience of life on board a moment longer than he needed.

Besides, he might just be able to catch up with some new Jamaican colleagues he'd had dealings with recently. It was possible they could be of further use. He had seen the approximate point to the west where the tender had landed Delgardo's consignment. What he'd like to know was who, precisely, the Colombian was dealing with in Jamaica. The Yardies? Who were they, exactly – and where did the cocaine go from there? To the US? To Europe?

Something told Dan that, in his current situation, it wouldn't hurt to have as much information as possible at his disposal, as long as it was discreetly obtained, in such a way as to not jeopardise his safety any further. One never knew when it might prove useful in some form of bargaining process, were things to begin to turn nasty in the future.

Dan talked through his proposed disembarkation up in Captain Symiakos' quarters a little later on. He still had no direct evidence, from what he'd seen early that day, to suggest that the Captain himself was involved. No officers had been in that area of the ship when the tender drew alongside; only a handful of sailors chatting away to each other in Spanish. Delgardo's 'couriers', no doubt. Yet, judging by the voices he'd heard, there were far more involved than the small number the Colombian had suggested. There was something else too: had he imagined it, or had the ship slowed a little at about that time? Were the lights he'd seen a signal? If so, surely there had to be some collaboration with the Bridge?

It would be fruitless, he knew, to directly confront the Captain about this right now. Besides, he daren't risk anything that might antagonise Delgardo should word of it somehow get back to the man himself.

Just then their conversation was interrupted by a knock at the door. Demitri entered briskly, in his usual fashion.

"Excuse me, Captain. There is someone here to see you – says it's important."

"Okay, send him in."

Demitri went to the door and held it open. Dan, meanwhile, muttering some brief final comment, stood up to leave. It would soon be time for the ship to sail. Time, in fact, he was out of here.

The door swung open before Dan reached it and the man walked in. Tall and stockily built, he was remarkable in more ways than one. Most noticeable of these, within the untidy frame of fair hair and frazzled beard, were the alarming set of bruises – his eyes peering out keenly from behind heavily swollen lids. Dropping his small bag down at his feet, the man offered a large hand in greeting.

"Hi," he said. "Name's Chuck Withers. So sorry I'm a little late getting here. Though believe me, gentlemen, I can explain."

Dan stood there dumbfounded, unable to take in what had just occurred. He rallied sufficiently, however, to shake the Texan's hand. How on earth had this been allowed to happen? How the fuck had those Jamaican guys managed to screw up so badly?

"We are extremely grateful you made it," said Captain Symiakos warmly. "To be honest, I had secretly given up hope. We are a long way behind schedule, but, with luck, it still might not be too late."

"Well, the fact is, Captain, I actually arrived on the island eight days ago – in plenty good time to join you as arranged. Trouble was, I got waylaid by a bunch of local Rasta fellas on my way up from Kingston, who decided to run me down a mountainside just for the hell of it. Luckily, I was thrown from the car before it went up in flames, though it seems I was unconscious for some time. Came to three days ago in hospital in Kingston. Took me a day or so to get my strength back, and here I am. Felt I just couldn't let you good folks down again."

"Let me just say, we certainly appreciate your efforts, Mr Withers," said Dan, by now reasonably recovered and trying his best to sound sincere. "But are you sure you're really fit? Concussion can be a serious business. Perhaps you'd best let the ship's doctor take a look at you, just in case. He's a pretty tuned in kind of guy."

211

"Glad to hear it," said Chuck. "There's a whole lot I'm planning to go through with him. The US Public Health like to see not only a well-run and orderly ship, but also an efficient and enlightened medical facility on board. But getting back to what you said, no thanks, I'll give the check-up a miss. Believe me, I feel great and keener than hell to get started. I want to look over your water system first, including that new desalination plant. I take it all the structural changes are complete?"

"Yes, but only just," said the Captain. "Though we'd like your advice on some filters we're still missing. Perhaps you could take a look and give us an idea of how crucial they are at this precise moment. As you can imagine, we're keen to get the new system fully operational just as soon as possible."

By the time Chuck Withers gave his verdict half an hour later, Dan Forsbrook had quite independently decided what it was he next had to do. The unexpected arrival of the Texan had opened up a whole new ballgame. And oozing enthusiasm as this guy clearly was, it was now plain there was a vastly increased risk of the ship's preparations being successful after all. Dan could think of only one simple method of sabotage that, at this point in time, was likely to have any chance of bringing about the desired result; especially, given what Chuck Withers had just been saying.

"So, you say it's essential to have these filters as soon as possible?" he said. "Well, if I take the relevant part numbers, I'll get onto it shore-side right away. I can have them sent on by special delivery to the next port of call ahead of you at the time. Any special instructions for pick up, naturally, I'll telex to you at sea. As you can probably appreciate, I would prefer it if we left as little to chance as possible from now on.

"In fact, Dr Darius," Dan continued, turning to Luke, who had been summoned to the group by that time, "I was just saying to the Captain a moment ago, it might be best to get one of you from the ship – someone who understands the absolute importance of these missing parts to our effort – to collect them in person from wherever in the port they happen to arrive. And I would say, Luke, you're probably the most available of all once we've docked. If you could arrange for your nurse to stay on board that day to cover you, I'm sure you could easily manage to slip ashore and make the necessary pick-up."

Chapter 19

I

It had turned out to be quite a night. So good a night in that West End club, in fact, Martin Darius' first thought on waking was very quickly pushed aside by another; how the hell did he get home?

He lay for a while in his large, brass-headed bed, trying desperately to piece together exactly what he'd done, when, and with whom. Approximately halfway through this process, the insistent ring of his bedside telephone cut in on his musings.

It was Hayden-Jones, his Campaign Manager, sounding unusually excited for that time of day. Martin forced a greeting then let him talk – his mind still lamenting some half-remembered dream. Gerald was asking him something about a newspaper. His silence now suggested he was expecting some sort of reply. Martin considered the point for a moment.

"Well?" said Hayden-Jones repeating the question. "Have you seen it?"

"No, I'm afraid I haven't," said Martin finally.

"Well, I advise you to try to get hold of a copy – you might find the article on page seven rather interesting. Somehow, the story about Windhope Hospital and the imminent ward closures has hit the national press. Someone has organised a campaign march which – according to this report – is set for Wednesday the twentieth. It's due to start at the hospital itself and end up down here outside our local offices. There'll be TV cameras, the lot."

"Christ, you're kidding!" exclaimed Martin, now very definitely awake. "But this is only a small, local issue. How could it have attracted such coverage? Gerald, we've somehow got to stop it. It would be an absolute, bloody disaster for our campaign."

"I think you might well be right. I managed to get in touch with the Union reps at the hospital just now before calling you. I get the feeling they might be open to negotiation. What they really want, apparently, is some kind of live public debate – an open forum on the subject. An idea which, I need hardly tell you, the Opposition candidate, Henry Moreton, has jumped at."

"If that's what it takes, I guess we'll damn well have to agree to it. Anything's better than a well-orchestrated public demo on our own patch – especially at this particular time. But, Gerald, listen; we don't want it televised at any cost, okay? See if you can get agreement on no TV cameras in the auditorium."

"I'll see what I can do. Oh, by the way, Martin, the other thing I need to report is that Sutcliffe, our treasurer, seems to think he's uncovered a shortfall of some £43,000 in our campaign funds. As you know, we've had quite a lot in recently from our various fundraisers and benefactors. He hasn't had a chance to look into it fully yet, but what I need to know is, do you want us to inform the police if it's confirmed?"

"God no, Gerald, not at the moment. After all, there could easily be some simple explanation for it. The very last thing we, as a party, need right now is that kind of publicity. No, tell him to leave it with me. I'll investigate over the weekend and discuss it further on Monday."

Fuck it, Martin Darius thought to himself as he dropped the receiver back. He needed this like a sodding hole in the head. The trouble with John Sutcliffe was that he was just too damned efficient. He certainly hadn't expected that money to be missed quite so soon, if at all. He'd only just borrowed it, and if all went well, hoped to return it within a couple of weeks – not days. Still, when those investments paid off, he'd be laughing; an opportunity, at the time, he clearly couldn't ignore. Problem was, what to do in the meantime? There had to be some way of replacing the money before Monday and covering his tracks. But what?

As for the hospital issue, that was by far the more important just then, threatening virtually everything he'd planned for politically. But how the hell had it suddenly managed to assume a position of such prominence nationwide?

If ever there was a time when he could do with Harriet Fursdon's help, it was now. If not to retract the proposed ward closures – as he'd previously suggested – then at least to appear in person at the debate to justify what were, after all, her own damn health policies. Only that might get him off the hook; only that might give him back the edge he most certainly had before this whole fiasco erupted.

There remained only one problem: how could he persuade her?

II

The seagull hung there calm and motionless above him as he watched, unflappable against the grey Victorian roofscape. It was fast approaching dawn in that deserted area of town, and Jeffrey West sensed he ought to delay no longer.

It wasn't the revenge he'd intended, but if the owners refused to divulge who had been driving his wife in the courtesy car that particular night, then sadly, they must endure the consequences.

He tossed the burning rag and the petrol trail ignited. As his car pulled away and he glanced back in satisfaction, flames engulfed the small, backstreet garage; like some ritual dance to the morning sky.

What Jeffrey West had failed to notice in his haste, however, was the innocuous-looking CCTV camera on the building opposite trained in his general direction. And, if he hadn't been quite so preoccupied, that the run-down building bore a sign.

Ten days later, when the police eventually came knocking, it became all too clear: that not spotting that innocuous-looking camera on the NORTH SOMERSET WOMEN'S REFUGE was, by some ironic twist of fate, to be his ultimate undoing.

III

Dr Cedric Bannister M.D., M.R.C.P., dialled the number noted down on the front of the case notes at his Harley Street practice and waited. It was a little optimistic trying so early in the afternoon, but one never knew. Besides, the sooner he could speak to Martin Darius, the better he would feel.

"Martin, is that you?" he said.

"Yes, who's speaking?"

Dr Bannister identified himself. Martin, who had been expecting a further update from Hayden-Jones on the matter discussed earlier, managed, despite his preoccupation, some warmth in his reply. Cedric Bannister had been a friend of the family for as long as he could remember. He was also his father's personal physician.

"Martin, I'm glad I've caught you. There's something I need to discuss regarding your father. The news, I'm afraid, is somewhat serious."

"Go ahead, Cedric. I'm listening."

"Well, this latest batch of tests your father underwent recently has unfortunately rather confirmed what I most feared. The CT scan, a couple of weeks back, showed a mass in the upper zone of his left lung, which looked suspicious. This week's bronchoscopy has confirmed not only that this is a bronchial carcinoma, but also that it is sadly already too far advanced to be operable. The histology confirms it to be a rather aggressive tumour. There are already signs of spread to his liver and the prognosis, I fear, is very poor."

"Does Father know this?"

"Yes, he does. I've explained the gravity of his condition fully to him."

"And Mother?"

"He says he wants to tell her himself. Now, the thing is, Martin, I think it's important that Luke should be informed too, as soon as possible. He will no doubt have a number of questions which, of course, I'll be more than happy to discuss with him. Can I leave it to you to get word to him? I'd prefer not to have to bother your mother with this just now."

"Yes, of course, Cedric. Leave it with me. I'll see what I can do."

IV

There was silence at the other end of the line. Martin Darius waited as the Health Minister composed herself:

"Naturally, I am very sorry to hear the sad news about your father," she said, slowly and soberly at last. "It's just that – and I'm sure you'll agree – your brother returning just at this moment, or indeed any time between now and the Election, could prove disastrous. Not only because of this 'Care in the Community' documentary you mention either. Why, only the other day, one of my colleagues pointed out an article in the Independent by some hack or other, picking up on some very similar points to those presented by your brother in the December issue of the British Medical Journal. Can't think offhand who it was that wrote the piece."

"There is little doubt at all about the problems his return might cause," agreed Martin, "but there again, Harriet, what can I do?"

"I really have no idea, Mr Darius. Only you know what you've been told regarding your father's prognosis. Only you know how much your brother might, as a doctor, be able to do to help his condition should he return immediately to this country. Only you would be able to make any sort of judgment on whether a delay in telling him might not be appropriate."

"I see what you're saying," said Martin slowly, trying to sound as if such an idea had never before entered his head. "Of course, such a course of action would be extremely risky. You see, Harriet, I am not a particularly medically minded man. Were I to delay passing the news on to Luke, there would always be the chance that, by the time I did, it might be too late for him to make it back to England in time. Of course..."

"Yes?"

"Of course, it might just be the kind of risk I would be prepared to take, if, for example, I felt comfortable enough with the level of support I was receiving from senior colleagues in my personal Election campaign – if you take my meaning."

"I think I understand you well enough, Mr Darius. You're saying that you are prepared to delay relaying details of your father's illness for as long as possible on condition that I – or someone from the Department here – attend this Windhope debate on your behalf. Am I right?"

"Extremely succinctly put, Harriet. I always knew we understood each other."

"Very well then; I accept. May I just say though, Mr Darius, you are an extremely callous and calculating man. I didn't appreciate it at first, but there might just be a future for you in politics after all."

Chapter 20

I

Dan Forsbrook's arrival in Cartagena earlier that day, less than twenty-four hours ahead of the Venus Prince, left him much less time than anticipated. Once checked in to the Hotel Capillo Del Mar – Dan's regard for the Caribe tainted now by the memory of Delgardo's visit when last there – he quickly set to work.

At 3.10 pm, he had located the parcels office, a small shopfront on the Calle del Arzobispado in the Old City. By 3.15 pm, the deal had been struck. Señor Montes, the proprietor, smiled a black-toothed smile and clawed the two hundred dollars unceremoniously off the gouged wooden counter. There was no one else in the shop at the time; no one else to witness his extraordinarily good fortune.

"Now Señor," said Dan, "you are clear? When this man comes tomorrow to collect, you will give him first this larger parcel – the one he is expecting – and then this other one. You will tell him it, too, is for the ship, even though it has no label on it to say as much, and that it has been here for some time now, waiting for someone to collect it. You will point out that it bears the word 'urgent' and, above all else, make sure he takes it with him when he leaves. Do you understand?"

"Don't worry, amigo; of course I understand," said the proprietor, stuffing the money earnestly into the back pocket of his trousers. "It will be my pleasure."

II

It had been a long four months for Ricardo Chavez. Four spectacularly unproductive months at that, there in that north-west corner of Colombia. As he drove through the crowded streets of downtown Cartagena, he began wondering about the months to come. Would he still be stuck there, failing just as badly in his mission?

Perhaps he wasn't cut out for this type of work, so far from home, after all. Perhaps he'd be better off serving the Drug Enforcement Administration in some other way – in some other relatively peaceful location, like central Miami or the Bronx. At least then, there could be some pretence of normality, there in his own country; some semblance of a home life even, in those brief, snatched hours away from the job.

Slowing suddenly behind the traffic up ahead, Ricardo found himself stuck squarely behind a bus – a brash multi-coloured affair, typical of the area – crammed to overflowing with passengers. He glanced anxiously at his watch. He was still in good time for his meeting with Miguel. Relaxing a little in the jostling stream, he followed the vehicle ahead closely along Calle 33 towards the Old City then turned off sharply for the Plaza Fernandez Madrid.

Would his friend Gomez have anything further to report, he wondered, as he parked the car on one side and wandered over to the Café-bar Alfredo? It had been almost a week since they'd spoken, which was unusual. Miguel, he knew, had been following up some leads in Barranquilla, some seventy miles to the northeast. He, in the meantime, had carried on in the more immediate vicinity, tying in with the Special Police every few days to help update their common database of cocaine movement in that particular area of Colombia. Despite this, though, it seemed they were little closer to achieving one of their original aims in being there – the precise whereabouts of one Ramon Alvez Garcia.

Ramon was one of their DEA colleagues – a man who had bravely volunteered his services on a highly specialised mission. As a consequence, he had been flown into Colombia some three months before both he and Miguel had been due to follow. That was now almost seven months ago, and little had been heard back from him for the past six.

Their own task, his and Miguel's, had sounded simple enough at the time it was first explained to them: to track Ramon's progress and, if at all possible, facilitate some kind of liaison. Thus, it was hoped that together, they would be able to relay important intelligence regarding 'narcotraficantes' in the area back to the relevant authorities. Only then, could realistic counter strategies be developed.

In Ramon Garcia's case, however – where silence had been the order of the day for such a time now – a great many questions remained unanswered. Was there, for example, any possibility at all that Ramon had so far been successful in his mission? Had he managed, against all odds, to achieve the unthinkable – to actually infiltrate the local branch of the Cartel, as he had always vowed to them he would? If so, why had there been no communication from him for so long? Or, like others before him, had he chosen to defect to a life of plenty – the vast sums of money at stake making this entirely comprehensible if it were so? Or, alternatively, had he been killed: simply snuffed out once detected; another nameless body in a careless litter of unidentified corpses?

A shiver ran down Ricardo's spine as he thought this through. He was prompted to scan the street scene round about him, quickly if not a little suspiciously, as he strode across the roadway. Then, pausing only to light a long overdue cigarette – one of his personal rules being never to smoke in the car – he blew a dense plume of smoke nonchalantly into the air and went on into Alfredo's place. There, over at one of the less conspicuous tables in a dark corner at the back, sat Miguel Gomez Vicario.

Miguel was about thirty-five, a Latino darker and cleaner-shaven than he himself. He did not look, or – just as importantly, perhaps – sound, in any way out of place here, so far from the USA. In fact, he had been chosen specifically among others, equally as talented, with this very attribute in mind. As, for that matter, had all three of them: Miguel, himself and Ramon; the same team that had made such a difference the year before, on the Mexican border south of San Diego.

But things were very different now. The team had been split and, as far as he could tell, able to make very little difference to anything out here. Surely, a breakthrough of some kind was bound to come soon, in some form or another? Perhaps Miguel might, even now, have some news.

His colleague nodded to him discreetly as he approached. They sat for a few minutes in relative silence as their orders were taken and a clutch of coins fed into the old juke-box on the wall opposite. Then, with fresh cigarettes apiece – and a low salsa drone providing just the right level of noise screen for their needs – they began to talk.

Miguel, it soon became clear, had no further word on Ramon. Nobody he'd met that week had been able to throw any light on his whereabouts at all. His trip to Barranquilla, though, had not been entirely wasted. Among other things, he'd learnt more of the power struggle fast developing between factions of the Cartel to north and south, and the possible future implications for that area of Colombia.

"From what I have heard, Ricardo, it would appear certain of the local Cartel old-guard are getting rather nervous, finding themselves under increasing threat from some of the younger, more impatient, rising stars. Word is, even Delgardo himself has now started becoming a little edgy. One or two of his 'apprentices' seem to have begun taking certain liberties, and he certainly doesn't like it. Seems they've been getting a bit slapdash and trigger-happy, targeting anyone and everyone who gets in their way. The final straw, I'm told, was just recently when they tried muscling in on part of his operation."

"You are right, Miguel; from what we know of Delgardo, he wouldn't take at all kindly to such a thing."

"They lack his organisational brain, of course; and you have to give Delgardo his due. As far as force is concerned, he's always kept to the unwritten protocol agreed by all the old families of the Cartel: no targeting judges or senior enforcement officers – unless really provoked, that is."

"So very kind of him. All designed, of course, to perpetuate what, in the past, has been virtually a state of symbiosis: you know, between the Cartel and the Government here, though no one would admit it. The vast revenue from the export of cocaine can never be truly ignored when faced with such a huge National Debt."

"But with these young upstarts out to make a name for themselves, there is very little chance that state of affairs will ever be allowed to happen again. Not with overseas pressure the way it is, particularly from the US."

"That's why we're here, after all, Miguel – as if I ever need to remind you. Though from what the Chief of Police announced last week, it seems as though Delgardo has managed to take care of at least one of these loose cannons in his camp recently. You know, the body found dumped out on that construction site near the airport. Though, of course, there's no way on earth it'll ever be identified."

"Always difficult without hands, feet and a head, I always think," remarked Ricardo drily. "But what was that thing the pathologist remarked on? Oh yes – that was it: the overpowering smell of fish."

"You know, the more I think of the Cartel's methods, the more I wonder what the fuck I'm doing here so far from home. And also, the more I fear for Ramon. That man is too brave for his own good."

"But, Miguel, you know as well as I do, there was no way anyone else could get a look in; not once he'd discovered what the special mission was about. Seemed almost like a man possessed."

"Can't say I'd have particularly fancied swapping places with him. Okay, so his tactics for infiltration of the local operation here were no doubt highly thought out, but realistically, there are just so many other things that could go wrong. And, let's face it, Ricardo, the longer his silence continues, the worse it looks for him."

"Listen, Miguel, don't talk like that. You know these things take time. Once in there amongst them, Ramon will have done all he can to build their confidence in him. He would, of course, be thoroughly vetted and tested – and, no doubt, have to be seen to be equally as ruthless as them to win their confidence. The unpalatable truth is that some of the less savoury incidents we have had to investigate recently might well have been carried out by Ramon himself. When we pull our guns at night, ready to open up on someone, that someone – there in the dark – might easily be Ramon."

"You're right of course – and don't think I'm not aware of it." Miguel stubbed his cigarette out pensively with a slow, purposeful twisting motion. "Still, if that's true, it's surely only a question of time before he is able to pass on some really good intelligence about Delgardo's whole operation. Admit it – we know precious little of real importance just at the moment. His current storage bases, for a start. That last one we came across over near Valledupar must have been vacated months ago."

"True enough. There's no way our team back home will be able to organise a successful intervention programme without some decent information coming in. Let's just pray Ramon gets in touch soon. At least he knows where we are. By the way, Miguel, what did you make of that anonymous call the Policia got earlier on this afternoon?"

"What anonymous call? Tell me, isn't virtually every call we get anonymous – or am I missing something here?"

"This one was about some guy or other, due to pick up a kilo or so from that parcels office over on the Calle del Arzobispado tomorrow, between one and three-thirty. Whoever it was thought the authorities ought to know so that he could be intercepted."

"Let's be honest, Ricardo, there could be a thousand fucking guys out there carrying around a kilo in Cartagena tomorrow. Hardly earth-shattering information, now, is it? More one for the local police to sort out, I would have thought – if they could give a shit, that is. Unless, of course, it was to lead us on to something else."

"You're right – either to a distribution point or, more importantly perhaps, to a source of some kind. In that case, it might be worth at least a little of our time tomorrow."

"I may joke but – anonymous or not – it really is quite novel these days getting any of the local populace here in Cartagena volunteering information like this out of the blue. Known traditionally to be quite a risky occupation."

"No, it wasn't a local making the call. It was some guy with a US accent – East Coast they seemed to think."

"Well, that's pretty interesting, for a start," said Miguel, perking up visibly at the news. "Could be a little more to this than meets the eye."

Chapter 21

I

Dan Forsbrook looked out from the large window of the Bar Olimpo on the top floor of the Hotel Capillo Del Mar and marvelled at the vantage point the revolving saloon provided. To the east was Cartagena Bay, to the north the Old City, and far below him – its toes dipping lazily into the wide Caribbean – the main beach of Bocagrande. Having risen late that morning, he had taken a leisurely stroll, adjourning there a little after 11.30. Dan had watched the Venus Prince approach and dock in a great many ports over the years. Few sightings gave him as much pleasure as the one just then – particularly now that his latest plan was both primed and ready. Now, some forty minutes and two single Scotches later, he spotted what it was he had come specifically to see.

He nibbled at a bar snack as the ship inched slowly in from the horizon.

Luke made his way along to the foyer half an hour later, clutching the telex he had received the night before with the address on. Up ahead, he noticed the Captain speaking quietly with three men. As he approached, Captain Symiakos turned to face him, then beckoned him over.

"Doctor, there is a favour I would like to ask while we are here in port."

229

"Certainly, Captain. What is it?"

"These gentlemen represent a very important local man here in Cartagena, who, they tell me, would very much like to see you this afternoon."

"You haven't forgotten, have you, Captain, about the box of filters I'm due to collect?" Luke proffered the telex. "You know as well as I do, they must be picked up today; and Mr Forsbrook, you recall, did entrust the job to me personally."

"I'm afraid, Doctor, this really is far more important. It must be viewed, I would say, as a crucial public relations exercise. Don't worry, I'll be able to have those filters picked up, no problem. Here, give me the address."

The car was waiting outside the cruise ship dock. One of the men gestured to Luke as they reached it, and held the rear door open for him to get in. Joining him in the back, he immediately directed his attention to the others in the front, speaking quickly in Spanish. Luke couldn't understand their words, but watched the interplay of gestures with some interest, surprised at the degree to which he was being ignored. Where were they taking him, he wondered, and why? Why him specifically? Eventually, he gave up watching them and instead, gazed out at the streets of the city as the car moved briskly along.

Once out in the dusty suburbs, the car pulled suddenly into a side street, then just as suddenly, in at what looked like some kind of factory entrance. One of the men got out. It was the tallest of the three – the one who had been seated, head slightly bowed, in the front passenger seat. He looked cautiously around him then walked over and began opening a large metal garage door – one of a pair. As he stood there holding it, the car edged in beside two other vehicles parked up inside. The tall man then pulled the garage door closed behind them and the other two got out, gesturing for Luke to do likewise.

Was this it, Luke wondered? They'd brought him to this place, but just what the hell was going on?

Things very soon became clearer. The driver of the car mumbled something to the others then jumped into the driver's seat of a hardy-looking four-wheel-drive truck parked alongside. As he started up the engine, the two other men suddenly turned to Luke – the question in his eyes quickly answered by the production and deft application of what turned out to be an impenetrably dark blindfold. His futile yells of objection came a poor second to the mechanical growl of the truck as it started up. They then bound his wrists. He was waiting for the gag: thankfully, it didn't materialise.

Once inside, the vehicle was soon picking up speed on the open road. A confusion of thoughts coursed through Luke's mind as they travelled. The way the changeover of vehicles had taken place, and the whole demeanour of the men throughout, led him repeatedly to the same conclusion: wherever it was they were taking him had to be highly secret. Was he in any personal danger, he wondered? It was unlikely, surely – given the way events had unfolded so far.

The frequent gear changes and subsequent alterations in engine tone suggested the terrain was less than level. Not long after, Luke sensed a more consistent inclination of the vehicle as they headed into the hills. Stones spat and scurried beneath them from the uneven road surface. A sudden chill came over him and he was aware of a dankness in the air as he breathed in. If he wasn't mistaken, they had now entered some kind of forested area. The truck trundled on and the men began talking more freely, more animatedly now amongst themselves, and with very much better humour; less concerned, it would seem now, about the possibility of being followed.

Twenty minutes or so later, Luke became aware of the vehicle finally pulling to a halt. Two minutes after that, he'd been led out – uneven terrain underfoot – across to a place fairly close by. As they approached it, he was able to make out other voices growing gradually in volume. And there – further in the background – intermittently, a woman's anguished scream...

It was then his blindfold was removed.

II

The man outside the parcels office on the Calle del Arzobispado, at about that same time, had little clue what it was he had come to collect. The message had reached him via a friend, one of the shipping agents in town. The instruction was simple: pick up a package that had just arrived for one of the ships in port that day, and make sure it was delivered in good time before that ship sailed.

The ship was called the Venus Prince, and this last-minute errand promised to be as straightforward and lucrative a piece of courier work as he had ever been offered.

The same man, on his way out of the parcels office a few minutes later, bore an expression few could have mistaken: he could hardly believe his luck. Not only had the proprietor insisted on his taking a second package for the ship, but he had also let slip some rather interesting information about it, too. It had been sitting there, apparently unclaimed, for several weeks. And, even now, it had not been the subject of any direct request. It was, therefore, hardly something expected when he turned up at the ship – unlike the other, larger parcel. It was something, in other words, that might well be worth hanging on to. Whatever it was, there was bound to be some kind of market for it. It was certainly worth taking a look at, anyway, especially as an old girlfriend he happened to know had an apartment he could easily drop it off at, down a quiet side street only a short distance away.

Luke stared dully into the space about him, the blindfold now removed – his eyes at first rejecting this latest trick of the light. Once again, from not far off, came that tortured scream.

He found himself standing inside a tent-like structure – almost army style in design. The men who had brought him, he discovered, had positioned themselves both squarely beside and behind him. In front of him, behind a rough trestle table, sat another man. It was clearly in deference to this man that the others were now striking such a transparently servile pose.

The man was older than the others by about fifteen years, Luke guessed – putting him in his mid to late fifties. His clothes were casual though obviously expensive, and he wore around his neck a gold chain of the chunkier variety. This was complemented by a bracelet of similar quality and almost comparable mass, worn loosely on his right wrist. Repeatedly, it clunked the table surface in front of him as he played idly with some keys in his hands. A small scar visible on his left cheek showed obvious signs of keloid overgrowth, Luke noticed – broadening it and raising its surface slightly, into a strange and irregular pattern.

Luke watched the man's face closely as he spoke in clipped phrases to the other men present, and again as he stood up and walked around the table towards him. Once more, from fairly nearby, came the distressed female cry he had heard earlier; this time though, louder and more piercing. Luke strained to hear who else might be involved – a man inflicting some kind of punishment, perhaps? For a moment, anger then fear passed through him. What was this place – and who were these people? The screams died away and, irrationally perhaps, Luke began to relax once more.

The man had now stopped in front of him, his face close up to his own. Luke felt uncomfortable by both the proximity of his presence and the warmth of his breath on his cheek. Luke edged nervously back half a step but found himself butting up sharply against the solid and formidable torso behind. The man was now staring squarely at him. Luke tried looking away a fraction to one side past him, but the power of the man's gaze quickly attracted his back. Before he knew it, he found himself drawn – a little too intimately perhaps – towards a pair of intriguingly hooded eyes.

"You are the doctor from the Venus Prince?" the man said gruffly at last, this time in English.

Two features about the man's eyes struck Luke almost simultaneously as he stood there. The first were well-developed xanthelasmata – lipid deposits on both upper and lower eyelids, towards the inner side of each eye. The second, the pale – almost-white – rims around the periphery of this man's otherwise deep brown corneas; a condition known medically as 'arcus senilis'. As suggested by its name, Luke was aware, this was not an uncommon physical sign in older people. In someone of this man's age, it was considerably more remarkable. Together with the xanthelasmata, Luke felt it likely pointed to hyperlipidaemia – a high blood-lipid level, possibly even diabetes. Presumably, the man would have been made aware of the significance of these features. Or would he?

"Yes, I am," said Luke, now widening his focus to take in the rest of the man's face. "And you are?"

The man laughed. "Let's just say, I am a friend of your good Captain." There was clearly broad agreement on this assessment from the other men present, as they too broke out into laughter. "You are here to repay a favour. Come with me."

With that, he turned and headed off past the table, through a flap in the tent wall and out into the open. Luke followed, looking around him keenly as he walked. They were in some kind of clearing in what was, quite evidently, thick rainforest. Another three tents stood in a group nearby, the closest barely twenty feet away. Just beyond those, a low, flat building adjoined two larger barn-like structures. The screaming that seemed to be coming from inside the low, flat building grew pitifully louder. Within ten feet of the door, the man in front stopped abruptly and turned to Luke.

"Wait here," he said then continued on by himself inside. The men following gathered themselves around Luke, who had now collected more questions than he could ever reasonably hope to get answered.

Luke allowed his eyes to wander around the clearing. The two barn-like structures, one more than a hundred feet away, seemed the centre of activity there that afternoon. Several men were loading something from inside the furthest building onto a waiting truck, half-hidden from his view. A harsh, deeply masculine voice – which Luke identified as that of his host – wafted out of the doorway nearby. It growled angrily and repeatedly in Spanish. It was followed by a female voice, thin and pathetic, and equally unintelligible, which lapsed ultimately into a whining cry and then a low moaning sob. If he wasn't mistaken, there was surely a second female voice too – older, possibly, and slightly deeper than the first. Angry at times, it was easily shouted down by the voice of the man who had recently entered. More from him, then that pitiful scream again.

The man emerged from the doorway and gestured to Luke. Beside him stood one of the women, a tired and shrivelled creature in her sixties.

"You may go in, Doctor – it's over to you now," he said rather cryptically. "Just shut her up before I am forced to. That damn noise is driving me completely crazy."

III

Curiosity finally overcame Dan Forsbrook. His vantage point at the top of the Capillo Del Mar had proved second to none in many respects. In others, though, it was found woefully wanting. For viewing the Venus Prince as it docked and departed, it could hardly be faulted. For watching the onward progress of those who had come ashore from the ship, it was pretty much a washout.

Not that he had ever really intended witnessing the fortunes of Luke Darius directly, there in Cartagena that afternoon. To hang out near enough to the parcels office up in the Old City to see what actually transpired would be sheer folly; tempting fate just a little too far. Were he, for any reason, to be spotted – at a time when he was not even expected to be in that country – questions might quite reasonably be asked.

Besides, all he had to do was wait. All would be revealed in good time. Following the doctor's anticipated arrest carrying that second parcel, delay in departure would be inevitable. Certainly, for as long as it took for the port agent to find some temporary replacement prepared to join the ship at short notice. He could witness the delay right there where he was now, with a glass of champagne in his hand to celebrate.

Somehow, though, this wasn't enough. He needed to know now.

It was a little chancy, he knew, but he felt sure he could pull it off. He went out to the payphone by the elevators and dialled.

"Señor Montes? We met at your office yesterday. I left some packages with you for the ship, Venus Prince. Tell me this – has the collection been made yet?"

"Si, Señor. A man came just before three o'clock. I made sure he took both packages as you instructed. I believe I told you yesterday, Señor, you can rely on me."

"Mr Withers, I am pleased to report that those filters we require have finally arrived; though the box they arrived in, for some strange reason, seems to have taken something of a battering."

Chuck Withers stopped what he was doing and straightened himself up. "Thank God for that, Captain," he said, raising the back of a large hand to his forehead. "That really is good news. Now, I believe there's nothing to hold us back."

Captain Symiakos walked off pondering these words. There was no question progress had been made, and plenty of it, since the Texan had come aboard. And Withers' optimism now, with this latest obstacle out of the way, was certainly encouraging. Something else, however, was on his mind.

What was the reason for Delgardo commandeering his ship's doctor, as he had that afternoon? Would Dr Darius be safe, wherever it was those men had taken him? Would they really deliver him back in time for the ship to sail as they had promised? And how much might Luke end up knowing about their little 'arrangement'?

He glanced at his watch. It was already ten past four.

The man who had delivered the filters had gone. At that moment, in fact, he was heading back to the apartment near the parcels office where he had quickly dumped the second parcel – as yet unopened – curious about what it might contain. He was also puzzled as to why the Police had insisted on stopping him on his way to the ship, tearing open the box containing the filters in the back of their car, and blaspheming loudly.

Whatever it was in the other package must surely be more valuable than he had ever seriously imagined.

Chapter 22

I

Luke was not having a particularly easy time of things just then, wishing more than anything that he had been warned to grab his medical bag at least before departing.

As he'd quickly discovered on first entering the room, the woman in such agony was in an advanced state of labour. How long she had been so, he had no idea. Her face appeared puffy and flushed, her look one of alarming detachment. As he'd perched himself there on the bed beside her, Luke could sense the stark dryness of her mouth and the sweet and very characteristic scent of ketones on her breath. This he knew was a clear sign of exhaustion and possible dehydration; the real danger being that, as a result, her uterus might become atonic, its contractions weak and ineffective. He needed more information and quick.

Trying his best to ignore her tortured cries, Luke set about the task of assessment. Abdominal palpation was simple enough. The baby seemed about full-term by size, with its head well-engaged, though no foetal movements were discernible just at that time. What then, Luke found himself wondering, was the cause of the hold-up? And how, more importantly, was the baby itself faring throughout all this? Could it, perhaps, already be too late?

Vaginal examination was a little more problematic, not simply because of obvious difficulties conveying to the bemused woman what it was he intended to do. Having finally got the timing right, however – avoiding the clamping thighs of yet another contraction – Luke soon discovered what was wrong. The woman's cervix, not quite fully dilated to the required ten centimetres, had developed what Luke knew to be termed an 'anterior lip', made up of oedema fluid. This had been formed in response to the woman pushing prematurely with her contractions before full dilatation had been achieved. The lip, in turn, was doing its own rather efficient job of obstructing the labour still further.

Somehow, Luke knew, the stalemate needed to be broken. It was clear the woman was bearing down almost reflexively in response to the intense pain she was experiencing. Attempts to get her to simply breathe through her contractions – as Luke repeatedly and exaggeratedly demonstrated – fell dismally flat. She continued instead staring concertedly ahead, locked deep into her own lost world.

Adequate analgesia was what was needed. Where, then, his armamentarium of suitable drugs? Where, while he was at it, the foetal scalp monitor and blood gas analyser needed at such a time as this? All thoughts on the subject brought him back repeatedly to the same conclusion. There really only was one solution. He stood up and made for the door.

The guard outside was on him immediately he emerged, ushering him brusquely back to his host.

"Hospital, Doctor? I'm afraid that is completely out of the question. We cannot take her to hospital."

"Why not, for God's sake?"

"For reasons that, for your sake, Doctor – never mind God's – I hope you never come to fully understand. Just do something for her quickly, or I might completely lose my patience. Between you and me, I have only managed to control myself so far because I have entertained some vain hope that the slut might be about to present me with a son."

"But you must surely understand that the baby, whatever its sex, might well not survive unless it is delivered as soon, and as safely, as possible? Here there is no equipment or drugs. I fear potentially major complications."

"Enough!" interrupted the Colombian, grabbing Luke angrily by the throat. "I do not want to hear this, okay? If that woman is about to give birth to my son, I want him delivered here, and I want you to deliver him safely. Do you understand me?"

Luke looked at the woman once more, there in the bed in front of him. She had just endured, as he watched, yet another horrendous contraction. A lot of energy had been expended on her part fighting it – both vocally with her strained cry, and in pushing even harder now against the oedematous rim of her cervix.

He examined her internally once more, the 'anterior lip' now clearly even more pronounced than earlier – even more of an obstruction to delivery. But how could he hope to relax her and prevent her bearing down? Could this ever be achieved while she was in so much pain? Little progress, he felt sure, could ever be made until this problem was somehow addressed. And time, he was aware, was ticking on.

Quite how he came to remember it at that time he would never know. It had clearly been buried there deep in the depths of his memory since it was first mentioned to him all those years before. It was nothing he'd ever read in any textbook of obstetrics, nor indeed anything he'd ever heard discussed in modern practice. The old retired district midwife, Iris Charterman, though, had been convinced of its effectiveness.

How might it work, he asked himself? Could it, perhaps, have anything to do with the 'Pain-gate' theory? Luke felt he might be better placed to comment on this if only he could remember what the holy fuck the 'Pain-gate' theory was all about. Perhaps, more simply, it was some form of distraction technique or even a hormonal thing. As things stood at that moment in time, if there was any chance at all it might work, who the hell cared?

The time was 4.35. Luke knew then there was no way he'd get back to Cartagena by 5.15. How long might the Captain be prepared to wait? Departure was almost certainly dictated by the tides; another area, he had to admit he knew absolutely sod all about.

The insistent cries of the woman sharply refocused his thoughts. There was clearly no time to lose. Luke swallowed hard and turned to his patient.

The old midwife had referred to it simply as 'pressing the button'. There remained only one problem, though, Luke realised, as he prepared to begin – the procedure in question involved fairly prolonged and continuous direct clitoral stimulation.

Luke sat on the left side of the bed halfway down, where he had positioned himself before to examine her. Her eyes, he was relieved in a way to note, still bore that same look of detachment. But what on earth would she think he was up to? How easily might his intentions be misconstrued? Who might she report him to later? Presuming, of course, she was lucky enough to survive both the birth and his Colombian host's threats. What if she produced the boy he wanted – would she then return to his favour? How then might this man respond to reports of such actions on his part, at a time when this woman was at her most vulnerable? Might the Colombian perhaps conclude that he, Luke Darius, had been out for some diversion of his own? Surely not, for God's sake?

Now, however, was not a time to be faint-hearted. If he was going to go through with it, he needed, above all, to act with conviction. That, and to get started before the painful hand-clamping of another contraction.

Slipping his right-hand fingers quickly into her vulva, as if to examine her internally once more, Luke this time allowed his fingertips to ease themselves slowly forwards. Tensely and apprehensively, they continued until they reached their objective – the tiny, flaccid mound of dormancy of her clitoris.

Having arrived there so easily, Luke suddenly halted, keen to take stock of the situation. He swallowed hard, certain that she could not fail to hear him. He could sense her next contraction about to start. There was little option but to continue...

And this he proceeded to do, stroking gently and rhythmically, circling at first in varied and hopeful orbit.

Then, tangentially in every conceivable and flowing permutation, eyes closed, tracing slowly over the relief map in his mind; eager and waiting for some response.

The sudden alteration in the urgency of her breathing was the first sign he noticed. Then, if he wasn't too much mistaken, a fragile tumescence just now apparent beneath his fingertips. Other signs he found less easy to interpret – the painful clamping of his hand by her thighs still, for example, and only the barest change in the timbre of her cries.

Luke's conclusion, once that contraction had passed – and he'd begun to get some feeling back in his hand – was that his stratagem had so far quite obviously failed. There seemed to be no hint of response whatsoever. But had he given it anything like a reasonable trial? So far, he had tried only when the contraction was already underway, but 'continuous' stimulation tended to imply the time between contractions too. This, then, would be the test – both for the method and for him. Not least of all due to one particular, rather unhelpful physiological response of his own, which he was just becoming aware of...

Resuming where he left off, it became clear almost at once he was making some kind of impression – in the form, at least, of her initial physical startlement. Suddenly, her eyes opened and a cold, questioning look followed. Gradually, wordlessly, this died away – her eyes now averted, slipping slowly back behind the comfort of her eyelids.

Relieved and slightly emboldened by this, Luke continued on. By the time her next contraction started, she seemed submerged – lost now in some other, altogether different world. By the time it had finished, Luke was almost convinced: the spell was finally working.

Subsequent contractions came and went with remarkable compliance. Gone now the distressed cry of earlier; gone the involuntary bearing-down. Instead, she remained relaxed, her breathing reasonably calm – building up to some degree, though, he was surprised to note, both in frequency and loudness, in the interval between contractions. In fact, she was almost panting now as he observed her, accompanied for the first time by a definite writhing of her pelvis against his hand – increasing moment by moment in intensity. Then, a long low moan. What was happening now, Luke asked himself? Surely not...?

"Just what the fuck you think you're up to? Don't you know it's too late for foreplay, Doctor – this woman is having a baby. You are here to deliver it, not to try to give her another one."

The voice came from behind him, causing Luke to stop dead what he was doing and turn rather guiltily to face it. How the hell had he not been aware of the guard coming in?

"How long have you been standing there?" he asked angrily.

"Long enough. So, you care to explain – or you prefer I fetch Delgardo?"

Luke preferred to explain – or at least to try. The only trouble was, even as he began to, he couldn't help thinking just how unconvincing it all sounded.

"Well, let me say this to you, Doctor:" the guard said after he'd finished, with open threat in his eyes, "you'd better start praying this will work – for your own sake."

With the guard now gone, Luke was left to take stock of the situation. It didn't help working under this kind of pressure, but his problems were as nothing compared to those of the woman in front of him, and the child she was trying to deliver. Even though his technique had clearly helped her relax through her contractions, he still didn't know if this had been enough to have any effect at all on the anterior lip of her cervix. He examined her rather apprehensively once again and was more than relieved to find that it had. The oedematous rim had now almost gone. Five minutes more and it would be time for her to push. That was if this poor creature had any fight at all left in her.

II

"Stavros, what word have you from our agent? Has he managed to locate a doctor here in Cartagena willing to join us?"

"I believe so, Ioannis. I understand they're on their way this very moment."

"Right. It is now 18.15. We really can't leave it much later. In twenty minutes, we will begin manoeuvres out of the bay. I have left instructions for a tender to bring them directly out to us, so we can get quickly underway from there."

"And the agent has instructions to look out for Dr Darius?"

"Yes. He will arrange his onward air transfer to join us as soon as possible."

III

Luke was trying to imagine just then what he might do were the ship to sail without him. Bundled back in the truck and crouched in the trundling darkness, once more in that world behind his blindfold, his eyes were open to all manner of depressing possibilities.

Shortly after the vehicle had left that forest clearing, Luke's Colombian host called over one of his aides.

"I am afraid to say, Alfredo, it was not a son after all."

"I am sorry to hear that, amigo,"

"You know what to do?"

"I can guess."

Half an hour later, her dress still moist and bloodstained, her crying baby clutched tightly to her breast, the new mother was summarily ejected into the darkening night.

IV

Dan Forsbrook was now rather enjoying the outlook. Even from the balcony of his hotel room, he could make out the characteristic funnel of the Venus Prince. Not only was the ship, therefore, still very much in port, but it was now almost an hour and a half late departing. This fact, coupled with the news from Señor Montes on the phone earlier on, could only suggest one thing: his plan had obviously worked.

He could imagine the chaotic scenes on board right now as they scratched around desperately for even the most temporary of replacements to enable the ship legally to leave. Later – when it became clear the ship's doctor was to be detained by the Colombian authorities for a considerably longer period – word would no doubt make it back to him via Head Office. If he was to be required by Jamieson to find an urgent permanent replacement, he wanted to be as far away from the area as possible.

The Far East sounded a good idea. He would meet one of their other ships, the Venus Princess, when it arrived in Hong Kong in two days' time. There was plenty he could find to do out there while he was waiting. As long as he managed to keep well away from back street casinos; and, in particular, men called Wong.

V

Luke looked at his watch once again now his blindfold had been removed, fearing the worst. In retrospect, he had no regrets at all about his involvement that afternoon – particularly as his totally unorthodox strategy seemed to have worked so surprisingly well in the end. Surprising to him, surprising no doubt to the guard, (sufficiently so, he hoped, for him to maintain his silence), and clearly surprising in its own way to the woman.

What he did regret fervently, however, was the way that poor creature had been made to suffer; and the baby too, when it came to it – blue and unresponsive for what seemed like an age – before it finally cried and its breathing at last became established. All this during what, in any hospital, would have been a relatively straightforward delivery. Once more, he found himself thinking about the man responsible. His name, he understood, was Delgardo. Who exactly was he – and what was his relationship with the Venus Prince?

Arriving at last at the dock, Luke leapt out, ran through the entrance building and along the covered walkway towards the quayside. At the far end, he emerged suddenly once more into the open. Looking around him in some bewilderment, he stopped dead. The space where the Venus Prince had been docked was now completely empty.

"You say you are the doctor for the ship? But a doctor left here by tender not five minutes ago, intending to meet up with the Venus Prince just outside the bay."

"You have a boat, I see. Could you get me to the ship right away?"

"It is possible, of course, but I'm afraid, Señor, it will cost you."

VI

"It came to nothing, then, I gather," said Miguel Gomez to his DEA colleague later that night.

"Afraid not. The Police say it was a false alarm. Just some guy taking a box containing equipment for one of the ships. Didn't check out at all."

"Which ship, by the way?"

"The Venus Prince. Strange though; that anonymous caller sounded so convinced the guy would be carrying product. The question that occurs to me is this: if the caller had been right, would the man have actually been taking the stuff back to the ship?"

"It's possible, of course," said Miguel, considering the point. "In which case, the Venus Prince might well be a vessel worth keeping an eye on. You never know with these things, do you, my friend?"

Chapter 23

I

At 5 pm on the afternoon of Wednesday, March 20th, just over a week later, word finally came through. Ed Jamieson, who had been able to think of little else that day – aware the result would determine the entire viability of his plan – was sitting in his office when John Warringer knocked.

"It's good news, sir," said Warringer blurting it out right from the doorway as he came in. Ed breathed an inward sigh of relief and smiled as the younger man approached. "Here's the telex – just in from the Captain. The Venus Prince arrived in Tampa this morning and has succeeded in fully satisfying both the US Public Health and Coastguard. It would seem they could find no reason why the ship should not include American ports in its future itineraries. Though, naturally, the standards now achieved will have to be maintained."

"That's great, John," said Ed standing up and clapping the other man forcefully on the back. "And thanks for all your efforts over the past weeks; yours and those of the rest of the team. At last, it's all systems go for this new itinerary."

At that moment the phone rang. Ed covered the mouthpiece with his hand and turned to the other man. "It's a private call, John. Would you mind leaving me to it?"

"Jack, is that you? Found out anything about our friend Mitchell?"

"Very little, I'm afraid. Nothing at all to directly connect him with the threat you received. Any further problems to report since we last spoke two weeks back?"

"None at all. I'm pretty sure, in my own mind, that whole thing was no more than an empty bluff. Besides, we've just had the excellent news that the Venus Prince has passed all its US inspections. There'll be no stopping us now. I mean, surely if the guy was seriously out to prevent the ship going out of Miami, he'd have tried some kind of direct sabotage before these checks?"

"And there was no suggestion at all of that being the case?" Jack Buchanan sounded a little surprised. "Didn't you mention something about that Texan guy, Withers, being waylaid en route to the ship? Anything behind that, d'you think?"

"Just a bunch of local Jamaicans out for a little sport, that's all. Even then, Withers thankfully wasn't held up for long. Turned out to be invaluable in the ship's final preparations. And Oceanway too – the firm that actually carried out the refit. They worked together well in some very difficult conditions."

"Yeah, they also checked out alright in my investigations."

"So, what of Mitchell then, Jack? No dirt on him?"

"As far as I can gather – speaking discreetly to some of his business colleagues, ex-employees, and an old attorney friend of mine down in the Miami area – his company's pretty straight. The guy's successful, sure, but he don't exactly flaunt it. His books are apparently well in order – according, that is, to a contact at the accountancy firm he uses – and there are no problems with the IRS. He has a nice home, well-guarded – but who wouldn't be, in his position? I even got speaking to a maid who used to work at his house. Says he was always charming and fair and paid well."

"Makes him sound like some goddam saint, don't it?" said Ed heatedly. "I must say, Jack, I'm disappointed. I'm still totally convinced he's behind that threat. And nobody else I know has a motive."

"There was just one thing I found out," said Jack Buchanan a little tentatively.

"What was that?" Ed had noticed the change in his tone.

"You ain't gonna like it, I'm afraid."

"Tell me, Jack. Is it something to do with Sophia?"

"Indirectly. Mitchell is having an affair with his new secretary behind her back."

"What?! You're fucking kidding me, right? How dare the bastard? Steals Sophia from me then treats her like that."

"Just thought you ought to know."

"Thanks, Jack. I owe you one, okay? But if that mother-fucking son-of-a-bitch thinks he's getting away with this, he's got another thing coming."

"What have you in mind, Ed – if I dare ask?"

"Not a lot at the moment," said Ed Jamieson ominously. "But, trust me on this one, Jack, I'll think of something..."

II

It was celebratory drinks all round, several hours later in the nightclub bar on the Venus Prince. The officers and staff had gathered directly after that evening's show. Captain Symiakos took to the floor and raised an authoritative hand to get their attention.

"I would just like to say thanks to you all for pulling together so well in this past few weeks to ensure our success today. In particular, I would like to thank my Staff Captain, Stavros, for his organisational help, and our doctor, Luke, for his work to ensure standards were reached for the Public Health inspection. Also, there is one other person – unfortunately no longer with us – who I would like to toast here tonight. He is, of course, our Texan friend, Chuck Withers."

Things had gone remarkably well in the end, Luke thought to himself as he raised his glass along with the others. There were few passengers in evidence just then – few, in fact, on the ship for this three-day repositioning voyage back to Jamaica via Cozumel. After that, there would be the resumption of the last cruises of the season. The first of these – for reasons he didn't fully understand – offered a slight variation to the usual route. The Venezuelan port of Caracas had been substituted for Aruba – with Grand Cayman dropped that week to accommodate it time-wise in the equation.

Not long after that would come the short vacation he had booked as a break from the intensity of recent weeks. He had even received confirmation of his replacement – the Colombian doctor who had ended up spending so brief a time onboard back there in Cartagena. The time he, himself, had been so badly delayed by Delgardo. Thinking back to it, Luke couldn't help wondering how that mother and baby might have fared since his involvement that day.

There had been someone else worthy of thanks that night there in the disco bar; someone who – due mainly to his station in life on board – had been passed over by the Captain. Luke, better than most, knew of the role he had played. In fact, if it hadn't been for Jose Gomez, a young Honduran sailor whom Luke had befriended, the stowaway discovered on board the previous day might easily have put paid to the whole affair. Sure, he'd had to shop the Costa Rican deckhand in the process – the one who'd arranged it all – but at least they'd been able to deal with the matter before the ship had reached US waters. One Costa Rican and one hopeful from Panama left ashore in Cozumel on the way; no big deal in the greater scheme of things. Luke had since heard from others on board – those with far greater experience at sea – that such a thing was not at all unheard of when a ship was planning to visit the US. A lot of money could be made if the attempt was successful – success, in this case, meaning the landing of an illegal alien on American soil.

Checking out the deckhand's cabin showed how the scheme had been managed. Closer inspection still had revealed the stash of cannabis he had also hoped to get ashore; its ejection overboard an obvious necessity.

Now, though, with all these concerns at last behind them, the feeling among those working on the Venus Prince was altogether more relaxed, with plans afoot for a special Crew Party that Friday evening after the show. From what Luke had been told of previous ones, it promised to be an occasion well worth waiting for.

He looked around the nightclub, its dance floor now heaving with bodies. A tap on his shoulder caused him to turn abruptly. The person standing there, he couldn't help noticing, was smiling broadly at him – the whiteness of her teeth strangely exaggerated in that flickering ultra-violet half-light. The intermittent curves of her body, too, stood out in alarming proximity as he looked. It appeared she wanted him to dance. He smiled back and swallowed hard in dangerous anticipation, recalling the confusion of feelings he'd had about her since first being on board.

The person in question was Sandy.

III

The letter was waiting for Dan Forsbrook at the reception desk of his Singapore hotel on his way back in that afternoon. The girl on duty extracted it from a pigeon-hole behind her, and, smiling, handed it to him. He was sticky and hot from the vast humidity outside. The slow-fanned and green-fronded coolness of the lobby engulfed him in an aura of mock colonial propriety as he made his way over to one side and sat down.

The communication, whatever it was, was not one he had been expecting. The simple fact was he was only just getting over the implications of the first message – the one from Head Office – received late the previous day. The one that told him of the success of the Venus Prince in the recent US checks; checks, it intimated, that he himself had so assiduously helped prepare it for.

To make things worse, there had been Jamieson's congratulatory tone – so effusive in its thanks that it almost choked him. There was no doubt his boss was delighted with the way things had turned out. How, in particular, his planned changeover of itineraries was now very definitely on course. So, where the hell did that leave him personally, now? Dan had spent a lot of time the night before trying to work this one out.

His first inkling that the latest of his ploys had ultimately failed was when confirmation of Luke Darius' arrest in Cartagena had not come through in the way he had expected. Somehow or other, that doctor had made it back to the ship okay after all. Dan still had no clue as to what exactly had gone wrong with his plan. So curious was he, in fact, that a few days after leaving Colombia, he had taken the opportunity of contacting Head Office directly from Hong Kong on some pretext or other. It soon became clear through their conversation that Head Office itself had nothing of burning significance to report on the subject of that, or indeed, any other ship's doctor.

Nor had time passed easily for him since that day. All he had really been able to do was effectively sit and wait to see what the outcome of the ship's inspections might be. He had not been entirely idle in the meantime, though. He had managed a couple of days, for appearances' sake, on their other ship, Venus Princess, as it had passed through. Then, he had flown on to Bangkok. His intention there was to meet up with Bill Newman – the guy Delgardo had so rightly identified as his partner – and, if possible, catch up on business.

What he discovered there, though, gave Dan fresh grounds for concern. The agency, Eastern Promise, no longer appeared to be in operation. Not only had the office been empty, but the hotel, Thai Orchid, too – the one they owned and used as part of their set-up. Newman himself was nowhere to be found. Dan recalled the problem Bill had specifically called him about in London. Was there any way he could have run into problems dealing with that – whichever of the two options he'd had to use?

The following day, Dan was to learn precisely what had happened. Having sought out Tai-Chin Wey, one of their local 'administrators', at his modest suburban home, Dan was quickly brought up to date with events. Word had got out the week before and Bill had, quite sensibly, acted at once. A team working for the National Criminal Intelligence Service's paedophile squad in the UK had apparently turned up out of the blue. Dan was well aware of their successes to date in computer-listing paedophiles convicted abroad, in an attempt to clamp down on the so-called 'sex-tourism' industry. Thailand and the Philippines were understandably prime targets. Not long before, he was informed, a team from CNN had also been snooping – which, if anything, being an American, alarmed him even more.

The last thing he needed was for his links with that particular business to be exposed in the media back home. He would tie up with Newman later. No doubt, even at that moment, Bill would be trying to get in touch with him.

Several of the street-boys were also in residence when Dan arrived in Thailand, being looked after until such time as the Eastern Promise operation could resume. Tai-Chin pointed out, in passing, one of the newer recruits – a young boy whose father had been, but was no longer, pestering them.

Soon after, Dan had left Bangkok and quickly made his way there to Singapore. Once settled in, he had let Head Office know, for obvious reasons, of his whereabouts.

And now this letter had arrived. Who could have sent it? Who else other than Head Office knew he was there?

Dan took it up to his room and opened it. What he read alarmed him greatly. It alarmed him still more that the sender knew so precisely his movements – even on that side of the world. The message was from Delgardo. It started out reminding him of their agreement. It ended, very simply, with a threat.

IV

The Crew Party on the Venus Prince that Friday night lived up to all expectations. As the ship steamed ahead south-eastwards towards Jamaica and the resumption of the remaining cruises out of Montego Bay, the workers on board took little persuading to get into the true spirit of things.

Even Captain Symiakos and the Staff Captain, in a totally unprecedented move, put in a brief appearance. They watched as Tassos, the First Engineer, and two other Greek officers, performed a dance from their homeland. This involved much leaping and bounding – seriously Zorba-like at times – against the rhythmic clap of those looking on. Tassos' large frame found the greatest difficulty pulling off the illusion, particularly once he began to tire. Leaping and bounding soon gave way – in his case, at least – to some pretty intrepid lumbering and stumbling. The audience loved it, nonetheless. Appreciation followed in the form of crashing white plates – their jagged fractions darting alarmingly outwards across the floor. Spent and inert, like so many used fireworks, they were brushed dismissively aside as the ouzo began to flow even more freely.

Luke awoke the following morning and felt, uncompromisingly, like shit. His mouth was parched, his head strangely buzzing. The ceiling moved as he glanced up at it – movement closely synchronised with the waves of nausea emanating from some point low down in his gullet. There could be little dispute: it had been one hell of a party.

It was only when he blindly turned to one side that he felt the body beside him. It was warm and soft, curled gently away from him. He opened his eyes with a start; this was clearly no dream. Blonde hair in an untidy cascade spilled over the adjacent pillow, only inches away from his nose. Whoever it was, was sleeping soundly. And from her obvious state of undress, there was little chance she had come uninvited. Many things he remembered of the night before, but not this. Even so, he knew instinctively who it must be. There was that scent, for one thing.

Amidst all of his other feelings at that point, Luke became aware quite suddenly of an overwhelming physical excitement. He tried desperately to recall the night before. They hadn't, surely – had they? If so, he would have remembered, wouldn't he – even in this state?

Luke propped himself up on his left elbow and gently leaned over her. Half-hidden under that hair, and viewed from such an unfamiliar angle and state of repose, her face in any other circumstance might easily have eluded him. Now though, knowing what he knew of the party – of how they'd danced and laughed and drunk together – there was virtually no possibility of error. From the top of her head to the tips of her toes – taking in all manner of nameless and palpitating delights in between – this woman was very definitely Sandy.

Luke looked at his watch. It was almost eight o'clock. The ship's engines were audibly still and he could hear the sound of deep Jamaican laughter from somewhere outside. Very soon it would be time to open up the hospital. The idea immediately alarmed him. The way he felt just then, there was no way on earth he was ready to face anyone – least of all Sandy herself.

Taking care not to disturb her, Luke quickly showered and dressed. The cabin door closed behind him, leaving her there still sleeping. His mouth cried out for coffee, the rest of his head for some more potent remedy. The hospital, he trusted, would soon have the answer to both.

An hour and a half later, well after disembarkation, hospital business had virtually petered out. Luke turned to Kate. She had been eyeing him oddly since he'd arrived – a look he interpreted as a knowing look, with a certain degree of amusement thrown in. What could she tell him of the party, and, in particular, its immediate aftermath? What, if anything, might she know that he didn't?

Having just prepared himself to ask her, and following the least obtrusive of knocks, Martina suddenly stuck her head round the door.

"You're still open, I see," she said cheerily. Kate replied in kind. The moment had been lost. He would have to delay his questions till later. "There's somebody out here to see you, by the way, Luke – just turned up at Reception."

"No problem, we're not busy. Send them right in."

Martina did as requested, and in walked Tara Scott.

PART 4

ODE TO ODIUM

Chapter 24

I

At about the time Luke Darius first awoke that same morning in such a state of physical compromise, George Mitchell, owner of Palm Cruises, sat himself down for breakfast in the garden of his Miami home. His wife, Sophia, had been up some time before and already taken her customary early-morning swim. George skimmed through the mail as Sophia poured the coffee and sat down opposite him at the large white table – there under the canopy on the patio – sipped hers, watched him and talked.

George was pretty well used to this kind of scenario by now. So much so that except for the odd timely grunt as he looked quickly through his correspondence, what she was saying hardly even impinged on his consciousness. Every so often, he had learned, it was best to look up and smile, and mutter something safe like, "Really?" or, "Is that so, Dear?" And sure, once or twice he'd been caught out; largely due to the gross inappropriateness of his remark at the time. Like when she'd slipped in that bit about her mother's illness and he'd replied with a grin and a "You-bet-ya." Very unfortunate for him and, later, it turned out – in an unconnected kind of way – for his mother-in-law too. He hadn't been allowed to forget it, either.

The envelope at the bottom of the pile looked little different to the rest. Nothing about it gave cause for concern. It had a New York postmark, but then so had two others.

The message inside was blunt, and in the anonymous hand of the typewriter:

WE KNOW ALL ABOUT YOU AND YOUR SECRETARY GEORGIE-BOY. AND PRETTY SOON SO WILL YOUR WIFE. DON'T WORRY – WE HAVE ALL THE EVIDENCE WE NEED. IT'S SIMPLY A MATTER OF TIME...

George read it through once again. Holy freaking shit, he thought to himself. He sensed Sophia's gaze coming at him from across the table and looked up, somehow forcing a smile.

"Some kinda problem, Darling?" she asked gently.

"No, not really, Soph," he lied. "Just business as usual. Though, as you know, I usually prefer to keep all work correspondence strictly for the office. The weekends are for relaxation, right? So, what have you in mind for us today, Honey?"

They talked on, the only concession on George Mitchell's part now being that, for once, he was actually making some effort to listen. The voice inside his head still cut in at intervals, reminding him of the potential gravity of this new development. What he needed was time to think. And to achieve that successfully, he had to appear as nonchalant as possible to the letter.

What the eventual outcome to all this might be, he couldn't at that moment even begin to imagine.

II

"God, this really is beautiful," said Tara as they sat there on the warm powder-fine beach of the Royal Caribbean Hotel early that afternoon. There were few other people about just then, and thankfully – much as he had anticipated – none of his colleagues from the Venus Prince. Her face was half-shaded by the broad-brimmed hat she wore, yet still there could be no mistaking the exquisite refinement of her features. Luke looked at her, still hardly able to believe she was there.

For whatever reason, the opportunity to develop things between them had arrived far sooner than he could ever have imagined. But how on earth had it come about?

"Funny thing is," she began to explain, "I've been agitating for a chance to go on one of the Company ships for weeks now. To be honest, though, I never really thought anything would come of it. Imagine my surprise then when out of the blue, Dan Forsbrook calls in from the other side of the world, and suddenly, it's all arranged. Just like that! Seems he'd come up with the idea I might be able to help with some kind of review of the passenger-satisfaction questionnaires given out during the cruises. Though, now I'm here and I've seen how little there is to do, it strikes me it was probably just some ploy to give me what I wanted – you know, being the boss's niece and all."

"Well, I'm not complaining," said Luke, smiling at her there on the beach mat beside him. She was wearing a light green one-piece that clung wetly to the curves of her body. Her hair was still damp, longer now than in London, swept back from her face; a face which, even without make-up, was equally as stunning – though in a different way – as the face etched for so long in his mind. Her eyes were shut now, and he allowed himself the luxury of observing her close-to for a while. Suddenly, she sat up, and he realised to his embarrassment that he'd allowed his gaze to drift way down from her face and that her features, as he looked, were now set in a definite frown.

"What's up?" he asked breezily, innocence trying to shove guilt quickly out of the frame.

"Oh, nothing really. I was just thinking of a close friend of mine back at Aberdeen."

"Aberdeen?"

"Yea – that's the military college I attended. I tried getting in touch with her yesterday afternoon before I flew out, just to let her know how things were going, but I couldn't get through. No one seemed any too helpful, either. Even had me wondering if it wasn't because somebody there maybe recognised my voice. I didn't give my real name; there were people there, you see, that I didn't see eye-to-eye with in a big way. The fact is I persisted, and after what seemed like ages, someone came on the line and told me Marianne was off on sick leave right now – wouldn't say what for – and that I'd best leave it at least a couple of weeks before calling again."

"And you're worried about her?"

"No, just puzzled, I guess. I can't remember her having even so much as a single sniffle when I was there. Admittedly, I wasn't exactly there for long."

Two hours later, they had left the hotel and its grounds behind them and were making their way leisurely back to the ship. It had been a calculated move on Luke's part going there that afternoon; calculated to give the best chance of avoiding others from last night's party. Including one in particular: Sandy. As they walked, Luke found himself acutely aware of the potential awkwardness that lay ahead. He hadn't managed to speak to anyone so far about the events of the night before. It was imperative, of course, that he did.

Only shortly after getting over his initial astonishment at Tara's unexpected arrival that morning, it had struck him: at that very moment, barely twenty yards down the corridor, a near-naked dancer lay in his bed. Putting all initial panic quickly aside, at the very earliest opportunity, he'd escorted Tara to her cabin – one, thankfully, some distance away across the ship from his own. While she prepared herself for their beach excursion, he cautiously returned to the hospital corridor and gently tried his cabin door. It was open, though nobody, he found with some relief, was now inside. The bedclothes were pulled up neatly, and a faint smell of perfume hung in the air; a perfume he had come to know quite well over the weeks.

Sooner or later, he would have to speak with Sandy – sooner or later, discuss what precisely had occurred between them. Even now that they had returned to the ship, he still had no idea at all whether anything of any real significance actually had.

He left Tara soon after they arrived back on board. She clearly had plenty to do getting organised in her cabin, and he had a mission of his own. Between now and the after-dinner show that night – when he next planned to meet up with her – Luke intended to get some answers; and preferably, from whichever third-party witness might be able to oblige – before the embarrassment, that is, of facing Sandy, herself.

In the end, it was Kate who provided the clue. Most others he approached appeared to know nothing. Kate didn't have all the answers though. She had, however, seen the lacing of the drinks. For whatever reason – pure devilment ranking high on the list of possibilities – vodka had been surreptitiously added where certain selected partygoers were concerned. Though admittedly, only until such time as those particular partygoers had become incontrovertibly legless.

Whether the same effect could not have been achieved by some alternative means – hypnosis or magic sprang most readily to mind in the case of the apparent perpetrators – Luke did not know. But Duane Dalton, the hypnotist, and the magician Rick Tucson, were certainly implicated. Kate, herself, knew little more than that.

Luke came across Duane setting up for the show in the Venturer's Lounge, soon after he'd closed the hospital for the evening. There was a curious smile on his face as he watched Luke approach.

"Okay, you scheming son-of-a-bitch, spill the beans. I've heard all about you and Rick fortifying last night's party brew. What I need to know is, what happened after the party – how the hell, for example, I ever managed to get back to my cabin?"

"Oh, that was nothing, really – just Rick and I doing our bit for a good cause, that's all. No thanks required. There you were, crashed out on the crew-mess sofa, with the delectable Sandy still in tow – after keeping her so well entertained throughout the festivities. So, when it came to dumping you back to your cabins, we thought why double our workload? You'd earned it, so why not leave you both back at your place to carry on your acquaintanceship? We certainly didn't hear any complaints from either of you at the time, when we suggested it."

"Probably because we were both out of our skulls by then, thanks to you two! Did you ever stop to think what might have happened had there been a medical emergency on board with me in that kind of state? I guess not. But tell me this: how come when I awoke this morning, we were both in an advanced state of undress?"

"Ah, now that I can explain," said Duane sounding considerably more confident on this point. "You puked all over your uniform trousers, so we thought it best to get those off you. Nothing worse than the smell of stale vomit to dampen a woman's ardour first thing in the morning, we always find. Anyhow, I found a clean pair of trousers hanging up in your wardrobe, so I left them out for you. The others I sent to the laundry. Don't say anything – I knew you'd be impressed."

"Very considerate, I'm sure," said Luke. "But that doesn't explain Sandy."

"Ah yes – well that, admittedly, was a closer call. You'd only managed a small spatter on her dress. Still, removing that was far more fun. Besides, we thought you might thank us for it by the morning. How d'you get on, by the way? – any good old Jolly Rogering?"

III

An hour and a half later, when Luke Darius next entered the Venturer's Lounge, the show was about to begin. Though the lights had already been dimmed, he could just make out Tara down near the front, in conversation with someone to her right. It was only as he weaved his way through the crowd towards her – or, more precisely, the vacant chair to her left – did he become aware of how strikingly handsome the man in question was. And then, in the instant that followed, how jarringly well they looked together as a couple.

Approaching as Luke had from behind, Tara didn't actually become aware of him until he had arrived and sat himself down deftly beside her. Only then did she break off from the other person and turn to him. If she had intended any introduction, the start-up of the band at that moment loudly precluded it.

Before he knew it, Luke's sense of self-consciousness suddenly heightened. Barely twelve feet away from him, looking as composed and overtly sensual as ever, stood Sandy. Only one row of the audience lay between them.

What would she be thinking when she saw him, he wondered? Or would the dimness of the auditorium prevent her from seeing him at all? Almost without knowing it, Luke found himself cowering down in his seat as the show went on. He would prefer to leave his intended discussion with her until the following day – and, hopefully, till such a time as Tara was very much elsewhere. He needed to clear the air; explain what he now knew had – and just as importantly, hadn't – happened the previous night.

The show limped painfully on as Luke sat there, slowed further in his mind by its now numbing predictability. His original intention that evening had stretched only as far as a seat at the back. There, with Tara, he could have relaxed, and, at intervals, possibly even chatted – far from the discomfiting gaze of even the most hypermetropic cabaret dancer.

Then, just when he thought he might have got away with it, it happened. It was only fleeting, but there it was just the same. The look in her eye as she caught his – in the one moment of recklessness he let his gaze stray upwards from its more usual point of focus where Sandy was concerned. How could he have done that? And her expression in that instant: more open and direct than he would have predicted; a smiling, well-considered quality about it. Unashamed even.

The sooner the show was over and he got himself and Tara out of the way, the better, thought Luke. They could go for a stroll to some quiet corner on deck, perhaps. Then, later, when the coast was clear, on to the nightclub possibly. Sandy rarely bothered socialising on the first night of a cruise, he knew; the make-up from the first show of the week, for some reason, by far the most laborious and time-consuming of all to remove.

No, tomorrow would be time enough for speaking to Sandy. Tonight, he had dedicated in his mind wholeheartedly to Tara. How long had he waited for such an opportunity?

Luke's plan started out smoothly enough. The show came to its raucous close amidst a reasonably heartening level of applause. As the entertainers disappeared backstage and the house lights came on, the audience began quickly to disperse. Not quickly enough, though, in Luke and Tara's case. Someone had spotted the ship's doctor – someone, it turned out, on behalf of someone else apparently in immediate need of his services.

As he reluctantly dashed off back through the Lounge, Luke couldn't help noticing somebody making his way over in Tara's general direction.

It was the handsome, fair-haired man who had been speaking with her earlier.

No more than fifteen minutes later, entering the nightclub, he spotted them at a table over in one corner. Tara waved to him as he approached.

"Well, that didn't take you long," she said cheerily, shifting her chair a little so that Luke could get round to one of the two still vacant. "Oh, by the way, this is Paul Curtis, a fellow American I met on the plane over. His was the seat next to mine. We'd been talking for hours but, would you believe, it wasn't until we were just about to touch down, we realised we were actually joining the same ship."

The other man got up as Luke stretched across towards him to shake his hand, and smiled; a flash of flawlessly white teeth against his tan. How had he come by that in the early British spring, Luke wondered? Tara, by comparison, looked positively pale beside him.

"Pleased to make your acquaintance, Doctor," he said in a charming, well-rounded sort of way. "You have a very nice ship here."

"Thanks. Glad you like it. You've come over from London too?"

"That's right. A business trip – nothing too exciting, I'm afraid. Though, I thought I'd make the most of some time owed me by my company and take a detour down here to the Caribbean on my way back. To be honest, I haven't had a decent vacation for two, maybe three years."

Luke watched as he talked. In part, he watched this Paul Curtis fellow himself, and, in part – though mainly by way of a series of quick glimpses out of the corner of his eye – he watched Tara and the way she was responding to her compatriot. If this guy was trying to cut in, he definitely had one or two quite reasonable things going for him. And not only his highly manicured good looks; there was their shared nationality too.

Tara had clearly enjoyed this man's company on the trip over. Even now, as he watched them communicate – only half-listening to their easy banter – Luke couldn't help but admit to a strange and uneasy feeling inside him.

Five minutes later, Paul Curtis excused himself and left for the restroom. Luke edged closer to Tara, determined to make the most of the opportunity. He slipped a hand onto hers. She did not pull away.

By the time the American returned, Luke – considerably more buoyant from the intimacy of their conversation in his absence – set off to the bar for more drinks.

It turned out to be a rather unfortunate piece of timing. Had he known Sandy was just about to enter the nightclub at that time, he would most certainly not have positioned himself so prominently in view. Had he known she was about to come from behind, grab his hand and drag him onto the dance floor, he would have tried putting up considerably more resistance. They needed to talk, not dance. They had danced enough, he recalled, the night before at the Crew Party.

Luke's dilemma was now pretty clear. The dance floor, although some distance away from where Tara was sitting, was nevertheless potentially well within view. If she was watching now, he had to ensure that he and Sandy remained physically apart; that no aspect of his body language towards her betrayed any hint of the purely physical desire he had allowed himself to feel on previous occasions.

And it was going okay for a while. What he hadn't predicted was the sudden change in the tempo of the music. Almost before he knew it – at the precise moment he had intended to thank her for the dance and make some excuse to leave – it had happened. So, there he was now, locked in a slow-dance embrace, Sandy's slinky torso wrapped around him with an alarming urgency he hadn't known before. What the hell ought he do? This was dangerous ground alright. Best get to the furthest end of the dance floor as soon as possible and hide behind as many other dancers as he could manage.

The idea seemed to work surprisingly well. No doubt a little to Sandy's surprise – and by a series of odd, individually protracted dance steps, mainly in the one general direction

– they were soon much more privately placed. As long as the other dancers remained on the floor, Luke had every hope he might just get away with it.

He heard Sandy's comment, but couldn't quite make out what it was she had said. His next mistake was to move his head back from over her shoulder to look her directly in the face. The kiss when it came startled him; more at first by its unexpectedness than its intensity. Soon after – as he tried to gently extricate his mouth from hers – the intensity issue suddenly left all other considerations behind. The trouble was it felt so good. And how could he manage to pull away without causing offence? He thought about it some more as her tongue danced playfully with his. Then, again, as it slithered more urgently deeper – ending up surely within barely an inch or two of his brain. His mind was bound to be affected.

When he was set free – there being little certainty he had in any way freed himself – Luke returned his head quickly to where it had previously been, and tried to act as though nothing had happened. When he opened his eyes to those around him, he felt reassured both by the numbers still present on the dance floor, and their apparent indifference to anything that may have occurred.

The excuse came to him in an instant. By the time the music faded off, he had perfected it in his mind.

"Listen, Sandy, I'm really sorry to leave but duty calls, I'm afraid. There's a couple over there, top knobs from the London Office, I've been detailed to entertain this week. Got a feeling I've kept them waiting long enough. They'll be wondering where the hell both I and their drinks have got to. Catch up with you sometime tomorrow, okay?"

But even before he arrived, it was clear something was wrong. The table itself was empty. Both Tara and Curtis had gone.

Chapter 25

I

When Luke awoke early – very early it turned out – the next morning, he couldn't believe how well he'd truly fucked things up. There was a lot he still didn't know, but that didn't stop him lying there restlessly in the tortured silence of his cabin, mulling over the various other ways he might have played it.

What he now knew for certain was this: Tara had indeed left with Paul Curtis, soon after the American had taken her off for a quick turn on the dance floor. What alarmed him most was just how much Tara might have seen at close-quarters. Had this been the reason for her leaving the nightclub so early without waiting for him? He had to see her to explain.

So much depended upon it.

One or two other things bothered him too. This fellow Curtis – what exactly were his intentions? Was he actively pursuing Tara? And could the timing of his invitation to dance have had anything to do with his having spotted Luke from afar, in such a compromising position with another woman? A position he felt Tara ought perhaps to be made aware of? And – just as worryingly – where had they both got to after they'd left the nightclub? Had he simply taken her back to her cabin, then left – or was there more?

Things might have been a little easier for Luke that day in his quest for Tara, had the medical department not found itself so busy. There were various times he had in mind he might get to see her. And various places he calculated she might well be, at each of those times. Unfortunately, things did not work out quite so simply. Either the times came and went without the opportunity to seek her out presenting itself, or – at the times those opportunities did arise – she was never at any of the places he had anticipated. There was, of course, one other explanation to consider: Tara Scott was avoiding him.

Once this thought took hold, Luke had great trouble fighting it off. The more he struggled to keep it at bay, the more other permutations on the same theme contrived to taunt him further still. If Tara couldn't be found, for example – could Paul Curtis? Was there any chance they might be together? What started out as a straightforward desire to find Tara soon transmuted into the most pressing need to locate Curtis himself – just to confirm Tara was nowhere there in sight.

By four o'clock, Luke was still none the wiser: neither of them had he seen. He had a feeling, though, that the situation would shortly change as he remembered the Captain's Cocktail Party. Also, an idea had struck him which, if it worked out, could guarantee him the chance of her company without that of the other man – at least for a significant portion of the evening.

Tara shook his hand and smiled, all quite formally, as she reached him along the line of officers – looking, if possible, even more bewitching than he had ever seen her before.

Yet, as she disappeared into the main body of the Venturer's Lounge, grave doubts now formed in his mind that he would ever be granted the chance to partake of her beauty close-to again. His only consolation just then was that she appeared to be alone.

Paul Curtis turned up a short time after, looking predictably impeccable in a tuxedo, smiling at Luke in the same open way he had the night before. Luke followed his onward progress with interest, out of the corner of his eye, pleased to note no immediate convergence of the two parties.

After the formal introductions had been carried out and Luke was free to mingle, he set off in search of Tara. A few minutes before, he had spotted her chatting in a small group at the back. Now, as he looked, she was no longer there. Paul Curtis, he noticed with some relief, still was.

The Catering Manager, Luigi, came straight over to Luke early that evening as he first appeared in the restaurant for dinner.

"I'm sorry, Dottore," he said, shaking his head gravely as he approached. "I amended the table listings as you requested..."

"And?"

"Unfortunately, the Captain has since intervened and invited Miss Scott to his own table instead. I'm afraid, there was nothing I could do."

Luke left the restaurant promptly after the meal and waited in the lobby for her to emerge. She was clearly surprised to see him.

"Tara – we've got to talk."

"Oh really? About what?" There was little discernible warmth in her reply.

"About last night. When I got back with the drinks, you had gone."

"That surprised you, did it? I'm a little amazed you even got around to noticing." The affected indifference of before was quickly giving way to something else. What that was exactly Luke had little time to analyse.

"Listen, Tara, that woman I danced with – presumably that's what you're referring to?"

"What about her? No – let me guess: you're just good friends, right?"

"Well, as a matter of fact, we are. It's just that, at the moment, she apparently doesn't quite see it that way."

"Is that so? And why do you think that might be? Could it have anything to do with the way you kiss her, perhaps?"

"Believe me, Tara. It just isn't like that." And with that, Luke attempted to explain. There were, however, things he felt were better left unsaid, like the Crew Party and its immediate aftermath. Sandy, he explained in simple enough terms, as someone emotionally frail from a recent relationship breakup, confusing her feelings for the one person on board who, by necessity, had shown a sympathetic ear. It was a story he hoped he could sustain for the rest of Tara's time with them there that week.

Eventually, and with some relief, he found her slowly beginning to soften. Only a touch at first, then thankfully more visibly.

II

When he arrived at the hospital the following morning, Luke was feeling considerably more buoyant in his spirits. Not only had he managed to secure Tara for himself after all the previous night, but things had gone tremendously well between them. Paul Curtis, he noticed with some satisfaction, had had to play very much from the sidelines. On the two or three occasions Luke had caught his eye, though, he found his look extremely difficult to interpret. Later still, he noticed him chatting quite affably with others who worked aboard – members of the band and cruise staff amongst them.

It was only then, that next morning, as he talked idly with Kate in between patients, that any clue emerged as to why.

"One of the passengers was asking about you last night," she said.

"Oh really?" he replied, without any great interest.

"Yes. Seemed particularly interested in you and Sandy, and what your track record has been with other women on board."

It was coming up to eleven o'clock now and Luke decided to go and find Tara. In the next hour or so, they would be docking in Caracas – a port he had never visited before. Although they had made no formal arrangements for going ashore together, it had been left that they would meet up beforehand to discuss it. He tried the Cruise Office.

"Well, she was here not long back, chatting away, happy as you like; next minute, she was gone," said one of the female cruise staff. "Looked a little upset, if you ask me."

"Any idea why? What were you guys talking about, anyway?"

"Only the Crew Party the other night; oh yes, and how Sandy still doesn't have a clue how she ended up in bed with you. You see, we haven't had the heart to tell her it was all a set-up."

Luke found himself hurrying, filled with a new urgency to find her. She wasn't in her cabin – or, at least, didn't answer his knock. Nor, as far as he could see, was she in any of the public rooms.

They were docking now and Luke could feel the massed ranks of passengers preparing for invasion. Perhaps he'd have an easier time finding her once they'd all departed on their shore excursions.

Shortly after, having returned to his cabin briefly to change out of uniform, Luke went up on deck hoping Tara might somehow be there too – having a coffee, perhaps, with some of the others. She wasn't. The Sun Deck did, however, provide some form of vantage point for keeping an eye on how disembarkation generally was progressing. Looking down, Luke could see Jose Gomez, his Honduran friend, manning the foot of the gangway. What he saw next made him almost choke on his mouthful of Coke. Leaving the ship at that very moment, was Tara Scott – and with her, ushering her protectively down onto the dockside, was the American, Paul Curtis.

Rick Tucson was saying something but Luke didn't hear him; there was only one thought now in his mind.

When Luke reached the main exit doors at the top of the gangway only a minute or two later, Paul Curtis was just getting into a waiting taxi. Tara, he noticed, was already seated in the back.

Luke stood transfixed, not knowing what to do. He could hardly dash out after them and make a scene. Not that he couldn't have caught the taxi before it pulled away – it had parked up extremely close by. Trapped agonisingly in the moment, all he could do was watch helplessly as it drove off. Jose, seeing him there, shouted a greeting. Luke waved a reply and suddenly an idea struck him. He dashed down to where the Honduran sailor was standing.

He wasn't quite sure exactly what was in his mind at that time, but the shock of what he'd just witnessed caused a host of odd emotions to well up uncontrollably within him.

"Say, Jose," he said, still a little breathless, "the couple who just left in that taxi – you didn't by any chance happen to catch where they were going, did you?"

"Si, Señor, now you come to ask, I did. The Café Medina – and I must say it surprised me a little."

"Why was that? You know the place?"

"Not the Café itself – but the area of town where the Café is situated. It is a very rough and dangerous neighbourhood, Señor Luke. Not a place for tourists."

"So why would she choose to go there?"

"It was not the Señorita who asked the driver for this place, Doctor. It was the man. And he spoke to the driver in very good Spanish. Gave good directions too, I seem to remember – once she was safely in the back, that is..."

Chapter 26

I

"Jose, can you explain to this driver where exactly the Café Medina is?" said Luke as the next speculative taxi pulled up close by just then.

The Honduran was quick to oblige, sensing the level of Luke's concern.

"Take care, Doctor," he said warningly, as Luke jumped in and the old Mercedes pulled smartly away.

By now, Tara Scott was mystified. She had watched patiently as she and her companion had been driven through one or two relatively majestic areas of the city, before ending up rather abruptly there. Surely the driver had made some mistake? She mentioned this to Paul, who seemed equally surprised. Then, as they stopped – a little to her embarrassment while she watched – he leapt out after the driver and embarked on what sounded like a furious verbal assault in Spanish, quite obviously for his error in bringing them there. Not content with simple rectification – getting the driver to take them somewhere more suitable – Paul then insisted on alighting and packing the fellow off with a thunderous flea in his ear.

The upshot of all this was quite clearly the need to call another cab to take them back. The nearest phone had to be in the café opposite. They could call from there. Paul suggested a quick drink while they waited. The next taxi along, he told her as he came off the phone, wouldn't be for about half an hour. They made their way a little tentatively through into a small, almost deserted, back-room bar.

Luke's taxi was making slow progress. The trouble was, he had now formed the distinct impression that the driver was out to give him a tour of the sights too. Whether this was some ploy to maximise on the fare or not, he didn't know. The only response Luke could find to this – to put the urgency of his trip across – had been to repeatedly tap his watch face with his index finger, together with the words "Medina Café – important."

Each time this happened, the man smiled at him for a moment then replied, "Si, si, Señor," with apparent enthusiasm, before reverting almost immediately back to his former manner.

Tara tried to disguise her apprehension as she looked around her – not least of all at the discomfiting macho stares their entry aroused. She also tried to ignore the smell – an earthy mix of tobacco, garlic and stale urine. Paul, though, seemed little put out, Tara observed, as he ordered a double brandy for himself and a white wine for her. He was smiling more, and gently cajoling her into making the best of things. An odd display of beer cans caught their eye, and they laughed together as they looked at them. She found his manner reassuring – his whole attitude since she'd met him on the plane over from London, refreshingly protective in an old-

289

fashioned kind of way. Independent, though, not stifling, as someone back home she once knew well had so unfortunately become.

Luke was getting nowhere fast. If there were any traffic jams in Caracas that afternoon which he hadn't one time or another been stuck in, he would have been surprised. Then, after a further ten minutes – when he was beginning to feel that certain of the roads they passed down were now oddly familiar to him from the first time round – he insisted on the driver pulling over and stopping.

He opened the door of the cab, gestured to the driver to wait, then dashed into a nearby hostelry. A minute later, he emerged with the first local he met inside who spoke any English at all, and who could be press-ganged into helping. In some desperation, he explained his plight. The man appeared to understand. Words were exchanged between the newcomer and the driver.

"He says this Medina Café is a bad place to go. He will take you if you insist, but will drop you off nearby and you can walk. He says it will only be a block or two away. He will wait there for your return."

"Okay, but we must get there as soon as possible. Does he understand?"

When the waiter came over to speak to them, Tara presumed it would be to do with the arrival of the taxi. The message relayed to her in translation through Paul, suggested it was not. The proprietor of the café, it appeared, wished to see them in his office upstairs. She could not imagine why. Paul had agreed almost before she knew it, shrugging his shoulders amiably as he looked at her, as if to say 'What the hell – why not?'

"You know, they're probably not used to having real tourists drop by," he said, smiling. "Maybe this guy can help speed the cab up for us."

The waiter, a dour young man in his early twenties with a leery smile and grimy fingernails, led them up a dark stairway and knocked on a door at the top. It opened almost immediately and a stocky, pock-faced middle-aged man beckoned them in.

"Señor Valez will see you shortly," he said in English. His face was mask-like as he spoke, Tara noticed; unimpressed, devoid of expression. Paul smiled at her as they waited, cracking a joke of sorts to ease the tension.

A door at the far end of the room suddenly opened.

"Go through," said the pock-faced man, turning to face them.

They did as instructed. He was holding a gun.

The room they were ushered into, Tara noted, was almost completely dark once the doors had closed behind them. She reached out for Paul's arm, wondering whether he, too, had seen the man's gun. As she found it there beside her and held on, her companion's voice boomed out loudly around the room.

"What the hell's going on here, then?" It was a question not intended just for her alone.

As if by way of answer, a powerful beam snapped on suddenly from one end of the room. Tara looked around reflexively, just able to make out the indistinct outline of a shadowy figure behind it. This, presumably, was Señor Valez.

"Tell me, if you would be so kind, what you two are doing here?" The words were English, pronounced with a certain proficiency.

"We are tourists," said Paul evenly, "from the cruise ship, Venus Prince."

"I mean, how did you come to visit this particular place – the Medina Café?"

"The taxi we came in brought us here by mistake. This is not the place we intended at all."

"I am afraid, Señor," said the voice, "this story you have come up with does not sound at all plausible. Who is it that you work for? You will discover that people in this neighbourhood do not take kindly to outsiders coming to spy on them."

"We are not spies," said Tara angrily. "We've told you we are quite simply tourists, here because of some kind of mix-up. The driver clearly misunderstood where we wanted to go. Tell him, Paul, where it was you asked for."

"I asked for the Medina Hotel – I believe it's reasonably well-known. A friend of mine recommended it. It has some renowned gardens, I believe. How the driver confused it with this place, I'll never know. Now, Señor Valez, our taxi should be arriving soon, and we only have a few, short hours until we sail. If you don't mind, therefore, I think we should go."

"Not so hasty, my friend," said the voice behind the light.

II

At last, the taxi arrived. Luke looked over questioningly at the driver, whose hand signals, at least, seemed to be indicating one block down and two to the left. Just what the verbal instructions that accompanied them were meant to convey, he would probably never know. He gestured back for the man to stay put, and there appeared to be general agreement on the point. Luke closed the car door behind him and set off, trying to ignore the fact that the taxi's engine had so far not been switched off. Any moment, he half-expected to hear it drive away. As yet, though, he had avoided parting with any money that was so far owing. It proved to be a good move.

The streets were largely deserted, the tarmac pitted and cracked where it hadn't already given way to gravel underneath. The buildings were run-down, some part-boarded. A dead dog lay stinking in the gutter. Some children played close by, apparently oblivious to the havoc being reeked by the maggots in its eye-sockets. Flies buzzed plump and black, weighed down by untold putrescence and the torpid heat of the afternoon. A dubious-looking couple chatted together on the sidewalk opposite, glancing suspiciously over at him as he walked by. Luke turned the corner, sensing only part of the danger he had been warned might lie ahead.

Five minutes later, Luke spotted the Medina Café up ahead. Two cars were parked to one side, both abandoned and without wheels; one picked clean, the human buzzards long gone. Was this really the place Tara and Curtis had visited, he wondered in disbelief? If so, why – and was there any chance they could still be there?

There seemed little activity coming from within as he walked nonchalantly by. Nobody had entered or left so far in the time he'd been watching and he could see only a handful of patrons through the grimy front windows. Clearly, no dress code applied. And as far as he could tell, Tara and her companion were nowhere in sight. Had they since moved on?

One thing in particular struck Luke as he watched. The building itself was clearly much larger than the front aspect alone would tend to suggest. Set on three floors, it had a depth which could only be appreciated close to, with a driveway running the full length of one side, down to what appeared to be an untidy, overgrown yard at the back. Rather than simply presenting himself at the front entrance he'd just passed, and running the risk of having to explain his presence to both Curtis and Tara were they indeed inside, Luke decided on a touch of reconnaissance first. Perhaps he could find out all he needed without having to interrupt them.

Glancing quickly around at the deserted street scene once more, and happy that no one so far seemed to have spotted him, Luke took a deep breath and set off cautiously down the driveway.

"You know, it is not often we are graced with the presence of such a handsome couple," said the voice behind the light. "A couple, no doubt, very much in love. It is extraordinary how much I like to see beautiful people in love. It gives me such a great thrill. And you, Señorita, you are beautiful indeed – that is, as far as I can see. Perhaps my friend Cortez here might allow me a fuller appraisal of your charms."

Tara wasn't quite sure what was meant by these words, though it didn't take her long to find out. The pock-faced man suddenly appeared right there in front of her from out of the shadows, his huge bulk totally eclipsing the light from the beam. She could feel his hands upon her almost at once, and the front of her dress rip open in one startling wrench. She could feel too the heat of his breath on her skin; skin covered little now by what clothing lay beneath.

"I was right, Señorita, your beauty endures throughout. And it is for this reason that I want you to help me. In fact, if you would like the opportunity of continuing your voyage at all – both of you – you will do exactly as I say. It may be of some interest to you to know that there is, at this very moment, a gun trained upon you. If necessary, I will, of course, not hesitate to use it."

"Who are you – and what do you want with us?" shouted Curtis angrily. "Show us your face, you fucking coward!" So saying, he lunged forward towards the source of the light, shielding his eyes with his hand as he did so.

A short burst of gunfire rang out. Tara watched in horror as her companion stumbled, then dropped heavily to the floor.

Luke had just completed his check of all the ground floor entry points of the building when he heard the muffled shots ring out. Nothing else was on his mind just then, other than he had to gain entry and quick. Whether they had anything to do with Tara, he couldn't possibly tell. But if there was any chance at all she was in danger, he knew he had to somehow intervene.

All the doors he'd tried so far were locked. Other than the main entrance itself, an absolute last resort, only one possibility now remained. He'd seen the fire escape round at the rear of the building a little earlier on but hadn't ventured up. The red door at the top, he recalled, looked promising; it was time to give it a try. Overcoming any urge to panic, he darted off, skirting the northwest corner of the building, keeping his head well down as he passed under each of the three windows looking out. If whoever was in there was unaware of his presence even now, it wouldn't do to give the game away. Surprise could be his most powerful weapon – or more precisely, his only weapon. And Tara's wellbeing, he knew, could depend on it.

He reached the foot of the fire escape and without any further thought, set off. Halfway up, he briefly stopped. The red door ahead of him, if he wasn't very much mistaken, now looked suspiciously ajar.

"That, my friend, was just a warning," said the voice behind the light. The pock-faced man, as Tara watched, stood over Paul Curtis where he lay face down on the floor. His knee was firmly planted in his back, the younger man's arms forced up roughly behind him. Now, ignoring his moans, he began tying Paul's hands. From where she stood, there appeared to be no signs of bleeding. She could only pray he had not been hit.

When he had finished with him, Curtis was made to stand up, looking badly shaken. Then, with a gun in his ribs, he was forcibly guided back to approximately his original position in the room. Tara looked at him questioningly. His look in return gave her no grounds for optimism. What on earth did these people want from them, she asked herself?

"Now, I think we understand each other," said the faceless voice coolly from about fifteen feet away. "The binding and gagging are perhaps a little unfortunate, but do, I think, add a rather intriguing slant on things. Now, Señorita, we will start with you. Do all I ask, and you will both go free. Do it slowly, as instructed, exactly where you are standing now. Do you understand me?"

"Yes," said Tara timidly after a pause, wondering just what was coming next.

"Okay, move closer to your boyfriend and kneel down in front of him. That's it. Turn your head very slightly this way. Very good. Now, listen very carefully: undo his trousers and take them down. Now the same with his shorts – both of them right down to below his knees. Do it slowly and try to make it look like you're enjoying yourself."

Once inside the door, Luke found himself in a narrow hallway. From somewhere close by, he could make out the sound of low voices interspersed with laughter. Holding his breath and listening closely, he tried to work out precisely where they were coming from. It appeared to be one of the rooms up ahead on his left. As he crept closer, he could tell the voices were in Spanish, one male and one female. Pausing for a moment outside the door to confirm this, he passed quickly on to a turn in the hallway. Almost at once, he was confronted with a choice: head further on, forward into the building, or take the right turn which had now presented itself?

Deliberating only momentarily over this, Luke's thoughts were interrupted by the sudden sound of the door behind him opening. The voices he had heard from within the room were now much louder and approaching. He made a quick choice and fled down the darker right-hand passage, far enough at least to find refuge inside the doorway of a clearly vacant room he passed on the way. The voices, though, kept coming – louder and louder as he stood there, out of sight behind the half-open door. He could just make out their features as they passed by – a youngish gravel-voiced man smoking a cigarette, and the badly wrinkled, sagging form of a woman in her late fifties wearing high heels and a mini skirt.

Breathing easier once they'd gone, Luke ventured out. He quickly decided though against that right-hand passage – it seemed to stop fairly abruptly further on at a door through which presumably the couple had just entered, with little sign of activity appearing to come from within. He quickly retraced his steps and ventured on down the main corridor. A stairway to one side made its way down two levels to the ground floor, and Luke stood at the top of it, wondering just what to do next. He glanced at his watch. It was now 3.15. The floor directly below seemed pretty quiet, so he tiptoed down, steeling himself for what might lie ahead.

On the landing, and listening keenly for anyone who might just happen to be coming up from the ground floor, Luke tried quickly to gain orientation. His mental processes, though, were almost immediately interrupted by the scream: a scream which – far from piercing on any vaguely appropriate scale of measurement – managed to penetrate right through his very being as he stood there.

For this scream, if he wasn't very much mistaken, belonged to Tara.

"That's it, Señorita – you can forget the tears. What I want is the demure look. Like you've never seen anything quite like it before in your life. And you, Señor: the little struggle – a very nice touch. And built like a stallion, too. God, we have struck lucky today, haven't we? Okay, I think we are ready for the next bit. Now, Señorita, I think you know exactly what I want you to do. Nice and slowly. Remember, he is powerless to resist. And don't be too shy now – for both your sakes – or Cortez might be forced to intervene once more. And I can tell he's getting a little excited himself right now."

Luke located the room easily enough, just there off to one side past a procession of old filing cabinets. He crouched behind one gratefully, looking over at the door, wondering at what precise point he ought to burst in. He remembered the gunshots from earlier. What danger lay ahead for him if he did just blunder on through? Surely there must be another way? Some kind of diversion, perhaps?

When the plan came to him, he wasn't in any way sure it would work. It was hardly sophisticated but had to be worth a try in the circumstances. He eased out from behind the cabinet and took a series of slow deliberate steps towards the door. The thick lump of wood he'd found – his makeshift baseball bat – was there in his hand at the ready. He raised his other, preparing to knock. He watched it poised, then, in slow motion, descend. What he didn't see, however, was it land.

All he saw instead was blackness. All he felt just then was the searing pain in his head.

The room Luke found himself in when he came round, was small and crammed like a storeroom. He had been dumped there, it seemed, like much of the other garbage strewn haphazardly around; a crumpled heap on the floor. He felt his head and identified the lump, then it came to him just how he'd come by it. He remembered Tara and those screams. How long had he been there? He looked at the time – no more than ten minutes or so, according to his watch. Surely there was still time to help her?

Luke tried the door. It was locked. He rushed over to the windows: there were two. These also were locked, though the old wooden frames, he noticed, were rotting and cracked. Forcing the locks wouldn't be difficult, if he could just find an implement of some kind to help him. The real question was, what problems would he face out on the roof trying to get down? And what, come to think of it, could he seriously do to help Tara once he'd succeeded?

Within five minutes, Luke was out on a ledge. Of the two windows available, the one he'd chosen definitely had the advantage. From where he was now perched, he needed only to negotiate a seven-foot drop onto a small flat roof below, with the backyard itself barely ten feet below that. Terra firma – though hopefully not too much of the firma when he landed.

Down on the flat roof, Luke thought he could hear voices. He crouched down low, out of sight, suddenly aware that one of the doors just beneath him was being forced open.

Somebody, he could hear, emerged agitatedly, trying to slam the door shut behind them. The door, though, sprang open almost at once and the person obviously in pursuit made a grab for them, trying to pull them forcefully back inside. Luke, alarmed by this, popped his head quickly over the corner of the roof to snatch a look. Just there below him was a swarthy Venezuelan, and clamped in his grip – trying her level best to head-butt him – was Tara Scott.

Surprise, as Luke had noted earlier, was his only possible weapon that day, and he could only pray it would work. He'd seen it done in the movies, of course, but presumed that was when they called in the stuntmen. The way he felt just then, however, little could have dissuaded him – particularly in this most critical part of the venture. With unexpected compliance, the unsuspecting hombre slumped down under him as he landed, like some really poor excuse, his head thudding audibly on the ground. Luke watched him lie there motionlessly for a moment then grabbed Tara's hand.

"You okay?" he asked. She nodded, looking totally bewildered by it all – by what had happened earlier; by the state of her clothes as she stood there trying to catch her breath and cover herself as best she could; by him simply being there right then. She went to speak, but he stopped her, motioning instead to the driveway and the front of the building they still had to negotiate.

"Not now – let's just get the hell out of here, okay?"

How they managed to make it successfully down the road, Luke would never know. He could hear a certain amount of commotion behind them as they ran, Tara's breathing a little laboured beside him. As far as he could tell, though – glancing back whenever he was able – no one was following them.

It was difficult, of course, to be sure...

Only when they finally reached the corner two blocks down – and he saw to his relief that the taxi was, in fact, still there – did Luke begin to feel in any way confident of getting away. The vehicle lurched forward towards them as they approached. For a moment, Luke wondered if it was some kind of trick. As he looked, pulling Tara abruptly to a halt beside him, he could make out the face of the driver inside looking distinctly alarmed. Then the car stopped. All appeared to be okay. Luke grabbed the door, and they were in. As the vehicle pulled sharply away, Luke held Tara close in his arms.

All he wanted to know now was what in God's name had just taken place there in the Medina Café?

"Christ, what about Paul? We should have waited for Paul," said Tara, when she had gathered her composure enough for the realisation to hit her. She turned in her seat, looking back through the rear window. There was no sign of Curtis, or indeed any sign of pursuit. She turned once more to Luke: "The police – we must get the police."

"Tara, what exactly happened in there? And why did you come to this café?"

"It was a mistake – one big, awful mistake. The taxi-man got the wrong place entirely. We only went in for a drink, waiting for another car to come for us. Then..."

"Then?" said Luke. There was no reply. "Then what, Tara?"

"Nothing. I don't want to talk about it – okay?"

"Is Curtis in some kind of danger?"

"Yes, I believe so. I must talk to the police."

"Tara, there's something you ought to know."

"What?"

"He arranged for you to go there – to that place, the Medina Café."

"No, he wanted the Medina Hotel."

"But he asked specifically for the Medina Café. He even gave the driver of your taxi precise instructions on how to get there. A friend of mine, one of the sailors on the ship, overheard exactly what was said from where he was standing. He realised immediately what a seedy area of town you were going to."

"That can't be right," she said. "Paul..."

"Think about it, Tara. How else could I have known exactly where to find you – here in this totally unfamiliar city?"

A strange silence followed as the taxi sped on back to the ship.

By the time they got there, Tara had changed her mind about the police. Instead, she strode off resolutely back to her cabin with hardly a further word to him.

Something of considerable significance had clearly happened to her that afternoon, Luke thought as he watched her go; something that had shaken her to the very core. There were a lot of questions this guy Curtis would have to answer when he returned to the ship. And his replies had better be good.

It was now 4.08 pm. The ship was due to sail at 5.30.

Luke went down to the foyer, as people were beginning to re-board. He spoke to Jose, still there on dockside duty. The tall American had not, so far, returned. Soon after, the main body of tour buses appeared and the stampede of passengers drove him back inside, well out of the way. His first patient at the hospital presented just then, and he went back there at Kate's request to deal with her. There was nothing else for it: he would just have to tackle this man Curtis a little later that evening.

Thoughts of Tara preoccupied him for the rest of that night. He desperately wanted to see her, to support her as best he could – as far, at least, as she would let him. It proved difficult, though; she seemed to be keeping herself determinedly to herself. She had not appeared for dinner, nor was she with any of the others in the public rooms. He decided against trying her cabin; if she wanted to be alone, he must respect her privacy. Besides, rest was probably the best thing for her just then.

What he had to tell her would have to wait. He was sure she'd be intrigued when she found out. He had checked once again with Jose – the American, Paul Curtis, it seemed, had not returned to the ship.

III

The next morning, after he'd finished in the hospital, Luke went in search of Tara once more. Yet again, she appeared to be in none of her usual haunts. He tried her cabin, determined now to see her no matter what. She'd had time enough on her own. If she wouldn't speak to him, then perhaps Kate might be able to help talk things through.

There was no reply to his knock. He tried again. Nothing. He listened for any hint of stirring from within. None at all. He tried the door handle. The door opened freely. Luke called her name and walked tentatively in. What he saw alarmed him. He just couldn't understand it.

Tara's cabin was completely empty. So tidy was it, in fact, it was easy to imagine she had never been there at all.

Luke rushed up to the foyer and into the Chief Purser's office. Soon all became clear.

"Ah, yes – Miss Scott, from the London Office," said the Purser suddenly remembering. "She called in and collected her passport yesterday at the very last minute before we sailed from Caracas. Then, without a word of explanation – to me, at least – simply took her bags and disembarked."

Chapter 27

I

"I'm sorry, Mr Jamieson isn't here right now. This is his secretary, Rachel Saunders speaking. Could I, perhaps, be of assistance?"

"My name is Dr Luke Darius – ship's doctor on the Venus Prince. I wonder if you might possibly have the home address and phone number for his niece, Tara Scott, on record? I need to get through to her urgently."

"As far as I am aware, Dr Darius, Miss Scott is working in the London office."

"She was until recently but flew out to join the ship here in the Caribbean three days ago. She left rather abruptly after some sort of upset. I've since discovered, through the shore agent in Caracas, that she flew from there to New York – presumably home. The thing is, I'm concerned about her."

"Where exactly are you calling from, Doctor?"

"Cartagena, Colombia."

"Can you hold for half a minute? I'll get the information you require."

It had been a trying few hours for Luke, made no easier by the temperamental nature of the shore-side payphones there in Cartagena that afternoon. Some luck had been with him, though, it turned out. When he did eventually get through to the agent's office in Caracas earlier, not only did the person he spoke to seem to understand his question but they were also, fortunately, in possession of the particular information he required.

Getting through to Head Office after that was considerably more straightforward. He now had one further call to make before the ship sailed. He held his breath as the ringing tone became audible down the line.

"Hello, may I speak to Tara, please?" he said, fairly confident that the voice that had answered was not hers.

"Who's calling?"

"It's Luke; Luke Darius – a friend of hers from the cruise ship she's just left in the Caribbean."

"I'm sorry, Mr Darius, but Tara's sleeping right now and cannot be disturbed. For whatever reason, she's made it quite clear she doesn't want to speak to anyone at all just now."

"I understand, Mrs Scott – I just wanted to check she made it back okay."

"I'll tell her you phoned. But please – at least for the time being – I'd appreciate it if you didn't call again."

Luke lay on his bed and stared at the ceiling, feeling little short of blind desolation. It had all gone so badly wrong. Whatever it was that had happened that previous afternoon had affected Tara deeply. Then, just when he wanted more than ever to be there and help her through it, a great geographical gulf had suddenly been thrust between them; one very much of her choosing. A sad indictment of the state of their friendship as it now stood.

Even worse, she had left still very much under the impression he had something going with Sandy. He'd sorted that out now with Sandy herself, not that it would do him much good. Told her nothing had happened between them on the night of the party, because, of course, he respected her too much and didn't really want a relationship just then anyway. It was a cop-out, sure. And there was no mention of Tara – but what the hell? It was kinder that way, and he wished her no ill-feeling. Just wished in a way he didn't find her body, at least, so outrageously exciting.

But getting back to Tara – what ought he to do? If he couldn't speak to her directly on the phone, his hands were tied. He either accepted things were effectively over between them or he took alternative action. And this, as it happened, was not entirely out of the question.

At the end of that particular cruise – in just four days' time – he had a week's vacation booked. He'd intended to explore a little more of Jamaica – or possibly take a quick trip down to Trinidad to look up an old friend from university days. But deep inside, Luke Darius knew his priorities lay very much elsewhere.

II

Helen Darius sat earnestly by her husband's bedside watching him. Little food had passed his lips for two days now, and it was as much as she could do to get him to drink. He was going downhill so quickly it alarmed her. Not that she hadn't begun preparing herself now for his eventual death. She had;

long before her son, Martin, had brought her the news from Cedric Bannister two and a half weeks back. She'd seen it in his eyes and heard it in the bite of his cough; a hollow, fruitless hack that had echoed painfully around the room, leaving him thoroughly exhausted.

And she knew that he knew too; and that he also knew that she knew. Yet nothing was said directly between them. A tacit understanding spoken only through their eyes, and tenderly reaffirmed every moment she was with him. He lifted his hand – bonier now than ever before, knobbly like rosary beads – and she took it gently in hers; and, when he wasn't looking, prayed.

In the background just then, Helen Darius could hear the sound of Martin arriving home. It seemed recently as if he'd almost taken up permanent residence there again at Wetherfield – presumably to support her. At times, though, she had to admit, it was not altogether clear. So many other things appeared to be on his mind. She left her husband's bedside and went out to see him. There was something in particular she needed to discuss.

"Hello, Martin. You've still heard nothing from Luke, I take it?"

"Afraid not, Mother. The cruise company tells me they telexed the ship several days ago with that second message. Must say, I'm a little surprised he hasn't called."

"I'm really worried. Father's definitely going downhill quite quickly now. Dr Bannister came this morning and started him on more antibiotics; told me he thinks it's just a secondary infection, but I've got my doubts. If he doesn't pick up a little soon and start taking food, he'll fade away quickly, I'm sure.

And Luke would never forgive himself if he wasn't here to say his farewell. If we haven't heard from him in the next couple of days, we'll have to find some other way of getting the message through. I can't believe for one moment he's too busy to respond."

Back on the Venus Prince, Luke mooched morosely in his cabin. His mind was fixed on Tara and little else. His main consolation now was that a clear plan of action had presented itself. Only two days more and he could act. His reservation had been booked using the satellite phone on board; the ticket arranged by the ship's agent in Montego Bay. He would be sorry to leave the Caribbean just then, but it couldn't be helped.

III

It was Saturday, March 29th, and New York City rejoiced in the initial surge of spring. The sun shone high over Central Park and people of all ages were out in force, warmer attire at last discarded in joyous overkill; coaxed from the hibernation of yet another long cold winter.

As the fleeting clouds passed on, the sun shone too over the body of Manhattan, the Hudson River and Jersey. It picked out the top of the Fairfax Building as Ed Jamieson approached, shining through the empty offices of Venus Cruise Lines on the sixteenth floor.

Ed made his way up and let himself in. He still had a little outstanding work to complete for that week. It had been an unusually busy time just then – bookings for the new cruise season running very close to his own, admittedly optimistic, initial estimate. He couldn't wait to see Dan Forsbrook's face when he pointed out how right he had been all along. He'd have to wait till the following week though, as Dan wouldn't be back in the country till then.

Preoccupied as he was with these and other thoughts – which naturally included somewhere amongst them his old rival, George Mitchell – Ed didn't immediately notice the parcel sitting there right on his desk. There was nothing garish in its wrapping to alert him – plain brown paper stuck with clear tape, and no label attached. Neither was it large – little more than eight inches by four and a half, and slim with it.

When he opened it not long after, Ed became aware of a strange feeling of foreboding. Inside was a video cassette and, perhaps more curiously, nothing else at all.

A feeling of relief immediately crept over him, followed almost as swiftly by a nagging uncertainty. What was this about – and who had sent it?

Ed took the tape through to the boardroom and shoved it into the resident VCR. As the images unfurled before him and he watched in disbelief, Ed's sense of puzzlement grew overwhelmingly.

It started out looking like a fairly standard porno film – not that he considered himself any kind of expert – but as he continued watching, aware thankfully that he was alone, something particular about it suddenly grabbed his attention. Once grabbed, he found it just wouldn't let go.

It featured a startlingly well-endowed young man and a girl. The girl for some reason looked strangely familiar, though he couldn't immediately think why. Only then did it come to him, the blow felling him like an axe. He swayed a little on his feet then struggled to steady himself. He stared again just to be sure. There could be no mistake.

The girl in question was none other than his niece, Tara Scott.

Chapter 28

I

Hugh Gotley's peaceful and highly ordered world was once again under siege. It wasn't the hardware store, though, there in Sheepshead Bay, that was in any way to blame. He had that side of things well and truly sorted. His shelves were neatly arranged and labelled, his latest promotions well thought out and displayed, and his stock control system second-to-none. Ask anyone who knew him. Not only that, he took pride in his bookkeeping and the general upkeep of the premises, and he couldn't really remember the last time one of his customers had serious cause for complaint. He'd learnt well from experience in the years since he'd taken over from his father. And, having evolved the best system, he could think of very little reason to change it now.

No, the hardware store there on Main Street was the least of Hugh's problems just then. Nor was it some of the other important facets of Hugh's life; things he really cared for, too: like the early morning fishing trips out into the bay with Sam from the hire shop – the freshest catch in New York, so they'd boast – or, of course, the Yankees. Then there was his religion, the close Catholic community thereabouts – but, come to think of it, the Yankees were a bit of a religion too. He'd followed them since he was just a kid – since his dad had bought him his first baseball outfit on his sixth birthday, and tossed him easy pitches out in the backyard. He'd followed them religiously, too, after he'd graduated High School and his dad had sadly pitched his last; and when he'd given up hope of ever playing College football and resigned himself instead to a life of simply running the store.

But two things of undoubted significance had happened in those past confusing months; things which threatened the calm of his very existence. The first was Tara leaving him after their being together so long and going off to work abroad. The second was the news just in from her mother that she'd returned.

When Mrs Scott phoned him two nights before, he had immediately jumped to the wrong conclusion: Tara was back, couldn't wait to see him, and all would be as it was before. Why his mind played such tricks he didn't know. It dawned on him fairly quickly into the conversation, though, that not only had he been a little too presumptuous over the inevitability of their getting back together, but Tara herself had absolutely no knowledge of her mother's phone call to him at that time.

Something, it transpired, had upset her while she was away – Tara wouldn't say what – and she'd come straight home. Now, it seemed, she'd given orders to the effect that she didn't want to see anyone at all. It was a sign of the special relationship he shared with her mother, he knew, that he had been afforded the privilege of even this information.

So often when he'd called on Mrs Scott after Mass on Sundays while her daughter was away – taking comfort from merely being there in Tara's home – she had told him. It was really all he'd had to sustain him; stealing into her bedroom at the top of the stairs just for a second or two before he left, on the pretext of using the bathroom. It had remained just as he remembered it, shrine-like almost – more so, it seemed, since the picture of the Sacred Heart had suddenly appeared there one day over her bed.

"Hugh, you hang on in there now, if you can. When she's finally got this crazy itch to travel out of her system, then Please God she'll be back," Mrs Scott had said encouragingly. He remembered the words; could recite them almost. "She's a good girl, Hugh – and, you know something? Between you and me, I think you two are right for each other."

So, he had waited, not really knowing how long it might take before Tara returned. Mrs Scott had been good to him. In fact, he felt almost as much a part of the family then as when he and her daughter were together. And she shared what she had heard with him – the gist, at least, of the phone calls and letters she'd received all the way from London, England.

At times he had almost given up; had tried dating other girls, but somehow it had never worked. No one he met seemed to measure up even slightly to the girl he'd lost. The girl who had now returned.

He wasn't sure how to play it exactly, now he'd been so secretly informed. Clearly, he had to drop round casually one evening on some pretext or other, and simply find her there; to his immense surprise, of course. And when he had – that previous night, in fact – he very soon became aware of the difficulty of the task ahead. Tara's reluctance to see him was evident, though she did soften a little after a while. She wouldn't be drawn on the nature of her problem though – just told him her work in London had been interesting, and that she'd seen a little of that country as well as learning more about her ancestors in her short visit across the Irish Sea. She was particularly vague about her return trip when he'd asked.

He remained curious even after Mrs Scott had offered further insights, in another of those clandestine calls earlier that same afternoon. It was Saturday and he'd just got over a busy spell in the store.

"Hugh – how you doing? Glad I caught you. Tara's told me a little more, so I thought I'd just let you know. Seems she was sent over to do some work on one of the cruise ships my brother owns – down in the Caribbean. The problem – and, you know, I'm still not exactly sure what it was – happened while she was there. I did manage to get from her that she left the ship a few days early and flew here direct from Venezuela, or one of those other countries.

"Now the other point, Hugh," she went on, barely stopping to take a breath, "is that some guy from the ship phoned long-distance to speak to her on Tuesday. In view of her instructions, naturally, I put him off. Tara sounded pleased I had when I told her. But now I know the problem was to do with her time on that ship, it kind of occurs to me it might be somehow linked to this man. You know what I'm saying here, Hugh?"

"You didn't happen to catch his name by any chance, did you, Kathleen?"

"Matter of fact, I did. It was Darius... a Luke Darius."

"Hmm," said Hugh gravely, noting it down on a piece of plain brown wrapping paper that just happened to come to hand. "At least, thank God, she's well away from the problem now."

"You're quite right, Hugh. But listen here, it's up to us to help her put it behind her, right? Though, be sure not to rush things, okay?"

II

Not so very many miles away, at about that time, Tara's uncle, Ed Jamieson, was just returning home to his house near Lincoln Park. Beside him – lying there on the passenger seat of his new 7-series BMW – was the video cassette left in his office.

Any doubts about it being some kind of practical joke – his initial thought when he discovered broadly the type of film it contained – were very soon put to rest. Not only had he been able, by closer scrutiny, to confirm that the girl involved was undoubtedly his niece, but he could tell from her expression throughout that she was there, very clearly, under duress.

What had shocked him even more – striking close to the very foundations of all credibility as far as he was concerned – was the apparent reason behind it all. The initial recording had been fairly brief, cut off rather abruptly not long after its natural conclusion. Then had come the message. Little finesse had been employed in its presentation; a crude scrawl on that placard in front of the camera. The point, though, was clear just the same:

WELCOME TO THE PREVIEW.
IN 10 DAYS TIME THIS WILL GO ON GENERAL
RELEASE UNLESS THE VENUS PRINCE REMAINS
ON ITS PRESENT ROUTE IN THE CARIBBEAN.
MAKE ALL NECESSARY ARRANGEMENTS AS
QUICKLY AS POSSIBLE.
WE WILL BE WATCHING YOU. DO NOT DELAY:
THIS IS NO IDLE THREAT, TRUST ME.
THINGS WILL ONLY GET WORSE IF YOU DO
NOT COMPLY.

One thing was certain; this was now some pretty serious stuff. He'd heard vaguely through Rachel at the office that someone had suggested Tara was back home, but he had no idea why. She hadn't exactly called him herself to let him know. If she'd been physically hurt or reported her ordeal to the police, surely he'd have been informed by now?

He must call her as soon as he got home – or should he? Perhaps he'd best talk to Jack Buchanan first. Jack would know how to advise him. This latest thing was clearly linked to that bald threat he'd received some weeks back. The threat he'd largely ignored – save, that is, for getting Jack to check out George Mitchell, and his own counter-threat on discovering the asshole was cheating on Sophia. But surely this video couldn't be the work of Mitchell? Much as he despised the man, there was no way he'd go this far. Or was there? One thing was sure: if it was him, this was now war.

As Ed let himself in the front door still deep in thought, his wife Ellen called out to him from the lounge. He stuck his head round the door to see what it was she wanted.

"Oh, Ed, your sister Kathleen called. Apparently, Tara's home and not feeling so good right now. She wanted to let you know she'd be staying a while and not returning to the London office just at the moment. I told her not to worry – that it was no problem at all."

"Did she happen to say what the matter was with her?"

"I did ask, and she said she didn't think it was anything too serious. Must admit, though, she did sound a bit vague."

Ed was relieved by one thing as he made his way through to his study and closed the door. At least, at the moment, he didn't have the wrath of his sister to contend with. She clearly had no idea what had happened to Tara – nor, thankfully, about the video. Could it be that his niece, too, was unaware at that moment of its existence?

It took Ed only a couple of minutes to bring Jack up to date with developments once he'd got through. He told of the video, its message, Tara's return to New York and the phone call taken by his secretary three or four days back from someone on the Venus Prince trying to contact her to check Tara had got back from Caracas okay.

"So, what do you think, Jack? You think I ought to call her – that we should maybe go round and find out from her exactly what happened?"

"Tell me, Ed: bottom line – are you happy, at the end of the day, to comply with what whoever's behind this blackmail wants?"

319

"No goddam way, I'm not! It could almost ruin me at this late stage. We're pretty heavily booked now, and the new season's only weeks away. There'd be the loss of business, compensation payouts – the whole frigging works."

"Well, it sure strikes me as soon as you bring this video to Tara's attention – especially with the threat of it going public – your hands will be well and truly tied. You'll be forced to give in. That is, unless you want a complete and permanent breakdown in your relationship with both your niece and your sister.

"Were this video ever to get public airing, and they later learnt you'd been in a position to prevent it – but wouldn't because of purely business reasons – your life wouldn't be worth shit. And seriously, who could blame them? If it went onto the Internet, for example – not just to the normal sleaze-pits that handle this kinda stuff – perverts the world over would have access to it for God knows how long; maybe forever. Trust me, they can do that now and quite easily, I'm told. Thankfully, from what you say, it only went so far and was a bit too brief to be anything like a full feature in itself. But it could still get exposure, right? Could still be extremely damaging to the girl for the rest of her life."

"So, you're saying I should keep quiet about it?"

"For the moment, yes. You've got ten days, so the message said. After that, if you can't convince whoever it is that you're taking them seriously, they may very well do what they say. But Ed, listen – if they do that, they still don't end up with what they want. If they do it anyway – just to show you they mean business – you would naturally try to convince Tara and your sister you knew nothing about it; that you'd never heard tell of any such video or received any such ultimatum. No, it's pretty clear to me whoever sent this knows quite a lot about you and your relatives. You've just the one sister and one niece – no grown-up kids of your own, right?"

"That's right."

"Well, my hunch is, if they get to see you're not playing ball with them, their next move might be to make Kathleen and Tara herself aware of the deal. Let them help out in the persuasion process."

"Shit, yes; I see what you mean. So, what the hell would I do then, Jack? It's taken me years to build up this business. I'm damned if I'm going to see it all go down the toilet just to protect a young woman's finer feelings."

"Ed, it's family we're talking about here. You must never forget family. And, besides, it's not her finer feelings we're talking about; it's her honour as a woman. Remember, this girl seems to have been the victim of a pretty horrendous criminal assault. And, from the sound of that message, if this fails to get them what they want, God knows what they'll resort to next. Whatever it is, it sure won't be pretty. Seems to me you've got to try to buy time somehow, Ed – ideally whatever time it might take for us to catch up with these scumbags. Just keep the ship on that Caribbean itinerary a bit longer – you know, in the hope we somehow get lucky."

"Guess you're right. Though, believe me, as far as I'm concerned right now, that's got to be the very last resort."

"Okay, agreed. So, let's consider where we go from here. Now, think, Ed: is there anything else you haven't told me so far? Anything at all strange that's happened since we last spoke – you know when I'd just got back from Miami?"

"No, I don't think so, Jack."

"This guy Mitchell – the one I checked out for you down there – seems a little extreme for him, wouldn't you say? Unless, of course, he's totally flipped."

Ed thought this through but said nothing. He hadn't told Jack about the anonymous letter he'd sent to George Mitchell on the subject of his infidelity. Surely that couldn't have tipped him over the edge, could it?

"I agree with you – can't believe it of him, either. But then, as we discussed before, who the hell else could it be?"

"At least this time there might be a little more to go on. Whoever it is seems to be getting more desperate now and taking more risks with it. That could well be to our advantage. The video itself will hopefully provide some clues; I'll need that off you right away. First, there's the guy directly involved – yes, I know from what you say it appears as though he, too, was an unwilling participant. But he was certainly aroused, right, from what you saw? He may well be able to answer one or two questions for us – given the right encouragement."

"You mean you think he might have been in on it too? Good God!"

"Anything's possible, believe me. Also, I'll need to know who it was from the ship made that phone call to your secretary. Check that out for me, will you, Ed? It's likely whoever it is isn't personally involved in this – judging by his willingness to identify himself and his apparent concern for Tara – but he might well be able to help out on some of the background issues. Then, there's the style and quality of the recording itself. Or any clues on the exact location it was shot, for example. I've got several contacts who could advise me there, both in the Department and on the streets. Drop the tape over tonight, Ed. I'll get straight on with it. Time, as they say, is now of the essence."

III

"What do you mean he's on vacation? Are you sure?"

"Quite certain, Mrs Darius. After your call earlier on, we contacted the ship and that is what they've reported back to us. Your son apparently left as soon as it docked in Jamaica this morning. It is understood he was intending to fly from there up to the States for a week."

"To America? Didn't he receive any of our previous messages? I know for a fact my other son has contacted you at least twice this past week alone. His father's condition is very critical now, and it's vital Luke comes home as soon as possible – before it's too late."

"As far as I am aware, we at the London office here, have no knowledge at all of any other such requests having been made. But trust me, Mrs Darius, I shall personally ensure that your son is informed, directly he returns."

IV

That following day, Sunday, at about 11.20 in the morning, a hire car pulled into the northern end of Saracen Drive, Sheepshead Bay, and slowly made its way down. Its driver hesitated a little halfway along, checking out the numbers as he went, then came to a halt finally a few houses further on. He turned the engine off and sat for a moment composing himself for what was to come. When the thought struck him, he checked his smile quickly in the rear-view mirror in the hope he might need it, and got out. Luke Darius was as ready as he was ever likely to be for his meeting with Tara Scott there at her home.

There were potential problems, of course. The first, and possibly most significant of these, was that Tara had no idea at all he was coming. His flight from Jamaica had landed in New York late the previous evening. By the time he got the taxi into Brooklyn from JFK and found his cousin Marie's house down near Prospect Park, it was too late to call and let her know. Certainly, by the time Marie and her family were through with him, anyway. It had turned into a wild night of catching up and fond remembrances. And, in the back of his mind, Luke had reservations about phoning again, especially after Tara's mother's guarded response when he last called five days before.

If he had arrived ten minutes earlier, he would have found no one in at all. Sunday morning in the Scott household was a time set aside for worship. Ten o'clock Mass at St Theresa's had attracted a typically full congregation that day, Tara and Mrs Scott amongst them. Hugh Gotley was there too, in the middle of the fifth row, offering thanks with considerably more purpose than over recent months. He had, he realised, a lot to be thankful for. His singing, too, possessed an added vim as it projected loudly and hopefully forward towards Tara down at the front. Then, after the blessing at the end, when he'd timed his parting genuflection to coincide with her arrival alongside him in the aisle, they'd walked out together into the sunshine. Mrs Scott had followed, adjusting Tara's imaginary train in her mind. Then she'd left the two of them to chat with their friends over coffee in the Parish Hall while she went home to start the lunch.

She had only been there five minutes when the doorbell rang.

"Mrs Scott? Sorry to turn up out of the blue like this. I'm Luke Darius. I called on Tuesday, you may recall, to talk to Tara. I've been really worried about her."

"I'm afraid, Mr Darius, she's out with Hugh, her boyfriend, right now. And, to be honest with you, I'm not sure how long for, either. I told her you called already, but I'm sorry to say it's very much like I told you on the phone: she doesn't want to speak with you, okay?"

Luke remembered little more of the conversation. He walked back to the car feeling stunned as the door closed behind him, then drove off down the road. Not long after, almost without thinking, he pulled over and stopped. He was close to the bay now; somewhere on Emmond's Avenue, with the crowded sidewalk cafés and the tops of fishing boats bobbing in and out of view as he sat there. Art works in some profusion dotted the sidewalk opposite, he noticed, there in the afternoon sunshine, their proud creators drinking in any jot of praise they could lay their hands on as folk strolled by. Remembered summer sunsets from dark winter nights, taking the air and testing the water.

Luke left the car, a small white Toyota, and walked for a while. More than anything, he needed time to think.

Mrs Scott took the opportunity after lunch, once Tara had gone to her room to change. She spoke quietly, not quite whispering, though it really wasn't necessary. Her daughter couldn't have heard her anyway.

"Hugh, that guy I was telling you about – you know, the one that called long distance from the ship? Well, he's here. Came knocking this morning just after I'd arrived home from church. I told him she was out with you and didn't know when she might return. Pretty sure we might not have seen the last of him."

It didn't immediately strike Luke that the man leaving might be Tara's boyfriend – the one mentioned earlier by her mother. It was now after four and he'd been sitting patiently in the white Toyota, a strategic distance away, for almost an hour. He was shorter than for some reason he'd expected, and physically less impressive; though he had a pleasant enough face, even if it was a little worried-looking just then.

When it did occur to him that he was, one other point hit home almost simultaneously. If that was the boyfriend coming from the house, then the two of them must have returned while he was away. Time to try again.

Luke could tell what Mrs Scott was about to say even before the words came out. He watched her immediate response as she opened the door – even watched in slow motion as she opened her mouth to speak. He'd heard them all before, and more or less in the same order – the only difference now being that they were choked, initially at least, by the sheer force of her indignation.

His own response, too, seemed painfully staid as he heard himself speak. What was needed was more passion.

"Please, Mrs Scott, I know she's in there. I only want to talk with her for a short time to see she's okay. We were quite close for a while, you know."

The woman looking back at him composed herself for a reply, when a voice came from behind her:

"Luke, is that you? What on earth are you doing here? Hey, Mom, let him in." Tara looked pale and drawn, with an authority in her voice he'd never really heard before.

"Please excuse my mother," she said, showing him into a small sitting room overlooking a shaded backyard. "She has a tendency to be a little over-protective."

"I noticed. She told you I called round earlier?"

"No, afraid not – must have somehow slipped her mind." Tara smiled as she said this, pursing her lips in her characteristic way.

"She did mention I phoned from Colombia the other day to see how you were?"

"Yeah, she did. I'll have to give her that."

"And how are you?"

"I'm okay. I'll survive."

"Something really awful happened that afternoon in Caracas, didn't it, Tara? What was it, exactly – can you say?"

"No, I really can't. Had a little bit of a shock, that's all. Thanks for your concern, anyway."

"If you're sure?"

"Quite sure. Now would you like some tea? I'll just go make some."

She returned soon after with a tray, and set it down on the low table between them.

"Your mother tells me you're back with your old boyfriend now," Luke ventured as she poured. "That right?"

"Just a little wishful thinking on her part, I'm afraid. Hugh and I have known each other for years. Used to go out together, but not now. Seem to have outgrown each other, somehow. Got to find him a bit too predictable, a bit too s…"

"Safe?"

"Settled, I was going to say. Safe and reliable I can live with right now."

Luke wondered at her inclusion of the word 'reliable'. Could that be some oblique reference to him and that fiasco with Sandy on ship?

"Listen, Tara, I know things didn't ultimately work out so well between us when you came aboard. But then you left so suddenly, and I…"

"Luke," she said interrupting him, slowly shaking her head. "Believe me, the way I feel about things right now, I don't want or need the complication of a man in my life. You're an extremely nice and very attractive guy, and sure, I've always enjoyed your company. But I think you'll agree, we never really got to know each other that well; had very little chance of each other's company right since that first night we met. Ours was more a kind of infatuation – the kind you might have on vacation, say. The kind that can remain pretty much undisturbed by such risky acts as actually having to spend time together. Of course, such relationships can be perfect in their own way. But never real."

"I'm sure you're right," said Luke, inwardly reeling under the blow, forced at last to confront the truth. "Now that I'm here – seeing where you live, where you come from – I realise there's precious little I do know about you."

"Nor me about you. You're older than me for a start. You could be married for all I know – despite your apparent independence."

"Divorced, actually – about a year ago now."

"There, you see? My mother would never accept you. Such a fervent Catholic – know what I'm saying?"

"And you?"

"Not so fervent, I'm afraid. I've yet to decide about religion. In fact, I've yet to decide about a lot of things right now. Any kids?"

"No, never managed. It's probably that, more than anything, which caused my wife and I to split. I wanted them: she didn't. Simple as that, really. I had my career: she had hers. Can't blame her for that. She's a paediatrician, by the way – so in one sense, of course, she has lots of children. Not long after, Rebecca – that's her name – started looking further up the career ladder instead. A job came along miles away from where we lived and my practice, and we decided to call it quits. Got to admit, though, it's the best thing that's happened to me for ages. Feel like I'm living again. Wouldn't have met you, for example, otherwise. And trust me, even though it now seems we can only be friends, I don't regret it for a moment."

"You're very kind. Strange how we met, wasn't it? Your being headhunted like that."

"What do you mean 'headhunted'?"

"Sorry – of course, you probably weren't aware." Here Tara hesitated. "I don't really know how to tell you this, but our meeting at that party wasn't quite as much by chance as you probably thought."

"Are you saying it was some kind of set-up?"

"I was asked to go talk to you, then let slip the bit about the job. Dan Forsbrook – he brought me along, if you remember – had heard you were a doctor looking for a job abroad. Told me he'd be interested to interview you, that's all. But hey, don't look so deflated; if you want to know the truth, I was really glad he asked me. Trust me, it was no hardship – in fact, the evening took a distinct turn for the better after that. Had a great time, thanks to you."

"So gracious of you. I won't say this hasn't come as something of a shock; it has. And there I was, foolishly harbouring some sort of vain belief in love at first sight and all that crap. But, joking aside, what concerns me a little more just at the moment is how Dan Forsbrook got to know about my intentions. I take it, it had to have been my brother."

Luke left the house half an hour later entrenched in a trough of stolid resignation, well hidden, he hoped, behind the smile he'd kept for their goodbye. They would remain friends and 'keep in touch' – whatever, in practical terms, that might amount to. Beyond that, he was forced to accept there was no more. Just the memories of the beautiful young woman he had met at his family home; memories that even now were tarnished by the basic deceit behind their first coming together.

He walked out of the gate, turned once, waved, and headed off to where his car was parked a little way down the road. A door closed distantly behind him. He relaxed a little, sensing he was no longer on show; relieved in a curious way that he at least knew precisely where he stood.

The man who appeared before him, he recognised from earlier. His face still had that worried look, distorted intermittently by the gum he was now chewing, but there was more to it this time. The man stepped forward, effectively barring his way to the car.

"Now you take my advice, Douchebag, and just leave Tara alone. You know what I'm saying here? I don't know who the hell you are, but you've caused her nothing but upset. If I ever find out what it is you've done to her, or I ever see you bothering her again, trust me, I'll..."

Luke wasn't quite in the mood for this. He'd had enough to deal with having just seen Tara. What he needed just then was some kind of snappy reply; short and to the point. There were, no doubt, many to choose from.

"Go fuck yourself," he said almost at once, not fully aware till he'd said it just what anger dwelt within him. It clearly wasn't quite the optimal approach, certainly not the most tactful. The man's face contorted and he came flying towards him, his right arm swinging.

Blocking the punch was simple; it was the simultaneous planting of his knee neatly in the man's groin that proved slightly more taxing. Luke managed it somehow, nonetheless. Hugh Gotley sank to the ground, a startled expression on his face. Luke stepped over him, got in the car and drove off.

As he looked in his rear-view mirror – the one he'd earlier smiled into so optimistically – he could see the man still curled up writhing on the sidewalk.

Putting swiftly aside any feelings of guilt he might have – which, at that time, were surprisingly few – Luke's mind gave way to other thoughts. A new plan for his vacation was emerging. He would stay with Marie another day or two, chew the fat, see the sights then move on. Much as he loved New York – its brashness and grandiosity, and the people, of course – there was someone else it occurred to him he might look in on before heading back to ship. She had proffered her hospitality down there in North Carolina. He hoped it might come also with a goodly helping of her very own brand of worldly wisdom. She was eighty-seven years old and hopefully still going strong. He'd met her soon after first joining ship. Her name was Eunice Charlton.

Another thought struck him as he drove along Shore Parkway, the Verrazano Narrows Bridge stretching away to the west as he passed it. A question from earlier reformed in his mind; a question he pondered over for the rest of his journey back to Marie's. Why had his brother Martin been so helpful in getting him the job on ship? Why, in other words, had he been so keen to get him out of the way?

V

"Hi – yes, I'm calling to enquire about a friend of mine, Marianne Carter. She was on Edgward, but I believe she's recently been assigned to Gateway. I called from London a

332

couple of weeks back and was told she was on sick leave and unavailable to speak to me. Two nights ago, I checked again, having returned to the US, and was informed you were unable to trace her. Now I've been told she's no longer at Aberdeen. So, tell me, just what the hell's going on here?"

"Who is that speaking, please?"

"My name's Charlotte Walters."

"Well, Ms Walters, your friend has unfortunately been suffering with a kind of stress syndrome we sometimes see here among the trainees. I understand she went home to recuperate and think about her future..."

Tara put the phone down angrily. Something about this just wasn't right. What was really going on down there at the Proving Ground?

What she really needed was to see Marianne face-to-face to find out.

With Luke gone, Tara Scott had been left to consider a number of things that night. Besides Marianne, there was her own predicament too. She had thought about it a lot already since her return home. She had re-lived in her mind the events of that afternoon in Caracas; thought about her companion that day, and, in particular, what she'd suspected after visiting his cabin to check whether he'd managed to get back to the ship prior to sailing.

It was Luke who had first opened her eyes to the possibility. It was he who had told her of the way this man had ordered the cab specifically for the Medina Café. But it was what she had found – quite by chance later that afternoon – looking through what remained of his personal effects, that had virtually confirmed it in her mind. The man she had known then as Paul Curtis had indeed been a party to what, quite disgustingly, she'd been made to endure that afternoon.

Tara went over to the top drawer of her bedside table and took out an envelope and the heavily folded letter inside. She had spotted it poking out from under his bed that day as she had quickly searched his cabin for some hint of a clue.

It was not a letter addressed to Paul Curtis. In fact, it bore someone else's name completely. And, interestingly enough, a Washington DC address.

There were too many questions that needed answering; too many times that she'd felt overcome by recent events; too many times she had been forced to play victim.

First, there was Aberdeen. Now, there was this.

Tara Scott came to a decision.

It was time she finally took back control of her life.

PART 5

OWED TO A TOAD

Chapter 29

I

From where he stood just then, Delgardo Santos Estremosa could sense that dark forces indeed had somehow played their part in the events of the past week. How else could all he had spent his entire life building up be so swiftly and successfully undermined?

It had all begun with the raid. Little warning, he'd been told. Enough only for those on site to cut and run. Consolation of sorts, perhaps, that they'd run quickly enough; or most at least. Those that hadn't, killed or incarcerated. Those incarcerated, grimly holding their tongues in the certain knowledge that he, personally, would see to it they were ripped out if they didn't. Not now, perhaps, but sometime. And so much that day had been lost – equipment, and his largest stockpiles of product to date, destroyed in one fell swoop; a bitter pill to swallow.

But something in particular about this raid alarmed him – and not just the vast damage to his operation. There had been other raids in the past, sure enough. Each time, though, he had somehow managed to read the signs early, sensed the very heat of pursuit, and acted almost teasingly to thwart them. Always in the past he had slipped away, long before they had closed in – then stood back laughing, setting up quickly once again in the vast rainforest elsewhere. He,

Delgardo Estremosa, once again had been ahead of the game and they knew it.

But now things were different. Something was very much amiss: his trusty network had failed him. A cog had worked loose in his machine and the whole operation – once so smooth – was now well and truly out of sync. Worse still, he was on the run, and in a poor position even to assess the damage, never mind fix it.

If he was honest, he had been aware of the tide of change for some time. Close aides had warned him, though he'd been slow to listen. Now, it seemed, he was paying the price. He was being squeezed from virtually every angle, though his pride refused him to accept it. His territory was now under threat; mainly from a bunch of ambitious and impatient upstarts out to make a name for themselves. Some had worked for him in the past; a few having practically learnt at his knee. There were those too he rather feared had gained insights into his weaknesses, both operative and personal. And such knowledge was potential power, no matter how one chose to look at it.

Then there were the other forces acting against him – the Special Police and the DEA. It was almost certainly both of these in liaison that had carried out the successful raid. But from where had they got their information? And how far did they intend to take their campaign against him?

Perhaps he had got too soft in his old age. Perhaps now was the time for a fight back.

There were certain problems, though. Not only were his equipment and huge stocks of product no longer part of the equation, but a large cache of arms also. Without them, he was more vulnerable than ever; ripe, in fact, for takeover. Had somebody sensed this might be the case, prior to tipping off the authorities – leading ultimately to the raid?

It was clear to him he needed to somehow shore-up his position – not broadcast his misfortune and invite opportunists in. He still had an inner circle he could trust. What he really had to do was keep his head down for a while and get a fresh and sizeable batch of weapons as soon as possible. He had a contact in Nicaragua he could use – someone who could easily and discreetly satisfy his arms requirements. It would be worth making contact as soon as he could.

Money would be handy, too – his own, preferably, untraceable by the accountants of the Cartel and all their prying questions. No, this was a problem he had to deal with himself; a problem his pride told him he must see through on his own. Money, though, of this kind – in the sort of amounts he needed – would not be so easy to come by.

It was then he remembered the man called Forsbrook and his failure to succeed in what they had secretly agreed between them for a price. It was a price, he recalled, roughly similar in amount to the sum that he estimated for his most immediate requirements.

Perhaps it was now time to call in the loan.

II

Dan Forsbrook's apartment on the northern outskirts of DC had tended, over the years, to serve more as a repository for his personal effects than any true home. Even so, on those rare and fleeting occasions he called on it to act as such, he felt curiously safe and at ease there. No one asked him questions, for, in truth, no one really cared. It was that kind of neighbourhood. The apartment was known to few and that was the way he liked it. And those he did speak to when there, knew him by a different name entirely.

It was, therefore, with considerable amazement that following morning that Dan Forsbrook opened his apartment door and found himself greeted by someone who clearly did know of him. Not only that, but the man in question had a gun. His invitation in followed quickly on once this point had been established.

When the man departed barely ten minutes later, Dan was left in no doubt exactly how the land lay. The message was clear: following on from his earlier warning, Delgardo now wished to see him. Not only that, but – accepting his failure in the assignment he had personally given him – the Colombian also wanted his money back.

Dan tried to set aside his immediate shock at the prospect. It could, of course, have been far worse. The messenger had made no threats, nor any mention of retaliation, just Delgardo's desire for the cash. Could it be, it had been accepted just how hard he had tried? If not, he would try to explain when he saw him there in Cartagena in six days' time. The other problem was the money. Of that, virtually nothing remained.

Dan found himself suddenly close to panic. How the hell could he raise such an amount in so short a time? And the messenger had been clear enough on that point – Delgardo wanted every last cent of it returned.

Just then, Dan remembered the meeting he had planned for the night after next – Thursday. He was due a payout then – three hundred grand or so, if the merchandise was up to par with previous stuff he'd supplied. And he had little reason to think it wouldn't be. Eastern Promise, thank God, had started coming through with the goods once more.

But his dilemma was clear enough. How could he turn three hundred thousand dollars into a cool, round million – with only four days after he was paid to do it?

Dan pondered this question for a while when a thought suddenly struck him. What if Jamieson finally backed down – would Delgardo then call off the heat? So far, though, it was clear his boss had hardly budged an inch. Bookings were on hold, but that was all. He'd been too generous with his deadline; that was the problem. Or perhaps the asshole really couldn't care less about his niece and that video?

He had seen what had been made that day in Caracas – not that he was there personally to advise. Professional quality it wasn't, but it should have been enough. Enough to show that spoilt little bitch suffering; enough humiliation surely to force any doting uncle to toe the line? Perhaps he'd totally underestimated Ed Jamieson. There were things about the man he couldn't explain at all. Why, for example, this obsession all along with a simple change of itinerary? Why was the man prepared to risk so much? What the hell was behind it all?

It came to Dan as he mulled over these questions that he had only one further trick left up his sleeve. It wasn't much, but there was just the chance it might finally swing it for him; bring the reality of that video threat home to Jamieson just a little more graphically.

As things stood right now, he had very little choice but to try.

"Could you put me through to Ed Jamieson, please? Tell him it's Jack Buchanan."

There was a pause as the connection was made.

"Ed, that guy in the film with your niece – we've identified him at last. Name's Brad Earlham and – wait for it – he's a porn star. Lives down here in DC where I am at the moment, and is known vaguely to one of my contacts in the City Police Department. He doesn't know we're on to him yet, but he pretty soon will. We're going in to bust his ass tonight and squeeze the little shit till he sings. Someone else must be behind it all, and I want to know who."

"Listen to me, Hugh – what I'm saying here is Tara's been going out a lot on her own lately and won't say where. Matter of fact, she's being kind of secretive all round. First, Sunday night, then all of yesterday. Didn't get back till nearly midnight. Now she's announced she's off again this afternoon and might – only might, mind you – manage to make it back tonight. I don't like it, Hugh. Frankly, I'm getting real worried about her. And, you know something? – I kind of hoped you might be too."

"Oh, I am, Kathleen – you got to believe me. But what can I seriously do? If she won't talk to you about it, there isn't a chance in hell she'll discuss it with me."

"But where's she going each of these times? You tell me that. I've been checking out the mileage on her car in between trips, and I tell you she's doing some distances, believe me. You know, I'm at my wits' end. She's been so different since she's been back – at times, almost like a stranger. Then, that man round here pestering her the other day. Say, you don't think it's him she's going to see, do you, Hugh?"

"Sure hope not," he said at last, rather weakly.

"Well, what you going to do about it?"

"What can I do?"

"You could always follow her and find out for sure."

"But I can't just up and leave like that, you know. You said yourself she might be gone overnight, and some distance away, too. What about the store? It won't run itself."

"Hugh, answer me this: do you really want to win Tara back?"

"Of course I do, Kathleen."

"Well, how can I put this to you simply? Ah yeah, that's it: screw the frigging store, Hugh. Get off your ass and find out what's going on with my daughter."

III

It was after nine that evening when Tara's car eventually pulled up opposite the tired-looking Georgetown brownstone there in DC. She carefully checked the contents of her bag, slung it over her shoulder and crossed the road. As she did so, the man following her – now almost as tired as that brownstone from his journey – parked up a discreet distance behind and watched. It was dark now and he noted, carefully from where he sat, the precise building she entered. Why she was there he had no idea. And what his next move should be, he had little clue either.

He would give her ten minutes to return then maybe investigate. Ten minutes passed and he gave her five more. Hugh Gotley, so far from home and his store, felt curiously lost as he sat there. He began wondering what had possessed him to come in the first place. He soon recalled Mrs Scott's entreaty earlier, and, in particular, its tone. It was perhaps this alone that finally stirred him into action.

A dim light illuminated the hallway as he went in. He strained his ears to listen, first outside one door then another – on one floor then the next. Voices of various resonances were audible as he stood there. None, he felt sure, was that of Tara; and no voice, as far as he could tell, that of her weekend visitor to Sheepshead Bay.

Arriving eventually outside apartment five on the second floor, Hugh noticed the door slightly ajar. Surely, then, this had to be the place? If so, what should he do now?

It was the timbre of her voice that determined it, not merely the content of her speech. The yell was deep, with a sharpness and authority he initially didn't recognise. Then, when the other voice replied, male and threatening, he knew he had to act immediately. If he wasn't mistaken, Tara was in some kind of trouble.

He could feel the urgency of the moment sweep over him as he eased the door open and quietly stepped in. The sight that greeted him left him almost totally speechless. There, over to one side of the room, stood Tara. On the other side knelt a man. His hands were handcuffed behind him and Tara was pointing a gun directly at his head. There, just as calmly as you please.

"Hi there, Hugh," she said, nodding briefly in his direction. "Had a feeling that was you behind me on the road."

"What the hell you doing, Tara?! Who is this guy, and where on earth did you get that gun?"

"I'm afraid I can only manage to answer one of your points at a time. Firstly, I've been asking this asshole some questions. Secondly, he's a complete sleazebag I met on the ship, and thirdly, it's none of your goddam business where I got the gun. Suffice it to say, Hugh, it has proved very useful in persuading him to talk. In fact, I think we've had enough answers for one day. I take it my mother insisted you follow?"

"Yeah, she did. So, what you going to do now?" Hugh spoke nervously. "Nothing too stupid, I hope."

"You're right: nothing too stupid. Don't worry, Hugh, I've been well trained with guns: I only hit what I plan to. Now, leave us, will you? Go wait down by your car – I'll come and find you in a few minutes."

Hugh could not imagine what was going on up there as he stood in a state of mild trance, looking up at the window of the apartment he'd just left. The light was still on, though subdued now behind the freshly closed drapes. Five minutes later, Tara appeared. She seemed somehow different – her mood lighter, a look of quiet triumph on her face.

"Good of you to come, Hugh – and uncharacteristically brave, if I might say so, to have followed me like this. May I perhaps advise a certain caution in these matters in future. You never know just what kind of person you might run into."

She smirked as she said this, stowing her bag deftly in the trunk. "First stop, by the way, is a motel for the night. We can talk once we're there."

"You're kidding me, Tara, right? Please say that's just some stupid joke." There was incredulity mixed with a kind of blind panic in his voice, as though he really couldn't handle hearing this. "None of that ever really happened to you, did it? Because you know if it did, I'm going to..." Whatever it was Hugh was going to do remained unclear as his voice trailed away into silence. "...I'm going to throw up," he said at last.

"Calm down, Hugh. It happened alright, just like I said. No more; no less. I wasn't badly hurt – and for that, perhaps, I've got to be grateful. But it doesn't end here – not yet. I need a few more answers and, with luck, I might just get them. Now, let's relax a little. Say, did I tell you how proud I was of you back there? Sometimes, Hugh, you know, you kind of surprise me."

He could count the nights they'd ever spent alone like this on the fingers of one hand. Though they'd had several years together as a couple, many of these were when Tara was still quite young and at high school – and such opportunities had seldom arisen. Not that he would have dared take advantage in any case: his faith wouldn't allow it and, besides, he respected her too much. And if he'd got any wild ideas about pre-nuptial bliss, he was sure Tara's mother would have quickly put him straight. He was afraid, too, to offend, quelling the powerful forces inside him with regular prayer and a discipline even Jesus Christ himself would have been proud of.

Now all this had happened and changed things entirely. Could he ever think of her in the same way again? It was not her fault, granted, but that itself couldn't stop the way he felt. She had to bear some responsibility though – all this travelling of hers, moving in such circles; putting herself in a position of such vulnerability. Then there was how she'd acted since returning home. He, like her mother, hardly knew her now. Then the gun, tonight – God Almighty, the gun; where was it now? And her language too, and the way she'd looked so cool and heartless when he'd walked in on her. And what in God's name had she done back there after asking him to leave?

These and a host of other thoughts coursed through Hugh's mind as he lay there beside her; her body relaxed, gently sleeping, her head on his chest. Something about the way she had nuzzled up to him as they'd settled for the night was different too. Coquettish almost, teasing him silently for his reticence, his staidness, his values. Values he believed she too, once shared. Goading him gently – towards what? Some act of sexual gratification, perhaps? An act of impulse divorced from love? What kind of high was this she was on? And did he really know this woman at all any more?

"I take it you're planning to stay on down here?" he said over breakfast the following morning.

"Yeah, a little longer, I think," said Tara, looking up.

"I'm going back. I'll tell your mother I lost you along the way. You can tell her what you like when you see her next."

He didn't relish the deceit, particularly after all Mrs Scott had done for him over the years. She was worth more than that. It was just the simplest way all round.

IV

Ed Jamieson arrived early for work that Wednesday morning, well in time for the business meeting later. He, too, was in something of a quandary. Time was ticking on since the video threat had first been made known to him. Jack Buchanan's news of yesterday had been welcome as a sign they were at last on the right track, but something else about it alarmed him even more. Okay, the guy with the ginormous dick was a porn star – his credentials, in a way, spoke for themselves. But, surely, the implications of this ran deeper? If the video had been produced by people in that kind of business, then their threat of distribution had to be very real and taken seriously. Could he and Jack, and a couple of guys from the Washington DC Police Department – whatever their level of involvement under Jack's direction – really catch the true culprits before the damage was done? God, how he hoped so.

His only real comfort was what Jack had told him when the threat first came. If whoever it was, was only interested in the itinerary of the Venus Prince, actually carrying out the threat would serve no useful purpose at all in getting them what it was they wanted. And he still couldn't imagine why anyone could want that so very desperately.

The second he entered his office he saw it. It was there on the wall opposite, and unobtrusive it was not. It was designed to shock, and shock him it did. Almost three feet by two, and featuring perhaps the most degrading shot of the entire video in all its close-up glory, the poster hung there openly for him

– and anyone else who just happened to come in – to see. Under the picture were the words:

**OPENING SOON AT A THEATER NEAR YOU.
DO NOT DELAY.**

As he stood gazing in disbelief, the phone on his desk began to ring. He snatched it up angrily. It was Rachel, his secretary.

"Thought I'd better warn you, Mr Jamieson, your sister, Mrs Scott, is on her way down right now. I tried to tell her you were busy this morning, but she just wouldn't take no for an…"

"Shit Al-fucking-mighty – you're kidding me!!" cried Ed, aghast, throwing the phone down and snatching wildly at the poster on the wall.

She left twenty minutes later, leaving him in no doubt at all as to how she felt. Whether she had truly been coming to the city to shop that day as she'd said, or made the trip especially to see him, he couldn't be sure. Although she still clearly lacked any clue as to what lay behind it, her concern over Tara was growing. The latest thing, apparently, was her going off for the night alone without saying where. As yet, she still hadn't returned.

Ed tried to sympathise and make it sound convincing. It was difficult, though, as all the time he found himself thinking about that screwed-up poster in his drawer and the very real dilemma he now faced.

This was still on his mind after that morning's meeting when Jack Buchanan got through to him.

"What you got, Jack?" he asked with some urgency.

"That guy Earlham – we picked him up okay, and he's squealing like a pig. Turns out he was working for some local porn distributor, name of Wayne Gibson. Unfortunately, that's all he could really give us. This fellow Gibson, by the way, is known to the Department here, though they've never really managed to pin much on him."

"What you planning to do now, Jack – have him taken in for questioning?"

"No, we need a good deal more evidence first. We're intending to stake out his place tomorrow – get in and bug it first, if we can, while he's out – then monitor things for a day or so. I know time is tight, Ed, but we've got to make sure any charges against him stick. Besides, there's obviously someone else he's acting for – someone with some connection to Venus Cruise Lines. And that's what we've ultimately got to find out."

"You're dead right," agreed Ed. "You know, I think I might even come down and join you guys – I can barely concentrate on anything else here right now. By the way, this porn star – did you end up having to use force on the filthy scumbag to get him to talk?"

"Afraid not – though I know how you feel, Ed. Strangely enough, turns out someone else – God knows who – seemed to have got there first. Someone, presumably, also with a gripe or two against him. No, Ed, we found the guy particularly shaken up, I'd say. Not only was he handcuffed and unable to move, but he had a fucking great pepperoni sausage sticking halfway down his gullet. Strange thing is, even after all that, the guy just outright refused to tell us who did it."

"Jeez, Jack, you're kidding me; kinda poetic, though, wouldn't you say?"

Chapter 30

I

Ed Jamieson stared once more at the date mark on the letter that had arrived at his home early that next morning. It had been posted on Sat 29th – it was now Thursday 3rd April. Not bad considering it had come all the way from one of the remotest regions of Ireland. He didn't re-read it just then, but recalled the general sentiments expressed by various of his family members from back home. Folk he'd hardly seen face-to-face in the last ten years, extending the hand of friendship so unwaveringly across the miles.

However, something in the content of the letter left him uneasy. It was that bit about Tara who had visited them not so long back while over in England. They'd been struck by what a fine young woman she had turned into, intelligent and beautiful – a credit both to her mother and to him too, obviously doing all he could to support her at this time in her life. But was he really? Was that truly what was happening? What might they think of him were they ever to discover the truth? He remembered then something Jack had said to him only a few days before. Family – Tara was family. And that was special. In that instant, he understood precisely what Jack had meant. Unfortunately, it served only to intensify his dilemma.

The phone call that followed didn't exactly help either. He took the details down feeling a little stunned, aware almost immediately afterwards there was perhaps more he should have asked before replying, almost mechanically, that he just wasn't interested. Something about it suddenly occurred to him, and he felt he needed to discuss it with Jack. He got through straight away to his mobile.

"Jack – how you doing? Listen, I don't know if there's any way it could be related, but I've just had a call from a group of financiers representing the APC Corporation. Seems they're interested in acquiring the entire cruise side of my company, and prepared to offer a good price too."

"APC – who are APC? Do you know them?"

"No idea, Jack. Never heard of them before. I've been thinking about it since, though. It's just struck me there could be some link between this approach and those threats I've been receiving. Say, for example, they came from someone aligned to this company; they could have been intended to wear me down to the point I might just welcome a takeover."

"Hmm," said Jack, "you're right – we'd better look into it."

Ed headed home early that afternoon. He needed to get some things together in preparation for his trip to Washington and the stake-out that night. He was a little in two minds as to whether to bother going, fairly certain he was unlikely to make any major difference by being there. The alternative, however, was to do precisely nothing – and that was even worse. The video release deadline, after all, was getting closer by the day.

When Jack phoned through with the news soon after, the final decision to go was more or less made for him.

"Ed, get ready for this. It wasn't easy, but my contacts have checked it through thoroughly. The man behind APC Corporation, it turns out, is none other than your old friend George Mitchell."

Ed Jamieson sat looking at the phone long after his conversation with Jack Buchanan had ended. An anger, ignited long ago when this man Mitchell had first stolen Sophia from him, now erupted in a volcanic rage. There was something he now knew he had to do before he left to join Jack that evening. He had held back up till now, giving Mitchell nothing more than simply the warning.

Now it was time for Sophia to discover the truth of his infidelity.

II

If Wayne Gibson had sensed there were three men set up across the way in the house opposite that evening, he didn't show it. He had plans for that night – an important meeting, in fact – and such was his preoccupation, he saw little reason to bother with such niceties as the early closing of the window blinds. Had he witnessed the fleeting glint of the telescope trained on his every movement in that side of the house, however, it is likely he might have viewed things differently.

Gibson had resided for almost four years now in this most respectable of Washington neighbourhoods. It had always provided the best form of cover, he believed – life among the young, equally affluent professional classes. As long as he fitted in, with his Porsche, slick suits and attaché case, who would seriously ever guess the truth?

Jack Buchanan, Charlie Vincente – his vice-squad colleague – and a recently arrived and still very shaken Ed Jamieson, were preparing themselves for a slow waiting game. Ed, who was not used to such things, found greatest difficulty settling in. Traffic movement through the wide, tree-lined roadway was monitored as well as possible. No cars, however, showed the slightest inclination to turn into the driveway of the large and impressive ante bellum house opposite. What Jack and Charlie were waiting for most of all was the opportunity – should Gibson leave – to break in and bug the place. Little, it seemed, could be achieved in terms of establishing hard evidence until this was successfully carried out.

They didn't have long to wait. Less than an hour later, Wayne Gibson could be seen leaving the house by its side door, and almost before any of them had a chance to react, the electric gates opened and a dark Porsche emerged onto the road.

Tailing Gibson, should he leave, had never seriously been part of the plan. There was the limited size of task force available, for one thing. However, what the onlookers noticed next caused a rapid re-evaluation of the whole question of pursuit.

As the Porsche began slowly gathering speed, another car, parked inconspicuously at the roadside further along from the house, suddenly started up and began to follow. At the very instant it passed by in front of him and he got a better view of the driver, something suddenly registered in Jack Buchanan's brain.

"Quick, Ed, take a look. See who's driving that car?"

"Oh my God," said Ed, hardly believing his eyes, "it's Tara."

For a man of his girth and general mobility, Ed did well getting down to his own car within the minute. As Jack and Charlie prepared for a quiet break-in over the road, Ed set off in pursuit. Something he'd only vaguely suspected up till now seemed more or less confirmed: it was Tara herself who had visited the apartment of Brad Earlham two nights before with such dramatic effect. How much had she managed to find out so far? And what was her intention with this guy Gibson?

Ed continued on at speed, intent on first catching her up, then – if possible – keeping her car within sight at all times. Something told him she could be in danger.

Wayne Gibson was making good time, unaware of the stir his leaving had caused. He had the money in his bag; he only hoped the man he was due to meet would have merchandise of a quality worth buying. His customers were getting impatient now: there had been a dearth of good material for some months. Hopefully, this guy – one of his most seasoned contacts – would be in a position to help change all that.

Ed Jamieson was doing his best. Problem was he really wasn't used to this kind of thing. He'd seen it done on the big screen, sure – but it was different somehow in real life. The road was busy and it was dark now, and the monochrome vista played heartless tricks on his aging eyes.

All might well have been fine if it hadn't been for those stop lights. He would have chanced running through them himself. It was just unfortunate he wasn't in a position to persuade the three other cars ahead of him to take any such similar gamble. All he could do was sit, watch and curse, as Tara's car disappeared out of view into a bend in the road up ahead.

He knew pretty well he'd lost her then. Three frantic minutes later, it was all but confirmed. All he could hope was that she wasn't carrying the gun Earlham had reported his assailant having, the night he'd been visited in his apartment.

The man Wayne Gibson was meeting that night nodded to him from afar, as he stood there waiting in the wide hotel lobby. Only when the elevator doors closed on them and they had begun their ascent did either chance normal pleasantries. Room 814, with its large-screen TV and VCR, awaited – essential equipment for the work in hand. An hour and a half later, a deal was struck and three hundred and twenty-five thousand dollars changed hands.

In keeping with his strict, though slightly desperate, timetable for expansion of assets, an extremely relieved Dan Forsbrook jumped into a cab and set off for the nearest casino.

Meanwhile, a frustrated Ed Jamieson, back at the stake-out, was now drawing what consolation he could from what the others had achieved in his absence. The house opposite had been bugged and, so far, at least, one incoming message on the answerphone had been monitored. What appeared to excite Jack and Charlie more than anything, though, was what they'd managed to sneak a look at whilst they'd been nosing around.

"Basement over there's crawling with the stuff, Ed: magazines and photographs, and an entire area stacked high with video cassettes. We daren't disturb things too much – just snatched what we hoped might be some kind of representative sample."

"Something tells me we could be onto something far bigger than we first thought," said Charlie, turning briefly round from his vantage point at the window. "A fair number of kids in those pictures, as you can see. Makes me want to get in there and tear the fucking place apart; and that scumbag, Gibson, too."

"I know exactly how you feel," said Jack. "It's no good, though, Charlie – we've got to stay cool. Got to somehow build up a profile of this guy, and, in particular, who he might have dealings with."

"And what the hell the connection is with Venus Cruise Lines," chipped in Ed.

The deadline for the video release featuring Tara, he was aware, was now less than four days away.

The night proved spectacularly unproductive. To Charlie and Jack, this came as no great surprise. To Ed Jamieson, it served only to bring home how thoroughly ill-prepared he was for this kind of thing at his time of life. By seven-thirty next morning, the desire for decent food, a shower and sleep proved overwhelming. By eight, he had made his excuses and left. Half an hour later still, he had checked into the nearest reasonable motel and was sitting down to a full-scale breakfast. He would return later to monitor the progress of the professionals in the case.

That night had not been overly bounteous as far as Dan Forsbrook was concerned either. Try as he would, any progress he managed at any one point at the roulette wheel was very soon overtaken by a loss. When he eventually called it quits at 4.30 am, he was more or less in the same position as when he'd started out. He still needed over $600,000 more to satisfy Delgardo when they rendezvoused that Sunday night. Perhaps, after some rest, he'd be ready to continue his quest at the private afternoon session he'd got himself invited to.

The pickings there, he knew, promised to be good.

III

When Tara Scott arrived back at her home in Saracen Drive, Sheepshead Bay, at noon that day, her mother was thankfully out. Though she loved her dearly and tried to appreciate all that she had done in singlehandedly bringing her up, there were limits to how much of her fussing she could take. She knew roughly the tone her questions would take when eventually she did return. The problem was, few answers she could offer might comfort her – and fewer still of those would be honest.

Over on the sideboard, the snapshot beckoned. Why at this particular moment in time, she really didn't know. It hardly stood out, especially from that distance. Its frame was tarnished and dull, the image small and long-faded. It had resided there beside the silver crucifix, derided then ignored, as far back as she could remember. Whatever reason her mother might have had for placing it there originally, its sole function these days seemed more related to emphasising the lot of the Selfless One: the parent who hadn't deserted them in their hour of need, all those years ago.

Tara took the small photograph out of its frame and held it in her hand. She guessed it was a 1960's Coney Island backdrop, and saw that he was smiling – a fact she'd never really noticed before. He was handsome, too, in a dark devil-may-care kind of way; this man, Johnny Scott, her father. And how come she'd only just noticed that? Could it be she was only now allowing herself to appreciate such things in him – outgrowing the strictly negative conditioning of her formative years? Perhaps, in other words, that she might at last be developing a mind of her own?

There was so much she wanted to understand. So much about him had been lost to her; irretrievable now with his passing. How she wished she'd known him. Though, as she gazed on, until the image blurred with the very intensity of looking, Tara knew instinctively that somehow, he was there inside her. And that, just then, was enough. Tears released as she blinked – a long overdue blink – and she let them run as she kissed the smiling image and slipped it into the warm breast pocket of her blouse.

"Well, you've sure gone and done it now, haven't you?" said Mrs Scott later that same afternoon. Tara had braved the initial skirmish on her return, but this, now, was a different tack. She pointedly said nothing, but knew this itself would be no deterrent to her mother in full flow.

"I've just seen Hugh with that girl, Gloria Wheatley, and, I've got to admit it, they do seem to be enjoying each other's company. Oh sure, don't get me wrong: she's a nice-enough young woman alright – sings in the choir and all – but Hugh is your boyfriend, Tara. Always has been. You'll lose him for good if you don't do something about it soon."

"Thanks for letting me know, Mom," replied Tara solemnly.

And for a while, Mrs Scott began to think there might just be hope after all.

At what stage prudence began to desert him that afternoon, Dan Forsbrook was unable to tell. Certainly, he had started out with the best of intentions. The seriousness of failure was self-evident; he needed no reminding. But any equation which attempted to predict the move the wisest of gamblers might make in any given situation, ignored one rather crucial variable: the very need to run risk. Ask Dan Forsbrook about it in virtually any other environment you might find him, and he'd call you crazy. Put him in front of a roulette wheel and it all too soon became clear: the real thrill for Dan Forsbrook came very soon after all logic had flown out of the window.

And once things began to go wrong, he was firmly locked into his own undoing.

On reflection, things had gone pretty slowly that day for Charlie and Jack as they watched and listened from the house opposite. Gibson was in – had been since returning in the early hours of that morning – but it wasn't till 3.30 that afternoon they got wind of the outgoing call on his phone. Jack set the recorder and they both listened in. What wasn't clear, though, was who exactly he'd got through to.

"You mean they took him in for questioning the night before last?"

"That's right, Wayne. You think he might talk?"

"No, he won't talk – not if he knows what's good for him."

"Still, best lie low for a while, eh? No point taking chances."

"You're probably right. Thanks for letting me know. Appreciate that."

"Sounds like we may have to pick this guy Gibson up sooner than we planned," said Charlie to Jack as Gibson put the phone down.

"Guess you're right. Pity we haven't been able to learn more, though. Ed's not going to like it one little bit. If the guy holds out on us and won't talk then we're still none the wiser."

"I'll get straight on to Headquarters for some back up. If he leaves now, we want to know exactly where he's going so we can bust his ass right there, along with any other sleazebag he happens to be hanging out with."

The car pulled out of the drive less than fifteen minutes later. They watched as Gibson packed the two suitcases and three other bags hurriedly into the trunk, praying that the unmarked police cars assigned to the task would arrive in time to follow. Even as the grey Porsche gathered speed up the road, it was still not clear whether this had been achieved. No doubt, they'd get to hear soon enough.

It was with great disappointment all round that Jack Buchanan passed on the news to Ed Jamieson when he arrived.

"I'm afraid, Ed, that's how things stand at the moment. We're going in again for a closer look round when some of Charlie's other colleagues from the Vice Squad arrive. There's a ton of stuff to be collected; there are bound to be clues there somewhere."

"Trouble is, it might take weeks to go through all that video footage. And no guarantees they won't carry out their threat against me, anyway – even if it's just for the hell of it."

They were preparing to leave when the phone began to ring once more in the house opposite. Gibson's answerphone cut in, gave of its message, then beeped. The agitated voice, faced with the machine, sounded momentarily at a loss:

"If you're there, Wayne, pick up the phone. Okay then, listen, it's me. You've got to help. I need more money and I need it fast. Can't tell you how important this is, Wayne – believe me, my fucking life may depend on it. Call me on my cell phone – you know the number."

"My God!" cried a stunned Ed Jamieson, turning quickly to the others. He tried to speak again but no words came out.

"What is it, Ed?" asked Jack, looking over.

"That voice – I just don't believe it. Play it back to me Jack, quick."

"You think you know who it is?"

"I might well be wrong, but I could swear that was Dan Forsbrook – my Head of Operations. And, if so, what the fuck's he doing calling that filthy scumbag, asking for money?"

Chapter 31

Saturday April 5th 1997

I

When Luke arrived back in Montego Bay to rejoin the Venus Prince that Saturday morning, he was feeling more or less at ease with himself once again. This had not been true of many of his days since leaving New York. Away from the infectious buoyancy of Marie and her family, he had experienced a sudden plummeting of spirits – most noticeable when the Greyhound bus first left New York's southern limits behind.

They revived a little with the passage of time on the journey – a compressed time in that travelling capsule, first affronted, then repeatedly bombarded by thoughts of Tara and her ultimate rejection of him. What galled him most was not the fact that she didn't want a relationship, but that she had been so accurate and dispassionate in her assessment of what had so far happened between them.

What had he really expected from such a tenuous liaison? Thoughts of their being together had sustained him for all of his time at sea so far. Could he blithely let them die the natural death they craved – overcoming, among other things, his professional instinct for resuscitation? And what would replace them – the physical presence of Sandy? Perhaps that was what he needed right now. But would the purely physical be enough? They had so little in common, he felt sure – not that he'd really taken time to find out. Could it be that the same forces that had driven him to idealise Tara so irrationally in his mind, had conspired equally to push Sandy far out onto the sideline? Perhaps when he returned to ship, he might address that very issue: he would spend time getting to know her properly. At least, once he'd got the physical bit well and truly out of his system, anyway.

His stay with Eunice Charlton had sustained him still further. Proudly, she'd introduced him to her coterie of friends and they had talked of this and that, on into the small hours. He'd accompanied her on trips into the countryside there near Wilmington, and on two of the evenings – to the amusement of all – he'd partnered her at bridge. When he left, she smiled a wrinkled smile and waved. Luke knew he had found a friend for life; though, at her age, daren't speculate quite how long that might prove to be.

He saw Sandy leaving the ship as he arrived early that morning, waiting to board a taxi, looking cool and sexy in an understated, carefree way; pink tee-shirt and tan, her slim brown legs daring his eyes to linger.

He felt somehow differently about her now – now that he had allowed himself to, with Tara no longer a consideration. She smiled as he approached, holding his gaze until he was right there in front of her. Only then, as he moved closer still and briefly hugged her, did he detect the slightest change in her expression. There was surprise there, yes, and a tinge of awkwardness. Little more than he could expect though, bearing in mind the way he'd chosen to define so coldly the limits of their friendship prior to his leaving. There was clearly work to be done in wooing her back, but the signs were good, nonetheless; and God, she did feel good. Though she was off to the beach now, he would make up for lost time later.

Luke bumped into Rick Tucson in the hospital corridor soon after, in an even more upbeat mood than usual. "Hi, Luke. Glad I caught you. Thought I'd better let you know, I'm just in the process of making a move on Sandy. I take it that's okay with you?"

Luke nodded as amiably as he could manage, and walked on, thinking over this latest piece of intelligence. Rick had signalled his intent, but how might Sandy respond – especially now that he was back on the scene and showing fresh interest?

Luke got Martina's message only minutes after he'd entered his cabin. He listened in silence, his mind totally numbed by the news. Up in the radio room, he got through to his mother on the satellite phone with unexpected ease. He allowed his breathing to relax into a series of controlled, sighing expirations only after he had heard for certain his father was still alive. Apparently, though, it was a close call.

Within half an hour, Luke was ready to leave for the airport once more. He was still in a state of some bewilderment when Duane Dalton came over to him in the foyer and, in typical form, failed completely to read his mood.

"You heard about Rick and Sandy, then?"

"Yes, I did," said Luke flatly.

"Rick had this theory you weren't interested in her because she's too much of an airhead for a man of your educated tastes."

Luke thought this over but said nothing. Could there be something in Rick's analysis after all? She was no genius, admittedly...

"Which shows you just how deceptive looks can be. Would you believe that girl has a Master's degree in English and two volumes of poetry under her belt?"

"You're kidding me – Sandy? Who told you that?"

"I've seen them – they're in her cabin along with a whole bunch of other books she brought along. Let me see – there was Updike, someone called Saul somebody and..."

My God – a true soulmate after all, thought Luke, forgetting momentarily the grave news he'd only just received. He was struck by a sudden thought: perhaps Duane could give him some hint of Rick's progress to date.

Duane seemed surprised. "Oh, didn't he tell you, then? He's been shagging her senseless for most of the past week."

II

It was about midday British time when Helen Darius got Luke's call from the Venus Prince. It was not unexpected – she knew roughly the time he might arrive back on ship – but she was relieved, nonetheless. Now, at last, she had something more than merely vague to report when, periodically, her husband emerged from the background stupor into one of his more lucid moments. All being well, Luke would touch down just after eleven. By midnight, he should be home and the family, perhaps for the very last time, would be all together again at Wetherfield.

Not that she'd seen much of Martin in the past few days. His life seemed little put out by his father's recent decline. The impending Election was doubtless his excuse – though she had the feeling if it wasn't the Election, it would have been something else.

Then there was that business of the message to Luke's company. Was that a genuine mix-up, or had Martin purposely avoided sending it? She wouldn't put it past him – but, if so, what possible motive could there be?

This whole sad business had taken its toll. All who saw her told her as much. Her face was pale and drawn, her hair tidy but no more, and, in her eyes, a tortured look. Regular food and sleep had long since become a thing of the past – the way she knew it had to be just now. There would be time for all that later, now that the end was in sight.

Sitting with him there – his hand in hers, inert and bony, his breathing strained and harsh – she tried thinking back to happier times. She remembered all the years they had been together and how, there in Wetherfield, they had first met. She was nursing then – his father in those days – which accounted, no doubt, for her recent sense of déja-vu. But she preferred to think back now to the handsome young man who had wooed her, and who, throughout his life, had shown the very same dignity he was now displaying in death.

When she heard the sound of the front door opening, her mind made an irrational leap and she looked up half expecting to see Luke. The absurdity of this struck her only half a second after she realised it was in fact Martin who'd arrived.

His breeziness caught her on the hop; so, too, his sudden concern.

"Mother, I'm very worried about you, and I'm not going to take no for an answer. Luke will be back late tonight, as you know, and you really must get some sleep. I'm here now – I can sit with Father for a few hours while you go up to one of the other bedrooms for a lie down. Needless to say, I'll call you if I'm in any way worried."

Martin took up position dutifully by the bedside as she left the room. With the recession of her footsteps, he smiled to himself. His mother had fallen for it beautifully. All he needed now was for his father to remain as blissfully detached from the real world as he was just then.

He had read about the syringe-driver from the leaflet that accompanied it and about the Diamorphine it was programmed to deliver. The 10ml syringe, when full, would be set to last twenty-four hours. A brief manual override would allow the small bolus injection he required. He could switch the machine off for a while later, after achieving his aim, in order to rebalance the timing – so no questions would be asked when the hospice nurse eventually came to reset it.

His father was quieter now, his breathing less urgent, and Martin felt free at last to carry on. His was a fact-finding mission and the main focus of his search would, almost certainly, be right there in his parents' bedroom. He went first to the bedside drawers, starting with those on his father's side, and was rewarded almost at once. It was what he hoped he might find: the bundle of life assurance documents, in a total amount almost worth dying for.

What he really needed next was the Will itself. He knew his father kept a copy there; he had made it his business to know, ever since that latest amendment three to four months back. Clearly, his old man knew he was on his last legs even then. He found it eventually, poking out of its large brown envelope, hidden there amongst a bundle of old correspondence. He scanned it quickly at first then began reading its more long-winded jargon with considerably more care. There were few real surprises – an even split between Luke and himself after the bulk had understandably gone to his mother.

It was the difficulty in closing the drawer that first alerted him to it. The jarring noise alarmed him for a moment and he looked over to see if his father had stirred. The old man lay motionless, the bolus shot he'd given playing its part well. Something was definitely jamming the works and closer inspection revealed precisely what: the bulging white envelope addressed to his mother in her maiden name, c/o Wetherfield House, penned in a hand he did not recognise. The envelope had slightly yellowed with age, the ink faded and the handwriting ostentatiously looped as from some bygone time.

It was when he opened it, however, and idly read the contents through, that Martin Darius suddenly began to feel that all his Christmases might just have come at once. He glanced back at the Will. There was still time for some favourable last-minute changes.

III

Ellen Jamieson suspected long ago there was something bothering Ed. He'd been acting strangely and rather secretively now for some weeks. Sure, he had offered some explanation of his moods, and the odd correspondence he had, at intervals, been receiving – not to mention all those phone calls. Okay, so he was a busy man, and yes, someone in his position was bound to have a lot going on. But things, more recently, had set her wondering if this was indeed all there was to it.

Those secretive phone calls out, for example – like the one he was making now, locked away in his study; supposedly to this old friend of his, Jack Buchanan. And, more worryingly perhaps, the nights away that week – something about a small hotel in DC. It just didn't add up.

Their home life had developed an interrupted feel about it and she couldn't remember when they'd last made love. The friends she'd confided in hadn't exactly helped set her mind at ease either. As far as they were all concerned the signs were clear enough: her husband, Ed, must be having an affair.

Inside his study, Ed Jamieson's mind couldn't have been further from that which was worrying his wife. He still hadn't been able to get over the revelation of Dan Forsbrook's involvement. And what he'd just learnt too in a recent incoming call, sparked off fresh concern in his mind.

"Jack, sorry I couldn't get back to you sooner – had my sister Kathleen on the line. Seems my niece, Tara, turned up at home yesterday, stayed for a few hours, then, when Kathleen was out, took off with her bags and passport. Not just that, though. Early this morning, Kathleen answered the phone, hoping it might be Tara. She was greeted by a man's voice saying threateningly, something like: "Better stay alert, bitch – we're on to you." Then they hung up. She hasn't a clue what that's all about."

"Hmm, kinda worrying, eh? Could be Gibson, of course. We still don't know what happened after Tara followed him like that. Trouble is, whoever it is, we can't exactly warn her now either. Did Kathleen say anything else – you know, about what Tara's been up to these past few days?"

"She knows nothing. The only thing she did mention was that Tara had gotten some kind of letter, two days ago."

"What was it about, does she know?"

"Yes; after she'd gone, Kathleen sneaked a look at it. It confirmed that Tara had been selected as a special prosecution witness in some military court hearing down in Maryland in the next few weeks. Tara, needless to say, hadn't discussed anything about it. You can understand Kathleen's concerns."

"Sure can. By the way, Ed, word is Forsbrook, too, is on the move, by all accounts. Left late last night on an Avianca flight to Colombia. We've had someone make a check on all local airports."

"Colombia? You think he's intending to meet the ship next Tuesday?"

"That we don't know."

"Hell, Jack, you don't think Tara might have learnt about Forsbrook too, and gone after him, do you?"

"Well, to be honest, Ed, this assault has obviously affected her pretty badly. Could be she's intent on revenge. The question is, how much does she know of the true motives behind what happened to her – how, ultimately, it ties up with you and your company? Earlham himself knows nothing,

372

except that he was employed by Gibson. So, he couldn't have helped her very much."

"And what about Gibson? How much do you think he knows? Could be, of course, the whole thing was done simply as a favour to Forsbrook."

"Gibson, I regret to say, got clean away yesterday despite our attempts at pursuit. We'll get him in time, no doubt – there are bound to be plenty of clues among all that stuff back at his house. The news so far, Ed, is that we've found a box with nine copies of the tape of Tara's ordeal. The one you've got makes ten. Could well be that's all there is – though naturally, it's difficult to say. What we really need is the master copy – the original from Caracas. Of course, it's going to take some time to go through all the rest of the material and it's unlikely we'll get any immediate light thrown on Forsbrook's angle in all this; why, in a nutshell, your own Head of Operations should be so outrageously keen for the Venus Prince to avoid the switch of itineraries."

"Unless, of course, he's acting directly for Mitchell," said Ed. "A ruthless bastard if ever I met one. This takeover bid; our longstanding rivalry; Sophia – it all ties up as far as I'm concerned."

"You could be right. But one thing's pretty clear: you won't be able to pin anything on Mitchell without first getting hold of Forsbrook. Without his confession, it's possible we might never know the truth."

"I'm one jump ahead of you, Jack. That's why I'm going down there after him. If Tara has followed, she could be in grave danger. He's obviously more ruthless than I ever imagined."

"And, if you don't mind me saying, in your niece's present state of mind, he too, could be in some danger. But listen, Ed, we don't want a global fucking chase on our hands, okay? We've got to act smart and somehow lure him back to US soil so he can be picked up and questioned. Sure, your niece needs watching – if indeed she has followed him – and warning off before any confrontation can occur between them. I can do that, no problem. But for you to go shooting your mouth off at him would be totally counter-productive. As far as he's concerned, at this very moment, no one really knows of his involvement. Presuming he does board in Cartagena as we think, it would be far better for you to be there, having, say, joined the ship the day before and have him return with you to Head Office here on some pretext or other – all perfectly normal-like. We can have him picked up at the airport just as soon as you arrive."

"You think it'll be as simple as that?" asked Ed nervously. The reality of what was being asked of him had just hit home. It was clear he didn't really know this man Forsbrook at all any more.

Chapter 32

I

Little had prepared Luke for how he might feel that night at Wetherfield. He had experienced terminal cancer in many of his patients over the years, but to see his own father in such a state of advanced emaciation shook him fully to the core.

He had arrived home as planned close to midnight, a cathedral silence pervading the house. He hugged his mother wordlessly and she ushered him directly into the downstairs bedroom. There was a strange calmness there; the low lights casting faint, still shadows onto the far wall beyond the bed. His reception he found particularly gratifying. As he stood there looking down at the skeletal man – who, in another form, he had known all his life – the closed eyes slowly opened, there was immediate recognition, and a weak smile rallied to greet him. There was contentment now on his face, and as Luke bent lower over him, he felt a hand rest on his. Roger Darius opened his mouth to speak but an overwhelming dryness prevented it. Luke propped up his father's head gently with his hand and held a glass of water carefully to his lips. His father gulped down several grateful but imprecise mouthfuls, panting after with the effort. He could speak more freely now, and did; his eyes assuming once more their usual playful glint, there in the shadows of the night.

And as the hours passed, they remained, Luke and his father; his father drifting in and out of sleep, Luke in an out of reality. It was a lot to come to terms with. He found himself struggling constantly with guilt for having missed so much; for putting himself in such a position where it was felt best not to call him sooner – wondering all the time why they had not. He should have phoned more frequently; though he knew in his heart his father would have wanted him to get on and live his life regardless.

His father was a little brighter with the morning, though still painfully weak. His cough tore right at Luke's heart, and hearing it, he cursed his inside knowledge of what this illness was doing to his father's body. Instinctively he knew it would not be long now. He had a feeling his father was privy to such information too.

Martin arrived like a gale – brash, cold and unfeeling, throwing the door back hard on its hinges. His bold strut was at complete variance with the ambience of the bedroom, and his greeting betrayed an almost cynical amusement at the scene going on before him.

He kissed his father dutifully, if not a little ostentatiously, then turned and walked to the foot of the bed. Luke and his mother were there too, startled by the sheer force of the intrusion. Helen Darius rose and spoke quietly to him, her body turned purposely away from her husband, sheltering him from the terseness of her words.

"Martin, have you been drinking? At a time like this?"

"Drinking, Mother? Why yes, I admit it: I have had a tipple," he said loudly. "But then, I often do when I've suffered a terrible shock like this."

"What do you mean, 'terrible shock'? And would you mind please lowering your voice – I don't want your father unduly distressed. Perhaps you might like to continue this discussion outside the room?"

"No, I would not, as a matter of fact." Luke had rarely heard his brother so openly disrespectful. It was puzzling. He watched as Martin took an envelope from his inside pocket and held it in his hand, making no immediate effort to open it. "And as for that shock, I'm afraid it's a subject that doesn't just affect me. It's something I personally feel that you, Father, especially, ought to be made aware of."

"What is it, Martin?" asked Roger Darius feebly, from his bank of pillows.

"What I have discovered has affected me deeply," began Martin, secretly happy now the stage had been set. "I've thought about it long and hard and decided that it can be kept from you no longer. Father, I'm afraid you have been cruelly deceived for many years by this woman you call your wife – and I, my mother. I have found evidence, quite by chance, that proves beyond any doubt that Luke here is not your son. Mother was already pregnant by another man when she tricked you into marrying her. No doubt she had her reasons – though I'm sure we can all guess what the true motive might have been. I'm sorry, Father, that you have had to find out this way. And you, of course, Luke."

Luke turned urgently to his mother and looked at her, waiting for her denial. It did not come. Instead, there was silence. A panic rose chaotically inside him.

"I'm afraid there is some truth in what Martin has said," his mother said flatly at last. Martin's face registered triumph.

Luke looked at his father, first in concern at how he might be reacting to the news, then in a confusion of emotions as he realised this man, whom he had loved so deeply all his life, had no biological link to him at all. His dad's face remained impassive.

"It's all here in this letter I found, Father," Martin went on, keen to press home his advantage. Roger Darius took the note weakly between his fingers and placed it gently on the bed cover beside him, making no attempt at all to read it. There was a certain finality in the gesture.

This was not entirely what Martin had intended. If his father hadn't the strength to read it, perhaps a brief summary of its main points would do instead:

"It's a letter from a man called Peter Simpkins. It was sent to Helen Frampton on April 26th 1958. It..."

"Who on earth gave you permission to go through my personal things?!" his mother cut in angrily. "How dare you?!" Martin ignored her.

"It states, and I quote: 'Darling Helen, do not fear. Before the child is born, I will be back and, of course, my love, I will stand by you. My choice for a boy is Luke. Perhaps you could think of possible girls' names?'

"Strikes me this chap Simpkins didn't turn out to be a man of his word, after all. Left you stranded, didn't he, Mother? And you knew a good thing when you saw it: a man of independent means like my father here."

"That will be enough!!" The power of the voice startled them all. For a moment, it was not clear from where it had come – such was its air of authority. By some supreme effort, right there from his sick bed, Sir Roger Darius had spoken. He looked angrily at Martin.

"I am sorry to disappoint you, Martin – you are obviously taking great pleasure in these revelations of yours. There are certain points, however, you have unfortunately failed to appreciate – such is your desire to shock. Peter Simpkins was a good man – a fine and honourable man who loved your mother, Luke, with all his heart. He would have returned to her, too, as he promised, if, on May 14th – only two weeks or so after that letter was written – he hadn't been killed in an accident while working for the Ministry of Defence. At least that was the official version." Sir Roger's voice tailed off but resumed soon after. He was clearly determined to continue.

"Your mother, Luke, was still very early in her pregnancy, working here at Wetherfield nursing my father. The truth was I had loved her right from the very first moment I saw her, but until then, dared not tell her so. I understood her plight soon after the news of Peter's death and offered to marry her directly and bring you up as our own. Never once have I regretted this action. I am so sorry you have had to hear it this way; we should, of course, have told you before now. My only regret is that my own biological son has turned out so differently to yourself – such a loathsome little shit." His eyes turned towards Martin, cowering now at the foot of the bed.

"Your motives are clear enough to me, young man," he went on. "I know well enough the utterly despicable way you work. As far as I am concerned, you can leave this house immediately, and not return while I am still here alive."

The door slammed loudly behind him. Through the open window, the sound of angry revving from the driveway could be heard, then the slow recession into silence.

Though still completely stunned by these revelations, Luke did his best to compose himself. His inner feelings had been cruelly assaulted, yet there was so much he knew he had to say to this man – this very generous man – who had brought him up as his own. And so little time to say it.

Luke moved forward and sat himself on the bed, as close as he practically could, and put his arms gently around him. His glaring weight loss, and how unfamiliar it made him feel, shocked Luke once again, but he turned his face to his and kissed him gently on the cheek. There were words to be said but he couldn't find them. Instead, he pulled back a little and placed his head gingerly on the old man's chest – not so heavily as to in any way compromise his breathing, just enough to feel and hear his heart beating closely inside. Luke felt a hand running through his hair and his own tears running in a short cut from the corner of his eye, slowly wetting the pyjama top beneath him. He sat up suddenly, peering resolutely into the old man's face.

There were still no words between them; only a feeble and knowing smile.

Sir Roger Darius did not die just at that time, but in a moment of relative peace an hour or so later.

Martin Darius, in an act of unconscious obedience to his father's last wish, was, by then, several miles from Wetherfield; and already otherwise engaged.

Cartagena, Colombia.

II

Not long after Sir Roger Darius' death at Wetherfield – on that Sunday, April 6th – two US DEA officers, Ricardo Chavez and Miguel Gomez Vicario, sat in a car in a quiet side street of Cartagena. It was almost noon local time and they were discussing the latest tip off they had received concerning the likely whereabouts of Delgardo Estremosa.

Things had been going pretty well for them so far. Their success in raiding his headquarters, way off in the hills to the south near Carmen, had renewed their enthusiasm for the task. Not only that but this operation, which had signalled the very height of their achievement so far since arriving in Colombia, had been possible only due to intelligence finally through from their deeply undercover colleague, Ramon Garcia.

Ramon was not only alive and well, therefore, but clearly functioning to his own exacting standards, having achieved – by whatever means it had taken – a position of significant trust in Delgardo's set-up. It was perhaps a little unfortunate that the destruction of so much of his equipment and cocaine stores had now forced the drug lord into hiding. As far as they could make out from Ramon, only a limited regrouping exercise had been possible so far – which, as it stood, had not involved him.

The information they had just received that day was once again from an anonymous call – and, as before, an American voice had spoken. It had told of Delgardo's expected movements that night – in particular, how sometime soon after ten, he would be leaving the Hotel Las Velas in possession of a briefcase full of drug money. If the DEA wanted him – as this caller had rightly surmised – he was theirs for the taking.

Dan Forsbrook arrived in the El Laguito area of Cartagena close to the Pierino Gallo Shopping Centre, at nine-thirty that evening, in good time for his meeting with Delgardo. He crossed to the Las Velas, got the key from Reception as arranged, and made his way up to Room 706.

Once in the room, Dan placed the briefcase down beside him on the bed and opened it. The money was all there in wads of $50,000. He closed the case, lit a cigarette and ambled over to the window. The gardens at the back, which he overlooked, extended right down to the main beach. He wondered how many men the DEA might have lying in wait for Delgardo when he left – presuming, of course, they had taken his tip-off as seriously as he hoped they might.

Dan turned abruptly when he heard them enter, feeling suddenly vulnerable there in front of the window. He prayed that this suite had not been chosen solely for its altitude and the relative quiet of the gardens below.

There was something in Delgardo's manner, he noticed, that was somehow different from before. Gone was the swagger, the cockiness of their last meeting. And, this time, there was little in the way of preamble.

"Mr Forsbrook – so glad you decided to come. You have the money, I take it?"

"It's all there." Delgardo motioned to one of the two men with him – the tall one Dan recognised from their previous meeting at the Caribe – who opened the case and flicked quickly through its contents. No attempt was made to count the money just then.

"Your ship – the Venus Prince – will be here, I believe, on Tuesday as usual. You will be leaving on it?"

"That is my intention, yes."

"I'm sorry you failed, Mr Forsbrook, in persuading your boss about the itinerary."

"I, too, am bitterly disappointed. I am sure you are aware, though, I did try many ways to get the result you wanted."

Dan was waiting for what might come next. His eyes darted from one to the other gauging their movements. His heart beat quickly and he could feel himself begin to perspire heavily beneath his bullet-proof vest. He'd at least attempted to impress with his humility. That and the money, of course...

Delgardo suddenly signalled to his companions. The tall man snatched up the case while the other went over to the door. He held it open, and Delgardo rose from where he sat. Without further word, they all left the room. Once more alone, and very greatly relieved, Dan Forsbrook slumped onto the bed and took several deep breaths. He then got up slowly and went over to the window to open it.

He didn't have long to wait. Less than five minutes later loud gunfire became audible. Several blasts from a variety of directions down there in the darkness, mingled uncomfortably with stark Latino cries. Quietness descended soon after, followed by the flashing lights of an approaching ambulance.

Half an hour later, Dan left the hotel behind him. He would need to vacate the area as quickly as possible. The hire car was parked close by in a side street. He would drive through the night now to the place he had chosen – outside Santa Marta, further along the coast. The Venus Prince might come, but he would not be leaving on it, as Delgardo now believed. In fact, by the time it did arrive, he would have left Colombia and his life in the USA far behind him. For how long? He did not, at that time, know. A lot would depend on the news about the ambush – whether Delgardo had been caught and whether the briefcase and its contents had, at the very least, been retrieved. If all went according to plan, Delgardo would never have had time to discover that the bulk of the notes he'd given him were, in fact, counterfeit.

Monday 7th April

III

Dan awoke at three the following afternoon. He had arrived, dozed fitfully for a while in the car until a more reasonable hour, breakfasted then checked into that small and slightly run-down coastal hotel at about ten that morning. He felt better for the further sleep he'd had, and more confident generally now that the time of his flight was only five hours away. In fact, he couldn't help thinking just how easy it had all turned out in the end.

The TV bulletin that afternoon spoke of two deaths there outside the Las Velas the previous night, but sadly, no more precise details. He would make further enquiries once he was safely out of the country, but with what he'd learnt so far, it was difficult not to feel a little like celebrating.

Down at the café-bar by the pool, a number of local youths were diving and splashing around and he watched their brown, carefree bodies as he sat there sipping his coffee. Two boys came and sat close by, clearly intrigued by the gringo newcomer, chatting to him and smiling innocent white smiles. They were poor here, it was clear, and Dan could sense in their easy banter the same practised enquiry he had witnessed so often in the Thai children who worked for Eastern Promise.

Dan Forsbrook had never considered himself truly weak in these matters – it was only ever a business arrangement, after all: simple payment for simple pleasure. His only question now was the timing. With the younger of the two off getting him a coffee refill at the bar, he made the deal with the other. A certain discretion was called for nonetheless, so they left him there to finish his drink before the planned rendezvous a little later back at his room.

What Dan hadn't counted on though, as he waited in anticipation of their arrival, was the degree of lethargy that had now suddenly come over him. It felt almost like he had taken a sleeping draught – but that was clearly ridiculous. Coffee, he seemed to recall, was supposed to be stimulant. No way, though, could this new feeling ever hope to stand in the way of his pleasure, so intense now was his arousal. He indulged himself with his young visitors in all those highly particular ways he had come to enjoy. Very soon after though, in a sudden final rush, drowsiness overcame him.

Dan came round sometime later, not totally dismayed by the situation he now found himself in. He was naked, yes – that he could remember – but he was now lying bent over the edge of the bed, his feet on the floor and his hands tied tightly behind his back. One of the young boys, was kneeling just in front of his face, smiling. As he tried to smile back, the boy began to urinate freely over him. Not only that – novel enough in itself, but not strictly to his taste – there was something else too. He was aware of a definite fullness in his rectum, slightly cold but nonetheless thrilling; six inches or so at an educated guess.

One thing, however, Dan Forsbrook failed to appreciate at that precise moment, was that this, in fact, was the long cool barrel of a Ruger .44 Super Redhawk handgun.

Chapter 33

I

Three hours after the Venus Prince left Aruba that same day – and Ed Jamieson had ensconced himself in a vacant suite to ponder his tactics for the next – a call came through for him on the satellite phone. It was Jack Buchanan ringing from Cartagena.

"Word is, Ed, Forsbrook certainly arrived here alright – took a hire car even – but that's as far as I've got. The local police have been pretty helpful, thank God. We can only hope we're right in assuming he'll be joining the ship tomorrow."

"And Tara – any word on her?"

"None at all. Naturally, we couldn't check all departure lists from the US, and arrivals information here is way less than accurate. So, it certainly doesn't rule out the possibility she might've come down here herself to confront him. You have your plan of action ready for when he arrives on board?"

"I'm just working on that now – though I've got to admit to you, Jack, I'm beginning to feel kinda nervous about this whole damn business."

Tuesday April 8th

When the Venus Prince turned into Cartagena Bay late the next morning, Ed Jamieson gazed anxiously towards the dock. As the ship slowly closed in on its berth, the figures on the quayside became gradually clearer. He could make out the tall, stocky, red-headed form of Jack Buchanan standing there amongst a small group of men, but Dan Forsbrook was nowhere to be seen. The men with Jack, it turned out, were Colombian Police.

"Grave news, Ed – Forsbrook's dead. His body's been found in some seedy hotel room a little way up the coast. These guys here need you to go with them to identify the corpse."

"Any idea who was behind it?"

"None at all at the moment. One thing you got to realise, Ed: Colombia's one hell of a dangerous place. There are all types of people he could've somehow crossed along the way. It was definitely homicide, alright. But the nature of his death: now that was a little unusual – even, I'm told, for these parts. Not only that, but whoever did it was kind enough to leave us an action replay. There was a video record of the whole event – minus the perpetrators, of course – left, for some reason, rather provocatively on top of his body."

II

Luke Darius had been particularly low since his father's death, but that Tuesday evening felt the need to get away from

Wetherfield, at least for a few hours. There was one person, in particular, he wanted to see – someone of sufficient sensitivity to appreciate his recent mood. He made his way to Chiswick hoping his journalist friend, Sarah Wright, might be in.

When the door opened, she was not only surprised but clearly delighted to see him. As the evening wore on, Luke knew how right he had been to come. She was particularly taken by the account of his brother, Martin's, last-minute revelations – both the content and its obvious effect on him, as well as the manner of Martin's doing so. What real motives, she wondered, might have lain behind it all, at such a sensitive time? Sensitivity, she appreciated, was hardly one of Martin Darius' strong points. Deviousness in all its diverse forms, however, was.

It was a theme, now they were on to it, which Sarah clearly wished to expand on. She described all that had happened since they had last spoken: of her attempts – almost matching Martin at times in duplicity – to expose him as the inept impostor she felt him to be in the celebrated Windhope Hospital issue. How she had helped stir local outrage and steer it towards the proposed public demonstration – commuted, she felt, a little too readily to the live debate. How he had managed to get himself personally off the hook, with help from senior Party members, she still had no idea. But she did not intend to let things go at that. The memory of the blows Martin Darius had so cruelly dealt her still rankled. She was, and would continue to be, firmly on his case.

Information, it seemed, had recently come her way incriminating him in a number of shady deals in the City – more, that is, than the standard 'failure to declare an interest'.

If she could prove it, Martin Darius would have some very serious explaining to do – to the electorate, his Party, and the police. Evidence, though, of any sort at all, had sadly so far proved elusive.

Through the wineglass in that dim light, Luke looked out from his inner confusion and saw beside him a woman he could not help but admire. She was independent and strong, yet sensitive and warm, too. And something – possibly a combination that included slight intoxication – made him move closer to her on that settee and slip his arm around her neck. She turned to him in surprise and tried to speak, but he stopped her with a kiss full on the mouth – then deeper. He closed his eyelids and sank into the swirling darkness behind them, only to find that rather abruptly she had pulled away.

"Luke, I'm terribly sorry," she said putting a significant sudden space between them. "I don't think you quite understand. I'm really very fond of you, believe me – and extremely flattered that you might find me in any way attractive. It's just I'm already in a relationship; one I happen to be fully committed to. No doubt it will come as something of a shock to you, but it just so happens to be with a wonderful and truly amazing woman."

Wednesday April 9th

III

Luke came off the phone to the Funeral Directors that afternoon happy that all arrangements had been made for the service the following day. He was due to fly out the morning after that, on the Friday, to join the ship once more in Jamaica. He made his way through to report one or two details to his mother when the phone began to ring. To his immense surprise, it was Tara Scott.

"Where are you calling from?" he asked, delighted to hear her voice but unable to imagine what might lie behind the call. He had worked hard so far to forget her – worked hard to get to where he was now.

"London. I started back at Head Office here again this morning. Earlier on, someone happened to mention you'd flown home to see your father. How is he, by the way?"

"He died on Sunday, I'm afraid. He was very ill."

"I'm real sorry to hear that. How long you staying in England?"

"Due back on the ship this Saturday."

"Is it possible I could see you tonight? There are things, Luke, I really need to explain."

As Luke made his way to Tara's flat in Chelsea that evening, he tried above all not to read too much into her call. There was little, really, in the content of their conversation earlier that gave grounds for any true optimism. Something in her

391

tone, though, suggested this was a very different Tara Scott to the one he had visited at her home in Sheepshead Bay barely ten days before. What, he wondered, could have brought about such a sudden transformation?

He held back a little at the point of greeting, allowing Tara to set the tone. She came towards him, kissed him quickly on the cheek, then led him through to the large Georgian sitting room.

She wore a short white dress revealing her bare legs – slightly tanned from those few short days in the Caribbean – and light-grey high heels. Her hair hung down long and straight, darkly framing those well-remembered features. There was something she wanted to explain – it was pointless construing it differently. Now that he had seen her again and sensed the fragility of his resolve, Luke began to feel it might have been better had they discussed whatever it was by phone.

"Luke," she said, when they were both seated. Luke had chosen one of the single armchairs away from the sofa where she sat. "I'm glad you're here. You know I really must apologise for how I acted when you came to see me at home. It was so good of you to make that effort – such a journey and all – and so ungracious of me to treat you as I did."

"Don't worry about it. It was clear you were pretty upset at the time."

"You're right, of course, I was. And I think I would've done well to have discussed it with you there and then. That business in Caracas – it affected me more than I first imagined."

"And now?"

"Things have happened since; things that seem to have helped me come to terms with it all – at least to some degree."

"You mean counselling – therapy?"

"You could describe it that way, I guess." Here, she laughed slightly. "Though I don't really want to go into that right now, okay? I do feel, however, I owe you some explanation of what happened at that place, the Medina Café. What I still keep asking myself is, 'why me?'"

Luke listened with growing amazement as she began to describe what happened that day. He watched as, bluntly and dispassionately, she spoke, sparing little it would seem by way of detail. Her eyes now were fixed, looking ahead of her, not at him – focusing only on her memory of that afternoon.

Luke fought hard to contain his immediate outrage. He marvelled at her calmness of speech and general composure, and was relieved to hear of Paul Curtis – or Brad Earlham's – eventual arrest. Her eyes betrayed a definite satisfaction as she reported this fact to him. He was disappointed that the man this bastard was apparently working for at the time had somehow escaped capture.

Tara herself felt better for having told him. It was not only cathartic to some degree; she found it interesting, too, comparing Luke's response with that of the very Christian Hugh Gotley when she had similarly confided in him. And Luke had not exactly been without his own troubles either. When she'd heard earlier that day of his father's death, a chord had been struck deep inside her. She too had lost a father – in her case, many years before. The memory of this man, Johnny Scott, was nevertheless one now very dear to her. She had rediscovered her dad and brought him very much back into her life. She was in a better position now to understand the loss Luke must be experiencing.

Then there was the business of Martin's callous revelations. How might they affect Luke in time to come? And what kind of absolute lowlife would engage in such a despicable act?

Luke was by now a little puzzled. Tara, it seemed, was clearly taking pleasure in his company. Was she merely being supportive, as the friend she promised she would remain – sensitive to the plight of the recently bereaved? Or was there more perhaps? If this were the case, he would wait patiently for the signs to become clearer. His experience with women over the past ten days had been dispiriting enough as it was. First, there'd been Tara's rejection of him in New York, then the reality of Sandy, in his absence, having been taken – in more senses than one – and no longer available to him. Lastly, and perhaps most embarrassingly, there was that drunken pass he'd made at Sarah. Tonight, he would make no such mistake. If, by any outside chance, Tara did want to resume their friendship on any more amorous grounds, he must be prepared to take it slowly. Anything more and he would almost certainly blow it with her forever. If he only remained where he was in that chair, he was surely bound to be safe.

"Care for a drink – wine, perhaps?" she said.

Grim recollections of the night before came flooding back.

"Just a beer if you have one."

He stood and looked around the room while she'd gone. It was high-ceilinged with ornate plasterwork, repaired in places, and a crystal chandelier. He was idly counting its

394

light bulbs when Tara returned and they flicked off suddenly leaving just the two wall-lights still on. She put the tray on the low table in front of the sofa and settled herself back down on it. Luke turned to watch her: those same high heels, those same glorious legs, the same exquisite Tara.

"Your drink's here, when you're ready," she said. He went over to take it. She patted the space beside her, gesturing for him to sit. This he did a little nervously. What had she in mind now, he wondered?

Luke sipped his beer slowly, using the time to watch her out of the corner of his eye. She appeared to be adjusting the cushions behind them. The advantage of this manoeuvre did not become fully clear until after he had replaced his glass on the table. Sitting back as he then did, in search of a more relaxed position, Tara turned to him, running her hands playfully over his chest. Then, almost before he knew it – suddenly and earnestly – they were kissing.

She was in control now, which suited Luke fine. As long as this remained the case, he could hardly be held to blame. He relaxed to savour the kiss; the gentle play of their tongues...

A hand settled on his thigh. It arrived there casually and ambiguously – then remained there motionlessly, keeping him guessing. Luke tried to ignore it, convinced at last of its innocence, cursing the degree to which it was threatening to arouse him nonetheless. This was not the sort of temptation he needed just then; he would have to think of something else instead.

It was not particularly difficult: there were so many other serious things happening in his life just then. Before he knew it, reality began to beckon. Suddenly and almost uncontrollably, he found himself being drawn back, locked in now to the cruel truth of recent events. How, with his father so recently dead, and as yet unburied, could he be here like this enjoying himself in such a way? His very own father – lying somewhere that very minute alone in waxy death, his coffin lid still unclosed. A sobering guilt crept over him.

Suddenly, she was kissing him once more – a deeper, more insistent kiss. Her eyes were closed now as he looked, her face flushed, her breathing more urgent. Deftly, she moved to sit astride him and he could feel his hand on her leg and her groin pressing down on his. He tried to focus his mind on the kissing: it was by far the safest option.

It was clear now that Tara had sensed his reticence. Rather than discourage her though, it appeared to be having almost the opposite effect. She was making all the moves and was clearly content to be doing so. It was a novel enough experience for Luke, too. In many a fantasy – right from his young teenage years, in fact – the forward and always highly revelatory older woman had figured strongly, relieving him of all responsibility for the encounter. If he just closed his eyes now and imagined...

Her hand fumbled and found his, and she was lifting it slowly now off her leg to he-knew-not-where. She knelt forward, more upright for a second, somehow busy, kissing him deeply, keeping him guessing. When she eased back down, his hand was magically there and she circled slowly around it; always in control. Luke gasped inwardly, his arousal now fully confirmed. Tara's intentions could be no clearer. How much longer could he hold back? Though, as things had gone so far, it might prove interesting were he able to continue to do so.

Her hands were busy again now, keener than ever to tempt him in the face of such open resolve. He could feel the waist clip of his trousers loosen and her lips detach from his. A flood of anxiety suddenly gripped him and he struggled to relax. Whatever apprehension he was showing just then, though, seemed once again to be spurring her on – like that eternal woman of his fantasy. He held his breath in anticipation...

With the most extreme act of willpower, he eased himself away, drawing her face to his, kissing her unselfish lips with thanks. Then, picking her up bodily – slim and delicate in his arms – he carried her through to the bedroom and gently laid her down. Slowly, he undressed her, cherishing the images he would keep in his mind of each startling moment. He looked up at her face, her eyes closed deep and lost now in a world he trusted might include him.

They had reached a different phase somehow, her body flushed and warm against his. She appeared more focused now – descending deeper and deeper, hypnotically almost; passive yet strangely more natural with it.

It was time to go onwards. There was no other way. It was right and fitting. Besides it would be almost rude not to.

He shifted slightly and edged forward, her breathing faltering in anticipation. Suddenly she twisted, and then with a forceful jolt, pushed him away – her eyes open wide in a kind of wild panic. She let out a soft cry.

"No, sorry, Luke," he heard her say, "there's just no way I'm ready for this right now."

As he looked at her now, sitting there beside him, her knees drawn up close to her body, she appeared startled by the force of her own dramatic reaction. At last, she spoke:

"You know, so much has happened recently, Luke. Only now am I beginning to appreciate how much it has truly affected me."

They sat in silence a little longer. Then, as he watched, she reached over for her blouse, lying there where it had landed on the floor, and pulled something out of the breast pocket. She stared at it a few moments then put it away.

As far as he could tell, it was a photo of some kind.

Chapter 34

Thursday April 10th

I

Luke was glad when the funeral was over – or at least the part of it so obviously stage-managed by Martin. A sizeable crowd had gathered at the cemetery that day, reflecting the same strange mix that had attended his father's party so few months before. There were reporters there, invited this time though, hand-picked by his brother for whatever political advantage he thought he might gain. A photo opportunity at this stage of the game definitely not to be missed.

Back at home afterwards, the mood amongst those gathered quickly changed. Sombre and reflective one moment; Election tactics the next. Martin once again at Wetherfield; his father no more.

Luke saw Tara that evening as arranged. She had news for him when he arrived.

"Something really shocking has happened," she said. "A telex came through today. Dan Forsbrook's apparently been found dead in Colombia. Uncle Ed had to identify his body; he just happened to be on the Venus Prince when it arrived there this Tuesday – the day after it occurred."

"Do they have any idea at all what was behind it?"

"None at the moment – at least, as far as I'm aware."

They talked later of other things: his return to ship the following day, and when they might see each other again.

"These are the last couple of cruises before we reposition to Miami. There's a week's break then before the new season begins. I'm sure we could arrange something for that time. What about your own plans, Tara – will you stay on here in England?"

"Probably only for a little longer. Firstly, with Dan Forsbrook's death, it strikes me I'll be a lot more use to Uncle Ed over in his New York office. He doesn't know it yet, so it'll be a surprise – though I have told Aunt Ellen about my intention to return. Secondly, it occurs to me, talking to you about your own dad, there's an awful lot I don't know about mine. I think I've reached that time in my life when I really owe it to myself to find out. And lastly..." – here she hesitated, "there's also been something else playing on my mind a lot lately."

"What's that?" asked Luke, eyeing her closely now.

"You remember me mentioning Marianne, my friend back at Aberdeen Proving Ground, that day I arrived in Jamaica? You know, the one I was told was on sick leave and unavailable to talk to me?"

"Yes, I do. It struck you as odd at the time."

"Well, I called a couple of times after I arrived back home. I eventually got out of them that she was suffering some kind of stress and had left the base and gone to stay with her folks to recover. This also didn't quite fit. So, before I came over here, I went to see her, you know, to find out for myself what was going on."

"And?"

"I never seen such a change in a person. Sure, she was pleased to see me – a hell of a lot more so than her parents, for whatever reason – but there was no disguising how withdrawn and frightened she looked. She wouldn't say at first what had happened, but I had my suspicions."

"Which were?"

"There've been things going on in the US military that you've probably heard little about. I'm talking here about sexual harassment against women which seems to start almost the moment the training programme begins. There were a number of celebrated cases a few years back, mainly to do with the Air Force – Tailhook, for example – but then things went quiet. Now, it appears all has not been quite as rosy as it may have seemed.

"At Aberdeen, over the past months, there have been, I understand, a vast number of allegations made by women recruits against male training staff. Some very serious, others not. We're talking here, by the way, in the most extreme cases, about such things as physical violence, rape and sodomy."

"My God," said Luke.

"I was only there six weeks and really experienced little of any great significance by comparison – a few minor beatings, victimisation, lewd comments and a little touching-up. Soon, I decided it just wasn't for me. When I quit, though, I got the distinct impression something real odd was going down. The staff seemed pretty jittery. Seems they might've got wind of just how big a case the whole thing could turn out to be; and took great pains to try to convince me that any complaint I might make wouldn't be worth a damn."

"And did you make a formal complaint?"

"Yeah, I did. I gave the fullest statement I could at the time – more for the hell of it really – then moved on, glad to put it all behind me. And glad too that I hadn't had anything more serious to report. I've since learned, though, that Marianne wasn't quite so lucky.

"She seemed to be doing great after I left, and had been there so long I'd no doubt she'd be able to stick it out to complete her training. They teased her a bit, sure, over her size and shape mainly – she's a beautiful big black girl, by the way – but that was all. Then, for whatever reason – probably when they could see she was actually going to make it – they turned. One night, they came for her and started fooling around, and before she knew it, she'd become the victim of what amounted to the most humiliating gang rape. She was stationed over on Gateway at the time, a restricted phase of training, where soldiers aren't allowed to leave the Company area. What made it worse was being told by the three instructors involved that if she dared report it, her career would be over."

"How, for God's sake?"

"Because the guys involved, two black and one white, had found out she once had a thing going with one of the officers on base – I know the fella: one hell of a nice guy. Unfortunately, recently, as a result, he was transferred out west."

"So what? They didn't like him? They trying to get back at him for something?"

"Not even that. No, it was purely aimed at her. You see, in the US military, what the rest of the world considers to be consensual sex, is illegal when it involves personnel of different ranks. Knowing what they knew, they had effective power over her; and one, in particular, decided to use it. Didn't take much effort to coerce others in the Boys' Club to join him."

"What have these guys got against women, anyway?"

"Seems to me to be an attitude that pervades almost the whole military. Some, no doubt, think we're not up to the job either physically or mentally, and only admitted in the first place on a wave of ill-judged political correctness. Others – some of them well-known political commentators too – have gone so far as to say that moving women into front-line positions has seriously weakened the nation's military capability."

"I see. So, getting back to Marianne – will she file a complaint?"

"No. She feels there's no way she can. She's put up with a hell of a lot so far, just to get where she is now, and doesn't want to lose it all. Then there's the pressure she's getting from her father."

"Pressure?"

"Yeah – to let the whole thing drop. He's a retired Colonel himself and thinks she's making way too much of the whole thing. Thinks women in the military should just learn to suck it up and 'fit in' with the men. Wants her to get back there and get on with it – not sit around moping at home. Marianne suspects the fact he's gotten certain political ambitions of his own might just have something to do with it."

"So much for parental support. That, then, I take it, is why you want to be there for her?"

"Yep – got it in one."

With Luke gone, Tara sat and reflected on those things she had decided not to tell him. Things that – though she tried repeatedly to put them out of her mind – simply refused to lie down.

Other aspects of the Aberdeen situation that Marianne had told her about, for example. How, even at that very moment, the defence lawyers were preparing their case: preparation that, by all accounts, involved the systematic discrediting of all main witnesses going forward. One by one, trainees Marianne knew to have strong grounds for complaint had decided to withdraw when threatened by aspects of their private lives being brought into the public domain at the hearings. Not only that, some had apparently become the subjects of further intimidation and threats.

Anonymous threats perhaps, Tara wondered? Like the mysterious call her mother had told her about recently when she'd phoned home – the one received the morning after she'd left Sheepshead Bay last Friday? What was that all about?

Then there was the information she'd extracted from Brad Earlham over the Caracas incident. The extreme lighting that day had made her suspicious. What he told her at gunpoint that night confirmed it: a video recording had been made of what happened that afternoon, and ten copies since. A porn movie, no less, which, if it got into the wrong hands could – among other things too horrendous to contemplate – be used to discredit her testimony. That, or warn her off appearing at all like the others.

But what chance was there that such a video would ever find its way into their hands? Incredibly slim, surely – bearing in mind the absolutely vast number produced each week across the nation. But could she take that chance?

Not necessarily such a slim chance, though, it suddenly occurred to her with some alarm. What if the video had been commissioned specifically for that purpose – to warn her off? Surely too far-fetched? And it would assume Forsbrook, inexplicably behind the whole thing, had some very specific link with the military. How could she find that out?

Unfortunately, she had failed to get the answers she wanted from Forsbrook when she followed him down to Colombia. The good thing was, he'd gotten his just deserts.

And, so far at least, no one even knew she had been there.

II

"Is that Sarah Wright? I understand you are a freelance journalist. I have some information that might interest you."

"What sort of information?"

"About Martin Darius and certain financial irregularities in the running of his campaign. The thing is, my name must not be identified as your source. Do I have your agreement on this?"

"No problem, Mr...?"

"Sutcliffe, John Sutcliffe. Until recently, I was treasurer of his campaign fund – until he had me sacked for no justifiable reason, that is. I suspect, however, it was because I'd identified various sums of money that had gone missing from the fund – followed, when discovered, by rather flimsy attempts at cover-up."

"You have evidence of these irregularities?"

"The evidence very conveniently disappeared from his campaign headquarters just before I was asked to leave. I now hear he's trying to point the finger at me. Much of the evidence, I feel sure, is still in his personal possession – in his flat, maybe – and could possibly be retrieved."

"What exactly are you suggesting here, Mr Sutcliffe – a break-in?"

Monday April 14th

III

Delgardo Estremosa's face, strained and pale, bore a distinctly haunted look. He hadn't been eating properly, that was the trouble, and his old stomach problem had returned with a vengeance to taunt him. It hadn't been easy that past week out there in the countryside, relying largely on peasant fare. His palate was used to finer things. As he took yet another swig of his antacid mixture, he thought back to those fine city restaurants he used so openly to frequent, and what little problem he had with his digestion then. For the moment at least, they would remain but a distant memory.

That he, personally, had managed to escape that night of the ambush at the Las Velas was perhaps blessing enough.

The other two hadn't made it – Capestriano and Recevez – cut down by a flurry of bullets as they were about to open fire. All ultimately, he reminded himself, to protect him. Such dedication to duty; his oldest and his most trusted friends. He would see to it that their families were well-supported once he was out of this mess and back on his feet once again.

There were definite problems ahead, though. The first was successfully to regroup – out in this desolate place, so many miles from the main centres, up here on the Caribbean coast. He would know soon enough who was still with him; he'd got word to most of the others about the meeting he'd arranged for two days' time. A certain restructuring would be necessary, that was clear: promotion within the team where promotion was due.

Then there was his current financial problem – hopefully, too, just short-term. Now that he was effectively in hiding, so far from the essential areas of his trade, obvious difficulties arose. Add to that the effects of the recent raid and destruction of his main plant and stockpiles, plus the undermining of his operation by those desperate to take over his territory, and the outlook appeared grim to say the least.

But he, Delgardo, was a fighter; and besides, he had his pride. Despite Forsbrook's trickery over the money, a compensatory amount had come his way almost directly after, from a most surprising source. He had enough now for the arms consignment he had planned to pick up in a week's time, but only a limited amount more, readily available. The lucrative secret operation he had going via the Jamaica link seemed set soon to die a death. He had little stock now available to ship out, and he'd had to accept, finally, the reality of the Venus Prince's change of itinerary, now almost upon him. So few other types of ship had managed to run the gauntlet of DEA surveillance over the years quite so successfully, he had found. It would be a difficult outlet to replace.

But he wasn't quite through with the Venus Prince just yet. No other vessel he could think of would stand anything like the same chance with the movement of arms into Colombia. Particularly, too, seeing his relationship with Captain Symiakos had always remained so wonderfully sound. A more obliging captain, he really couldn't have wished for. He would warn him of the intended detour that would be required very soon.

Tuesday April 15th

IV

As the Old City of Cartagena became visible in the distance as they approached, Luke Darius became aware of a feeling almost akin to that of revisiting an old friend.

She was standing on the quayside as they came closer – the slender form clutching the bundle to her chest. There was a man with her of similar complexion, and an anxiety in both their eyes. Luke recognised the face even from that distance, though couldn't quite place it. Studying her more closely as they came alongside, it suddenly came to him. This was the woman whose baby he had helped deliver, all those weeks back. But why was she here? From her face alone, he could tell this was no pleasure trip. And the person with her – who was he? One of Delgardo's men?

Luke made his way down to the foyer and watched the passenger hordes depart. He went to the top of the gangway. The woman and her baby, and the man with them, were already half-way up. Greeting and basic introduction were simple enough, but it soon became clear the language problem precluded any deeper conversation. He was still puzzled as to why they might be there. Consuela, it turned out – for that, Luke discovered, was her name – had come prepared for such a situation. Delving into a pocket, she thrust a crumpled note into his hand.

Luke began to read the translated message. When he had finished, he looked up at her. Before he could think of what to say, she spoke:

"Please, you will help me?" she said in English. Luke nodded.

"If I can," he said. An idea struck him: he needed an interpreter. "Wait here," he said, gesturing, and went off to find Jose Gomez, his Honduran friend.

When he returned, Luke led the small party down to the ship's hospital. It was unlikely at this time they would be disturbed. As they walked, he thought about the note Consuela had given him. Her brother was missing: nobody she had asked could tell her anything. He'd worked at one time for Delgardo but neither he nor his henchmen had seemed able to throw any light on the subject at all when she'd enquired. She had discovered, though, that he had gone to work at sea – on this very ship, the Venus Prince, some six months back.

Relieved at first when she'd first heard this, she became worried when he still failed to make any form of contact. Further enquiry revealed he was no longer on the crew list, and no other shipping company admitted employing him. It was inconceivable, she felt, their being so close, that he might have gone to work away without first letting her know. She now feared something had happened to him – but, if so, why wasn't she being told? Why this veil of secrecy?

Luke went over these points and several other background details with Jose's help there in the hospital. They sat in a group, chairs arranged accordingly, and Luke scribbled down a few notes, mainly of relevant dates. He looked up into her strained, worried face and knew he wanted to help her. He was no detective – simply hoped he might eventually be able to offer some assurance of her brother's well-being, at least during the time of his stint there on board the Venus Prince.

With the imminent change of itinerary, it occurred to Luke he had best take an address where he could write to her. It was more than likely he wouldn't have any answer by that following week – the last time the ship would be calling into Cartagena.

Consuela thanked him gratefully – almost to the point of embarrassment – for the help he was offering. Luke gestured towards the baby and she handed her to him. He was a little alarmed at what he saw. The child, now almost five weeks old, was clearly undernourished, and through Jose once again,

Luke asked questions about the child's feeding and health in general.

As Consuela and her friend prepared to leave, Luke pressed two one-hundred-dollar bills into her hand. "Your child needs more food – here..." he said.

"Thank you, Doctor Luke, thank you. I will never forget this."

"Jose," said Luke when she had gone, "I might need your help on this one. Ask around the crew, if you can – though, at all times, be discreet. See if you can come up with any information on this man, German Bocuse, during the time he worked on board. I'll tie up with you soon."

Thursday April 17th

V

Back in Head Office two days later, Ed Jamieson couldn't help but feel that all was going his way at last. He had just had the latest figures in and bookings for the new itinerary were running apace. There was little doubt he had been right all along in his decision about the route change.

Now that news of Dan Forsbrook's death had quickly filtered through the cruise-industry grapevine, he was sure George Mitchell would be running scared. He was as convinced as ever the two of them had together been plotting against him. What other reasonable explanation could there be? George Mitchell would now just have to prepare himself for viewing Venus Cruise Lines' success at close-hand – right there in Miami under his nose. It would teach the bastard a lesson.

Okay, so with Forsbrook dead, Mitchell might just get away with it. There was little, so Jack had said, to really link him in with this whole sickening business. Their only hope was if, in combing through the evidence from Gibson's house, something might somehow expose the connection. It would be better still if Jack had managed to locate Forsbrook's own apartment in DC – something that had so far eluded both him and the DC Police Department too.

Even their concerns about Tara had proved unfounded. Sure, she'd gone off without saying much – but hadn't she turned up soon after at the London office fit and well, having apparently visited friends along the way in the meantime? His sister Kathleen's relief, he knew, had been immense, hearing from Tara as she had direct from England.

After the worry of recent weeks, he could now look forward to getting his home life more in order – spend more time with Ellen for one thing – now that the stress factor had been so greatly reduced. It helped too that they were now able to switch their home security back to a vastly less restrictive level.

All in all, life was looking good once more.

When Rachel's call came through to his office, Ed was still enjoying that same buoyant feeling.

"Mr Jamieson, I have someone here to see you. A lady – very sophisticated-looking too. Wouldn't give her name: says she wants to surprise you. In fact, I see she's already making her way along to you right now."

Ed was intrigued. Who could this be – this sophisticated lady? It was perhaps a sad indictment on his social life nowadays, that he knew so few.

The knock when it came, came gently at the door. He rose to answer it, a token sweep of his hair in the mirror as he went – just why, he wasn't exactly sure. The voice that greeted him was intriguingly familiar:

"Guess who, Eddie-babie?" it said playfully.

"Sophia! What you doing here?" He hadn't seen his ex-wife Sophia for the best part of seven years: one hell of a shock all round. "Come – come on in," he said, before she could seriously answer.

"Eddie, I'm sorry to turn up here out of the blue like this after so long. I just couldn't think who else to turn to."

"Why, what's wrong, Sophia?" Ed asked with concern. There was a pause. She lit a cigarette and took a slow, elegant drag; long slender fingers and painted nails. "I've left George – it's over between us."

"What happened?" Though he asked this, Ed was beginning to see the light. "I found out – don't ask me how – that he's been cheating on me. Been screwing that secretary of his now for the past year or more. It's going to mean divorce, alright – and, trust me, I'm going to take him for every penny I can get. Just you wait and see." Sophia paused and looked over at him. "You know something, Eddie?"

"What, Sophia?"

"I should never have left you. You were so good to me. You didn't deserve what I did to you, running off with George like that. We were right together, you and me. You know, I've often thought about you since – though, I guess it's unlikely you'd have ever thought of me..." She left the statement hanging, daring him to respond.

"Sure I have, Sophia, often. But you see..."

"Oh, Eddie, I'm so glad I came back here to New York. I really do want to start over. It is, after all, where I belong."

"Where you staying at the moment?"

"I've checked in to the Plaza. It's expensive, but what the hell – let that asshole George pay. I've got what he wants and he knows it, so why not let him sweat a little?"

"What exactly are you talking about?"

"Shares – shares in his goddam company, that's what. Enough, at least, to leave him feeling pretty damn nervous right now, I should think."

Ed became aware of a sudden curious thrill creeping over him. He had barely time to analyse it when Sophia was speaking again:

"One heck of a nice hotel room, Eddie-babe – views over the Park and all. You will come and visit me there, won't you? Room 403. I'll sure be lonely if you don't."

414

PART 6

HELL AND HIGH WATER

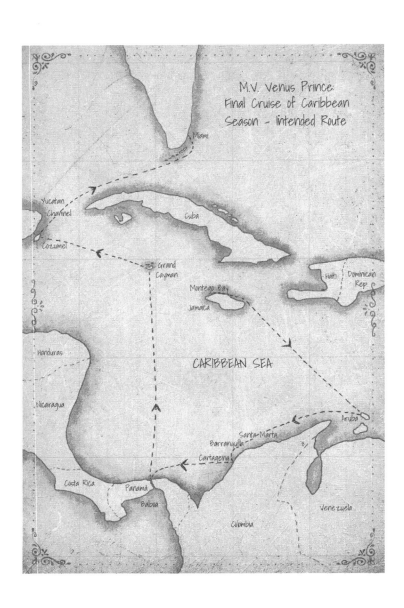

M.V. Venus Prince:
Final Cruise of Caribbean
Season - Intended Route

Miami

Yucatan
Channel

Cozumel

Cuba

Grand
Cayman

Haiti

Dominican
Rep.

Montego Bay

Jamaica

Honduras

CARIBBEAN SEA

Nicaragua

Aruba

Santa Marta

Barranquilla

Cartagena

Costa Rica

Panamá

Balboa

Venezuela

Colombia

Chapter 35

Tuesday April 22rd.

I

There was an almost eerie calmness to the waters of Cartagena Bay that evening under the heaviest and most threatening of skies, as the Venus Prince departed for the final time. No band was there on the quayside to play it off; no banners of farewell. Instead, a cluster of regulars – faces Luke Darius recognised from various of their stops over previous weeks. The men in the main were shore agents and port workers – practical and unemotional beings, already preparing in their minds for the next ship due. But there were women as well, slightly fewer now, Luke noticed, than on previous departures; those eternal smiling beauties, practical and unemotional too, save where the reality of further lost trade impinged directly on the wellbeing of their dependents. The crew of the Venus Prince had, after all, proved more than accommodating.

His main regret about that day, Luke reflected, as the ship made its way out into open sea, had been the lack of information to report back on the lost brother of Consuela Bocuse. It had now been a week since she'd come aboard to seek his help. Neither he nor Jose, however, had managed to find out anything of any real note during that time.

A number of Colombians had been working on the ship over the months, but for some reason, their names had not appeared on any crew register as far as Luke could ascertain. They had tended, by all accounts, to keep themselves very much to themselves, and thinking back, Luke could recall no dealings, professional or otherwise, with any of them. Over the past three weeks, they had all, for whatever reason, apparently left the ship en masse. None now remained for either he or Jose to question directly. Not that this, as things stood, would have proved the most advisable way forward.

Luke's thoughts that week, he had rather guiltily to admit, had been commandeered largely for more personal and selfish objectives. Getting back with Tara, surprising and wonderful though it was – at least up to a point – had done little for his general state of ease. Memories of their evening together, in flashes of startling clarity, revisited him when least he expected them – mid-diagnosis once (quite embarrassingly), and mid-sentence often. As he had fought to regain his footing on each of these occasions – struggling against the emotional conspiracy he had unwittingly been sucked into – a montage of concerns framed and re-framed themselves in his mind.

How successful would Tara be in addressing those clearly unresolved issues relating to her father – and how might their relationship run on from there? Had there been something about he himself, that had perhaps triggered in her such a response that evening at her place? Could it be that he represented – however unconsciously in her mind – a sort of father figure; pigeon-holed into some safe and asexual part of her brain? And once pigeon-holed...

Luke's main consolation since his return to ship had been the thought of being able to see her again so soon. It would be less than a week now – six days, in fact – till they arrived in Miami. Then their precious week together. But what after that? He was virtually committed now to one further season on board – the contract signed weeks back – but could he seriously stand being separated from her again? And for so long?

The route that week, through to the following Monday, was similar to the one the Venus Prince had taken up to Florida for the certification checks five or so weeks before. Reaching Cayman as usual on a Friday, they would head north-west towards the Yucatan Channel instead of south-east to Jamaica. Stopping off briefly at the island of Cozumel – a little to the south – they would then make their way through the Channel and, skirting Cuba, sail on north-east to Miami. If all went to plan, the ship would arrive in good time for all necessary servicing to be carried out, ready for the new season.

On shore but not strictly on the quayside that afternoon, watching the Venus Prince leave Cartagena, were a number of other onlookers – some more interested than others. Two, in particular, studied attentively its progress out into the Caribbean; two men who had been alerted long before to its potential significance among cruise ships visiting that Colombian port. At that particular time and with little really to go on, they had failed to follow it up. But Ricardo Chavez and Miguel Gomez Vicario, the two DEA officers in question, had just now discovered the part it was to play in Delgardo's immediate plans. Their colleague Ramon had been clear enough on this point when he got the message through to them just an hour before. Even then, he could supply few details. Delgardo, it seemed, was now playing his cards extremely close to his chest. They were, however, keener than ever not to miss this very unique opportunity, off Colombian soil, for nailing the man once and for all. The fact there were so many passengers also on board at the time did, unfortunately, tend to complicate the picture just a little.

When night began closing in two hours later, amidst the dense and sullen contortion of cloud overhead, Luke Darius was otherwise engaged, working away busily in the ship's hospital. Like most others on board that evening, he remained blissfully unaware of the tender pulling up alongside the Venus Prince in the enveloping darkness.

So, too, despite the proximity of their entry point to his place of work, was he oblivious to the men who boarded from it. They were a dozen or so in number, disparate and intriguing-looking, with an array of baggage to match. Their leader, a short, stoutish man in his mid-fifties, was greeted warmly if not a little warily by none other than the Captain himself. It was to be their final collaboration. After that, both he and his ship would finally be free.

Captain Symiakos could only pray it would run as smoothly as all previous ventures he and this newcomer had so far undertaken together.

Wed April 23rd: New York

II

At about the time the Venus Prince was wending its way slowly through the three Gatun Locks at the northern end of the Panama Canal early that following afternoon, Tara Scott had just arrived home by taxi from JFK.

"It was Hugh, wasn't it?" her mother said as she opened the door. "You two had some kind of tiff, to make you rush off so suddenly like that?"

"No, Mom, you couldn't be more wrong. Hugh and I, as I've told you before, are very much a thing of the past."

Her mother looked smugly unconvinced which annoyed her, but she decided to leave it at that just then. Later would be better. She'd think of something later.

"You may have wondered where this got to," said Tara after dinner that evening. "I took it with me to London." The snapshot of her father, out of its frame, looked pathetically small and insignificant in her hands.

"Yeah, I noticed alright," her mother said flatly. Tara waited for the question she felt certain would follow. No question came. She could not let up now though.

"What was he like – really like, I mean?"

"Much as I've always told you – wayward, undependable and ultimately extremely selfish. I guess the drink accounted for most of it."

"But why did he leave us, Mom? Did anything happen to drive him away?"

Her mother looked over at her questioningly. Something in her eyes told Tara she was at least edging in the right direction. She had asked little, but, on reflection, had never really asked so much before. She waited patiently for the reply.

"I guess now's as good a time as any to tell you – though I'm afraid there's no easy way of putting it. Your father, Tara, always had a real attitude problem, and turned out to be an unpredictable and dangerous man – especially if anyone dared cross him. Four police officers came for him one night – that was the first I knew of the trouble he was in – and he spent the next four years in the State Pen. Seemed easier to tell you he'd left us – particularly as he didn't seem too bothered about returning once he'd been released.

"I heard some time later he'd died, supposedly of natural causes, but you know, somehow I have my doubts. You see, if there was one thing that man couldn't control, it was his outrageous urge for revenge. Once somebody crossed him, he just wouldn't let it go. One prison psychiatrist's report claimed, I seem to recall, that when provoked, your father displayed very definite psychopathic tendencies."

At about that very same time, over at his home in the Bronx, Jack Buchanan poured himself a beer and sat reflecting on the one point that was troubling him more than any other just then. He had avoided mentioning it to Ed at the time – though quite why, he wasn't sure. And what he ought to do about it just then, he wasn't sure either.

The small silver bracelet, broken at its clasp, bore the inscription T.S. That itself was not so remarkable. Finding it, as he had, searching that Colombian hotel room, where not long before had lain Dan Forsbrook's lifeless body, however, was.

III

Luke did not become aware of the Colombians on board until he was informed by Jose that night. The Venus Prince had left the Panama Canal a little earlier than usual that day – quite unaccountably it seemed – and his Honduran friend had come to seek him out and tell him the latest. He appeared a little excited.

"You know you were saying, Doctor, only the other day, how all the Colombian crew have left the ship? Well, we seem to have acquired a few more from somewhere overnight. They've taken over that whole row of cabins up by the Bridge."

"Really?" said Luke. "These are passengers, then, we are talking about?"

"That's where it becomes a little unclear. These men, they dress like passengers, but something one of my friends said made me wonder. He said he recognised one of them as someone he last saw here as a worker on board – a humble sailor, like myself. Now, this man is strutting around looking like he owns the place – fancy suit and tie, the lot."

Luke laughed at Jose's clear indignation at this upset of the ship's social order and the little mime that accompanied his words. Jose too, it seemed, was a man who knew how to strut. It was intriguing, nonetheless, what Jose's friend had said. Could they perhaps enquire of this man about Consuela's missing brother?

"And there is something else, maybe more important, you ought to know, Doctor Luke," Jose continued, his voice suddenly quieter now. "This friend of mine, when he saw this man again, became a little worried. I asked him why, and at first, he wouldn't say. Finally, he admitted something had happened at that time on this ship, all those months ago, among the Colombians on board."

"What exactly was it – did he say?"

"A death of some sort, apparently. The guy had fallen – from some height it would seem – right down onto the engine-room floor. Looked pretty messed up, he said, when he was sent with another of my compatriots to move him."

"He didn't happen to know the identity of the dead man, by any chance, did he?"

"Unfortunately not," said Jose. "Don't worry, that was one of the first things I asked him. There was one thing, though…"

"What was that?" asked Luke keenly.

"He admitted that he and his colleague were paid to move the body to the cold store, and keep quiet about it being there."

"The cold store? You mean the mortuary, don't you?"

"No, it was definitely the cold store, Doctor Luke – you know, the refrigerated hold where the meat and fish are kept. What's more, the body was apparently still there the following day, despite the fact we'd stopped in Aruba in the meantime."

"But why not the morgue?" puzzled Luke. "It surely wasn't full at the time? And where did the body leave the ship? Cartagena then, presumably, if the deceased was Colombian."

"I gather so," said Jose.

"Who paid your compatriot not to mention it – the Captain?"

"The Staff Captain, apparently; though it seemed the Captain was in on it too."

"You're kidding me," said Luke. Now this was getting interesting. "Well, there should have been full records kept of the incident, nevertheless. You know, medical reports; reports to Head Office; entries in the ship's log, etc. Well done, Jose – I think we might just be onto something here. See if you can speak again to your friend; and maybe, even, to the other man who was involved. Try getting his account of things, too."

"That is not possible, I'm afraid. I'm told he left ship and returned home not long after this thing happened."

"Shame. Well, see if the guy on board can give you any idea at all of the approximate date we're talking about here, and get back to me as soon as possible. A lot of those records I mentioned are kept down here in the hospital area; it'll save a hell of a lot of time when it comes to going through them all tomorrow. From what you've said, asking these Colombians now on board might be exactly the wrong thing to do."

Thursday April 24th

IV

When Luke turned up at the hospital at eight the following morning, he – like just about everybody else on board – was completely unaware that the ship was now travelling in entirely the wrong direction. There were no visible landmarks to orientate him – not that he was particularly looking – and whatever internal compass his body was supposed to possess failed miserably to convince him they were travelling in any direction other than north to Grand Cayman as planned.

He had slept soundly that previous night – so soundly, in fact, his consciousness had not been stirred in the slightest by the ship grinding to a halt and dropping anchor close to the Islas del Maiz, three hours earlier. Nor indeed stirred by the burst of activity that followed, as the consignment of arms, under Delgardo's watchful eye, was transferred swiftly from the smaller vessel then alongside, still under cover of darkness.

Had Luke even been aware of their existence, he might have also known that the islands were Nicaraguan. It was here that Delgardo's contact had brought the requisite supplies the fifty or so miles over from the mainland; not merely guns but ammunition, explosives and detonators too.

If all went according to plan and they maintained their present course to the southeast, it was Delgardo's guess they would hit that secluded spot on the Colombian coast near Coveñas by midnight. Off-loading shouldn't take long and the ship would hopefully be on its way north again almost before anyone noticed. Only when it became clear the Venus Prince had had to skip the Cayman stop due to lack of time and make its way directly on to Cozumel would passengers become aware of a problem. Though not necessarily, Delgardo thought to himself with some amusement, the extent of the detour which had caused it.

At 10.30, the hospital now closed, Luke stayed on and went over to the main filing cabinet in the office area. He took out several bundles of reports, homing in on those pertaining to the month Jose had just reported might well be that of the incident they had discussed the night before. According to Jose's compatriot, it must have been December, though he couldn't recall exactly which part.

That was something at least, thought Luke, as he set aside those documents relating to the six weeks or so prior to his arrival on the ship. What struck him first was how sketchy they were. Then, as he began reading them through – when he could actually decipher what was written there, (English of sorts giving way repeatedly to confident foreign scrawl) – how scant in essential detail they turned out to be. And how poorly any one of them might stand up in a court of law, should it ever prove necessary.

Slowly and painstakingly, he worked. Eventually, it became clear that none related in any way to the death on board that Jose's colleague had so recently admitted knowledge of.

Luke was puzzled. Had this death been truly accidental, then surely half the available file space would be taken up with information about it? The Company, after all, would have an important insurance case to prepare for, and a number of angles to cover. Why the apparent secrecy here, then? Surely there couldn't really have been any more sinister cause – murder even? Just the very possibility of this made Luke's flesh creep. There had to be a simpler explanation – but what exactly? Here, Luke had to think. He worked through various permutations in his mind. How about, for example, that the guy who died had been working on board secretly, illegally even; someone who didn't appear on any legitimate passenger or crew list? Much more likely, he concluded, and felt immediately easier dealing with this thought than just about any other so far.

This state of contentment, though, didn't last for long. If this was the case, he began to argue – thinking it through a little further – and this man's body had been put ashore in Colombia as he and Jose had surmised, how come even his own sister hadn't got to hear of his death? This was presuming, of course, that the man in question was indeed German Bocuse. As it currently stood, neither he nor Jose had any evidence at all to suggest that it definitely was.

Might the Captain's log hold any clue as to what had actually happened that day? Even if it did, what chance did he have of ever finding out? He couldn't just go merrily up to the Bridge and nose through the log wherever it happened to be kept. Only the Greeks themselves seemed to have ready access to it. And how many Greek officers could he seriously call on to help him out in a situation like this?

There were only two at the most: Kypros, the junior radio officer, and Tassos, the First Engineer – the most decent out of the lot of them. Tassos would have more excuse to go looking through the log, but could he fully confide in him? What about his loyalty to the other Greeks? Would he be willing to help unearth something that might ultimately expose the Captain and Staff Captain, and God knows how many other officers besides?

Even if he wouldn't help directly with the log, something else just occurred to Luke. Being an engineer, Tassos spent long stretches down in the engine room daily. Might he have seen or heard anything first-hand relating to the death – if not exactly how it happened, then at least the identity of the victim? That, in itself, would be something.

Luke decided to go and find Tassos there and then. Word was he was working somewhere up on deck. Halfway there, a man came alongside and stopped him in his tracks. He had a serious, slightly worried look about him.

"Doctor?" he said.

"Yes," said Luke. The man spoke with a heavy South American accent.

"You must come with me. My travelling companion, he wants to see you."

"He is unwell?" The man did not answer. Instead, he turned, motioned for Luke to follow, and set off briskly towards the fore-end of the ship.

"Come to your hospital for an EKG? No way, Doctor! That will not be necessary."

Here, Delgardo laughed, a loud mocking guffaw of such energy that Luke began to wonder whether his suggestion might not be a slight overreaction, after all.

"I have had this stomach problem for years. Besides, you are mistaken: there is nothing wrong with the heart of Delgardo Santos Estremosa – a fact which, when I return to my country, I intend to prove to all who ever dared doubt it. They will see."

When Luke returned with the proprietary antacid mixture from the hospital as Delgardo had requested, he took the opportunity of bringing his bag along too. As it turned out, he really needn't have bothered. The Colombian wouldn't let him anywhere near with his stethoscope, not to mention the portable sphygmo for checking blood pressure. Instead, grabbing the bottle of white medicine determinedly from him, he wrenched the lid off and took a long deep swig. His face assumed an air of immediate contentment as he began wrestling playfully within himself with the belch he knew intuitively would follow. When eventually it did, he smiled triumphantly at Luke; his countenance transformed as much by this as by the chalky-white residue which had already dried on his lips.

When Luke left, he did so to the sound of Delgardo's disparaging chides at such clear diagnostic failure. His words became lost, however, in the sudden overhead roar – progressively louder by the second, up to a short-lived, mind-numbing peak. Delgardo's response was immediate – a flood of barked orders to the empty corridor – following which, doors all along sprang open and men darted out,

430

jabbering loudly amongst themselves in Spanish. Luke could not follow what they were saying, though it was clear their level of excitement was intense. They rushed off past him onto the nearest deck.

Luke also wondered what precisely the noise could have been; a helicopter, surely? But why would one be out there, flying so close overhead? Wouldn't it be almost out of range, there on their present course? He followed after Delgardo's men and just caught sight of the Coastguard helicopter moving off into the distance. Delgardo, he noticed, was making his way quickly up onto the Bridge. What on earth could be going on?

It would be several hours more before things became clear to Luke Darius that day. Behind the facade of calm, much was happening – a lot of which, he would only get to hear of later. He knew little of Delgardo's conversation with the Captain, for example and little of the terse incoming messages to the radio room. Little too of what the radar suggested might be waiting to greet them up ahead on their present course.

What Luke did become aware of very soon after, though, was the very radical shift in direction that the Venus Prince next went through. The vessel listed alarmingly as the long sweeping manoeuvre round to the south-west was carried out. Then, about an hour or so later came the tannoy message. It was Captain Symiakos:

"May I have your attention, please. Would all passengers go immediately to the Venturer's Lounge. I have some important information to give you. All passengers must attend. I repeat – all passengers must go immediately to the Venturer's Lounge."

As those nearby him on deck began making their way down to the main lounge, Luke became aware of the distant sound of the helicopter approaching once more. This time, though, it seemed to be coming from behind them. He located it with some difficulty from the stern of the vessel and was surprised to see below it, crouched low on the horizon, what appeared to be a small group of ships following them.

Almost before he had time to consider the possible implications any further, the next tannoy message came:

"Would all Senior Officers and Heads of Department go immediately to the Lido deck. I repeat..."

Already there on the Lido deck, Luke watched as the Captain and Staff Captain came down from the Bridge, accompanied by Delgardo and several of his men. Two, at least, he noticed were carrying machine guns.

V

The call that came through for Ed Jamieson at five that afternoon was startling to say the least.

"The DEA? Get outta here, Rachel. What would a man from the DEA want with me? Okay then, put him through."

The voice, despite the imminent message, was upbeat.

"Mr Jamieson? Hi, this is Felix Reutner, Head of the US DEA. I have some rather important and serious news for you about your ship, Venus Prince. Sorry to have to break it to you like this, sir, but it appears the vessel has been hijacked by a group of Colombian drug-traffickers led by one Delgardo Estremosa. As far as we understand, all passengers and crew are currently well. The ship is being tailed and, at this moment, is heading south towards Panama."

"Panama? – but it was only there yesterday," said Ed quite irrationally, as though this fact alone might have some sort of bearing on things. "What do they want with it?"

"We understand it was used to pick up an arms cache from Nicaragua early this morning. This guy Delgardo – we've been after him for some time now – is a wily bird if ever there was one. We know the Colombian Policia Nacional have been pressuring him a great deal lately, and, though he's been in one or two tight spots, he's somehow always managed to slip through the net."

"Presumably, he's dangerous?"

"Unfortunately, he does have a fairly impressive track record where violence is concerned – though our sources in Colombia tell us he has mellowed considerably over recent years. As to how much danger those on board are in, it's hard to say. We have a team of psychologists working with all available information on him, right this minute. You can no doubt imagine what a tricky situation this is, all round. He's got five hundred and forty-two US nationals alone on board and many others, and that's some bargaining tool, believe me. We'll have to play this very smart indeed; the potential for disaster here is enormous."

"What do you intend to do, exactly, Mr Reutner?"

"I'm afraid we need to keep our cards very close to our chests on this one. Naturally, we're taking advice at the very highest level. This man Estremosa is important to us, but not that important – not when so many lives could be in jeopardy. What we need from you right now though, Mr Jamieson, is as much information about the layout of the ship as you've got – fax it through as quickly as possible on the number I give you. The most detailed plans you can lay your hands on, its full specification, and anything else you feel might help."

"Help what, exactly? You planning on sending a boarding party?"

"Sorry, I can't comment on operational tactics. One other thing, though..."

"Yes?"

"We need to keep this whole thing under wraps for the moment. The last thing we need is to be pushed into doing anything rash by the groundswell of public opinion here at home. These terrorists, by the way, are very much aware of our presence, even though we're holding well back at the moment. The next move will come, I guess, when they try landing at one of the Panamanian ports. No doubt their list of demands will follow soon after."

When Ed Jamieson put the phone down three minutes later, he immediately called John Warringer through to his office.

"John, there are two things I want you to do. First – get me all the plans we've got on the layout of the Venus Prince; and second – go home and pack some things. Whatever your own plans might've been for tonight, forget them. You see, you and me, John, we're going for a short trip down to the Caribbean."

Just after midnight, the Venus Prince slowed to a halt at the Cristobal breakwater. Ricardo Chavez and Miguel Gomez Vicario, in the DEA launch a discreet distance behind, were frankly puzzled. Why had Delgardo chosen to return to the Panama Canal rather than go for one of the ports? What exactly could be in his mind? If he went through the Canal, he must surely know they would have craft waiting at the Balboa end to intercept him?

"I don't like the look of this at all," said Ricardo. "I'm not sure what our venerable bosses might think, but in my mind, this smacks of the grand gesture. Can't help thinking our old friend here might be out to make something of a name for himself."

"You could be right," agreed Miguel, putting down the night-vision binoculars he'd been using and drawing deeply on a cigarette. "Let's just hope all this fancy psychological profiling they're into at the moment doesn't distract from the blindingly obvious."

"I wonder how Ramon's getting on onboard. Keeping his head well down, I hope."

"If he has any sense. Say, Ricardo, did you see that? The lights at the aft of the vessel – they've suddenly all gone out."

"By God, you're right!"

"And look – seems someone's trying to signal: a pretty weak beam, admittedly. Got to be Ramon. It's Morse, I think. I wonder what he's trying to tell us. No, I can't quite make it out. Whatever it is, he sure as hell better keep it brief, for his own sake."

As things stood on the Venus Prince just then, few indeed were aware of the lighting deficiency so recently affecting that section of the ship. The curfew had been in operation for almost four hours now and all passengers and non-essential crew were confined to their cabins. They had taken the Captain's explanation and plea for calm extremely well earlier on in the Venturer's Lounge, where they had congregated as asked.

"If we follow the instructions we have been given, I have been personally assured no one will get hurt. In fact, things will be a lot easier for us all if we comply. And, ladies and gentlemen, please – no heroics. This situation will be resolved very soon, I feel sure. Then, we can get on with our cruise up to Miami. You may continue to move around the ship as normal until the curfew at 8.30 this evening, as mentioned earlier. The deck area near the Bridge has been cordoned off and is out of bounds. So, too, is the radio room. Any further instructions will be given over the tannoy. Please be sure to comply with the curfew call promptly."

Now, as he responded to a cluster of cabin-calls – relating mainly to stress and anticipated insomnia – Luke strolled the lonely corridors, bag in hand. Turning back towards the hospital, he became aware of a minor commotion up ahead. A small group of Delgardo's men had gathered by the rear stairway, machine guns at the ready. A brief conference followed, after which they split up, darting off in different directions. One rushed down the stairs and two up. Luke continued on his intended course and suddenly noticed another of the Colombians emerging breathlessly from the stairwell as he reached it. The man pushed by him, almost as if he wasn't there, disappearing quickly out of sight.

At the hospital, Kate was restocking her visiting bag. Luke related what he'd seen, though it was still far from clear to either of them what precisely was going on. The ship, quite obviously, was no longer moving. They peered out of the hospital port holes, but all they could make out was an array of lights not far off in the distance. They were close to land – but where exactly?

Delgardo, soon after curfew, had decided to commandeer the Captain's cabin. One of his men knocked just then and walked in.

"Those lights that went out at the rear of the vessel? No accident, it would seem. Someone was there in the darkness, signalling. We interrupted him, but I'm afraid he got away. One thing I did notice, though – the strongbacks had been removed from one of the shipside doors down that end. Whoever it was either planned for an accomplice on the Bridge to secretly release the hydraulic mechanism, or he intended to do it himself later. Don't worry, I've left two armed men down there ready to warn off anyone attempting to board."

"Pedro – he was on duty there, wasn't he?" asked Delgardo.

"Yes – hit on the head from behind. We found him unconscious. He came round shortly after, but remembers nothing."

"Okay, Santiago. Get him checked over by that ship's doctor, and keep me informed of any further developments."

"Yes, Delgardo, of course."

As the man left, Delgardo leaned back in the Captain's chair and slowly bit his lip. Something he had always feared now seemed highly likely. The evidence, at least, was strongly suggestive. First, there was the raid on his headquarters, then, the obvious tip-off that had caused the ship to be followed in the first place. Now this.

If he wasn't very much mistaken, it would appear he had a spy in his camp.

Chapter 36

I

It had been more than half an hour since that signalling episode, but still its purpose remained unclear to those on board the DEA launch nearby. It was Ricardo Chavez's turn with the binoculars, though, besides the resumption soon after of normal lighting on the Venus Prince, there was little else to report. Miguel was just finishing up on the phone to their immediate superiors in the area.

"Any news?" asked Ricardo keenly. "Do we know what he wants yet?"

"Afraid not. Our Colombian friend seems strangely reticent about his demands just at the moment. It appears, though, he definitely wants to make a transit of the Canal, and the US Government naturally has agreed to pick up the tab. They're currently using all the influence they can to get the Administrator of the Panama Canal Commission to agree to the transit. He's bound to be reluctant, naturally, knowing the potential security risk to the Canal Operating Area. However, with nearly nine hundred lives at risk – and so many of them American – I've no doubt he can be swayed."

"I still can't understand why Delgardo should have made such a move. Of all the places he should pick to go to, he has to choose one with virtually the highest density of defence sites in this part of the world. Just at this northern end of

439

the Canal alone, according to this map at least, there's Fort Sherman and Fort Davis – both US bases until the handover in the year 2000 – and Fort Gulick."

"A lot of troops, apparently, have already been put on alert, and our own boys from the department should be down here and in position within the hour."

"What about the owners of the ship? They been informed of what's going on?"

"Yes, we've managed to contact the owner – some guy in New York – who's on his way right now. Must've come as a bit of a shock to him hearing about all this."

On the Bridge of the Venus Prince, Delgardo was getting a little impatient.

"What's the delay, Captain? Why are we waiting here?" In the distance, the intense floodlighting of the Gatun Locks was just visible above the tree line. Intervening clusters of lights proclaimed Cristobal harbour to the east and a group of large vessels dotted about ahead of them.

"We are awaiting clearance procedures. Problem is, we contacted Cristobal Harbour only six hours ago with our ETA. Hopefully, in our case, they'll dispense with routine visits by Port Health and the Admeasurers. Next thing, then, would be the arrival on board of the pilots to guide us through."

"And these pilots – they stay on the ship for the whole of the transit period?"

"That is correct," said the Captain. Delgardo seemed suspicious.

"Can't you and your crew take the ship through?"

"I'm afraid not. It is a highly specialised job and these pilots have years of experience. Without them, it would be almost impossible. If you are concerned that they might try sending bogus pilots instead, have no fear. It would be obvious straight away that one or other did not know what they were doing."

"Hmm," said Delgardo, not entirely convinced.

An hour later, Delgardo was still on the Bridge, now pacing irritably up and down. One of his aides came bursting in.

"We are next to go; the pilots are on their way. The Americanos, too, are on the phone again, keen to find out what it is you actually want."

"I'm sure they do," said Delgardo sardonically. "But I'm afraid they will just have to wait."

Within twenty minutes, the pilots had boarded and been shown directly up onto the Bridge. They were clearly apprehensive at the strangeness of the set-up, not least of all the machine guns being brandished by their escorts. Delgardo's own suspicions grew further still when – with the ship now on the move once more – the pilots separated, one to each side of the Bridge, and began preparing themselves for the task ahead.

"These radios they have – not just one, but two each. What game are they trying to play with me, Captain?"

"You will see soon enough, when we approach the Gatun Lock system, how they will need to speak almost simultaneously with each other, as well as to the locomotives guiding us on each side of the lock. Minor alterations have to be carried out almost continuously to steady the ship through:

the tension in each of the connecting lines, or 'wires' as we call them, the speed of each of the locomotives and control of the ship's own power during transit."

The passage through the locks was slow and, for many reasons, once underway, began to show every appearance of being uneventful. No ships were following immediately behind as they'd insisted, and, besides what the Captain reassured him was a normal quota of Canal personnel around the lock system, there appeared to Delgardo little sign of any imminent rescue attempt. Reports from his men around the ship confirmed all was quiet there too. Almost too quiet, he began to think. And then there was that other consideration.

"Santiago," he said to one of his men as he moved to leave the Bridge.

"Yes, Delgardo?"

"Bring that doctor to see me. I'll be down in the Captain's cabin."

When Luke arrived, the clock on the wall said 5.30. Delgardo looked up and gestured for him to sit.

"Doctor, this man you saw earlier, Pedro Berrio – the one who suffered the blow to the head. How did you find him?"

Luke thought back for a moment to his examination of the man a few hours earlier.

"He was dazed, certainly, but as I recall, there were no abnormal neurological signs as a result of his trauma. He was okay when he left the hospital. Why – has he deteriorated since? If so, I must see him immediately."

"He's fine – but tell me, did he have any bad contusion on his scalp?"

"No, none. Just a headache and some temporary drowsiness."

"Any local marks at all, to show that he had in fact been hit?"

"No, come to think of it, he didn't. Why do you ask? You suspect that maybe he wasn't hit at all? You don't even trust your own men?"

Delgardo looked at him irritably now. He was just about to answer when one of his men knocked and came in. Delgardo's attitude changed immediately.

"You have given over our list of demands?" he asked.

"Yes, Compadre. They say we should hear back within the hour."

"And how long before we are finally through this lock system?"

"Half an hour more at the most, I am told."

"You know exactly where I want the ship brought to a halt?"

"Si, Señor. I haven't informed them yet, but I will soon."

"And the other little job – it has been carried out?"

"Just finished. When you are ready, just give the word and the timers will be set."

"Excellent. It will certainly give them something else to think about when the helicopters arrive."

Having successfully disengaged from the locomotives on leaving the last of the three locks, the Venus Prince began making its way slowly out into Gatun Lake. The expected pick

443

up of speed, however, did not materialise. After little more than two hundred yards – and to the puzzlement of all those watching out of sight in the wings – the ship pulled suddenly to a stop. One of the least verbally reticent of the onlookers, the DEA officer Ricardo Chavez, was not slow to voice his thoughts:

"What the fuck they doing now?" he said simply.

"I wonder...," began Miguel, but his words remained hanging as he pondered the point further.

"Wonder what?" said Ricardo impatiently.

"Well, we've had his demands, right – the money, the helicopters?"

"Yeah, so what?"

"And he's clearly very keen for a reply as soon as possible. Remember, he didn't like it one bit when we told him it might take some time to get those things he asked for organised – especially the five million in cash."

"Right."

"Well, stopping the ship there as he has, might in fact turn out to be quite a shrewd move on his part – particularly as it's very much blocking the Canal to other users. Think about it, Ricardo: as time goes on, more and more ships will be backed up causing huge delays all round. And were it to continue for more than a day or so, I should think there'd be a pretty sizeable loss of revenue too. All this, presumably, until his demands are met in full. To his credit, Delgardo still hasn't said anything specific about actually harming the passengers. Though, I accept an omission like that from a man like Delgardo is hardly cause for complacency at this stage of the game."

"But surely, presuming his demands are agreed, transfer to the helicopters would be a far riskier business with the ship in its current position. He'd be safer a good deal further into Gatun Lake."

"You're right, of course – and doubtless Delgardo knows this too. Either, he'll move the ship once the demands are seen to be met, or..."

"Or, what?"

"Or, my friend, he has something else up his sleeve instead."

II

Luke Darius, at that moment, was still sitting opposite Delgardo in the Captain's cabin. The aide who had been present with them had just left, and having heard what had been so cryptically mentioned before about the setting of timers, Luke felt the best thing he could do just then was leave as soon as possible too. Whatever it was sounded serious: a diversion of some sort planned for when Delgardo was set to leave the Venus Prince. What in God's name could it be? Some kind of bomb, perhaps – either somewhere in the ship itself, or maybe even planted in one of the locks, if that had been possible during transit? If he could just get away now, with luck, there might be some chance of finding out. Then, at least, they might...

"Relax, Doctor – you're staying put," said Delgardo, sensing his restlessness.

"You really think you'll get away with this? The Canal area hereabouts must be absolutely crawling with military personnel. How far do you really think you'll get before they intercept you in your helicopters and shoot you down?"

"I don't think that will happen, Doctor. You see, we shall take hostages – US citizens like yourself." Luke did not choose to correct him on this point. "In fact, if you haven't guessed already, I can tell you that you have been chosen to be one of them. You, the smart-arse doctor, who doesn't even know simple indigestion when you see it."

Luke was shaken but in combative mood. He could take the insults, no problem, but there was still a lot he didn't understand about what was going on.

"Why have you done this? I mean, why are you even aboard this ship?" The words came out louder and more heatedly than he'd intended. Delgardo's expression remained amused.

"This, my friend, is a good ship. At least, it has been a good ship where my interests are concerned, over the past few years. Today, it is carrying arms, but this, in fact, is the first time. Before, it was a different cargo entirely."

Luke knew precisely what he was referring to. So, he'd been right – the ship had been used for cocaine trafficking. Another thought struck him just then; that bit about their current cargo. What exactly did the consignment consist of – and what part was it to play in the little diversion they had planned? Where then might it be stashed?

"So, why do you need all these arms?" he asked after a pause, trying to make the question sound as innocent as possible.

"I have my reasons," replied Delgardo succinctly. His mood though, as Luke had already judged, was far too garrulous to leave it at that. Luke had caught him on a roll. For some reason, at this particular time, this man seemed to enjoy his presence there as an audience. Why, from a psychological viewpoint, might this be? What was going on in his head? And, if he could continue in his current, non-threatening role as an effective outsider seemingly in awe, how much more might he get to learn?

"You see, Doctor, back in my country I have many enemies. Not just, as you might think, the Colombian authorities or the US law enforcement agencies, who seem particularly keen at the moment to help the Administration in Washington score political points. I'm talking about people I once thought of as friends, as my equals – in the same sort of rank regionally in the Cartel. And, of course, the young, eager upstarts they bribe into carrying out their dirty work."

"Like German Bocuse?"

"Where did you hear that name?"

"His sister, Consuela, you may recall, I once met. It was her baby you had me deliver that afternoon. She told me her brother was missing. She is naturally distraught. Then I heard of the death of a Colombian sailor on board. Was it him?"

"The trouble with German was that he listened to the wrong people. He was ambitious, certainly, but weak and easily swayed. They talked him into actions they themselves were far too scared to try. Sadly, he paid the price."

"And Dan Forsbrook – did he too pay the price?" It was a bit of a long shot, but definitely worth a try.

"Oh, he paid the price alright," said Delgardo with some relish. "Make no mistake about it."

"But what could a man like him have possibly done to you to warrant such treatment?"

"Forsbrook was a fool, but, worse than that, he was a gambler. He gambled once too often. He tried to deceive me."

"So, you had him killed?" said Luke incredulously.

"Forsbrook was paid a large sum of money to ensure that this ship remained on its present itinerary – an itinerary which, as you can guess, served my business interests well. As a matter of fact, it was a little business I had on the side, well apart from the Cartel; the money my own. My own personal pension, so to speak. Not only did Forsbrook fail to persuade those he needed to that the change they proposed would be a bad idea, he also blew the money I paid him on gambling and tried to trick me with counterfeit notes in return."

"So, he had to die?"

"But that, my friend, was not all. He also arranged to have me ambushed by the Policia Nacional in Cartagena at the hotel where he handed over the fake money. Two of my closest and most trusted colleagues were killed that night. This kind of behaviour in my country is not without consequence. But death, in his case, you may be interested to learn, was not strictly down to me. There was someone else – another person, an outsider, equally keen on revenge where Mr Dan Forsbrook was concerned. So keen, in fact, that this person was prepared to pay handsomely for the chance to have it carried out in my territory. Inventive too, so it transpired.

"This man Forsbrook, you probably didn't realise, Doctor," Delgardo continued, "had an agency out East for sex tourists interested only in children. 'Eastern Promise', it was called.

These children were videoed too – there in the act, so to speak. The person I referred to earlier, who came to Colombia seeking revenge, had somehow or other learnt of this set up, and devised a method of death particularly suited to a man of Forsbrook's certain persuasion. It involved the use of a few of what I term my 'Junior Squad'. And, as the video of his death shows – if you ever get to see it – they did an excellent job."

"And who exactly was this person who came to Colombia and wanted him dead so badly?" asked Luke.

III

Tara Scott had found it particularly difficult to sleep that night. There had been a whole host of things on her mind as she lay there in the small attic bedroom of her home in Sheepshead Bay.

In fact, sleep had become difficult most nights now, since her mother's dramatic revelations about her father. Those, of course, and what she'd now managed to find out about the man she knew to be ultimately behind her ordeal in Caracas. Even now, as she lay there in that protracted early-morning silence, time seemed in very little hurry. She tried once again to fit all this latest information into the puzzle her life had become. At 6.55, she finally gave up on sleep and flicked on her bedside radio. She needed some kind of respite from those interminable thoughts.

The song currently in full swing soon came very unslickly to a close, giving way to the seven o'clock news. The first headline was enough to ensure her fullest attention:

"News just in tells of the hijacking of a cruise ship in the southern Caribbean. The Venus Prince, a twenty-one-thousand-ton vessel carrying over five hundred American citizens and three hundred others among both passengers and crew, has been boarded and taken over by a dangerous Colombian drug baron and his gang. The ship has recently come to a standstill in the Panama Canal and the hijackers are demanding five million US dollars and two helicopters to enable their escape. It is assumed that hostages will be taken, but no further details are currently available. Nobody is thought to have been hurt so far."

Tara jumped up, hardly believing her ears. Her immediate thought was for Luke and his safety. Thank God nobody had so far been hurt. She then remembered her uncle. Surely, he must have already heard the news?

"Mr. Reutner, I have the President for you." The statement was a little redundant, particularly as that protected phone line was used by no other person. Reutner took a deep breath. This was the call he'd been expecting – provoked in part, he guessed, by his timely involvement of the media. A voice familiar to him came on the line.

"Felix, listen. I want this hijack cleared up as quickly and as safely as possible. Offer these assholes whatever the hell they want – just get them off that ship. The last thing this Administration needs right now is a human fucking disaster on its hands.

"I know you've been after this Delgardo Estremosa for some time, Felix, but with so many US nationals on board and potentially in danger, I think we've just got to ignore the broader drugs issue for the moment. Therefore, Felix, you will continue to liaise with the other agencies involved as you have been doing – with Ted Jerome at the CIA, and the FBI director, Jim Wallace and his boys. I'm afraid, though, they will now be taking over control – at least until the passengers and crew are safe.

"If we can get Estremosa successfully off the ship though, responsibility for dealing with him and his team will once again move back to you. I understand you already have men and all other necessary resources in place?"

"That's correct, sir. May I ask what the situation will be if, as we suspect, he takes hostages?"

"I think, in that case, Felix, we might have to accept the situation as being a little more uncertain. Okay, so he takes a small number of hostages – the equation then will have become completely different. Sure, we must be seen to act with the hostages' interests primarily in mind, but at that point, the American people will also want to see this man caught and dealt with appropriately. The main thing is not to do anything too rash – or at least, not be seen to be doing it, anyway. Be patient, Felix, okay? If you're going to take them, choose the time and place carefully."

Felix Reutner put the phone down, pretty well satisfied with the way things were now looking. He had suspected this might be the President's response, and it was right on cue – particularly as news crews were, no doubt, at that very minute, setting up for what otherwise might be a lengthy encampment outside on Pennsylvania Avenue. All efforts were now being made to give Delgardo what he wanted, which was fine by him.

Now that all required forces were in place to deal with them once they were off the ship, the fate of Delgardo and his men, as far as he was concerned, was effectively sealed. His team had come too far in their mission to fail at this late stage.

IV

At 08.45, final word of agreement on terms reached the radio room of the Venus Prince. The news presented to Delgardo shortly after – along with details of the special transfer arrangements to the helicopters – was received with surprising relief. He had never really planned for a long stand-off. It was clear now that he was seriously undermanned for this latest situation he found himself in – for all but the most acquiescent of crews and placid group of passengers. So much so, that any challenge from within would almost certainly have to be dealt with in the severest of terms: a clear posting of intent should anyone else wish to chance their arm in the hero stakes.

So far, he'd got away with it. But night had kept a good many of the practical problems at bay. Now, though, a restlessness was becoming apparent among the passengers – to the point that some were even daring to venture out of their cabins in the mistaken belief that, as the ship itself had stopped, all previous problems on board must somehow have been resolved.

Now that the helicopters were on their way, Delgardo called his men together for one final briefing. Less than ten minutes later, each knew what they had to do and what, in general terms, was expected of them. There were to be two teams of six, the first led by Santiago – his most trusted remaining colleague – and the second by Delgardo himself. Two of the four hostages were to be taken by each team, strategically positioned in front and behind them so as to dissuade possible sniper fire. The one point Delgardo failed to elaborate on was the deliberate placement of Carlos Montes in Santiago's team, with the secret instruction for him to keep a close eye on Pedro Barrio, the man Delgardo still suspected of being a traitor; this despite his claimed blow to the head the night before.

Montes, although fairly new to the group, had, nevertheless, shown himself to be loyal and trustworthy – as well as ruthless when the situation demanded it. He had proved his usefulness in other ways too, his first-aid skills from military training days high amongst them.

Luke had been sitting alone in one of the cabins below the Bridge for what felt like an age now. There had seemed little point in attempting to resist at the time he was first delivered there. As the key turned in the lock, however, and it struck home for the first time that he was actually being restrained, a sense of outrage grew within him.

His mind was in something of a whirl following Delgardo's revelations: he still couldn't take in all that he'd been told.

Suddenly, voices became audible approaching. As he held his breath and listened harder, the door of the cabin shuddered momentarily then burst open. Two people initially – a man and a woman – were shoved roughly over the threshold, followed a few moments later by a dishevelled, sobbing, younger woman, hurled inwards and landing fully in Luke's arms. It was Sandy. Her clothes were badly torn and there were deep scratches on her arms.

"What have they done to you?" he asked in alarm.

"Those bastards out there followed me back to my cabin and grabbed me. If it wasn't for the fact Rick happened to come by at the time, I think I would have been raped. Instead, when he tried to intervene, they simply beat him senseless while I watched. They didn't even stop when he was unconscious."

"He's still there in your cabin?"

"Yes, they just left him – crumpled up on the floor. Luke, I hope to God he's okay."

There were other sounds now in the distance; not simply the usual Gatun Lock-side noises he'd become so accustomed to over the weeks. A new set of mechanical sounds were becoming audible, getting slowly louder. Luke tried to ignore the implications of the fact that they sounded remarkably like rotor blades. There seemed little doubt that soon the four of them would be called.

In the event, when the heavy footsteps reached the cabin door not long after, it was only him they wanted.

"Doctor, come with us quickly." Luke obeyed, puzzled, managing what he hoped would be a reassuring wink at Sandy as he left.

Delgardo was lying on a couch as he entered. He was pale and sweaty, and clearly agitated by his predicament. It did not prevent him, though, from barking orders at his men in his usual way. Two, Luke noticed, were seated at the Captain's desk with a small open suitcase to one side.

"It's all there, Delgardo – every last dollar," said one of them after a pause – the one Luke recognised as Santiago.

"And you're certain it's not fake? I'm not getting stung again."

"It's legitimate alright, as far as we can tell."

"Good. Now, Doctor...," said Delgardo a little breathlessly, turning his attention to Luke, "some more of your medicine please – and fast. In fact, bring several bottles. We have the money we demanded, and, as you've no doubt heard, the helicopters have arrived. We must get going at once."

"Permit me to give my medical opinion," said Luke, "not just my medicine. I believe your problem has nothing at all to do with your digestion. I think, in fact, you are, at this very moment, having a heart attack and need immediate hospital attention. Even here on the ship, we can help."

"Nonsense. You are a fool. Just get me the medicine. Go with him, Carlos, and be quick."

When Luke entered the hospital, he was delighted to find Kate there restocking her bag. Despite his escort – whom he felt sure would not allow him too much leeway to speak with her – he did manage a brief general enquiry as he looked through the medicine cabinet close to where she was standing. Her reply was encouraging.

"Fine – but that poor man in cabin 376?" he said with an urgent wink. "Dealt with him, yet?"

Kate looked back a little blankly at first. Then something registered. Room 376 was Sandy's.

Luke returned with the man called Carlos and the medicine but clearly Delgardo was worse. One deep swig followed closely by another saw an intensification of his breathlessness and a look on his face changing slowly to one of disbelief. The pain was of an intensity he had clearly never experienced before and the medicine just wasn't working.

"He must be taken to the hospital immediately," said Luke, taking his pulse.

With a telling lack of protest now from their boss, his men silently acquiesced.

Once down in the hospital, Luke felt it best not to have too many of Delgardo's men buzzing around him, getting in his way while he worked. One of his aides, Carlos – the one who had accompanied him earlier to the hospital – seemed to appreciate his concern. With his help, Luke ushered the others out into the waiting room and closed the door. Only two remained – Carlos and Santiago, whom Delgardo insisted should stay close at hand. Kate, thankfully, was not there when they arrived.

The aide named Carlos clearly had some knowledge of nursing techniques, taking sterile packs from the shelves and passably setting up one of the dressings trolleys. Almost predictably though, as soon as Luke got an IV infusion going, the cardiac monitor on and the diagnosis all but confirmed, Delgardo suddenly sat up on the examination couch claiming he was better, and why the hell all this fuss? He called Santiago over to him.

"My friend, it is time we left this ship and got away from here," he said. "Set the timers for thirty minutes, then get the money and the men together at the rear shipside door where the tender will arrive. I will be there to meet you in fifteen."

Luke looked over at Carlos as Santiago left. He was busy drawing up the diamorphine Luke had taken from the locked Controlled Drugs box and placed on the trolley. He was clearly as unimpressed by his boss's sudden recovery as Luke himself.

Delgardo next began feverishly pulling off the monitor leads and tried to stand. It was during the attempted disconnection of the intravenous line, however, that he suffered the relapse, clutching his chest in sudden, uncontrollable agony.

Carlos helped Luke get him back on the couch and quickly they reconnected him. Luke gestured for the diamorphine: it was urgent now that it be given. Adequate pain relief was vital.

Carlos had already finished drawing it up, checking it with him against the empty vials Luke had watched him break open earlier. Handing him the syringe, Luke inserted it into the side slot of the cannula in Delgardo's forearm and began the slow intravenous injection. At this point, Luke noticed, Carlos was leaning over talking calmly to Delgardo in Spanish.

What intrigued Luke more than anything at that moment was the vigour of Delgardo's response. He had anticipated Carlos' words, however they translated, to soothe and reassure his patient. Instead, they appeared to agitate Delgardo still further – an agitation which became more and more acute with the increasing speed of Carlos' word flow. Finally – with nothing short of pure terror on his face – Delgardo struggled to get himself up. A combination of weakness and his aide's restraining hand quickly prevented it.

Luke continued the injection hoping that as the drug took more effect on his pain so his agitation too would subside. The monitor, Luke noticed, was showing a tachycardia – the speeding up of Delgardo's heart rate – which was followed very soon after, by a loud, agitated scream. Carlos was still talking animatedly to him in words Luke had little chance of understanding, his face now bent low, close to that of his boss. As his voice finally tailed off, he turned triumphantly to watch Luke giving the last of the injection. Luke nodded to him, still a little perplexed – at which point Delgardo suddenly began to convulse there right before them, then slip more and more deeply into coma.

What the hell was going on, Luke asked himself, turning the Colombian roughly into the recovery position and trying desperately to take stock of the situation? The convulsions had now stopped, at least for the time being, but the tachycardia, though not vast, persisted. There were no new changes on the heart monitor but the blood pressure was now raised well above the base-line level checked earlier. Also, it was clear Delgardo's pupils were now noticeably dilated.

Luke was stumped. Had he perhaps had some kind of stroke?

Just then, Luke could hear Santiago returning and beckoning the men in the waiting room to follow him to the exit point as arranged. Time was ticking on. So too, Luke realised with sudden alarm, the timer that had obviously now been set. There were less than twenty minutes until whatever explosive device had been planted, went off.

A knock came at the door. Carlos gestured to him to stay quiet and went to answer it – opening the door, Luke noticed, little more than a fraction. Santiago and another man were outside. Carlos mumbled something to them which included the phrase 'ten minutes', and they left. Clearly, he did not wish to share with the others the precise severity of Delgardo's condition. But why the deceit?

"What did you say to them?" Luke asked.

"I told them Delgardo was okay and we would be with them very shortly. You and I, Doctor, will have to work fast."

Two things struck Luke almost simultaneously as the other man spoke. The first was surely that Carlos was aware that no amount of time – let alone ten minutes – would be enough to render Delgardo fit to make his escape. The second was the degree of change in the voice of the man speaking: Luke could hardly believe it was the same person.

"What do you mean 'work fast'? And who are you, anyway?"

"My name is Ramon Garcia. I am an undercover agent for the US DEA. I will explain everything later. At this moment, we must quickly vacate this place and lock it behind us. If they return, they will hopefully be fooled, initially at least, into thinking Delgardo too has left. In the meantime, we each have a separate and highly important job to do. You must try to make it up to the Bridge where the other officers are tied up. Release the Radio Officer and get him to put out a message to the effect that Delgardo is now dead, and to storm the ship directly. If we're in luck, that will coincide more or less with the time these men discover the truth about their leader."

"And you?" asked Luke.

"I have something else to do. There are almost twenty pounds of Semtex waiting to blow several sizeable holes in the bottom of this ship anytime now. If it goes down here in this spot, as Delgardo intends, it will effectively block the Panama Canal for God knows how long. Not only that, but we might well have an absolute disaster on our hands if we can't somehow prevent it."

V

Luke set off at pace, tracing his way along the most obscure corridors he could find. At every corner, he stopped, peering round cautiously, making sure the way forward was clear. He had almost made it as far as the foyer when he could hear voices behind coming up from the rear stairwell towards the hospital. If it were Delgardo's men, would they take the locked door at face value? How long before they returned to smash it down? And what state would Delgardo be in then – still comatose, or even worse?

It went against all his instincts as a doctor to desert an ill patient in this way, no matter what their station in life – or, in this case, degree of villainy. But it was clear to him now that so much more was at stake; so many more lives – perhaps even his own. He'd been right about the explosives, though. Would Carlos or Ramon – or whatever he was called – really get to deal with them in time?

The foyer, he was relieved to find, was deserted. So too, most of the corridors to the fore of the ship. Breathless yet determined, Luke attacked the forward stairs with every remaining ounce of energy he possessed. So far so good. Could he really make it all the way up to the Bridge without being noticed? The last bit would be the most difficult, close to the Captain's cabin – particularly if any of Delgardo's men were still in last-minute residence. Just then, he heard a noise from behind him.

Luke paused for a moment, flattening himself against the wall at the top of the stairway. He found himself dividing his attention almost equally between who, if anyone, might be following, and whom, if anyone, he might encounter taking the next few steps through the doorway ahead of him. The noise below, as he waited, seemed to drift away to nothing. Breathing a momentary sigh of relief, Luke pushed the door gently and stealthily made his way through. He held on to it as it closed to avoid any giveaway noises. The corridor he entered was silent.

As he approached the Bridge, all was silent too. Pausing for a moment, he suddenly pulled open the Bridge door a fraction, ready to slam it quickly and run – not quite sure who might be there to greet him. What he saw convinced him the DEA man had been correct. Forming a sitting line along two of the perimeter walls were all the other ship's officers and the two Panamanian pilots – painstakingly, but simply, bound and gagged.

Luke's arrival – and subsequent commentary whilst busily untying Savas, the Chief Radio Officer – appeared to provoke at least some animation amongst them. This was particularly so when he came to mention the latest regarding Delgardo

461

and the threat of imminent explosion and scuttling of the ship. Next to the Radio Officer sat Tassos Demetriou. Judging by the look in his eyes, he was eager to help. Luke untied him too, glad to have some muscle on their side. As the Radio Officer was briefed on the message to be sent, the Captain was also freed – then left, rather unceremoniously, simply to untie the others.

They reached the radio room to find some of the equipment damaged. Luke and Tassos stood watch, while Savas struggled to get the message out. Just then, footsteps, then voices, could be heard nearby. Looking below, back towards the corridor used by the Colombians, Luke could make out one of Delgardo's men escorting the three other hostages from the cabin where they had been locked in. The Colombian walked behind, his large machine-gun held confidently at bay. It did not appear he was expecting trouble. He was certainly not expecting what happened next...

Motioning his intent silently to Luke, Tassos waited patiently until Sandy and the other two hostages had passed by below them. Then, without any discernible warning, the startled Colombian found two hundred and forty pounds of normally amiable Greek landing squarely on top of him. As the machine-gun skidded across the floor away from him, Luke found himself leaping wildly from his perch to retrieve it. Though he held it as confidently as he could while the man was taken up to the Bridge for detention, it was – as Tassos later remarked – in the manner of someone balancing a large turd on a shovel, hoping all the while it wouldn't fall off.

Sandy, though still shaken, was clearly glad of the intervention – as indeed were the others. They remained rooted to the spot, still there when Luke returned barely two minutes later. As he reached them, he noticed Savas coming out of the radio room.

"Any luck?" he asked anxiously. He watched the man's lips form the reply. His words, though, when they came were interrupted by several loud bursts of gunfire from the other end of the ship. Luke glanced at his watch, then quickly back at the Radio Officer who was now nodding. Gunfire, yes, but thankfully, so far, no explosion. It was surely now overdue.

Were they safe?

Ten very anxious minutes later, it appeared to be all over. The deck was suddenly awash with friendly troops, swarming quickly but methodically towards the Bridge. Luke found himself clutching Sandy where they had crouched, tightly in relief. As he pulled back and looked into her eyes, he could see the anxiety locked in behind the smile, and remembered.

"Quick, let's get down to your cabin – Kate might still be there with Rick."

It turned out she wasn't – though nor was Rick. They were, however, both down in the hospital. Bruised, and still considerably blood-stained, Rick was helping Kate with another casualty of the affray – the victim of a bad gunshot wound to the leg. It was Jose, the Honduran.

"He'll be okay," said Kate, sensing Luke's concern. "Apparently ran into one of the Colombians setting up some kind of explosive device right down in the bowels of the ship.

Didn't say a word – just took a shot at him. Shattered his lower femur, but his vital signs are good."

Luke took Jose's hand and squeezed it gently. One thing was patently clear – there was no way Jose would be able to work on ships for some considerable time to come. How might his family back home cope now this had occurred? Then another thought struck Luke. If Jose was there on the examination couch, where was Delgardo?

He looked further round the room. There was quite a crowd now gathered. Over to one side, Sandy was embracing Rick. Thank God he was okay. They made a nice couple. Then, another familiar face became visible at the far end. It was the man called Ramon – undoubtedly the hero of the hour. Beside him, looking generally very pleased with themselves, were two other Latino types – colleagues of his, no doubt. And Delgardo?

Ramon indicated the body over on the first of the two hospital beds as Luke approached. No sheet covered his dead form, nothing to detract from the striking poignancy of that moment. Luke stood in silence and looked on, staring at the lifeless, glazed-eyed form lying there – cold and unblinking like a large stranded fish.

"Doctor Darius – meet my two good friends, colleagues in the DEA. This is Ricardo Chavez, and this, Miguel Gomez Vicario. We have been working towards this day for a very long time." Luke shook their hands warmly then quickly took Ramon off to one side. He needed a quiet word.

"Tell me one thing that's been puzzling me," he said.

"Of course, Doctor."

"What was it you were actually saying to Delgardo while he was lying there earlier? Whatever it was, it seemed to be getting him as agitated as hell."

"Interesting you should ask. The fact is, my friend, I was simply telling him that the doctor to whom he was at that moment entrusting his life, was just then injecting – in all good faith – a drug he believed to be diamorphine, to treat his heart attack."

"What do you mean, 'believed to be'?" interrupted Luke incredulously.

"I then went on to explain that I, personally, had switched syringes at the very last moment for one I had already prepared for such an opportunity. That one contained the sort of huge dose of crack cocaine that killed my own son barely three years ago."

"Cocaine?!" exclaimed Luke. "My God, you're joking. No wonder he reacted that way when he realised what was going on."

"Indeed. He also knew by that time – and I must admit it gave me great pleasure to inform him – that I had infiltrated his operation specifically to exact my revenge: to give him a taste of his own medicine, so to speak. You see, Doctor, the cocaine which killed Hank, my son, had been supplied, I discovered, by none other than this man, Delgardo Estremosa himself."

Chapter 37

I

It made great copy.

"Just the kind of thing the world needs to hear right now," commented Carl Silvers of CNN as he prepared for the special news report that evening.

"Absolutely. There's a kind of poetic justice to it," agreed his colleague Andrea Kimble, glancing at her autocue. "Drug Lord killed in massive cocaine overdose – every news editor's dream."

"Clearly knew he'd finally been caught this time round. Not as though he didn't have ready access to the stuff."

"That the official verdict?"

"Yeah – according to the statement from the DEA. Turns out it was entirely within the range of what they might've expected of him from the psychological profile they'd built up."

Saturday April 26th

II

Luke Darius stood on the deck of the Venus Prince the following day and gazed out once more at a familiar and constant sea. They were heading north now – almost straight for Miami – attempting to salvage something at least from this last cruise. It would mean missing out on Cayman, but they could manage a few brief hours at Cozumel and still make it back as planned on the Monday. Hearteningly, passengers had, in the main, elected to stay on, though Ed Jamieson had made the offer to fly all those who wanted directly back to the States following their ordeal.

Luke had only seen Jamieson briefly earlier on, in company with a man called Warringer. Even then it was clear his company boss had other concerns on his mind: finding a replacement Captain and Staff Captain for the remainder of the trip for one thing, and more permanent replacements for the new season ahead due to start in about ten days' time.

Chatting as he had with Ramon Garcia before the ship sailed out of Cristobal Harbour very early that morning, it seemed the DEA now had quite a lot on the two Greeks and their involvement with Delgardo. Not just the 'arrangement' of using the ship, but details of regular money transfers to their individual offshore accounts. They had learnt too of the death on board of German Bocuse and the involvement of these two, in particular, in its cover up. A signed statement apparently had been obtained from Jose's compatriot, Hernando Veso, giving details of the special storage arrangements used on board for the body. In time, Ramon had said, they might even get round to looking up a certain Dr Pedro Rodriguez, who had provided what they believed to be false medical certification for the corpse. At this stage, though, they accepted it would be virtually impossible to prove anything about the true cause of death.

Luke found himself wondering about Jose. He had been a good friend. It was sad to see him leave – particularly in that state. The arrangement had been that he be taken directly to the hospital in Panama City for emergency surgery. From there, when fit, he would return to his home on the outskirts of Managua. His address was there in Luke's diary. Two days from then, when they finally reached Miami, Luke would be flying directly to New York to meet Tara. He had spoken to her only briefly from a payphone in Cristobal that previous evening, but there was a lot more he knew he had to say.

Ed Jamieson's mind was also taken over by a number of concerns just then. His mode of travel back to the US, though, afforded him less time to dwell on them. In under four hours now, his plane would touch down at JFK and he would be faced once again with the other major dilemma affecting his life just then.

He was pleased this business with the ship had been so painlessly resolved. Thankfully – as far as he could tell, at least – the media hadn't cottoned on to the story of his ship's involvement with Delgardo Estremosa before the hijacking occurred. In return for all his assistance, the DEA man, Garcia, had assured him they would do their best to prevent that bit becoming public knowledge. Ed dreaded to think what effect such information might have on his company should a leak ever occur.

Ed's other problem was what to do about Sophia. Life had become so complicated now she had reappeared on the scene. Not that unconsciously he hadn't been wishing for such a thing since the very day she'd left him all those years ago.

468

When he was with her, he could feel all the old feelings rushing back. He hated himself for it, yet found himself transfixed by her power; by this control she had over him. He despised her, too, for her blatant disregard for Ellen. Or was that his fault as well, for not taking a stronger stand on Ellen's behalf?

And what of Ellen – dear, trusting Ellen? Had she possibly guessed there was now another woman on the scene? Why hadn't he told her of Sophia's return to New York and her cry for help? He was, after all, only doing what any old friend would do in the same situation. Or was he? Who did he really think he was kidding?

What then was he to do from here? Clearly, some kind of decision would have to be made. On the one hand, there was Ellen – warm, sincere and reserved, her beauty fading, almost lost now behind a comfortable exterior. Then there was Sophia – outgoing, pretentious and calculating; an up-front personality with a sexuality to match. And there was one other attribute too, which Ed found great difficulty in ignoring – those shares she owned in George Mitchell's cruise company.

III

"My name is Jack Buchanan. I am a long-time friend of your Uncle Ed's and I need to speak to you. May I come in?"

Tara vaguely recognised the name, and, though her mother was out, showed the big, broken-nosed Irishman into the lounge.

"What can I do for you, Mr Buchanan? Is Uncle Ed okay?"

"He's fine, though, as you know, he's been through one hell of a lot lately with the hijacking of his ship, and before that, Dan Forsbrook's death."

"A terrible business that, by all accounts. Left Uncle busier than ever, I should think, with the new season..."

"I've come to return this," said Jack stepping forward. "It's yours, I take it?"

"Oh that? Yeah. Where did you find it?"

"On the floor of Dan Forsbrook's hotel room in Colombia. The one where he'd been killed."

Tara looked stunned.

"Does anybody else know of this? Does Uncle Ed?" Her voice faltered as she spoke.

"No, he doesn't; nor, as far as I am aware, do the Colombian authorities. The local police didn't strike me as overly-fazed by what had happened, either. They clearly didn't go overboard searching for clues. So, would you care to explain?"

"I didn't kill him, if that's what you think," replied Tara quickly. "Though I still ask myself what might have happened if I'd gotten there first."

"He was dead already?"

"It was shocking, really. I couldn't believe the scene when I arrived. I'd intended to surprise him, yes. To confront him, certainly. To..." Her voice trailed away into silence.

"How did you know where he'd be? Such an out of the way place like that."

"I followed him – right from when he first left DC. I was there ten rows behind him on his flight; a little disguised, perhaps, but there all the same. It wasn't easy tailing him once we were in Colombia, but I was determined. That bastard."

Jack knew what it was she wanted to say – sensed the very strength of feeling that lay there still painfully raw behind her words. He even knew what she didn't – why Forsbrook had involved her in that appalling set up in Caracas in the first place. And though he'd have liked to come clean over all they had learnt, his hands were tied in this respect for Ed's sake. Instead, he let her talk. Only after she'd finished did it finally occur to her to ask about his own involvement in the case.

"I was brought in by your uncle to investigate some of the more dubious aspects of Dan Forsbrook's rather amazing double life. Not only was he a serious gambler, but also – as I believe you've discovered to your cost – someone heavily involved in the sleaze industry."

"You know about Caracas, then?"

"I have discovered something of what happened; though I have to tell you, your uncle Ed is still very much in the dark." It was better this way, figured Jack.

"Perhaps it's just as well – the fewer that know, the better I'll feel. A video was taken that afternoon, you know. And ten copies made since, according to that sleazebag Earlham when he had a gun in his groin."

"So, it was you at that apartment in Georgetown? Nice touch the pepperoni, by the way. If it's any consolation, we've found all ten copies of the video when we raided Wayne Gibson's house in DC. Only problem's the master copy – we still haven't traced that yet. We suspect it must be in Forsbrook's apartment, wherever the hell that is. We know he's got one, but we haven't the slightest clue where in the Washington area it could be."

"You know, I've got a feeling I might know. I don't have the address but I can show you. I tailed him there about four in the morning one time – the night he'd met with Gibson at the Magellan Hotel and then went for one of his late casino sessions. I should remember the street when I see it – I spent the rest of the night there in my car."

"Terrific! What a lucky break. Say, are you free tomorrow? I'll get one or two of the boys from the DC Vice Squad. We'll go then."

"You know, I've often asked myself why it was me targeted like that in Caracas."

Here Jack shrugged and awkwardly met her gaze.

"I do, however, have a theory. I doubt there's really any easy way of proving it, but let's just say locating that master tape is absolutely vital. I couldn't make the connection at first, but then I made a couple of very interesting discoveries about our old friend Dan Forsbrook."

IV

It came as something of a shock to Ellen when she saw it. Just when she'd got it into her head that she had completely overreacted in the first place; when it was clear enough it was the hijacking of the ship that had taken Ed away so secretively like that this time. She even managed to reconcile other of his recent nights away as being legitimate business obligations too. But what she saw there in front of her that

Saturday afternoon as she pulled out Ed's clothes from the laundry basket was enough to convince her she had been right all along in the first place. The lipstick on the back of his shirt collar was not her own – a garish shade she wouldn't be seen dead in. Then, as she held the garment up to her nose, the other tell-tale sign hit home, blatantly and brutally; its scent.

When she recovered – at least to the point where she came to a decision and bundled the shirt into the washing machine along with the rest of the whites – Ellen left the laundry room and made her way through to the lounge. Her husband, she knew, would be back later that night. She poured herself a stiff drink and sat thinking, twice glancing over at the framed wedding photos on the mantlepiece. It would be their sixth anniversary in only two days' time – Monday April 28th – a date etched firmly in her mind at least. Would her husband manage to remember it this time round – with business, and now this other love interest, competing for his attention?

She ought to confront him, she knew; ought to have kept that damn shirt to shove in his face when he walked through the door. She knew equally well though, this was not her style. No matter how she tried, she could never bring herself to act in such a way. She would cry, yes, but only when he wasn't watching or wasn't there; when precious memories of their life together resurfaced and cruelly taunted her; when she realised her future had all but evaporated, leaving behind little more than a void.

Monday April 28th

That Monday afternoon, Ed thought he'd surprise her. It was almost four when he phoned – plenty of time for her to get ready for the dinner he had planned.

"Happy anniversary, Hon. Guess you thought I'd forgotten. I purposely didn't say anything this morning just to keep you guessing. Well, get your glad rags on. We're going out tonight – and no, I'm not telling you where. I'll be back to pick you up at eight."

Ellen put the phone down and smiled to herself in relief. Ed had remembered, after all. It was a small thing, admittedly, compared to her other concerns just then, but significant enough nonetheless. His voice had been warm and loving – so too his manner ever since he'd returned from his mission down in Panama. And, as she thought about these things and the evening out that they would have together, Ellen Jamieson could almost convince herself that all was really going to be fine between them after all.

The phone in his office rang at 7.15 pm, just as he was about to wind things up for the night. The table was booked and the flowers ordered – the kind of surprise Ed knew for sure she would appreciate. So, who could this be calling now?

"Ed, glad I caught you – it's Sophia. I need to see you – can you come over right away? I've got something arranged I think you'll be more than pleased with. My lawyers have drawn up transfer papers for those shares we talked about.

I want you to have them, Ed – I know what a lot they mean to you."

"Hey, that's wonderful, Sophia, but do you think it might wait 'til tomorrow? I'm just on my way home – you see, I'm due to take Ellen out tonight. It's our anniversary."

There was an awkward silence at the other end of the line. Sophia's voice, when she spoke, was different. Ed knew the tone well enough.

"Hell, Ed – it'll only be for a few minutes. Just need you to read them through quickly and sign. That's all there is to do. Jonathan, my lawyer, is here to sign his part. C'mon Ed. You know, I thought you'd be grateful."

It was bound to leave him late. As Ed drove through Manhattan's early evening traffic towards the Plaza Hotel, his mind was fixed on one thing and one thing alone: those shares in Palm Cruises. There was a lot he still didn't understand about events happening lately – about the threats over the change of itinerary and the video involving Tara. One thing he was still certain of, though, was that somehow, George Mitchell was behind it all and that Forsbrook had been working for him. Mitchell's failed attempt at taking over his company had all but confirmed it in his mind.

By way of retaliation, Ed recalled with a certain satisfaction, he had so far managed to bring about a successful break up of Mitchell's marriage – a break up which, if it went on to divorce, threatened to prove very costly indeed. But, somehow though, even this wasn't enough. He wanted to see Mitchell much more directly squirming there in front of him – like, for example, on the day he would turn up at his Miami office and introduce himself as a major shareholder in his company. If all Sophia wanted in return was for him to join battle against Mitchell on her behalf, then he was more than equal to the task.

The door opened and she welcomed him in. There was no one else in the lounge just then, so he took a seat while she fixed him a drink then disappeared into the bedroom to check the papers were ready. Jonathan, or whatever her lawyer's name was, was clearly working overtime. Ed looked once again at his watch. It was now almost twenty to eight. He heard her call him through and gave a forceful sigh of relief right there into his gin and tonic. If he got the papers signed now and rushed back to Jersey, all might not be lost.

When Ed walked in through the door, a number of things suddenly became apparent to him. The papers were there on the bureau, certainly, though no third party was there at all. And though Sophia was holding the pen invitingly and gestured for him to take it from her, it was clear that signing documents was not exactly the only thing on her mind. For Sophia was not standing by the bureau but lying on the bed. She was no longer clothed but completely naked. And the pen, as he moved forward uncertainly to take it, disappeared teasingly out of sight behind her back.

V

Despite its grand name, the hotel Luke Darius' budget allowed him to check into on arrival in New York that night was one far more modest than the Plaza. He had booked it from the airport and called Tara at home to arrange a rendezvous time for a little later on. Luke had decided against staying with his cousin Marie this time round. At least a hotel room, however basic, would afford them some privacy together for the short time he was there.

When Ellen Jamieson went to bed that night, she slipped off the dress she had specially worn, shot home the bolt on the bedroom door and cried herself silently and wetly to sleep. If the phone call – the second from her husband that day – had been intended to pacify her, it had failed dismally. He may well have told her how unavoidably detained he was at the very last minute by his work, but she hadn't been fooled. He may have promised to make it up to her and take her out for that celebratory dinner the following night instead, but his words sounded completely hollow to her ears.

For it wasn't only his words that had been audible during that telephone conversation. There, in the background, wherever he was at that precise moment, was the unmistakable sound of poorly restrained female laughter.

PART 7

A CERTAIN RESOLUTION

Chapter 38

I

Luke didn't sleep particularly well that night. It wasn't due simply to the lateness of the hour that he and Tara had ended up chatting to, nor indeed to the supreme lumpiness of the mattress in room 87 of the Majestic. Even the central Brooklyn traffic, which paid scant regard to the time, had little direct effect. For though Tara lay there peacefully beside him, Luke's mind couldn't help going back over certain largely unresolved issues still bothering him.

He was glad, in a way, she'd fallen asleep so soon. This was only their second ever night together, but with memories of their first still there to haunt him, he had been keen to avoid any further broaching of the sexual issue. It was not the time and this very modest hotel, hardly the place. And besides, there was this other business she'd been involved in too. In the grey light of early morning, Luke gazed closely at her quiescent face, wondering just how it was she had ever become embroiled in so sordid an affair.

Thinking back to various of the things he'd learnt one way or another over the weeks, Luke felt he had managed to piece together most of the jigsaw. The complete picture, however, would continue to elude him unless one or two rather crucial points were somehow explained. But was that ever likely to happen?

He was due back on ship in less than a week. Not a lot of time, no matter how one looked at it. How, he wondered, glancing over at Tara once again, might their relationship go forward from there?

Then, as always in the background, there was home. There was his mother, now recently widowed, but no father; a reality he still hadn't fully come to terms with. It had only been a little over three weeks now, admittedly, and so much had happened in that short period to hamper even the initial grieving process. He wondered how his mother was coping and whether Martin might have been there for her. When it came to him suddenly what date it was that day, Luke made a simple computation and came up with the most likely answer; a resounding no. The British General Election was only two days away – that very Thursday.

When, some hours later, the two of them left the hotel, Tara headed home directly to Sheepshead Bay while he made the trip across to Jersey and the Head Office of Venus Cruise Lines on Palisade Avenue.

II

Luke arrived at 10.33, exactly twenty-seven minutes early for his appointment with Ed Jamieson. Ed, for his part – totally unaware of such precise details of timing – was already tied up in an impromptu meeting with Jack Buchanan, who had dropped by to give an update on how things were going. So keen was he to remain undisturbed through all Jack had to say, he had even gone so far as to take his phone off the hook; a virtually unprecedented move on his part.

This, though, soon posed a problem for Rachel, his secretary. Her usual practice – following his own previous strict instruction on the subject – was to call to inform him promptly the minute anyone arrived to see him. Having failed to get through, she deliberated for a second or two before following the second part of the protocol – directing the visitor along the corridor to take a seat outside Mr Jamieson's office.

Sitting where he was, Luke could not help but feel a little uncomfortable. Though the door was tight shut, he found it increasingly difficult to ignore the fact that he could hear virtually all that was being said from within. His first thought was to move away, but he wasn't at all sure where to go as an alternative. As he sat there, though, it suddenly dawned on him just what it was the two men were talking about. And very little of it had much at all to do with the cruise industry:

"Mind you, as I say, this is only the initial report from the Washington vice-squad – and very much as we originally suspected, this thing's gonna be big. The paedophile ring turns out to involve a large number of people – some quite easily identified, others not. Naturally, a lot aren't American; these ones here, for example. We're not sure who they are yet – and realistically may never know – though shots will be circulated to police forces throughout the world. These photos we have, by the way, are stills taken from videos produced secretly by the Eastern Promise agency."

"The quality's surprisingly good." This voice was Ed Jamieson's. Luke was still puzzling over the name 'Eastern

Promise'. Where was it he had heard it mentioned before? Had it been Delgardo?

"Incredible, isn't it? They've all undergone some kind of computer enhancement, of course. Let me tell you, Ed, these people come from all walks of life. Quite a lot from the professional classes, if you can believe it; politicians, lawyers, teachers and even one leading paediatrician. All part of what we believe might prove to be a vast international paedophile network. Things have been kept pretty much under wraps so far, but trust me, there'll be one hell of a stir when the arrests begin. Even now, I believe the Thai authorities are moving in on some guy called Newman, Forsbrook's partner in Eastern Promise, and busting the whole operation from their end. I understand he is also wanted for murder."

"You know, as far as I'm concerned," said Ed, "every goddam one of these filthy scumbags ought to be dealt with like Forsbrook. Whoever it was thought of shooting him butt-naked with a gun up his ass, sure cured him once and for all of his particular affliction."

"It's good news from your point of view though, Ed," said the other man. "That videotape made of the assault on your niece – we're certain all copies have now been located. We've confirmed that there were only ten ever made; nine we picked up at Gibson's house after he vacated it, and the other one sent to you. As for the master copy, we finally found that at Forsbrook's apartment in DC – with a little help from your niece."

"Tara helped? You mean she actually knows about the video?"

"The video, yes. But nothing about your involvement – neither the attempt to dissuade you over the itinerary change nor the threat to go public if you didn't comply. At this moment, she isn't even aware you know anything about her assault at all. We weren't getting anywhere finding the master copy, and, although it was a bit of a long shot, mentioned it to Tara to see if she might've learnt the whereabouts of Forsbrook's secret hangout. Turns out we were lucky. She and a couple of the guys from the vice squad searched the place from top to bottom, and there it was."

"Wow, I bet she's relieved – and I got to say, Jack, so am I."

"Yeah. She's meeting with them later today to witness the destruction of all the tapes. You wouldn't believe what she thinks the motive is behind it all..."

"What?" cut in Ed.

"She's somehow got this wild idea that the whole thing might have been masterminded by the US military in an attempt to discredit any testimony she might give at the Aberdeen hearings – you've heard about those, I guess. She's recently found out – so she was telling one of the guys – that Forsbrook had significant links with the military. Not only has she discovered he was decorated in Vietnam – apparently, he was down at Soc Trang in the Mekong Delta – but at one point, some years back, was actually based at Aberdeen. It would be such a shame to set her straight."

"Damn right it would."

"Now it's all over, I guess you're glad, Ed, you didn't give in to Forsbrook's blackmail."

"You bet I am. It goes without saying, Jack, I'm indebted to you for all your help and guidance in this whole matter."

"You're welcome. There are unfortunately still a few things we don't yet know about the whole sicko business. We know Forsbrook was directly behind the video threat and almost certainly behind the first, rather vague threat you received. We know the video was prepared through his business partner in DC, Wayne Gibson, who, in turn, employed Brad Earlham – alias Paul Curtis, the porn star – to bring his expertise and gargantuan personal attributes to the role. Then there were the local contacts in Caracas, almost certainly engaged by Forsbrook himself, having neatly arranged it that your niece would be on ship at that time. What we don't know is who Forsbrook himself was working for – if indeed he was."

"It's got to be Mitchell, surely?"

"Possible, but far from certain. You see, other than your old rivalry, Ed, and his failed but rather tentative takeover attempt of your company, there is really nothing to suggest it was him."

"But as I see it, he's always remained the only one with any kind of motive."

"Perhaps, but take it from me, obvious motives can be deceptive. It could be that someone was trying to set the whole thing up to make it look like it was him. My own guess though is that, if that were the case, it would probably have been done far more convincingly. We don't know all Mitchell's other enemies, but it would have to be someone pretty ruthless to go that far to ruin him. Who really might hate him that much?"

"I can think of one person who's not particularly enamoured of him at the moment, and she can be pretty ruthless – but no way to that degree."

"Who's that?"

"Sophia, my ex-wife. She's left him now. Somehow found out about that affair with his secretary. She's up here in New York and out for revenge. Wants to transfer shares she holds in his company over to me. At least, that's what she says – though she's playing her usual little games at the moment."

"Why not keep them herself?"

"Haven't quite figured that one out. Probably feels I would fight her corner pretty well."

"My advice, Ed, is tread very carefully before accepting any such gift. There are bound to be strings attached."

"Point taken – I'll definitely give it some thought. There's one other thing, though, that hasn't been explained; Forsbrook's death. Surely that's got to be tied in somehow, too?"

"I was coming to that. Truth is, we are absolutely none the wiser. Find the answer to who killed Forsbrook and I'm sure we'll be a long way to solving the whole puzzle."

"Gentlemen, perhaps I could be of some assistance," said a voice from the now open doorway. "I'm sorry, but I just couldn't help overhearing."

III

"Who the hell's this?"

"I'm Luke Darius, ship's doctor from the Venus Prince."

"You know who killed Forsbrook?" Ed Jamieson looked at him incredulously.

"I do."

"Tell us, then."

"All in good time. But now I have your attention, I'd just like to say how interesting I found one or two things I overheard whilst waiting out there. They've helped considerably in filling in some of the gaps in my understanding of events up till now. I knew, for example, of Tara's ordeal in Caracas – she was naturally reticent at first, but eventually described to me what happened, though perhaps not in the greatest of detail." He looked around at their stunned faces.

"I guessed Forsbrook was behind it," Luke continued, "when I learnt recently of his desperate need to persuade you not to change the itinerary of the Venus Prince. What I didn't know, however – until now, that is – was that a video of Tara had been made that day recording the assault and sent to you in an attempt to finally sway you in your decision. In particular, I would never have guessed that you, her own uncle, could have ignored the threat of that video being broadcast over the Internet – just so your company plans could go ahead.

"You realise, of course, that Tara has already suffered untold psychological damage from what happened that day in Caracas. Can you even begin to imagine how much more damaging the effect would have been had Forsbrook's threat actually been carried out?" There was outrage now in Luke's voice.

"It's not something I'm particularly proud of," said Ed Jamieson quietly.

"I should damn well think not. How do you think she will feel about her favourite uncle when she learns he was prepared to jeopardise her entire future – her entire psychological well-being, in this way?"

"Dr Darius, she must not be allowed to find out. And you must not tell her – not ever. Do you understand me?"

There was a pause.

"That, Mr Jamieson, rather depends."

"On what?"

"I have one or two things in mind."

"So, you too, Doctor, are in the blackmail business?"

"I do believe in what you might call 'a certain persuasion'."

"So, what exactly is it you want to guarantee your silence?"

"I will tell you. In the past six months, you may or may not be aware, a murder was committed on your ship. The victim was a Colombian working for Delgardo Estremosa, the guy responsible for the hijacking last week."

"Murder? – a death, yes, but murder?"

"Indeed. Delgardo admitted as much to me before he died. It was kept secret, of course. The Colombian had been one set up by others in an attempt to oust Delgardo from his position in the Cartel. Whereas I have absolutely no sympathy at all for the dead man, I do happen to know that his only living relative, his sister, is completely devastated by the loss. She is extremely poor and can barely even afford to feed her baby daughter. My first condition for silence is that a substantial sum of money be paid to her in compensation – we can discuss the exact amount later."

Jamieson was silent, further stunned by the news of the murder on board. Thank God, he found himself thinking, there had been no publicity about that at the time.

"A fact I'm sure you're well aware of by now, Mr Jamieson," Luke continued, "has been the use over the past three to four years of the Venus Prince by this man Delgardo for drug-trafficking. He had an agreement with the Captain and Staff Captain – which, as you know, is primarily why they're being detained at the moment by the DEA. Cocaine was delivered to Yardie contacts in Jamaica in an arrangement even the Cartel didn't know about. Delgardo Estremosa had sensed his position was under threat, even at that time, and wanted a secret stash of money as a sort of insurance policy just in case.

"Your proposed change of itinerary suddenly threatened the viability of the whole arrangement and forced Delgardo to approach Forsbrook to get you to change your mind. He failed, as you know. Then things began getting vastly more difficult for Delgardo when the squeeze came from just about all sides – the Cartel, the DEA, and the Colombian authorities themselves. And just when he needed the extra money, he found his secret Cayman account had been traced and frozen."

"So why hijack the ship?" asked Jack Buchanan who had been watching Luke silently all this time.

"The truth is, it wasn't really intended to be a hijack; just a detour arranged with the Captain to enable him to get much needed arms from a secret contact in Nicaragua. These, of course, to attempt to defend his position back home, in true Colombian style. He was a proud man, Delgardo – that much about him I've learnt. He had no intention of going down without a fight. When he realised the DEA boys were on to him on his way back to Colombia, and about to intercept the ship, he was forced to change course. The rest is much as you know."

Luke had no particular wish to go into the precise details of Delgardo's death: best stick with the authorised version.

"There were, as you know, Mr Jamieson, a couple of casualties – employees of yours, injured on board during the hijack. The first, one of the entertainers, was badly beaten up and will almost certainly be unable to join the cruise next season for several weeks. I want his position kept open for him on full pay until he decides he is fit enough to return to the ship. The other casualty, as you know, was Jose Gomez – the Honduran sailor shot by one of Delgardo's men. His situation is far more serious. He will be out of work for months – if, indeed, he is ever fit to work again. I think a fairly sizeable compensation sum would be appropriate in his case."

"Are you through, or does your list go on?" asked Ed Jamieson, a little irritably now.

"Only one more item."

"And that is?"

"That Tara be offered a position on the Venus Prince for the coming season."

"So you two can be together?"

"Precisely."

"Let me say, Dr Darius, you are very generous indeed with my money. The causes you outline are undoubtedly very laudable, but the bottom line is that I don't really believe you would ever dare tell my niece about the threat of that video going public. My guess is you care for her too much."

491

"Perhaps you're right. Perhaps I wouldn't want her to have to go through life knowing she has such an absolute shit for an uncle. However, if pushed, I would have very little hesitation in informing the press of your ship's role in drug-trafficking with its Captain's consent – or, indeed, about the murder on board and its cover up; both things, I fear, potentially ruinous to your Company's good name. The sums I have in mind are, I'm sure you will agree, a small price to pay for my silence."

There was a pause.

"Very well then, I accept," said Jamieson at last.

"So, getting back to Forsbrook, Dr Darius." This from Jack Buchanan, who had been listening closely to all that had so far been said.

"Well, as I mentioned earlier, Delgardo was particularly keen for you to change your mind over the new itinerary, Mr Jamieson, and so paid Forsbrook a large sum of money on condition he succeeded in persuading you to abandon it. As you rightly guessed, it was Dan behind the threats. When it was clear he had failed to convince you, Delgardo wanted his money back. His other funds were blocked as I explained, and he needed money desperately – not least of all for that consignment of arms.

"The trouble was, Forsbrook, as you may have been aware," continued Luke, quite enjoying the undivided attention he was now getting from the two men, "was an inveterate gambler. He had started out with huge debts, but even with the money from Delgardo, still managed to build up even more, in various places around the world. Not having the money to pay back Delgardo when it was demanded of him, Forsbrook tried tricking the Colombian with high-quality counterfeit notes. To make matters worse, he also decided to tip off the DEA as to Delgardo's likely whereabouts at the time of the payout. They unfortunately failed to catch Delgardo but did apparently shoot dead both of his most trusted henchmen. Not surprisingly, Estremosa wanted revenge."

"So, it was he who killed Forsbrook, then?"

"Surprisingly enough not – at least, not directly. At that time, it turned out there were others seeking revenge too. One of them was prepared to pay Delgardo handsomely – a sum large enough to purchase those arms he so desperately wanted – for the killing to be carried out on Colombian soil on his behalf. And, so I'm told, in the precise manner he prescribed."

"And this man was?"

"A man who, along with other members of his large family, had been crossed one too many times by Forsbrook in his outrageous gambling career. Someone so intent on avenging the near-fatal stabbing of his young cousin some months back in Hong Kong, that he flew over himself specially to oversee the proceedings. A man by the name of Wong."

IV

Luke was just leaving Head Office when word reached him that he was wanted on the phone. The call was from London.

"Luke, is that you? I've been trying to reach with you all day."

"Sarah? What's happened?"

"Nothing much. I really just wanted to update you, that's all. As you know, the Election's the day after tomorrow. With regard to your brother, though, it's a case of 'so near, yet so far away'. I've been following up reports, secretly leaked to me, of financial irregularities in the use of local Party funds, suggesting he is to blame. In order to get any kind of supportive evidence, however, a photographer friend and I had to break into his flat one night when he was out. We're just going through copies of various financial statements we managed to find there now."

"Anything of interest so far?"

"Only a set of cash deposits into his personal account which reflect, quite well time-wise, monies missing from the campaign fund. These deficits are rectified, to some degree, by a small number of what seem to be individual payments made later, directly into these local funds. Some of these sums, incidentally, are quite large. We're just going through them at the moment, in a last vain hope. I know it's a bit of a long shot, Luke, but do any of the following names ring any bells with you?"

"Fire away," said Luke.

"Brady?"

"No."

"Harlow?"

"No."

"Vesey?"

"No, I'm sorry, Sarah."

"Forsbrook?"

"What?! Dan Forsbrook paid money into Conservative Party funds?"

"Yes – about £40,000 in one single payment back in March. You know this person, then?"

"Let me just tell you, Sarah – I think you've finally got your story."

Chapter 39

Wednesday Apr 30th

I

Luke arrived outside 28, Ravenswood Rd, Chiswick, West London, at eight the following morning. He was jet-lagged and tired, having managed little sleep since his arrival at Heathrow sometime after midnight. He had checked into a nearby hotel, partly for convenience and partly so as to avoid disturbing his mother at Wetherfield at so late an hour. London, he noticed, had that strange air of expectancy so typical of the day before an Election.

Sarah was ready for him when he arrived and quickly surveyed the documents he had brought to show her.

"These could be just what we need. Courtesy of the Washington DC Vice Squad, you say?"

"Unofficially – yes."

"Now, how the hell did you manage that?"

When he left just over an hour later, it was clear she was eager to get on. Not only had she to complete her story, but successfully hawk it in time for inclusion in the next morning's press. She would have to work fast to beat the deadline.

When Luke did eventually arrive at Wetherfield, his mother, he discovered, was out. The house was silent now too, much in the manner of his previous arrival. For an instant, he thought he could hear his father's voice speaking to him again, but it did not disturb him. Instead, he found comfort, knowing those memories too had somehow been locked there deep into the ancient walls around him – along with all the music and laughter from happier times.

II

Tara was feeling concerned. Although she and Luke had no fixed arrangement to meet the previous evening, it had seemed reasonable on the basis of how things were left, to assume they would. She had stayed close to the phone, but no call came.

At ten, she'd got through to the Majestic, but with little satisfaction. Either there had been genuine confusion in the mind of the switchboard operator as to the room number, or she'd been correctly connected and the phone answered by a female voice professing a true ignorance. Only later still did it occur to her that Luke might have checked out – the person she'd spoken to being merely Room 87's latest incumbent. Another phone call had confirmed this to be the case. So where had Luke gone? And why, even by that morning, had he still not called?

Marianne Carter, poised outside her father's study and about to knock, could tell he was busy on the phone. Hardly approachable at the best of times – and even more so recently for whatever reason – interrupting him just then could, she knew, prove costly. Instead, she waited, trying to determine from what she could hear when he might finish. What became obvious pretty soon, though, was that this was no ordinary phone conversation.

Two things about it struck her almost simultaneously. The first was the succinctness and content of the message he was imparting; the second, equally surprising, was the strange way his voice sounded imparting it. She stood, rooted to the spot, realising only at the last moment that he had finished and was about to leave the room. Scurrying off, she remained out of sight long after he'd gone; long after he'd grabbed his car keys and driven off. Only then, alone in the house, did she emerge and cautiously enter the study. There on the desk sat the phone. Curiosity quickly overcame her. She picked it up gingerly, held her breath, and pressed REDIAL.

"Hello." The voice was one strangely familiar – but from where?

"Who am I through to, please?" Even as she was saying it, the answer suddenly flashed in her mind. "Tara – is that you?"

"Marianne? You sound kinda worried. Is something wrong?"

"You've recently had a call, haven't you?"

"Yes, I have – another threatening call. This time it was quite openly about the hearings. A man's voice. Said something like: 'If I were you, bitch, I'd think long and hard before testifying. You know it'll be the worse for you if you do.' How did you know that, Marianne?"

"I'm using the very phone it was made from – here in my father's study."

"It was your father?! Good God, why? You knew about this?"

"I only just found out – overheard him and when he was gone, pressed redial. As to why, I can only guess. I know he feels very strongly about the damage these hearings could do to the army, and madder than hell that they'll attract such publicity. Why, only the other evening at dinner here with some of his friends – political allies and one or two quite high-ranking serving officers – conversation seemed pretty much stuck on the subject. Got him real riled up, it did. The repercussions of these hearings, it seems, could be enormous – finding their way right up the chain of command. Some of these guys are coming up to retirement and couldn't live with tarnished reputations; others just see their careers going down the toilet. They particularly fear an avalanche of other complaints that could so easily follow on the back of these hearings."

"But your father's retired; why should he care?"

"You're right, but he's not immune. Not with his sights set on Congress. If you ask me, he's got one or two skeletons in his own closet, just waiting to break loose."

"But why me?"

"I'm afraid your name came up the other night too. You're a key witness now, if you hadn't realised it – with so many others successfully warned off. One of the few 'clean' key witnesses left, is how they described you. I take it that means they've not managed to get anything on you so far."

"Do you think it could have been him that made that threatening call to my mother?"

"Quite possibly. He could've found your home number easily enough in my diary. Do me one favour, will you, Tara?"

"What's that?"

"Say what you have to say at the hearings – don't let the bastards wear you down."

"I will. But what about you, Marianne? What are you planning to do now?"

"I'm going back to complete my training. Not to please my father, either; more to spite all those cretins back at base. Then, I intend to do all I can to get things improved all round for women in the military. And the way I figure it, the best way I can help is from the inside. There's no question about it: something in the system's got to change."

"Way to go, Marianne. But hey – tell me this – did your father ever happen to know, or have any dealings with, a man called Forsbrook?"

"Well, I've known most of Dad's friends over the years and nearly all, one way or another, since he's been retired. There's no way I can be sure, Tara, but I really don't think he did."

Tara's thoughts were interrupted, a little later on, by the arrival of Hugh Gotley. She showed him in, though it took her a little while to understand why he was there. She had hardly spoken to him at all since confiding details of her experience in Caracas all those weeks back. Surely, as her mother had so often reminded her, he had taken up with Gloria Wheatley and would soon, no doubt, be wed? When the truth finally emerged, Tara found she could hardly believe her ears. She replied calmly, hiding perfectly her incredulity at what he'd just said.

"I see, so what you're saying, Hugh, is that you want me back, and that you're prepared to forgive me for putting myself in such a position that I could be taken advantage of like that. Am I right?"

"That's about it, I guess. So, what do you say?"

"Well, Hugh, really, this is most generous of you," she began. At that moment, however, the phone in the next room began to ring. Tara rushed through to answer it. It was, as she'd hoped, Luke. To her amazement, he was calling from London.

"So, I guess there's little chance of seeing you again before you rejoin the ship."

"Actually, if all goes according to plan, I'll be back in New York in a couple of days. But as regards the ship – why not come with me?"

"That's impossible. You have a job on board – I don't. Besides, I've just been notified of the times of the Aberdeen hearings: I'm due to testify next week. What's this with the ship, anyway?"

"You have a job on the Venus Prince if you want it. Your uncle, when I asked him, was more than happy to oblige."

"Really? How did you manage that then?"

"Just my good old British charm, I guess. A very obliging man, your Uncle Ed, when you get to know him. I'm sure, though, the offer would still hold after the hearings. How do you feel at the prospect of testifying, by the way?"

"Let's just say, I'm feeling more determined than I've ever been."

Tara returned to the sitting room and switched the radio off. Hugh, she noticed, had made himself at home, lounging

501

on the sofa with his feet up. What she didn't know was that he was rather hoping just then that she might come over and join him there, just like in the old days. She remained where she was, smiling sweetly.

"Well, Hugh, thank you so much for forgiving me in the way that you have. I think it tells a lot about the kind of man you are. There are, however, two things I'd just like to say. The first is that there is absolutely no way on earth I consider I've done any wrong, so I'm in need of no one's forgiveness – least of all yours. The second is, perhaps, a little more revealing about my true feelings for you..."

"What might that be, then?" asked Hugh curiously.

"It is simply this: get the hell out of this house you self-righteous, small-minded asshole. It never occurred to me before you were so utterly full of crap."

III

Dr Fredrikson came out to greet her, then ushered her into his office in his usual charming manner. He had known Ellen Jamieson for some years now, even before her marriage to Ed. One glance told him something significant was wrong.

"Come, take a seat, Ellen. How may I help?"

She had thought long and hard before coming, and, now the opportunity to unburden herself had arrived, she found the precise words eluding her. As much in embarrassment as anything, she turned her head slightly away from him as tears coursed silently down her cheeks. Karl Fredrikson waited patiently until she was ready.

Ellen had not known who else to turn to just then. She had girlfriends, yes – but none she felt she could share this with. In a moment of harsh reflection, it had struck her forcibly just how few of them and their husbands existed totally independently of Ed; and how few indeed might remain as friends should her marriage finally break up. Sleep – anything, that is, more than the odd fitful hour – had been a serious problem too.

She and Ed had been out for their belated anniversary meal – more because it was easier to go than say no – but her heart wasn't in it. He might have guessed something was up – might have bothered delving past her initial limp reassurance that really everything was fine – if he hadn't been totally caught up in his own thoughts and the dominant silence that so often prevailed.

Finally, Ellen began to speak. Dr Fredrikson listened without interruption, knowing that to do so at that moment would serve only to stifle the flow.

When she left his office half an hour later, she did so with a feeling of almost monumental relief at having told him. It was tempered very soon after, though, by the flooding realisation that despite it all, her real problem endured. She tried to recall the practical suggestion he had made. Besides supportive words, it was all he could really offer just then, he had said, without Ed's agreement to participate in full marriage counselling. But that, of course, implied confronting him. Given the option, it was something she preferred not to do just yet. She would at least try the other way first...

IV

Luke guessed Sarah must be having problems. It was over two hours now that he had been trying to get through to her – over two hours that her phone was engaged. She had obviously finished the story; it was simply getting someone to take a chance with it when so much other news was vying to dominate Election Day headlines.

He was sitting idly watching television when his mother returned to Wetherfield. She looked well, he thought, considering all she'd been through. He wondered how she'd been managing. Her nod towards the TV screen answered part of his unvoiced question.

"You know, he's hardly spoken to me at all since the funeral. In fact, I only get to see him on television these days."

It was Martin, his brother, at what appeared to be the opening of some local children's home. He was surrounded by a sea of young smiling faces – innocently sucked into his last-minute pre-Election publicity machine.

"How's his campaign doing?"

"He's very confident – opinion polls have him way ahead. What amazes me though is the amount of air time he's getting. He obviously knows all the right people."

Luke finally got through to Sarah at six-thirty that evening. He could tell immediately from the tone of her voice that she was disappointed.

"No takers, I'm afraid," she said dolefully.

"No one even wanted to listen?"

"Oh, one or two, yes. But, you see, breaking a story like this at such a late stage means taking chances. To take it on at face value, without careful corroboration of the facts, is understandably fraught with risk. It's not as though I'm a well-known and trusted hack. One editor, who wanted some background on me as a journo, contacted Sam Reynolds, the guy I used to work for at the Herald. Needless to say, after that, he wouldn't touch the story with a barge pole."

"Anyone left to call?"

"A couple, but time's running out."

"Keep trying. I'll be over at nine."

Sarah was waiting for him when he arrived, breezing past him as he still stood there at the door.

"Come on," she said. "We're off."

"Off where?"

"Off to see your brother at his campaign headquarters. I can't take any more. I've just seen the smug little shit on TV; he's returned there, so he says, to prepare for his victory party tomorrow night."

Sarah's driving, from Luke's passenger seat perspective, was more than a little erratic as they made their way out to Woking. He understood clearly enough how she felt after the way his brother had treated her: she and her son had had to live with the consequences for months now. What he didn't understand was how she intended to play things from there.

Sarah made her way in through the local Party faithful – her role of well-wisher taken at face value by the person on the door. Optimism within quite clearly abounded, bordering, at times, on euphoria. She pressed on, determined now she'd started, to see this thing through. Martin Darius, she soon discovered, was not in the large main ground floor reception room of the building but on the phone in a smaller room down the hallway. Sarah paused outside the door for a moment and listened.

"Well, thanks again for all your assistance. I'm sure we'll be able to work just as successfully together in the future."

He put the phone down, smiling, and turned to find Sarah Wright standing there behind him. His expression altered instantly as he remembered just where it was he'd met her before.

"That was Harriet Fursdon, I take it," said Sarah scathingly. "Saved your arse completely with that business at Windhope Hospital, didn't she? How'd you ever manage to convince her to help – or is that some kind of Party secret?"

"Who the hell let you in? Get out of here before I have you thrown out."

"Like you got rid of me that time from your father's party? Like you had me effectively thrown out of my job? You and Sam Reynolds are pretty close, huh?"

"You deserved it; snooping around like that, you pathetic amateur. Now, are you going to leave quietly, or do I have to call the police?"

"Call the police, by all means. They might well be interested in this, for a start. In case you're wondering, it's a set of financial statements showing how you've been siphoning off money, almost at will, from your campaign fund; some paid back, but quite a lot not."

Martin glanced at the papers she held out towards him and his face dropped.

"Where the hell did you get those from?" he yelled, recognising one of them as his own personal bank statement and trying desperately to snatch them from her. She stepped back neatly and held them away from him in triumph.

"Not so fast, Mr Darius – that isn't all. We also have evidence of your undisclosed involvement in several city institutions."

Martin glared at her venomously.

"Okay, how much do you want for all this stuff, then?" said Martin Darius after a pause. "What's your price?"

"How much do you think this evidence might be worth? Enough to compensate me for loss of earnings from my job at the Herald? Who knows when I might get another regular post as good as that? Forty thousand pounds, perhaps?"

"Make it fifty and be done."

"No need for greed – forty will do. You have your cheque book handy?"

"Yes. Here – take the cheque," said Martin signing it and handing it to her. "And we'll hear no more about it."

"Not about that, anyway. However, tomorrow, Mr Darius, you and the rest of the country can read the main story. No, I'm not divulging which paper has taken it – you'll just have to be patient. What it will say, though, is that someone identified as running a lucrative sex-tourism outlet and international paedophile network, has made a sizeable financial contribution to your campaign fund."

"Who do you mean?"

"A man called Forsbrook."

"You can prove this?"

"I have signed statements here from members of the Washington DC vice squad, as well as photos from his special agency out in Thailand known as Eastern Promise."

"But this is scandalous: I had absolutely no idea."

"Whether you did or didn't, I'm sure you'll have ample opportunity of putting your side of things to the British people. Unfortunately, such explanation would, almost certainly, have to wait until after the electorate has voted. Shame that, isn't it?"

Martin Darius lunged wildly towards her, grabbing her furiously round the neck. He was ruined now and knew it. He felt his hands squeezing uncontrollably tighter...

The blow on his chin sent him reeling. The next one, considerably lower down, rendered him completely helpless on the floor. Standing over him, as he looked up, was his brother Luke. One of his arms, he noticed, was supportively around the girl; and there was a look of complete triumph on both of their faces.

Chapter 40

Thursday May 1st

I

Luke's meeting with his senior partner, at the practice in Weston the next morning, went much as he'd anticipated. Little he had to say seemed to cause Dr Clive Walsh the least surprise. The letter of resignation from the partnership, when handed over, was accepted with the same amiability he had shown Luke ever since that day four years ago when he had first attended for interview.

"Between you and me, Luke, I'm sure you are doing the right thing. You're still young and free. Experience life while you can. If there ever comes a time in future when you decide you might like to give general practice in this country another try, I'll be more than happy to give you a reference."

Luke sought out the other partners and bade them farewell. So, too, the rest of the practice staff and other colleagues in the building. For a moment – and since it was clearly vacant at the time – he stepped into the first-floor consulting room that had once been his daily haunt. Standing over by the window, he pulled back the net curtain and looked out. His gaze took him on over the dull brown rooftops to the grey corrugated sea and beyond. On this occasion though, he realised, his spirit no longer seemed quite so restless.

II

Ellen Jamieson was at a particularly low ebb when Tara happened to call late that same morning. The prospect of at least someone to talk to just then pleased her greatly. The loneliness of yet another two nights with Ed away – he'd left the afternoon before, apparently to oversee work on the Venus Prince in Florida – was almost as much as she could bear.

"But I thought you said your worries about Uncle Ed acting so mysteriously last week had proved groundless. Wasn't he secretly down in Panama helping the DEA?"

"He was. Unfortunately, things have happened since then – and I'm afraid the prospects for our relationship don't look at all good." Ellen told Tara about the lipstick and perfume, and the female voice in the background when Ed had rung to postpone their anniversary dinner. She told her too about seeing Dr Fredrikson.

"What did he have to say about it all?" asked Tara.

"He said that unless I confront him, and find out whether or not he's interested in trying to save our relationship, marriage counselling would not be possible. The thing is, Tara, I just don't know how to broach it with him."

"But what alternative is there, if you don't tell him of your concerns?"

"Dr Fredrikson's advice there was pretty basic, I'm afraid; and even he didn't hold out much hope of success. He said one tactic might be to try to imagine back to the time we first met – to the time we were first attracted to one another. If I could then somehow help rekindle in Ed's mind, too, some of the feelings we had back then, it might just possibly help rejuvenate our relationship. I've thought about it repeatedly since, but I've got to admit, I'm getting nowhere fast."

"Well don't give up hope yet, Aunt Ellen. You're still quite young and attractive, you know, with a really great figure if ever you chose to capitalize on it. Listen, I've got a little time on my hands: let's talk this thing through..."

Chapter 41

Friday May 2nd

I

Luke stood at his father's graveside with his mother the next morning, taking time in quiet contemplation and his own special farewell. He would be flying out again that afternoon, back to Tara and another season on the Venus Prince. Although he was sad to be leaving his mother again so soon, particularly after this latest family crisis, she remained typically stoical.

"I'm sorry to say this, Luke – I know Martin's my son, but I really don't feel the slightest compassion for him."

"Knowing him, he'll probably manage to get off fairly lightly – one way or the other. His political career, of course, is completely ruined, for what it was worth. What we'll never know is just what contribution such startling last-minute revelations might have made to the Conservatives' dramatic fall from grace in the polls yesterday. As for Martin himself, it wouldn't surprise me in the slightest if he didn't bounce back somehow in the fullness of time. Unfortunately, people like him often do."

Sarah phoned soon after he arrived home. She had recovered well from Martin's brief attempt at strangulation the night before last, and was itching to tell Luke something before he left.

"You'll never guess who just called."

"Let me think – the Pulitzer Prize Committee?"

"Not quite. Though, to be honest, just about everyone else. My phone hasn't stopped ringing since early this morning. You wouldn't believe the work offers I've had. The person I'm referring to, though, is Sam Reynolds, my old editor – wait for it – offering me my old job back at the Herald. Seems he's suddenly immensely impressed with my work. Thinks I'd now be well able to handle subjects of a little more substance."

"What did you tell him?"

"To go fuck himself – as, I believe, you might well have expected. Anyway, Luke, thanks again for flying straight over like that with all that stuff about Forsbrook and Eastern Promise. You know, I believe my career might have finally begun to take off."

"You deserve it – and, by the way, it was a pleasure. Keep in touch, Sarah, eh?"

II

A number of things had been on Ed Jamieson's mind while he was away on business in Florida. The first of them – and the one from which so many of the others stemmed – was just how much his ex-wife Sophia seemed to have changed since she had left him. She was scheming and ruthless, but worse still, dangerously determined. Following the debacle the other evening when she had lured him over, knowing full-well he had that anniversary dinner arranged with Ellen, he still hadn't managed to get those share transfers signed. By the morning, she had put it on the line: it was Ellen or her – and the shares on offer relied entirely on this decision.

Since then, other things had become clear. Sure, her husband, George Mitchell, had attempted the takeover of his company – that much was indisputable – but he hadn't been behind the original threats nor in any way behind his niece, Tara's ordeal. In fact, other than their old rivalry involving Sophia, there was little real impetus now for revenge. What concerned Ed more was the possibility, slowly dawning on him, that perhaps Sophia had not changed – that, in fact, without him being aware of it, she had been the same scheming bitch all along.

If that were indeed so – Ed found himself thinking sometime later as he arrived back in New York and headed straight for Head Office – had she been such a prize for Mitchell to steal away from him in the first place?

III

Luke's plane took off from Heathrow at 3 pm London time and arrived at a similar numerical hour in New York. The letter he had written in a quiet moment the day before, he kept for posting in the USA, figuring it would probably get to Colombia sooner than from England.

There were two things in particular he had to tell Consuela, and he tried as he journeyed to imagine how she might take the news. Firstly, there was the truth about her brother and his death at the hands of Delgardo's henchmen. That would hit her hard, he was sure – she had almost certainly been Delgardo's concubine at the time. No doubt news of Delgardo's own well-broadcast death, the week before, had affected her to some degree already. Secondly, and on a brighter note, there were details of the offer he'd got Jamieson to agree. More than enough to guarantee some kind of future for both herself and her young daughter.

Tara was there to greet him and they sat in the airport lounge, drank coffee, and talked. He related his experiences in London and she listened quietly, wondering secretly over the possible extent of Martin Darius' business relationship with Forsbrook.

"Changing the subject though, Tara," Luke said suddenly, rising to his feet, "I think it's time I found myself a hotel. One better than the Majestic, at least: still got that crick in my back from the last time. I take it you'll be staying at home with your mother?"

"No, actually I've got a better idea," said Tara, pulling something from her pocket. "This is the key to Uncle Ed's holiday cottage in the Catskills. I was talking to Aunt Ellen yesterday and she insisted I take it. The car's already packed and ready. We can be there in no time." She stood close to him now and kissed him. "I really want you, Luke Darius, if you didn't already know it. And besides, I think we have a little unfinished business to attend to, don't you?"

Ed Jamieson was totally astonished when the call came through. It was 4.20 that afternoon and he was just thinking about leaving early for home. This was perhaps the very last person he expected to hear from just then.

"Ed Jamieson? This is George Mitchell. Say, listen, I know we've had our differences in the past, but I thought I'd just ring and say good luck on your new itinerary. As you know, I've been running ships out of Miami for years now. If there's anything I can help you with, you just give me a call, okay?"

"I appreciate that. It's extremely generous of you, thanks," said Ed, more than a little embarrassed. "By the way, how's Sophia these days?" Despite everything, now he had the man on the line, it was a question he found hard to resist.

"Not so good, I'm afraid. She left me a few weeks back over some stupid affair I had with my secretary. Between you and me, though, Ed – and I'm sorry to have to say this, knowing how close you two once were – I'm glad to be rid of her. When you get to our age, life's too short to be stuck with someone you just don't love."

"Guess you're right," said Ed pensively.

"Strange about Dan Forsbrook, though, wasn't it?" said Mitchell. "You know, it always amazed me why you took him on out of the blue like that, in the first place. By that time, we'd been trying to get rid of him for months – terrible gambling habit, you know. I'd have warned you, of course, if you'd asked."

The next call Ed received – just as he was on his way out of the door – was from Sophia. She wanted to see him again that night, and didn't take too kindly to his excuse.

"Listen here, Ed, I need to see you. And you need to see me if you want those shares."

"No, you listen, Sophia. I've had just about enough of you and your scheming ways. If you've got a problem with your husband, go sort it out yourself – or find some other sucker to help you. If you have a problem with your social life, may I suggest you perhaps do the same. As for those shares you keep on about, I've decided I'm really not that interested any more, so please don't come bothering me again."

IV

His house there near Lincoln Park appeared empty when Ed arrived home. Not a sound could be heard anywhere. No radio or TV there in the background; no shout of welcome from his wife. The lounge was tidy – far tidier than normal, in fact – as he found, too, was the kitchen into which he ventured next. If Ellen was out, he couldn't remember why – that is, if she'd told him or, if indeed, he'd been listening if she had.

This was all so unusual, Ed thought to himself. It was almost like...no, it couldn't be, surely? If she had somehow suspected there was something going on with another woman – in this case Sophia – she'd have said something, wouldn't she? Not simply walk out on him like this?

Ed found himself suddenly gripped by panic; a panic that rose wildly inside him, making his heart palpitate and his throat muscles tighten. This was not how he'd intended it. He had made his decision now and he was sorry. It was Ellen he wanted, and should have wanted all along. From what he knew now about Sophia, no question should ever have arisen.

He found himself running from room to room, calling her name. If she had left, where might she have gone? How much, indeed, might she have found out? Had she had him followed, perhaps? He couldn't imagine her ever being as devious as that. Yet he had been – without a thought for how she might feel. Was it too late, or was there any chance at all she might forgive him?

By now, he was on the upstairs landing, pushing each door open as he went. There were other possibilities for the silence in the house, it occurred to him – one or two, far too awful even to contemplate. The guest rooms were empty, so, too, the bathrooms. There was only one door ahead now and that was of their bedroom. How happy a place it had once been.

The room was in relative darkness, the thick drapes fully closed across the windows. This surprised him as it was still quite early. The room was large and as he ventured in, he could see her still form, there on the bed. He called her name but there was no reply. He rushed towards her and took her head in his arms, now very much fearing the worst. The pill bottle was by the bedside. He blasphemed loudly, then looked more closely at it; it was completely empty. What were they, in any case? And how many had there been to start with? He turned to her again and shook her frantically, knowing that more than anything else, he mustn't lose her now. He'd been a fool all along, about everything – the ship, Tara, Mitchell, Sophia and most of all, Ellen. He deserved to be punished, that he knew – but please God, not like this...

When the paramedics arrived and transferred her to the ambulance fifteen minutes later, Ed stood awkwardly aside, still very much in shock. He answered what he could of their questions, though found himself a little preoccupied by something he'd noticed earlier – something that, in the confusion that followed, had only just now fully registered with him. As he thought about it once more, Ed became aware it posed one of the most intriguing questions of all.

What on earth could have been going on there that afternoon for Ellen to be found dressed like that – wearing, of all things, that old air-hostess uniform from way back?

~ THE END ~

Printed in Great Britain
by Amazon